A Castaway in Cornwall

JULIE KLASSEN

BETHANYHOUSE
a division of Baker Publishing Group
Minneapolis, Minnesota

Published by Bethany House Publishers
11400 Hampshire Avenue South
Bloomington, Minnesota 55438
www.bethanyhouse.com

Bethany House Publishers is a division of
Baker Publishing Group, Grand Rapids, Michigan

Printed in the United States of America

Library of Congress Cataloging-in-Publication Data
Names: Klassen, Julie, author.
Title: A castaway in Cornwall / Julie Klassen.
Description: Minneapolis, Minnesota : Bethany House, a division of Baker
    Publishing Group, [2020]
Identifiers: LCCN 2020029195 | ISBN 9780764234224 (trade paperback) |
    ISBN 9780764234231 (cloth) | ISBN 9780764236204 (large print) | ISBN
    9781493428076 (ebook)
Subjects: GSAFD: Christian fiction. | Romantic suspense fiction. | Historical
    fiction. | Love stories.
Classification: LCC PS3611.L37 C37 2020 | DDC 813/.6—dc23
LC record available at https://lccn.loc.gov/2020029195

Unless otherwise indicated, Scripture quotations are from the King James Version of
the Bible.

Scripture quotations labeled NKJV are from the New King James Version®. Copyright
© 1982 by Thomas Nelson. Used by permission. All rights reserved.

Scripture quotations labeled ESV are from The Holy Bible, English Standard Version®
(ESV®), copyright © 2001 by Crossway, a publishing ministry of Good News Publishers. Used by permission. All rights reserved. ESV Text Edition: 2016

Cover design by Jennifer Parker
Cover photography by Mike Habermann Photography, LLC

Author is represented by Books and Such Literary Agency.

20   21   22   23   24   25   26   7   6   5   4   3   2   1

To Marietta and Ted Terry,
prayer warriors and friends,
with love and gratitude.

During severe weather yesterday three vessels were wrecked near Trebetherick Point, beaten by the waves, and gone to pieces.

—WEST BRITON, FEBRUARY 1818

Obscurest night involved the sky,
Th' Atlantic billows roared,
When such a destined wretch as I,
Washed headlong from on board,
Of friends, of hope, of all bereft,
His floating home for ever left.

—WILLIAM COWPER, "THE CASTAWAY"

"What woman, having ten silver coins, if she loses one coin, does not light a lamp, sweep the house, and search carefully until she finds it? And when she has found it, she calls her friends and neighbors together, saying, 'Rejoice with me, for I have found the piece which I lost!'"

—LUKE 15:8–9 NKJV

Prologue

OCTOBER 1813
NORTH CORNWALL, ENGLAND

Flotsam or jetsam?

According to the heavy old volume of *Dr. Johnson's Dictionary* in my uncle's study, *flotsam* is any goods floating on the sea where a ship has sunk or been cast away, while *jetsam* is anything purposely cast out of a ship when in danger, in hopes of saving it, or at least lightening the load.

Almost daily I walk along the shore, eyes keen for either one.

I step, and sometimes leap, from rock to rock pool, from beach to beach grass. Looking, looking, always looking, my gaze pinned not on the unfathomable horizon or heavens but on the practical earth at my feet. Up, down, and over I go, across craggy rocks, shifting sands, and slate shelves with nary a misstep or hesitation.

All around me is the sound of the sea. Not a roar but a rhythm—a watery hum, strumming like a vibrating chord, a quickened heartbeat. The Atlantic rolls in, lapping and slapping at rocks with percussion, punctuated by the mournful cries of gulls.

Even with the chill of autumn pressing in, dainty stoic flowers—purple, orange, white—grow on the otherwise barren rock. Beauty amid harsh conditions. Life where nothing should thrive.

Can I say the same for myself? Am I thriving, or merely surviving?

Sometimes I wonder how I ended up here in Cornwall, so far from my childhood home. I feel like a castaway, set adrift on the tide by the long-ago deaths of my parents, and left wanting answers. Is there a plan in all this? Does God truly hold my fate in His hands, or has my life all been happenstance, the mysterious ebb and flow of chance?

I don't belong here, yet here I am. Washed up on this strange shore with its strange ways. Here, anyone not born and bred in Cornwall is eyed with suspicion and viewed as a foreigner. I have lived among them now for eight of my three and twenty years, yet I still don't belong . . . and doubt I shall ever belong anywhere again.

Standing on a rock, wind tugging at my bonnet, I wonder once more—am I flotsam or jetsam?

On Monday last the brigantine Star of Dundee was wrecked near Padstow. Her crew of five took to their boat which soon upset, and melancholy to relate, they were all drowned.

—WEST BRITON, NOVEMBER 1811

Chapter 1

L aura!" twenty-one-year-old Eseld called from the coastal path above the beach. "Mamm is angry and bids you come. You left something foul in Wenna's best pot again."

Laura's stomach sank. How could she have forgotten? She called back, "I was soaking a leather purse I found. Could be saved with proper care."

"The only good purse is a full purse to Mamm. You know that. Come on! I don't want her angry with me as well."

Laura sighed and picked up her basket. "Coming."

As they trudged up the steep footpath to

Fern Haven, Eseld said, "I don't know why you come down here every day. It would be one thing if you found gold or valuables we could sell."

Laura didn't remind Eseld that she *had* sold several things to the antique and curiosity dealer in Padstow. She'd not earned a fortune but had contributed to her upkeep and begun saving for a voyage she dreamed of taking one day.

Before selling anything, however, Laura felt duty bound to wait the prescribed "year and a day," in case the owners might come forward to claim their property. Eseld always shook her head at the precaution, parroting the local saying, "What the custom and excise men don't know won't hurt 'em."

Even Uncle Matthew, a kindly parson, saw nothing wrong in helping himself to anything that washed ashore near Fern Haven. "'Tis God's bounty, my girl. It isn't as though we're stealing," he'd say. "The crates and barrels come to us. Gifts from the Giver of all good gifts."

Between treacherous Trevose Head, Stepper Point, the Doom Bar, and the rocks off their own Greenaway Beach, wrecks were a common occurrence, claiming many ships and many more lives. In fact, from Trebetherick Point, near their home, Laura could look down onto the rocks and see the remains of more than one shipwreck, the wooden pieces half buried in the sand like carcasses—the spine and ribs of giant ancient birds. Many local dwellings and outbuildings had been built of salvaged ship timbers.

Reaching Fern Haven—a two-story white-washed house with a slate roof and dormer windows—they passed through the gate, also built from salvaged timbers, and climbed the few steps to its covered porch.

"Wipe your feet," Eseld admonished, sounding very much like her imperious mother as she did so.

Laura obliged, wiping the worst of the sand and seaweed from her worn half boots.

As they paused, voices from within reached them.

Eseld's mother, Mrs. Bray, said, "Thank you for the kind invitation, Mr. Kent. Mr. Bray and I, and Miss Eseld, will happily join you for dinner."

A lower masculine voice said something that included her name.

"No, I don't think Laura will wish to come," Mrs. Bray replied. "She doesn't like family occasions, not being one of us. And I believe she has a cold coming on. Best to leave her home, especially as the weather has turned decidedly chilly."

Eseld rolled her eyes, gave Laura an impish grin, and pushed open the door with a bang. "We're ho-ome, Mamm dear." She winked at Laura and sallied into the modest parlour, where Mrs. Bray was talking with two male visitors: handsome, golden-haired Treeve Kent and his younger brother, Perry.

"Ah, here is Eseld now," Lamorna Bray said with a smile, a smile that quickly faded when she turned to Laura. "Laura, child, you look a fright. Your face is nearly as red as your windblown hair. Roaming the beaches again, I suppose?"

"I . . . yes."

"Why must you go scampering about the countryside? You look wild . . . almost blowsy!"

Laura felt her cheeks heat, but Treeve Kent smiled at her. "Actually, madam, I think her eyes and complexion are quite brightened by the exercise, and her hair shown to best advantage."

Was the handsome man mocking her? Laura wondered. He must be.

"Forgive me," she said. "I did not realize we were expecting callers."

"We've come unannounced, I'm afraid," Treeve replied. "Unpardonable to a Town miss, I suppose?"

Laura blinked. "I . . . hardly know." As a

child she had lived in Oxford, not London, but the local Cornish youths often called her an "up-country girl" or a "Town miss," as though a great insult.

Treeve turned to his shorter and quieter brother. "Speaking of manners, I am not sure if you've met my brother, Perran. He's been away most of the time you've lived here, I believe, either at university or training at Guy's Hospital."

Guy's Hospital, Laura knew, was a London teaching hospital. Her own father had trained there as well.

"We have met," Laura said. "Though I don't expect he will remember."

The dark-haired man smiled shyly at her. "Yes, I remember you, Miss Laura."

"And what about me?" Eseld asked with a coquettish fluff to the blond curls framing her face.

"Of course I remember you, Miss Eseld." Perry bowed.

Eseld dimpled and dipped a curtsy.

Treeve went on, "We have just come to invite you to join us for dinner. All of you."

A moment of awkward silence followed, marked by the ticking of the clock. Mrs. Bray said nothing, did not even look her way, but in her stony profile, Laura saw her irritation. The woman probably thought Laura would jump at this chance to override her wishes and experience an evening with the local gentry. But Laura knew too well that Mrs. Bray did not want her anywhere near this particular gentleman.

Instead, Laura said, "Thank you, Mr. Kent. But I shall have to decline the pleasure. I feel a cold coming on, and the weather has turned rather chilly."

Treeve's eyes glinted knowingly. "You look perfectly healthy to me." He turned to his brother. "What say you, Perran? You're the professional."

"I am not well enough acquainted with Miss Bra—"

"Callaway," the older woman swiftly corrected. "Laura is my husband's niece through his first marriage."

"Ah. That's right. I forgot." Perry shifted from foot to foot, his face reddening.

"Never mind," Eseld soothed. "It's a natural mistake. And Laura *is* practically my cousin, living together as we have these many years now."

Laura felt weak gratitude seep into her heart at the young woman's words. *Dear Eseld.* She was probably only saying it to curry Treeve Kent's good opinion, but to her credit, Eseld *had* always treated her like a cousin, and not an unwelcome addition to the family.

For as Mrs. Bray pointed out, Laura was not really family. She was not related by blood to any of them. If not for Matthew Bray acting as her guardian after the deaths of her aunt and parents, Laura would be all alone in the world.

While Eseld and her mother dressed for dinner at Roserrow, the Kents' home, Laura helped Wenna in the kitchen—her penance for using their elderly cook-housekeeper's favorite pot to clean one of her finds.

Wearing a pained expression, Uncle Matthew appeared in the open doorway and beckoned Laura into his study. "I am sorry, my girl. I think you would have welcomed an evening out. You enjoy far too little entertainment or society."

"That's all right, I don't mind. I think I shall walk over and visit Miss Chegwin."

He gave her a rueful look. "The society of a woman in her seventies was not what I had in mind."

She reached up and adjusted her uncle's cravat, noticing his softening jaw, long silver side-whiskers, and kind hound-dog eyes. How the years and loss had aged him. Fastening the collar of his greatcoat, she said, "Button up. It's a blustery night."

"Yes, the wind is rising. If I don't miss

my guess, we'll be hearing Tregeagle before the night is out, wailing for his lost soul. . . ." He cleared his throat. "If I believed in such things, which, as a learned man of God, I do not." He winked. "Mostly."

He was referring to the old legend of the wicked man who sold his soul and had been wandering the coast and moors ever since, bewailing his fate. When the wind rose to its worst, its howl *did* sound almost human, hauntingly so. Cornwall, Laura had learned, was full of such myths, though the fierce storms and deadly gales were all too real.

"If Mrs. Bray did not have her heart set on a match between Eseld and Mr. Kent, I would beg off," he continued, "but she won't hear of us not going. I pray to God we don't regret it."

"Be careful," Laura urged. Uncle Matthew was the closest thing to family she had left, and she didn't want to lose him too.

"We shall be." He patted her hand and reached for his hat, then turned back. "If you go out tonight, take Wenna or Newlyn with you. I don't like the idea of you out alone after dark on a night like this. It's not safe."

"I can see Miss Chegwin's cottage from here," Laura protested.

"Please. For my sake, all right?"

"Very well, though it shall have to be

Newlyn, for I dare not ask Wenna. She is still cross about her pot."

"Wenna is always cross about something." He grinned. "Good thing she's an excellent cook."

Laura let herself into nearby Brea Cottage as she always did, her neighbor long ago insisting she treat their home as her own. Moreover, Miss Chegwin might not hear a knock above the howling wind.

Short, plain Newlyn sat resolutely on the small bench in the entry porch, refusing to go any farther.

"You can come in, you know," Laura said. "She does not bite."

"No, but Jago might." The seventeen-year-old housemaid shuddered.

"Silly creature. He is harmless."

"All the same, I'll wait here."

"Suit yourself."

Laura entered the snug sitting room, and the old woman looked up, delight written on her craggy features.

"Good evening, my lovely. How are'ee?"

"I am well, *Mamm-wynn*." Laura called her Grandmother as a term of affection and respect, for she knew it pleased her.

Mary Chegwin smiled, the lines of her wrinkled face softening under her halo of white hair. *"Meur ras,* my dear. And what brings you out on such a foul night?"

"I came to see you. The others have gone to Roserrow." She glanced around the humble sitting room. "Where is Jago?"

"Out looking for firewood." Trees were scarce in the area and firewood dear.

"I see." Laura sat down near the dying fire, keeping her cape fastened around her.

The woman watched her. "And did you not wish to go to Roserrow?"

"I . . . would rather see you."

The blue eyes, still keen, glinted knowingly, but she did not press her.

"I brought you something." Laura stretched out her hand.

"What is it?"

"A coin purse. See the embroidery there?"

The old woman squinted. "Pretty. Now if only I had a farthing to put in it!" Mary giggled like a girl. "Did you find it today?"

"No. That one is still wet. This one I found a year and a day ago."

Mary gave her a crooked grin. "You'll have to become less exacting if yer ever to be a Cornish lass."

"If I have not become one by now, I doubt I ever shall."

"Well, there are worse things, though I can't think of any at the moment." She cackled again.

"I also brought you some cake." Laura handed over a napkin-wrapped bundle.

Mary's eyes widened. "Wenna sent me cake?"

"No, I saved mine for you."

"I can't eat yer cake."

"Of course you can. You like it more than I do. But it will cost you."

Mary's wiry brows rose. "Oh?"

"Another tale."

The blue eyes twinkled. "I've already told'ee about the merry-maid's curse, but have I told'ee about the jealous piskies?"

Laura shook her head, eager to listen.

The old woman nibbled the cake, and then began the tale. "One night, during a harvest moon, the captain of a schooner called *Sprite* saw lights dancing on the waters and followed them to his demise. You see, those naughty piskies were jealous of the ship's beautiful figurehead, so they gathered a big jarful of glowworms to lure the unsuspecting mariners onto the Doom Bar. By morning, the sailors was drowned and all that remained of the ship was that figurehead, scarred by the rocks and no longer beautiful. It now marks the grave of all those lost on the ill-fated *Sprite*."

When Mary finished, Laura asked, "Is any of that true?"

"'Course it is! Have'ee not seen the grave along the coast?"

Laura had. But like most of Mary's tales, a liberal dose of fancy was woven among the facts.

Laura rose and put the kettle on. A few minutes later, refreshed by tea and shared cake, Laura urged, "One more?"

Mary smiled. "What shall it be this time? Smugglers? Pirates? Shipwrecks?"

Laura nodded. "Yes, please. All three."

Outside the wind continued to rise, and Mary began another story.

"One night, a large three-masted ship was drove under Trevose Head. Her lading was all sorts of warlike stores—muskets, bayonets, boarding pikes, and the like. All hands were lost except for three men. What country these men belonged to was not known." Mary leaned nearer and lowered her voice to an ominous pitch. "They was supposed to be pirates, and—"

The back door flew open and Laura started. Jago came in, a load of driftwood in his arms.

"*Meur ras*, Jago," Mary said. "Close the door dreckly, please. It's mizzling. I can feel the damp from here."

The tall, broad-shouldered young man dropped the wood near the hearth, then retreated into the kitchen to shut the door.

When he returned, he bent to build up the fire.

"Say good evening to our friend Laura," Mary prompted.

The big man with a prominent jaw and forehead shyly looked her way. "Evening, our Laura."

Some said Jago must be related to the Cornish giants of old. Some people, like Newlyn, were afraid of him due to his size, while others ridiculed him, assuming he must be slow of mind because he rarely spoke except to friends. But Laura knew him to be a gentle, thoughtful soul.

She smiled at him. "Good evening, Jago."

"Yer supper is on the stove," Mary added.

He nodded and turned to go, ducking his head to avoid hitting the lintel.

"I am sorry," Laura said. "Did I interrupt your supper?"

"Not at all. I ate while Jago was out foraging. Took him longer than usual to find enough wood to last through the night." She drew her shawl closer around her. "Sure to be a long winter this year. Thank God for Jago."

Jago, Laura knew, was not Miss Chegwin's natural son. Mary had worked for many years as a midwife and had never married or had children of her own. She had found the boy as an infant, abandoned in the church-yard.

She'd once explained, "I don't know why his mother abandoned him. Perhaps she was simply unwed and frightened. Dr. Dawe told me I was wasting my time, that the boy was too small and weak to survive, let alone thrive. Now, how I dearly enjoy parading my very tall, hale boy past him at church on Sundays."

From the kitchen, the sound of fork scraping against plate was followed by a festive tune—Jago playing his hurdy-gurdy. The music brought Laura back to the present. The wind now rattled the windowpanes, and water speckled the glass.

She stood. "May we finish the story another time? Newlyn and I had better go before the rain worsens."

Mary nodded. "*Meur ras* for the visit and the cake. *Nos dha.*"

"*Nos dha,*" Laura said, echoing the phrase for *good night*. She understood more Cornish than she spoke, but very little of either.

As she and Newlyn left, Laura drew the edges of her cape closed against the stinging wind, and Newlyn grumbled and held on to her bonnet. The wind moaned its ghostly wail, and Laura shivered from more than the cold.

"It's Tregeagle, miss, I know it!" Newlyn cried. "We're doomed."

"We are not doomed," Laura assured her, though any ship on open water might be. From the sound of it, a dreaded north-westerly gale had risen.

In the dark distance, a gun boomed and a voice shouted, "Ship, ho!"

Newlyn grabbed Laura's hand. "That's my pa."

Desperate ships frequently tried to navigate into Padstow's harbour to find shelter during storms. Many were carried onto the sands of the Doom Bar, where relentless waves either caused the ship to founder or sent it onto Greenaway Rocks to be pounded to kindling.

Laura hurried out to Trebetherick Point, Newlyn following reluctantly behind. From the overlook, Laura scanned the churning water below. A dark shape loomed off the rocks. It was difficult to see through the mist, but it appeared to be a ship thrashing in the waves.

Laura's stomach tightened, and her heart began to pound with a combination of fear and determination. "Come. Let's go down to the beach."

"Are'ee certain, miss? I don't think yer uncle—"

"I'm certain. Come on."

Laura turned and started down the narrow path, slipping on the wet sand and stumbling over a rabbit warren but managing not to fall.

Others were on the beach before them, gathering to wait. To watch. To hope.

From there, she could see more clearly. Weak moonlight now penetrated the rainy gloom, and streaks of lightning cracked the sky and illuminated the vessel. A ship a few hundred yards offshore was struggling. She rocked back and forth, listing too far to one side. She'd run aground on the rocks, and if she didn't lift off soon, the waves would tear her to pieces. Laura had witnessed it before.

Seeing a stocky fisherman nearby, Newlyn ran to his side and clutched his arm. "Oh, Pa!"

"Steady on, my girl."

Most local men were either fishermen like Mr. Dyer or boat builders, or employed as crews of sloops, loading and unloading vessels that traded in Padstow. Others worked in local slate and lead mines.

As Laura watched, small male figures on the ship's deck heaved crates and barrels overboard. One wiry youth climbed to the rigging to evade the encroaching water, but a huge wave struck the ship, washing him off the topsail yard and into the sea. He did not rise again. Had the crew already lowered their boats or had the sea torn them loose? Had they no way of escape? Few people Laura knew swam, but even if the sailors knew how, the waves and rocks were likely to crush them before they reached shore.

"Dear Jesus, help them," Laura cried. She wished there were something she could do. Something anyone could do.

Their parish had no rescue apparatus or official lifeboat. However, Cornish gigs manned by experienced pilots often acted as lifeboats, their size allowing them to maneuver into dangerous coves to reach victims. Why had no pilots responded tonight? Yes, the risks of rowing out in heavy seas were great. Many had paid with their lives for such bravery in the past. Had they not heard the shouts? The ship's gun signaling its distress?

As if reading Laura's thoughts, John Dyer looked around. "Where are the dashed pilots?" He called to a group of men loitering nearby, "Come on, lads—let's try to get to 'em."

"Pa, no," Newlyn pleaded. "It's too dangerous."

The brawny man loosed himself from his frightened daughter's grip. "Someone has to try."

Most men hung back, but three brave souls climbed into Dyer's boat and took up oars.

Laura thought of her own father—gone to sea in a ship and never returning—and grasped Newlyn's hand.

The men rowed hard, but the pounding surf drove them back. Twenty yards out a wave flipped the boat over as if it were a toy.

"Pa!" Newlyn cried, squeezing Laura's fingers tightly.

The men disappeared beneath the boat, beneath the waves. Laura held her breath and prayed. One by one their heads began to reappear, struggling to keep their mouths above water and return to shore. Other men on the beach, more motivated to help their own than some unknown sailors, grabbed a rope, and the bravest among them sloshed into the surf to help the struggling men. Thankfully, all four would-be rescuers made it back to shore, tired and bruised but alive. The boat, however, had suffered damage.

"How's Pa to fish now?" Newlyn wailed. "To support the little'uns? To live?"

More people gathered on the beach, lamps or torches in hand, others carrying pickaxes. Laura surveyed the torch-lit faces, heard the stomping of feet against the cold, and saw the eager rubbing of hands.

The first discarded barrel floated to shore, and the people pounced on it, circling it like ants to a spill of honey. This was followed by one crate and then another. With their axes, they pried them open, finding treasures like salted fish, a crate of figs and another of oranges, then a cask of wine. People exclaimed and called to their neighbors, some helping themselves then and there to the wine, others filling their pockets with fruit and fish. The scene took on the atmosphere of a macabre village fete.

Laura glimpsed golden-haired Treeve Kent among the revelers. What was he doing there?

He made to turn away, but realizing she'd seen him, he sauntered over, saying archly, "Home with a cold, I see."

"Entertaining my uncle's family, I see," she countered.

He smirked. "Evening grew boring without you there. I . . . went out for a pint, heard the gun, and came down to see what was happening." He avoided her gaze as he explained, she noticed.

"How long until the agent arrives?" she asked.

"Sooner than any of us would like, I imagine."

"You too?"

He sketched a shrug. "Why not?"

Laura held her tongue and returned her attention to the foundering brig.

Apparently having seen the wiry youth washed overboard and drowned, the rest of the ship's company remained on board. She counted nine or ten men and a boy, screaming for help. A wave crashed over the deck, sending others into the sea. One of the brig's two masts fell, and as it floated toward shore, Laura saw a man hanging on to it with one arm, his other wrapped around a comrade, trying to keep the man's head above water. Another wave swept over them and both men went under. The foremast popped up a few yards on, coming dangerously close to impaling one of the men in the shallows.

A desperate hand appeared above the water, before sinking again.

"He's close now, lads. Let's get 'im!" Newlyn's father called. He tied the rope around his waist and strode bravely into the water, while the others held the rope. Stretching as far as he could, Mr. Dyer reached down and grabbed the man by the back of his collar and dragged him toward shore. An incoming barrel knocked them both underwater, but friends came to John Dyer's aid and finally both men fell onto the sand.

Mr. Dyer rolled to his back, panting. Newlyn knelt at his side. But the other man lay unmoving.

Tom Parsons—an infamous wrecker and smuggler—strode across the beach toward them. His sandy-red hair stuck out in unkempt curls beneath his hat. He had faded freckles and deep scowl marks between his brows. He must have been a darling child, but as a man of fifty, he made Laura's skin crawl.

Seeing the unresponsive victim, Tom prodded him with a careless boot and muttered, "Good thing."

Laura looked around for help. If only Dr. Dawe had not gone to visit his sister . . .

"Roll him over," she said.

Mr. Dyer was too tired to move, and no one seemed willing to cross Tom Parsons to do so.

"Someone help me!" Laura bent and attempted to push the man over herself. A waterlogged adult male was heavier than he looked.

"Let 'im be," Tom commanded.

She looked up and saw the wrecker looming over her, cudgel in hand.

Horrified to think anyone would strike a helpless person, Laura felt righteous indignation steel her nerves. "No, *you* let him be."

In the past, people had the right to claim cargo from a "dead wreck," with no survivors, but the law had changed over thirty years ago. Now, goods washed ashore were supposed to be handed over to the rightful owners or duchy. Even so, many country people clung to the old ways, especially when their families were hungry, or worse, when there was a profit to be made. The penalties for wrecking ranged from fines to death, but perpetrators were rarely caught and convicted.

Laura shoved with all her might and rolled the man onto his side and then onto his stomach. A great deal of salt water came out of his mouth, and a little life began to appear.

Tom's voice remained deadly calm. "Back away, lass."

With a wary eye on the cudgel, she leaned protectively over the man. "No."

He raised the short, heavy club.

Treeve Kent stepped between them. "Everything all right, Miss Callaway? Ah. Good evening, Tom."

Parsons froze. "What'ee doin' here, Kent?"

Treeve gave the man a strained smile. "Same as you, I imagine."

"Doubt it. This don't concern'ee."

The shipwreck victim sucked in a watery breath and stretched out a hand, grasping at the sand.

"Newlyn!" Laura called. "Hurry and fetch

Jago, and tell Miss Chegwin to meet me at the house."

"But—"

"Now!"

Though Laura had rarely used such an authoritative tone with anyone, she had no other choice but to do so now, to assert herself as mistress over the timid servant. She would not leave this helpless man lying on the beach a moment longer than necessary. Unless she did something, she doubted the victim would live much longer, exposed to the brutal Atlantic and cold night air, let alone Tom Parsons's cudgel.

Whether due to her resolve in remaining at the fallen man's side or the presence of someone from one of the parish's leading families, Tom Parsons backed off, turning his attention to the barrels, casks, and crates instead, no doubt determined to salvage all he could before the duchy agent or a customs officer showed up.

A short while later, Jago came lumbering across the sand, drawing a few curious or disapproving gazes from those he passed. Fortunately, most people were too engrossed in rummaging through crates or going through the pockets of drowned men to pay him much notice.

"Jago, please carry him to Fern Haven."

The big man nodded, sank to his knees, and picked up the survivor as though he were a child.

Laura followed Jago across the beach, then turned back to Treeve. "Dr. Dawe has gone to his sister's. Please ask your brother to come as soon as he can."

"You think Perran can help?" His brows rose in surprise. "I suppose it's possible. Though I'd rather you asked me to call."

"Are you a doctor?"

"No. But if you want me, you need only ask." The handsome man stepped nearer, an impish gleam in his eye. "I am yours to bid."

Laura hesitated. Treeve might flirt with her, but she could not imagine his intentions were serious.

She met his gaze straight on. "Somehow I doubt that," she retorted, and hurried from the beach.

The captain, half drowned and unconscious, was carried up to a nearby house in the hope of [reviving] him.

—Bella Bathurst, *The Wreckers*

Chapter 2

The man had looked small in Jago's arms, but he looked larger laid in the modest guest-room bed. His shoulders were noticeably broader than his trim waist. He was perhaps thirty years of age with thick, wavy brown hair and a slim nose. Whisker stubble a shade darker than his hair shadowed the lower half of his face. He wore basic breeches, stockings, a shirt of cotton lawn. If he'd had shoes, hat, or greatcoat, the sea had claimed them. Nothing about the garments gave her any clue to his identity, though the fine shirt might be that of a gentleman.

"Let's get him out of these wet things," Miss Chegwin said.

With Jago's help, the older woman stripped

off his clothes and began washing the sand and blood from the injured man. Laura carried the wet garments down to the laundry.

Before she settled them into the tub, Laura searched for but found no identifying marks in the neck of his shirt or waistband of his breeches. As was common, the breeches had a buttoned fall flap that covered the front opening. This broad flap concealed a hip pocket. In it, she found three gold guineas and a silver pocket watch. The face displayed the usual Roman numeral hours and nothing else.

Leaving the clothes to soak, Laura returned to the guest room.

There Miss Chegwin was examining the man gently and methodically, his lower torso covered by a sheet.

After her years as a midwife, Mary Chegwin had worked as chamber nurse for Dr. Dawe, attending patients during their convalescence or journeys to eternity. Dr. Dawe had insisted she retire a few years ago due to her age, but the woman knew a great deal and had far more experience than Laura, especially where shipwreck victims were concerned.

The fact that she was needed again seemed to buoy Mary's spirits, and she suddenly appeared younger than her years, bending over her patient and testing the wholeness of his limbs.

"Ankle is swollen and bruised. I don't think it's broken, but can't be sure. Rope burns on his wrists. Maybe he tried tying himself to some wreckage. There's also an abrasion on the back of his head. Perhaps the mast or some other debris hit him."

She paused at a cut in his side. "Oh now, here's the worst yet. Deep it is. We'll have to clean and bandage that. Good thing he's out of his senses, for salt water stings something fierce."

Mary opened her old medicine case and began treating the wounds with murky tinctures and odoriferous salves while Laura assisted. Laura had been rather young to be of much help to her physician-father, but she had done what she could and had seen him working with enough patients that the actions now seemed natural.

Newlyn knocked and announced, "Mr. Kent, miss."

Perran Kent entered, a leather case in hand that gleamed as though brand-new. Laura introduced him to Miss Chegwin.

"Sure and I know'ee, lad. Nursed'ee through the croup years ago. Never knew a lad to cry so much. I hope you've outgrown it."

Perry cleared his throat. "I have."

He examined the patient much as Mary had, taking in the bruises, abrasions, and swollen ankle, which he declared was only sprained. "This is my first shipwreck, thank God, so I don't know if such injuries are common or not."

Mary nodded. "Could be much worse, as I've seen."

"Then thank heaven for small mercies." He frowned at the deep wound in the victim's side. "We had better stitch this up. I am no surgeon, mind, but I learned to do a bit of everything at Guy's."

He laid a hand over the man's brow. "He's very cold. Better build up the fire too."

Laura hurried to do so, but Jago was there before her, bending to the hearth. Seeing Newlyn hovering in the doorway, Laura said, "Please ask Wenna to send up a warming pan."

"Yes, miss." Newlyn hurried away, likely glad for a chance to distance herself from Jago as well as the stranger.

Perry gathered supplies from his bag. When he hesitated to pierce the skin, Miss Chegwin took the needle from him and began doing the stitching herself. "Women are better with needles, I find. We've had more practice."

Perry nodded in relief. "It's a mercy for

him that he has yet to regain his senses. Though if he doesn't soon, he may not at all. He might have gone without air too long."

Laura drew a deep breath. *Please, God, no.*

Old Mary's fingers were bent and frail, but they worked deftly. After a few minutes, she snipped the thread.

Perry studied her work. "Well done, Miss Chegwin. If I decide to stay and practice here, I would be honored to have you as my chamber nurse."

"Dr. Dawe says I'm too old."

"Then Dr. Dawe is a fool."

Mary grinned at that but neither agreed with nor refuted the claim.

The young man straightened. "I have to go. My parents will be worried. But I shall return in the morning to see how he fares."

Laura walked him to the door. "Thank you, Mr. Kent."

"Perry, please. Mr. Kent is my father. You make me feel ancient."

"After tonight, I should call you Dr. Kent."

He looked up at her humbly from beneath a fall of dark hair. "Then you would be the first—other than in jest, at any rate."

Laura smiled. "Very well. Dr. Kent. You deserve the title."

"Thank you." He looked back toward the

patient. "Keep him warm, and if he survives the night, well, we'll see."

Miss Chegwin watched him go, and when the door closed behind him, she tsked and shook her head. "That lad is worth two of his brother, but sadly ain't half as handsome."

"There are more important things," Laura replied.

"I agree but am surprised a young lady would. Well, you heard the doctor. Let's keep this poor soul warm."

Laura fetched a nightshirt from her uncle's dressing chest, and with Jago's help, the three of them managed to get it over his head, laced his hands through the sleeves, and worked it down over his body. Laura stepped back when Mary lowered the sheet, seeing only a flash of muscled, hairy legs before they were covered once again. Then Jago took his leave.

Mary shook her head. "Goodness, how he shivers. Where is that girl with the warming pan?"

They layered heavy wool blankets and a counterpane over the sheet. Even so, the man's shivering mounted to tremors.

"We could warm the bed the old-fashioned way," Laura said. "Did not servants once lie in their masters' beds to warm them?"

"Oh, iss, it were the way of things. And

only a few years back, a poor widow took in a half-dead sea captain after a wreck. She tried to revive him with brandy, and when that failed, warmed him in her own bed. Her country medicine worked. After he recovered, he credited her with saving his life and rewarded her handsomely. Twenty gold guineas! But you ought not do so, Miss Callaway. Yer a lady. And worse, damp through."

Yes, the rain and surf had soddened her skirts. She was near to shivering herself.

Thankfully, Newlyn came in with a warming pan—a closed container that held heated stones, sand, or embers from the fire.

"Good, you're here. Wrap this flannel around that and slide it under the bedclothes near his feet—but be careful not to scald him."

Newlyn did so, and after a few minutes, the man's tremors subsided.

Uncle Matthew and Mrs. Bray appeared in the doorway, still dressed in their coats and hats from their evening out. Eseld hovered in the background, trying to peek over their shoulders, but her mother shooed her away. "Go to your room, Eseld. This isn't a sight for you."

Eseld sighed dramatically but acquiesced.

"We learned of the wreck while at Roserrow and left as soon as we could," her uncle said. "Wenna tells us you brought a survivor here."

"Yes. I hope I did right."

"Right?" Mrs. Bray echoed. "I am not happy to find a stranger installed in my home, without so much as a by-your-leave. Did you not think to ask us first?"

Laura was not surprised Mrs. Bray was reluctant to have a stranger in her home. To be fair, the woman had welcomed her when she first married Matthew Bray, but that welcome had worn thin over the years, especially as Laura grew into womanhood and attracted the notice of Treeve Kent.

"You were away," Laura defended. "And the man needed help immediately."

Her uncle soothed, "It's only right the poor soul should find shelter in a clergyman's home." When Uncle Matthew moved from Truro to North Cornwall to marry Lamorna Mably and become vicar of the local parish, the bishop allowed him to live in his new wife's larger, brighter house instead of the damp old vicarage in St. Minver.

"We know nothing about him," Mrs. Bray insisted. "He might carry some foreign disease or be a criminal."

"Now, my dear, no need to jump to conclusions. I must leave to help with the dead, but this poor man poses no risk in his current state."

"Well." She huffed. "I hope you and Miss Chegwin can manage it yourselves, Laura, for I am going to bed. And I don't want Eseld in here either. Don't enlist her aid in nursing a strange man. Understood?"

Mrs. Bray turned to go but tossed over her shoulder, "For all we know he might be dangerous."

Seeing there was nothing else they could do for the man presently, Laura sent Miss Chegwin home to sleep, and asked Newlyn to sit with the patient while she helped her uncle lay out the bodies for burial. She promised to relieve the girl in a few hours' time.

Newlyn reluctantly agreed but moved the chair near the fire and far from the man, eyeing him warily, as though at any moment he might leap up and grab her by the throat.

Upon reaching the beach, her uncle paid the sexton and a few local men to carry the bodies to his cart and deliver the morbid load to St. Enodoc.

The small chapel was one of three churches in the parish and the nearest to the wreck site. It had become partially buried by sand dunes over the years and was no longer regularly used for divine services. Burials, however, continued. To enter the churchyard, one passed through a roof-covered lych-gate with its solitary slab or "coffin rest," used to lay out a single body before burial. But in cases like a shipwreck, with many sailors to be buried, they carried the bodies to the sexton's shed beyond the west hedge instead.

Reaching the shed, they hung a lantern high on a hook to illuminate the space and aid them in their work, and then laid the poor souls on the floor. Some of the victims had been badly battered by the rocks, while others looked as though they were simply asleep. Several had lost their shoes and coats or had them taken by wreckers.

Years ago, when she'd first seen a woman pulling boots from a drowned man, she'd been shocked and offended. Her uncle had calmed her, saying, "He won't need them where he's going. And she has six growing sons and not enough money to keep one well shod, let alone a half dozen."

But Uncle Matthew had been the one surprised when Laura offered to help after a wreck. Overworked as he always was, he'd agreed. She found the experience sad but not devastating. Perhaps it was because she was a physician's daughter who had seen the injured and dead on many occasions in her childhood, or possibly because she felt she could be of service to her uncle and, in a small way, to the recently departed.

Even though she knew anything of value had probably already been taken from them, she always looked for any identifying possession or mark that might remain. If there were survivors who could identify the dead, she recorded their names—her uncle was a horrid speller. And if there were no survivors, she wrote down brief descriptions of each victim, in case some loved one came to inquire after the bodies had been buried.

On naval ships, officers could often be identified by their uniforms. Even on a merchantman, the captain might wear a distinctive coat with epaulets. But the mates, carpenters, and ordinary seamen were far more difficult to classify.

Now she knelt beside each man, once again looking inside garments and pockets and writing descriptions:

Man aged 40–45. Grey hair. Green eyes. Rotund. Still wearing apron. The cook?

Man aged 25–30. Black hair. Brown eyes. Strawberry birthmark on his left brow. Initials T.O. inside his waistband and the collar of his shirt.

Laura paused. *T.O.?* The letters struck a chord. Were they his initials or something else? The answer tickled at the back of her mind. Surely it didn't signify what she thought it might. She tucked the suspicion away for later and moved on.

Boy aged 13–15. Red hair. Blue eyes. Freckles.

Tears blurred her vision as she wrote the words. So young. Thinking of his mother, wherever she was, Laura's heart ached, and she tenderly closed the boy's eyes.

When she had finished the list, Laura rose and handed it to her uncle.

"Thank you, my dear." He prayed over the men, asking God to have mercy on their souls, and then they spread a cloth over each body. They kept the cloths in the sexton's shed for just this purpose and, sadly, had used them several times.

"Eight men and one boy." Two less than she'd seen on the ship, though she might have miscounted.

He nodded. "The shroud maker shall be busy tomorrow."

He locked the shed behind them, to protect the bodies from further harassment, and the two started home together.

Driving away from St. Enodoc, Laura thought back to her first Sunday in the parish. She recalled her amazement at seeing her uncle lowered through the roof of the partially buried church, and her disapproval of the boisterous behavior of those gathered on the nearby mound. It had certainly not been the reverent atmosphere of a divine service she had come to expect. Mrs. Bray had accused her of looking as if she'd eaten a sour Italian lemon and cautioned her against criticizing traditions she knew nothing about. Eseld, however, had taken her hand and gently defended the strange custom, explaining that the vicar was required to conduct a service there at least once a year to maintain tithing rights and consecration.

Now, as they traveled back in the cart, Laura felt a little embarrassed to think of how naïve, and yes, judgmental, she had been as a sheltered youth. She still struggled to understand her Cornish neighbors, but she had grown rather fond of many of them. Even though her uncle had been new to the parish of St. Minver too, he had been born and raised in Cornwall, and so was not seen as an incomer. He had endured the strange new experiences with his usual patient stoicism. Dear Uncle Matthew. Always so kind and patient with her as well. At the thought, a wave of affection washed over Laura, and she laid her head on his shoulder for the rest of the journey.

When they reached Fern Haven, a vaguely familiar man came riding up the road. "You go in, Laura," her uncle said. "I'll just have a quick word with Mr. Hicks first."

Laura nodded, too tired to argue.

Returning to her room physically and emotionally exhausted, she stripped off her damp pelisse, unpinned her front-fastening gown, and wriggled it off her hips. Then she loosened and stepped from her damp petticoat, removed her half boots, and yanked off her sodden stockings. Finally, dressed in her mostly dry shift and stays, she washed her hands, wrapped her dressing gown around herself, and tiptoed to the guest room to ask Newlyn to unlace her stays, and to see how their patient fared.

Quietly opening the door, she found Newlyn asleep, slumped in the chair, and the fire burned to embers. The man, she quickly saw, was shivering again, his lips blue by candlelight.

She pulled the cold warming pan from under the bedclothes and carried it to the fire, quickly filling it with smoldering embers. She wrapped it in the flannel and slipped it between sheet and blankets, safely away from the man's legs. Then she bent to add more fuel to the fire, poking it back to life.

"Newlyn," she whispered, gently shaking the girl's shoulder.

The maid mumbled something and went on sleeping.

Laura gave up. She watched the man for a few minutes, but his shivering continued. Remembering the story Miss Chegwin had told her about the poor widow who saved a sea captain, Laura pulled back a corner of the bedclothes and carefully climbed in beside him.

She had never been in bed with anyone before. What did one do to warm a cold body? Was proximity sufficient, or was physical contact required?

She edged closer, until her shoulder touched his arm and her hip his leg. She was covered, she reminded herself, and so was he—well, except for their legs. And he was insensible, so really, she bolstered herself, there was nothing scandalous in her actions.

His convulsive shivering lessened but did not stop altogether.

She rolled to her side, her face near his shoulder. Reaching out hesitantly, she put her arm over his torso, relieved to find his chest rising and falling with regularity. She felt the hard muscle of his arms beneath the nightshirt, and the leanness of his belly. Her own body flushed, embarrassed by the intimate position. Hopefully, her nearness would have a similarly warming effect on him.

As if vaguely aware of a presence, the man turned his head toward her and murmured something into her hair. A name, perhaps. Honora? Three syllables murmured too softly and too quickly for her to gather any impression of his speech. Then he slackened again and said no more.

Being so warm and tired, Laura felt her eyelids grow heavy. She decided she would close them, just for a few minutes.

Sometime later, she heard a gasp and jolted awake. Morning light shone through the shutters.

Newlyn stood nearby, staring at her, brows high and eyes round as *O*'s. "Miss, what'ee doing? What would yer uncle say?"

What would Mrs. Bray say, is the more frightening question, Laura thought. She whispered back, "He was shivering again. The doctor said we had to keep him warm."

Deciding to refill the warming pan, Laura folded back the blankets and swung her legs from bed.

Just as the door opened.

Her uncle and Mrs. Bray stood framed in the open doorway and drew up short to see Laura sitting on the edge of the man's bed. Eseld's wide eyes appeared over her mother's shoulder.

"What is going on here?" Mrs. Bray demanded.

Laura stood, thanking heaven they had not entered a few minutes earlier.

Her uncle's brow puckered. "Is he wearing my nightshirt?"

"Sorry, Uncle," Laura said sheepishly as she retrieved the pan. "We were following doctor's orders to keep him warm. Newlyn, please refill this." Laura turned her burning face away, tucking the blankets more securely around their patient.

"Doctor? I thought Dr. Dawe was still away?"

"He is. I meant Perran Kent."

"Ah . . . A boy delivered a message about the wreck last night, and Perry dashed out without a word of explanation."

"A boy? Did not Treeve Kent deliver the message?"

"Treeve?" Mrs. Bray frowned. "Why should it be Treeve? He left the house earlier, some important meeting of the parish council, he said. Rather ruined our evening, first Treeve, then Perry leaving. A sorry party for Eseld."

Important meeting? Laura doubted it.

"You saw Treeve?" Eseld asked, expression anxious.

Laura didn't want to hurt her feelings or

raise her jealousy, so she said, "Only in passing. He . . . must have left his important meeting when the ship fired its guns. People came running from all directions."

"Including you."

"Yes."

Mrs. Bray's disapproving gaze moved from the still man to Laura. "Well. It isn't seemly for you to be alone in here in your dressing gown."

Laura gestured to the tongue-tied maid, cowering in the corner. "Newlyn was with me all the while."

Her uncle stepped nearer the bed. "No sign of regaining his senses?"

Laura shook her head. "He murmured something in his sleep, but that is all."

Mrs. Bray lifted a warning hand to Eseld and then followed her husband farther into the room, staring down at the stranger. "I don't like the look of him. Like a pirate. Or a foreigner. He might be a spy, for all we know."

"I don't think so, my dear," Uncle Matthew said. "The captain's chest washed ashore, and by it the ship has been identified as an English merchantman called the *Kittiwake*. I talked to Mr. Hicks, the agent, after you were in bed. He will determine what to do with the cargo his men are able to salvage."

Laura said, "Precious little, I imagine,

after Tom Parsons and his lot were through with it."

Mrs. Bray narrowed her eyes. "Remember, it's not your place to judge, Laura. You're not Cornish and don't understand our ways."

No, Laura did not, but she wisely held her tongue.

Chapter 3

Later that morning, Uncle Matthew returned to the churchyard to select a
grave site, and the sexton began digging.
Until five years ago, bodies washed ashore
were not legally permitted burial in conse-
crated ground. The usual practice had been
to bury shipwreck victims anywhere and any-
how, often in a common grave near the site of
the wreck—on the cliffs or the grassy verge of
beaches. Thankfully, a local MP had worked
for a change in the law, and that practice had
been abolished.

Miss Chegwin, looking well rested and
eager, came over to sit with their patient that

morning, telling Laura to get some sleep or fresh air.

She gratefully acquiesced, dressed warmly, and with her basket in hand went for a walk, starting at Daymer Bay. As Laura strolled, she searched the sand, among the faded clumps of sea thrift, between the rocks, and in the rock pools. She saw nothing of interest.

Moving on, she returned to the wreck site.

On Greenaway Beach, there were still signs of the melee of the night before. Broken barrels and crates and shards of pottery littered the sand. An old man was leaning against an overturned cask, sleeping off his overindulgence.

She continued on, farther from the site.

At the far end of Greenaways, dark rocks bordered the beach, and here and there lay purple slate with faint green stripes. Against this lighter background, she spied an object like a small black animal or perhaps a wad of material. She drew nearer, bent and studied the object, and then gingerly picked it up. A black two-cornered hat. Nothing frightening, yet it filled her with an odd foreboding.

Silly creature, she remonstrated with herself. She had lived among superstitious people for too long.

Laura knew hats like these, being valuable and looking alike, often carried a man's name embroidered within, especially among the military. She had found other cocked hats and *chapeaux bras* before. She looked inside the crown, and there was indeed a bit of embroidery: *A. Carnell*. The name meant nothing to her.

She put it in her basket. The salt water would do it no favors, but perhaps if she cleaned it quickly, it could be salvaged.

A. Carnell. One of the dead? Or the living?

When she returned to the house, she found Miss Chegwin hovering over the patient. The man moaned and turned his head one way, then the other.

Laura's pulse quickened. "What is it? What's happened?" She set aside her basket and untied her bonnet strings as she hurried forward.

Miss Chegwin laid a hand on his forehead. "He's burning up with fever."

From freezing cold to burning hot? That could not be good.

Fear gripped her. "Shall I fetch cool water and cloths?"

"Iss, thank'ee."

"What do you think it is?" Laura asked. *Please don't let her say "putrid or malignant sore throat. . . ."*

"Putrid throat, mayhap. Lord willing, not scarlet fever or typhus."

Lord willing, indeed.

Hurrying to her task, Laura came back a few minutes later, basin and clean cloths in her arms.

The man continued to thrash.

Old nurse Chegwin spoke in gentle, cooing tones, trying to soothe him with words Laura didn't understand. She was speaking in her first language, which few people still spoke.

Laura set the basin on the side table and dipped and wrung out the first cloth. "Why do you speak to him in Cornish? Do you think he doesn't understand English?" She thought of Mrs. Bray's fears that he might be a foreigner.

"I doubt he understands anything at this point. The words don't matter, not in the state he's in. It's the reassuring tone that helps. Leastways, that's what I've come to believe after sitting at sick beds all those years. Besides, it comes natural to me to speak the Kernewek. I can hear my own mamm speaking to me so when I were a wee girl."

The man continued to moan and jerk his legs. Laura hoped he wouldn't tear his stitches. She handed Miss Chegwin the cool cloth.

Mary laid it on his brow and then, with the second one Laura offered, began dabbing his cheeks, his neck, and the hairy vee of his chest visible in the open neckline of the nightshirt.

"Shh, my 'ansome . . ." the old woman hushed, and again began soothing him in her native tongue, Laura catching a few words but not many.

Eyes still closed, the man murmured a low reply.

Laura did not understand his response either.

Mary stilled, glancing over at her. "He answered me. In Kernewek! He understood me—I know he did."

"What did he say?"

"Ill as he is, it were a bit garbled, but I believe he said, 'Thank you, Granny.'" Her eyes brightened. "Don't often hear young people speaking the old language anymore. Does my heart good. He must be Cornish."

How unexpected. And the news should quell Mrs. Bray's suspicions that he might be a foreigner.

When the patient's fever continued to climb despite their ministrations, Miss Chegwin said, "Can't believe I'm saying it, but I wish Dr. Dawe were here. Perhaps we ought to send for that young man again."

"I agree." Laura rose, wishing there were

a faster way to summon him than walking to Roserrow. But Mrs. Bray and Eseld had gone shopping in Wadebridge, and her uncle had taken their only other horse on his rounds to the three churches in the parish.

Seeing her hesitate, Miss Chegwin said, "Take my donkey cart. Jago will harness it for you."

Laura nodded. "Thank you."

A short while later, Laura was again dressed for the brisk outdoors and on her way to Roserrow, about a mile and a half away, between Trebetherick and the church town of St. Minver.

The donkey was old and the cart rickety. She hoped they were traveling faster than she could have on foot.

After passing through Trebetherick, with its village shop and forge, Laura crossed a small bridge over a stream, then turned onto a sandy track, following it until the tall gables of Roserrow came into view. The two-and-a-half-story grey stone house was crowned with squat chimneys, while heavy columns braced its entry porch. Other than that, there was little ornamentation either in the architecture or grounds.

As she reached the drive, a groom came out to greet her, clearly looking down his long nose at her humble mode of transportation.

Treeve Kent, dressed in a well-cut riding coat, buckskin breeches, and tall leather boots, was just coming from the stables. His face brightened upon seeing her.

"Miss Callaway, what an unexpected pleasure." He diverted his steps in her direction.

"Mr. Kent, is your brother at home? Our patient has taken a turn for the worse. A fever of some kind."

"Horrors. Exactly the sort of thing Perry likes. Just don't tell Mamma or she'll forbid him to go. What kind of a doctor he'll be if he refrains from visiting the truly sick, I don't know, but Mamma would prefer it, sure he'll bring home some foul disease like malignant sore throat."

Laura shivered at the thought. She had lost her baby brother to that very malady.

He led her into the house and invited her to wait in the hall. "Sit here, if you like. This settle is about as comfortable as a pile of rocks. But then, you might like that, being something of a ruddy turnstone, pecking along the rocky shore for treasure." He winked and strode away.

Laura had never been compared to a sea bird before and was not sure she liked it.

She sat on the hard settle and looked around the austere hall. Few pieces of art—statuary or paintings—were on display. Only a dozen stern-looking portraits of Kent ancestors.

A few minutes later, dark-haired Perran came trotting down the stairs, bag in hand and expression somber. "Miss Callaway, Treeve said something about our patient taking a turn?"

"I'm afraid so. He has come down with a fever. Miss Chegwin is with him now."

"Then let us waste no time."

He donned his greatcoat and followed her out to the stable yard. He took one look at the ancient donkey and even older cart and called to the groom, "Saddle Lightning and quickly."

He turned to her. "You get started. I'll ride separately, if you don't mind. That way, I'll arrive sooner and won't have to walk back nor ask you to venture out again with that nag."

"If you think taking the time to saddle another horse will be faster?"

"Undoubtedly."

As they stood talking, a fine barouche arrived. Laura recognized the mineowner Mr. Roskilly and his daughter inside.

Treeve came out to greet them, all charm and warmth.

"Ah, Mr. Roskilly and Miss Roskilly, welcome to Roserrow." He offered the thin, dark-haired woman a hand down. "Come in, come in. My parents are eager to greet you.

Sadly, my brother will not be able to join us after all."

But Treeve did not look the least bit sad, and neither did pretty Miss Roskilly.

Laura turned to climb into the cart. Perry belatedly realized he should have offered her a hand, and ended up awkwardly cupping her elbow. Laura sent the young man a reassuring smile and urged the old donkey into reluctant motion, down the drive and back onto the sandy track that led to Fern Haven.

Sure enough, a few minutes later, Perry galloped up behind her on a black horse. She directed the donkey to the side and waved as he passed and rode on ahead, bag strapped to his saddle by leather cords.

Lightning indeed, Laura thought, impressed.

When she reached Brea Cottage, Jago was waiting for her and took charge of the cart and donkey. Laura thanked him and hurried up the rise and across the road to Fern Haven.

Perry was already in the guest room, pouring some liquid between the man's lips.

"What do you think ails him?" Laura asked, panting to catch her breath.

"Lung fever, I believe. His lungs certainly sound congested, which is no wonder after nearly drowning. I've bled him and given him fever powder and an expectorant. He'll need rest and quiet. There's little else I can do."

"I will help Laura nurse him," Miss Chegwin said. "Together we shall see him through. He's a strong Cornish lad, after all."

Perry's dark brows rose. "Is he?"

"Miss Chegwin spoke Cornish to him," Laura explained. "He seemed to understand, even replied in kind."

"Interesting. Well, I wish there were more I could do. I'll return tomorrow to see how he fares."

"Thank you. I would appreciate that. We all would."

He closed his bag and looked up at her with a tentative smile. His smooth skin and large dark eyes gave him a sweet boyish appearance. As Miss Chegwin had said, he was not nearly as handsome as his older brother. Seeing him look at her the way he was now, however, a girl could easily forget he even had a brother.

But then Laura realized he was not looking at her but past her. She turned and saw Eseld in the passage just beyond the door. She was the recipient of Perry's admiring gaze.

Unfortunately, Eseld saw no one but Treeve.

After Perry left, Miss Chegwin murmured, "All he can do, perhaps, but not all *I* can do."

The old nurse worked steadily. She alternated between building up the fire when chills racked his body and having Jago help her submerge the man in a cool slipper bath when the fever spiked once more.

"We called it winter fever in my day," she said, "seeing as it seems to strike when the weather turns cold, the old and the very young most of all."

To help relieve his congestion and labored breathing, Mary asked Newlyn to bring in pots of boiling water. She placed them near the bed and left another large kettle steaming over the room's fire. But Wenna complained to Mrs. Bray about the maid's usual work falling to her, so after that Laura and Miss Chegwin split the work between them.

In the hearth, Mary burned a combination of herbs harvested from hedgerows and her own garden: comfrey, peppermint, and eucalyptus.

Later, she spread a plaster of her own making over the man's chest—aromatic and potent.

At Mary's instruction, Laura made the man sip liquids as often as he'd take them—tea, water, broth, and elderberry syrup.

They tended the patient all that day and the next. Eventually, his breathing eased and both his fever and chills subsided.

"You've done it, Miss Chegwin," Laura exclaimed. "His fever has broken. Now, do go home and get some sleep. You've worked yourself ragged, and we don't want you falling ill as well. We need you."

She patted Laura's hand. "Feels good to be needed again."

The woman did as Laura bid, adding, "But send for me if he worsens."

"I shall."

After Mary left, Laura sat at the man's bedside, gently pressing a cup of water to his lips at regular intervals. She recalled doing the same for one of her father's patients long ago. Mamma had been out somewhere that day when the summons came, and Laura had asked Papa if she might go along. He had hesitated, but soon gave in to her request, as he often did, and the two set out together. After he'd examined the elderly woman, he'd asked Laura to sit with the patient while Papa went to tell her husband the melancholy news—his wife was gravely ill and hadn't long to live. Even with Laura's small experience of sickness, she saw how much restless fever there was in the woman's speech, and some instinct prompted her to tell a long story to distract the old dear, describing their recent visit to the seaside, her new frock for the trip, her baby brother's antics—all in an easy flow of talk that proved very soothing to the patient, giving her something to think about beyond her immediate suffering.

The woman had liked her and asked Dr. Callaway if Laura could come again. Papa agreed, pride evident in his expression. After that, she had visited the woman daily, helping as much as she could, explaining the finer directions of her treatment and diet to the rotating nurses, and talking to the patient about everything and nothing until she passed peacefully in her sleep.

As Laura again leaned near to help the man sip from the cup, Mrs. Bray came in but remained near the door.

"How is he?" she asked. "I do hope you don't catch something, Laura. Really, you should leave the nursing to Miss Chegwin."

Hope flared. Was that maternal concern in the woman's voice? But Laura guessed Mrs. Bray was more concerned about her passing on some infection to Eseld.

Defensiveness rose. "Mary can't remain awake round the clock."

"She must have done, when she worked for Dr. Dawe."

"But she is over seventy now, remember."

"Yes, well. I am as charitable as the next person, but I will want our guest room restored to us soon. There must be . . . institutions for shipwrecked souls like him."

"None near here."

"Very well. Just . . . do all you can to move him along."

"I shall do everything in my power to help him recover, rest assured."

Eseld's bright, inquisitive face appeared in the doorway beside her mother. "What is going on?"

"Stay out, Eseld. I won't have you falling ill."

"Of course not, Mamm. But Laura here is perfectly expendable." She winked.

"I did not say that." Lamorna Bray lifted her chin. "It is her choice to risk her health. I am not her mother to command her. But I am yours, so take care."

"Yes, Mamm. I'll just stand here and keep Laura company for a time."

"If you must, but be careful not to take a chill."

When Mrs. Bray had gone, Eseld looked mischievously down the passage to be sure they were alone, then tiptoed into the room, closer to the bed, though not too close.

"How old is he, do you think?"

Laura shrugged. "I would guess thirty, or a bit more."

"Too old for me, but just right for you."

Laura huffed. "I am only two years older than you are."

"In numbers, perhaps, but in other ways you are far older."

Laura could not disagree.

Eseld pushed the candle lamp closer to the man. "Hard to see if he is handsome or not, covered in all those whiskers." She tilted her head to one side as she studied him. "He has a good nose. Thin and straight. Aristocratic almost. And a very pleasant mouth. See how his lips are fuller at the center?"

Laura had noticed but did not admit it.

"He needs a shave and haircut," Eseld added.

"Are you offering?"

"Me? Heavens no. I wouldn't know how. A shame your uncle hasn't a valet."

Laura used to cut Uncle Matthew's hair after her aunt Anne, his first wife, died. So deep in grief he'd been, he had not cared a whit about his appearance or much of anything else. But since he'd remarried, his wife insisted he go to the barber in Black Rock.

"Well, this man will not be going to a barber for the foreseeable future," Laura said.

"Is he very poorly?"

"If you had asked me yesterday, I would have been hard-pressed to hold out hope, but he seems much improved, thanks to Miss Chegwin and Perran Kent."

"Did Perry help?"

"Absolutely."

"Will he be a good doctor, do you think?"

"With experience, a very good doctor, I predict."

"Then perhaps you should marry him, Laura. It would be perfect, your being a doctor's daughter and all. That would leave Treeve for me. Perry isn't as handsome, but he's twice as clever, which is just as you like."

Laura reared back her head in surprise but did not argue. She admired intelligence, that was true, but she was not immune to a handsome face.

Eseld looked around the room and took a deep breath. "Well, it certainly livens up the place, having a mysterious man living under our roof. Or would do, if he would hurry and come to his senses. Do you think he is married or single?"

"No way to know."

"Yes, a pity men don't wear rings. It would help a girl to know whom to flirt with and whom to ignore."

Laura chuckled at that.

"Mamm is right about one thing," Eseld went on. "He looks like a pirate with that dark beard and wild hair. Do you think he might be one, or at least a smuggler?"

"No, I do not. The wreck was a merchant ship from Yarmouth."

"Perhaps he sneaked on board, killed all the crew, and then ran the ship onto the rocks to cover his crimes."

"Heaven forbid." Laura laughed. "What an awful imagination you have."

"All right. If you don't like that . . . perhaps he is no ordinary sailor or merchant . . . but a man in pursuit of the woman he loves." Her lively eyes brightened with her tale. "He'd met her briefly once. She told him she was a sea captain's daughter, but she disappeared before he could ask the name of her father's ship or their home. And now he sails from port to port, just hoping to find her again."

Laura groaned. "Oh, bother. That is worse than the last."

"Is it?" Eseld sighed. "Sounds romantic to me."

"Sounds like a great waste of time to me."

Uncle Matthew came in. "Girls, how is our visitor? Good to see you showing an interest, Eseld."

"He has improved, thankfully," Laura replied. "The fever has broken."

"Good, good. I have been praying for him and will continue to do so."

Newlyn knocked on the open door. "A Mr. Hicks to see you, sir."

"Ah. That's the acting ship's agent. Show him in, please."

Laura knew that in the case of shipwrecks, a local agent for the duchy would attempt to salvage all possible cargo and the vessel itself and then be reimbursed accordingly. Salvaged cargoes of imperishable goods like copper ore, iron, or timber would either be shipped on to their intended destination or auctioned off for what could be raised to cut the owner's or underwriter's losses.

A small, well-dressed, balding man appeared, leather portfolio under his arm. This was the man who had stopped to talk to her uncle the night of the wreck.

"Laura, Eseld," Uncle Matthew began, "this is Mr. Hicks, the wreck agent."

The small man bowed. "Good day, ladies. I am curious to see how yer visitor is getting on. I'd like to report his name to the owners, if I can."

"He is some improved, thankfully," Laura said. "But still not sensible, as you see."

Mr. Hicks glanced at the bed. "A pity. Well, in the meantime, I have written to the owners for an official list of the crew and cargo, so a reckoning may be taken of what we manage to salvage, and the next of kin might be notified. Hopefully, our friend here will awaken and be able to give us all the information we need, though he'll no doubt be grieved to hear his mates have all perished."

"True." Her uncle nodded sadly. "A rude awakening awaits him indeed."

Laura sat at their patient's bedside that evening, trying to read about that famous castaway, Robinson Crusoe, but kept nodding off. She couldn't remember the last time she'd been so tired.

Nearby, the man rested peacefully, and Laura began to long for her own bed.

She picked up a book of hymns and tried reading aloud to keep herself awake.

> "God moves in a mysterious way,
> His wonders to perform;
> He plants his footsteps in the sea,
> And rides upon the storm. . . ."

Growing weary of reading, Laura rose and paced around the room, then fingered the man's pocket watch again. An idea striking her, she pried open the back, held it near the lamp, and by its light saw the winding stem. Also etched there was the name of the watchmaker: *L'Epine*. Not so surprising.

French fashions were in demand, after all, war or no war.

Newlyn appeared. "Miss? The Kent brothers have called. They're in the parlour with Mrs. Bray and Eseld but ask if they might come up and see the patient." The maid grinned and lowered her voice. "It's really you they want to see, but they be smoothin' Mrs. Bray's feathers."

"Ah. Well, certainly," Laura said, glad for the company. She surveyed her reflection in the mirror, pushing a loose strand of hair behind her ear.

Treeve entered first. "Good evening, Miss Callaway," he said with a gallant bow.

Laura curtsied in reply.

He glanced at the sleeping man. "I would ask you to introduce your new friend, but he seems . . . otherwise engaged."

Perry stepped in after him. "How is he?" he asked, moving to the bedside.

"Better, thank heaven."

The young medical man seemed surprised to find the patient's brow cool and his breathing easy. "You're right. No sign of fever. God be praised."

"Yes." Laura added with a grin, "And Mary Chegwin be praised as well."

Perry nodded. "Hear, hear."

Laura looked from one to the other. "What brings you two here tonight?"

"Begging compliments, Miss Callaway?" Treeve smirked. "It isn't like you."

"I was not—"

He held up a conciliatory palm. "Only teasing. You are ever so diverting to tease."

"I came to see our mystery man, and Treeve invited himself along," Perry explained.

Treeve spread his hands. "How could I resist an opportunity to call upon the lovely ladies of Fern Haven?"

Perry, she noticed, rolled his eyes.

No one could deny that Treeve was charming, likable, and generous with his compliments. But Laura knew he liberally shared his flattery with many females so paid it little heed.

Perry turned from studying the patient to her. "You look tired. Do you feel all right?"

"I am well—just a bit weary."

"No wonder, caring for this man around the clock."

Laura looked down, feeling self-conscious. "Hardly that."

"Yes," Treeve said, "you've been devoting too much of your attention to this veritable stranger while all but ignoring your old friends. I begin to grow quite jealous."

She shook her head. "I doubt it."

Eseld appeared in the passage, bright smile belied by her clasped hands. "Treeve? Do come down. We hoped you would make a fourth in whist."

"Very well." He backed from the room with a Shakespearean bow complete with rolling hand. "Pray excuse me, Miss Callaway. The fair Eseld beckons."

Eseld dimpled and giggled and led the way downstairs. This time it was Laura's turn to roll her eyes.

Perry's forlorn gaze followed them from the room, and then he turned his attention back to her. "Are you certain you feel well?"

"Yes."

He reached a hand toward her. "Do you mind?"

She stilled, unsure, then relaxed as he laid cool fingers on her brow. "You don't feel overly warm, but you ought to get some rest— I would not want you to fall ill. Our patient is out of danger, so go and get a good night's sleep, all right? Doctor's orders." He softened the command with a grin.

Laura exhaled deeply. "Sounds heavenly, I admit. Thank you again for all your help."

"I did very little and was glad to be of assistance. Do let me know if there is any change."

"I shall. Good night."

The next morning, Laura drank tea and buttered a second piece of toast while her uncle prepared to depart. She would normally accompany him on his calls or walk the beaches if she wasn't needed, but today she went up to the guest room. A few minutes later, Miss Chegwin returned with a bowl of broth she'd prepared at home. "Don't tell Wenna." She winked and took a chair near the bed.

"I'll sit with him for a bit," Mary said. "See if I can get him to drink this broth. You get some sleep."

"I slept most of the night, since Dr. Kent declared him out of danger," Laura said, "but I could use some fresh air."

"Go on, then."

Dressing warmly, Laura again went strolling on the beaches near Fern Haven. She walked along Greenaways as before, then expanded her search. Sometimes things washed ashore over a longer distance. She climbed the grassy cliff and descended into the next cove. There she again looked among the rocks, and all along the sandy stretch of Polzeath Beach until she reached a rock pool at its other side.

In the water trapped there after the tide

receded, something metallic glinted up at her. She bent and looked closer. A bottle?

She reached into the pool and drew out a flask of pewter or tarnished silver bearing a fine scrollwork design. Might be worth something. She gave it a little shake—empty—then placed it in her basket.

"What'ee find?"

Laura whirled, startled to find Tom Parsons looming above her. She'd not heard him over the wind and surf.

Uneasy at finding herself alone with the man, she chose a friendly approach. No use in angering him. "Just an empty pewter flask. You?"

He studied her expression, and she forced herself to look back. He finally broke eye contact, wincing into the morning sunlight.

"Nothing today, though I found plenty the night of the wreck before the agent and customs man came."

"Well, all the best to you." She turned to go, but his voice held her as forcefully as a hand on her arm.

"If'ee find something o' value, like a lockbox or chest or somethin,' you let old Tom know, won't'ee?"

His eyes glinted, and she barely resisted the urge to step back. "If I find anything like that, I will certainly let the appropriate people know."

She held his piercing gaze a moment longer, nodded, and then turned to go.

"I'll be watchin'ee, up-country lass," he called after her.

She felt his eyes searing holes through her back, through her soul, but she kept walking at a calm, steady pace away from him, even as she longed to run all the way home.

The gig, a six oared boat, is almost as traditional to Padstow as is the May Day 'Obby 'Oss ceremony. The gigs also acted as lifeboats to stricken vessels and also as salvers for the Doom Bar victims.

—BRIAN FRENCH, *WRECKS & RESCUES AROUND PADSTOW'S DOOM BAR*

Chapter 4

After her encounter with Tom Parsons on the beach, Laura returned to Fern Haven with a long exhale of relief. She took off her outdoor things and hung up her bonnet, then walked to the guest room to talk to Miss Chegwin.

She found the room empty, except for the man in bed, head propped on pillows.

She drew up short and gave a little gasp of surprise. "Oh!"

His eyes were open, and blue-green like the sea.

"Good morning," she said.

He did not reply, but those striking eyes watched her with wary interest as she crossed the room.

"I am Laura Callaway," she began. "And you are . . . ?"

He did not respond.

She swallowed, excited and nervous at once. "Do you know where you are? I imagine it might all be a muddle. You are in a house near Trebetherick. It's a small hamlet, so you probably have not heard of it. But larger Padstow is two miles from here, across the Camel Estuary."

His brow puckered in confusion or deep thought.

Clasping damp hands together, she said, "I'm afraid your ship was wrecked. The *Kittiwake*? Perhaps your captain tried to navigate into the harbour to shelter from the storm. The ship may have struck Stepper Point or the Doom Bar, and then waves carried it onto the Greenaway Rocks. Does any of this sound familiar?"

Miss Chegwin came in, bowl of gruel in hand.

"Ah, yer back, Laura. Good. I went to ask Wenna for something more substantial now that our patient is awake. Has he spoken?"

"Not to me."

"Nor me," Mary said. "And I tried both English and Cornish."

Laura turned back to the man and said, "This is Miss Mary Chegwin, our neighbor and an excellent nurse. She and I have been caring for you. Oh, and Dr. Kent, but he is not here right now."

The man blinked but seemed to be struggling to make sense of the scene, of finding himself in a strange bed with two strange women looking down at him.

Miss Chegwin tried again. "Yer in Cornwall. *Kernow.*"

"*Kernev?*" He imperfectly echoed the Cornish word for the county.

Mary shook her head. "Ker*now*," she repeated, emphasizing the final syllable.

He looked down, expression troubled. Did he not understand? Was he a foreigner after all?

Jago came in with more wood—wood foraged from shredded ship timbers, she guessed.

The man looked up at him in alarm. Did Jago's size intimidate him, or was it something else? It might have been her imagination, but he seemed nervous.

"This is Jago," Laura hurried to explain. "Our friend and neighbor. He lives with Miss Chegwin."

"My adopted son, really," Miss Chegwin added with a friendly smile. "Don't let his size worry you. He wouldn't hurt a midge. Well, maybe a midge, but not a person."

Jago laid more wood on the fire and then quit the room. The man relaxed slightly, but still his eyes seemed distracted and distant. She could almost see his mind whirling behind them.

"You have nothing to fear from us," Laura assured him. "We are friend, not foe. My uncle is the vicar here, and a good man."

His Adam's apple rose and fell as though with effort.

Seeing it spurred Laura into action. She poured a glass of water from the pitcher on the dressing chest and carried it to him. "You must be thirsty. Here."

He slowly reached out for the glass and raised it to his lips.

"Don't gulp it," Miss Chegwin warned. "You'll be sick."

Drawn by the jingling tack of a horse and wagon outside, Miss Chegwin turned to look out the window.

"Pray excuse me. I've a load of seaweed bein' delivered. So good for next year's garden, I find." She handed Laura the gruel. "I'll be back dreckly. You can help him with this, I trust?"

"Of course. Take your time."

After Mary left them, Laura set the bowl on the side table and asked, "Can you sit up a little, or I could help . . . ?"

How would she help—put her hands under his arms and try to haul him up? She doubted she was strong enough to do so. A shame Jago had left.

Before she could try, he propped himself up on his elbows and pushed himself into a half-sitting position. His face seized into a grimace of pain. Alarmed, he tossed back the bedclothes and yanked up the nightshirt on one side as though a hot coal lodged there.

She saw ribs and firm flesh before averting her gaze. "Sorry, I forgot to warn you. You've got a nasty wound in your side. Miss Chegwin stitched it up per Dr. Kent's instructions, but neither is an experienced surgeon, I'm afraid."

He stared down at the stitches a moment longer, then slowly lowered the shirt.

She stepped closer and rearranged the pillows behind his head. "I don't think it will hurt so much if you lie still."

She waited until he had raised the bedclothes once more, then retrieved the bowl and sat on a chair beside the bed.

"You must be starving." She dipped the spoon. "Shall I . . . ?"

He reached out unsteady hands for the bowl and spoon, took them from her, and began shoveling in the watery gruel.

"Slow down. Remember what Miss Chegwin said. You don't want to make yourself sick." She added on a teasing note, "Our cook would not like to see her *fine* gruel wasted."

He looked up at her, saw her wry grin, and returned it.

He did understand English, then. The corners of his eyes crinkled with laughter lines, or perhaps he'd spent a lot of time in the sun at one point in his life, although at present he was quite pale. Either way, even that small smile lent attraction to his face, and she glimpsed dimples through his whiskers.

He resumed eating, though more slowly.

While he did so, she explained, "You also suffered from lung fever, but you seem to be well on your way to recovery."

When he'd scraped every morsel, she handed him a table napkin, and he wiped his mouth as politely as any gentleman.

He handed back the bowl, pressed his lips together, and appeared to be gathering himself for a great speech. Then he said in a stilted manner, "Thank . . . you."

She smiled. "You are very welcome, Mr. . . . ? I wish I knew what to call you."

Again the dropping of eyes and careful thought before he replied. Then he slowly and carefully enunciated each syllable, "Alexander Lucas . . . "

"Mr. Lucas, a pleasure to meet you."

"And, em, you."

He stilled and patted his chest as though for pockets and then looked over at the side table, expression pained anew to find it all but bare.

"My . . . belongings?" he asked, his voice hoarse from disuse.

"Oh." She went to the dressing chest and gathered the few things she'd discovered in his pocket. "I found these in your pantaloons." She added awkwardly, "When we were laundering them, I mean." She did not want to be thought a wrecker.

He accepted the coins and watch and studied them on his palm. "This . . . is all?"

His English was excellent, yet there was a faint accent she couldn't quite place.

"Yes, I am sorry. You wore no coat when we found you."

He winced, then opened the watch.

"I cleaned and dried it as best I could, but it has stopped, I'm afraid. Perhaps a watchmaker might repair it. We haven't a watchmaker here, but a larger town would."

He nodded, but said no more.

Alexander stared at the watch and few coins in his hand, trying to remember. Where had the rest of his money gone? And his possessions—one possession in particular? Had it even been his? He'd held it in his grasp so fleetingly. . . .

He looked again at the watch. His father had given it to him before he left home. It was precious to him, yet looking at it now brought only pain. Even so, he was glad it had not been lost to him, as had so many other things: his freedom, his brother, the *Victorine*, Enora, and nearly his own life.

He glanced up at the lovely young woman sitting beside him. Her voice was already familiar—he had heard her reading to him—though this was the first time he could see her face clearly. Before now, she'd seemed a figment of his imaginings—his fevered imaginings, apparently.

He'd thought he'd been dreaming. The *Kittiwake*'s cook had told him the local legend of a beautiful mermaid who'd lived in the estuary between the Atlantic and Padstow's safe harbour. Centuries ago, a young man fell in love with her, but when she refused to marry him, he shot her in a jealous rage. In revenge for his vile act, the mermaid cursed the harbour by throwing sand into it, and ever since then, sailors had been dying on the sands of the Doom Bar.

In a haze of confusion, Alex had seen the blurred image of a red-haired woman bending over him, her windblown hair falling around her face, her eyes like amber pools. He'd thought the legend of the mermaid had invaded his dreams.

Now he knew the woman was real and had a name, although he'd already forgotten the whole. Laura something.

He ran a finger over the coins and another piece of memory returned. He'd used several coins to buy passage on a ship. And not only passage for himself, but for his closest friend. His heart began beating dully within him. Where was his friend now?

He wanted to blurt out all his questions and demand answers, but he refrained. He must tread carefully. He had not reached his hoped-for destination but had instead been cast ashore in unfamiliar territory. The woman had tried to reassure him, saying she was friend not foe. But loyalties, he knew, could change. It took only one glance at his stitches and rope-burned wrists to prove that fact. He would not trust again so easily.

After careful thought, he set the coins and watch on the side table. Then he took a deep breath and asked, "The other men?"

The young woman's expression remained somber. "I am sorry to tell you they all died in the wreck. You were the only survivor."

Waves of shock and grief washed over him, stronger than any gale. He felt a dozen vicious stab wounds, this time to his heart. *No. God, no.*

"We buried them in the churchyard," she went on gently. "Everything was done properly, rest assured."

She gazed at him, her golden brown eyes glimmering with compassion. "Were you . . . close to the others?"

He nodded, no longer seeing her, but rather Daniel's face. He murmured, more to the departed man than to her, "My friend, my good friend . . ."

Then he looked at her again, an ember of hope flaring. "Are you certain?"

She hesitated. "What did your friend look like?"

He thought, then said, "Shorter than I am. Straight black hair. Dark eyes."

She winced apologetically. "That is a fairly general description. Give me a few minutes, and I shall bring in my list."

She soon returned and flipped through a

bound journal until she reached a certain page and then began to read, "'Man aged 40–45. Grey hair. Green eyes. Rotund. Still wearing apron.' Perhaps the cook?" She glanced up at him for confirmation.

He nodded. "Yes."

She continued, "'Man aged 25–30. Black hair. Brown eyes. Strawberry birthmark on his left brow . . .'"

Alexander's heart deflated and his face crumpled in grief. "Yes. He had such a mark." *Oh, Daniel. I am sorry, my friend.*

His eyes filled, and he turned his face away. Would she think less of him for weeping? At the moment, he did not care. He wiped his eyes with the napkin and held out his hands for the journal.

She handed it over, and he read through the rest of the list himself.

Initials T.O. inside his waistband and the collar of his shirt. Alex stilled, nerves prickling through him. Did she know what those initials meant?

He read further.

Boy aged 13–15. Red hair. Blue eyes. Freckles. "Oh no." He groaned. "The boy too?" *Dear God, why the boy? So young . . .*

He read on, recognizing descriptions of the captain and several others of the crew. There was one more description he'd expected to see. He turned the page, but nothing else was written.

"This is all?" he asked.

"Yes. We buried nine—eight men and a boy."

"There was at least one more." He flipped back and read through the list again. "Did one man have a scar on his left cheek, like a shepherd's crook?"

He drew the shape on his own cheek.

"No. I would have noticed and written it down." She reached over and tapped the page.

"Are you sure? He had long dark hair and fair eyes."

She paused to consider. "I suppose it's possible I missed such a detail. Some of the bodies had been battered by the rocks, sorry to say. But I am . . . fairly certain."

Alexander muttered an epithet under his breath. "Then one man is not accounted for."

"Bodies don't always come to shore immediately. He might wash up farther down the coast. And some never reappear at all."

Uneasiness filled him. He grimaced but said no more.

She rose. "I know this has been difficult news, so I will leave you for a while. May I bring you anything before I go?"

He shook his head but did not meet her

eyes. There was only one thing he needed, but he feared it was lost forever.

Laura left Alexander Lucas to grieve. She wished her uncle or Miss Chegwin had been there to deliver the somber news and comfort him afterward. Either of them would have done it more tactfully, she imagined. Her heart went out to the poor fellow.

She recalled how he had avoided her gaze before she left the room. Embarrassed to be seen crying, or hiding something? Laura had been surprised but touched to see a grown man weep.

He has just learned his friend died, she reminded herself. *He is understandably upset. Don't read too much into his evasiveness.*

She had not seen a man cry since her aunt Anne passed away. She remembered how devastated Uncle Matthew had been when she died. He had not been himself for months afterward and had not rallied until he met the charming Lamorna Mably. The two had bonded quickly over their shared loss of spouses and their love of Cornwall. Mr. Lucas would recover in time as well.

Still feeling uneasy, Laura went to join her uncle, Mrs. Bray, and Eseld downstairs. When she reached the hall, she heard laughter coming from the parlour. "Laura has no fear of strange men or fever," Mrs. Bray was saying, "but remember how frightened she was at her first May Day festival?"

Eseld and Uncle Matthew chuckled.

Laura instantly felt awkward and left out, the butt of their jokes.

She knew all too well what they were referring to. She remembered with discomfort and embarrassment her first visit to Padstow during the annual Hobby Horse, or "Obby Oss," festival on the first of May. Laura had gone expecting flowers and a Maypole and a friendly celebration of the coming of spring. She had *not* expected the raucous crowd, the crude shouts of drunken men, the incessant drumming, and the terrifying face of the Obby Oss. She saw nothing of a horse in the costume. Tarred canvas stretched over a large hoop with a long black skirt formed the horse's body like a big black pot lid. Its masked face was painted, supposedly, to resemble a horse. But to Laura, with its black, red, and white lines, it looked more like a dragon or a devil.

Most upsetting, the Oss tried to catch maidens as he danced through the narrow streets lined with onlookers. He lifted the bottom of his costume and cast it over young women's heads, trapping them beneath the skirt. Eseld had warned Laura very sternly to avoid being caught. She'd said, "If you are caught and end up with black tar on your clothes, you will fall pregnant or be married by the end of the year."

To a young innocent, this was terrifying in the extreme.

As Laura stood with Uncle Matthew, Mrs. Bray, and Eseld, the Oss came toward her, its mask menacing, the beady eyes focused on her with seemingly evil intent. Laura screamed and went running into Uncle Matthew's arms and begged to be taken home. Around her some in the crowd had laughed while others scorned her foolishness. Mrs. Bray had shaken her head, disapproval twisting her thin lips. "Will she spoil the day for all of us?"

In the parlour now, the chuckles faded at the recollection. Laura waited a moment, then entered the room. Seeing the three of them sitting close together in warm companionship, Laura felt a stab of loneliness, as she often did.

"Our guest has awakened," she said.

Hearing the survivor had come to his senses, Uncle Matthew and his wife went upstairs to meet him, Mrs. Bray insisting Eseld wait until she had first ascertained his character. The couple returned ten minutes later, satisfied and even impressed with their guest.

"Such excellent diction and well-bred manners," Mrs. Bray exclaimed.

Uncle Matthew nodded. "I agree."

"Did he say anything more about where he is from or where he was bound?" Laura asked.

"No. We have only just met him, after all, and did not wish to pry," Mrs. Bray said.

Uncle Matthew looked at her, brows furrowed. "Why do you ask, my dear. Are you . . . concerned about something?"

Laura hesitated, then replied more casually than she felt, "Not at all. Simply curious."

The next morning, Newlyn met her in the passage.

"Letter for you, miss." The young maid handed her the missive, postmarked *Penzance*.

It took Laura a moment to recollect the significance of the town, but then it dawned on her. She had written to a man there with news of his wife's death. She'd been able to identify her from a case of calling cards found in her reticule, still attached to her wrist after a cutter had been wrecked on the Doom Bar.

Laura almost dreaded opening the letter and seeing into the heart of a man in the painful depths of grief. She hoped he would not take out his angst on the messenger for announcing such unwelcome news.

She unfolded the page, steeling herself.

Dear Miss Callaway,

Thank you for tracking me down and taking the time to send news of Prudie Truscott's death.

You wrote with trepidation, I know, hating to be the bearer of what you must have deemed news of the most grievous nature—a man losing his better half. His helpmeet. His true love.

But in this instance, your letter had the exact opposite effect of the one you no doubt dreaded.

I was relieved to read it, even happy.

Before you judge me to be heartless, allow me to confide that Prudie left me for a smuggler more than two years ago. They met while he was here in Penzance, and he convinced her to sail away with him. She was sure great adventure and romance awaited her. She did not go off in secret, but brazenly announced her plan and asked for whatever remained of her modest dowry to help fund her expenses. She was not worried that the amount was small, certain her new lover would be able to provide for her richly from the spoils of his nefarious trade.

At the time, I was hurt—my pride and my heart. But since then, I realized she had not loved me in years, if ever, for all of my misspent devotion. All the same, I would have gone on providing and caring for her had she stayed. But she did not.

Since her departure, I have slowly formed a friendship with a neighbor, an upstanding widow of sterling character. A godly, church-going woman. Ruth Hodge has accepted my friendship and occasional companionship over a meal or friendly game of draughts, but no farther. I have fallen completely in love with her and wished I'd had the sense to marry her or someone like her years ago when I'd had my chance.

As it was, Ruth would not have me. She was fond of me, I knew. Even loved me. But as long as I had a wife living, she would not consent to be mine. For my wife might return any day, she reasoned, beg forgiveness, and ask me to take her back, which according to Ruth, I would be obligated to do.

So I have been trapped. **We** *have been trapped in a torturous, yearning purgatory of Prudie's making.*

Now, after receiving your letter, Prudie's calling card, a lock of her auburn hair, and the clipped article from the **West Briton** *newspaper, my dear Mrs. Hodge has at last agreed to become the new Mrs. Truscott. My genuine better half, helpmeet, and true love.*

I am the happiest of men, and it is thanks to you.

I realize the chances are remote, but we invite you to our wedding breakfast on the third of the month, or to visit us should you ever be in our part of Cornwall. I will happily reward you for your kind offices, a reward I dare not include within for fear of theft, but yours for the asking at Quayside Cottage.

> *My deepest gratitude,*
> *John Truscott*
> *Penzance, Cornwall*

Laura's emotions swung from disbelief to amazement. Reading the final lines a second time, she blew out a breath of relief. Of all the responses she'd anticipated, she'd never expected this. She had written several letters during her years on the coast but had received few replies. This ranked as one of the most surprising.

Her spirits buoyed by the letter, Laura walked into the guest room with a lighter heart and a smile on her face. She was pleased to find their guest sitting up and wide awake, a breakfast tray on his lap.

"Good morning, Mr. Lucas," Laura said. "How are you feeling today?"

"Better, thank you." He studied her. "What has you looking so happy this morning?"

"I received a surprising letter—rather diverting, actually."

"Oh?" he said. "May I ask what about?"

She began explaining the gist of the husband's letter about his wayward wife, but seeing Mr. Lucas's expression harden, she broke off. "Sorry. I should not speak lightly of another shipwreck victim when your loss is so new."

He stared at the wall. "I can relate to the man's emotions, but I am afraid I don't find the circumstances at all amusing."

Laura's chest suddenly felt heavy. "Pray, forgive me."

"Not your fault. I asked."

Miss Chegwin came in and beamed at the pair of them.

"Sitting up and talking! Now, that is what I like to see. That is what I call progress."

Laura was relieved at her arrival and the change in topic. "Mary Chegwin, this is Alexander Lucas."

"Well now. I suppose this means I shall have to stop calling you *my 'ansome*. How do'ee feel, Mr. Lucas?"

"I hardly know."

"Well, the mind is sometimes the last to heal."

"He asked about the other men," Laura said. "I told him of their fate."

Mary Chegwin's face fell. "Did'ee? Ah." She clucked. "Poor dear."

The older woman studied her patient. "Know what'll make'ee feel better? A good wash and shave. Maybe a haircut." She lifted a tray upon which Laura saw scissors, a razor, and the like.

Mr. Lucas reached up and rubbed his cheek, then tugged at the whiskers on his chin. "I've never gone so long without shaving. I must look uncivilized."

Laura removed the oval mirror from the wall and carried it to the bed.

Regarding his reflection, he muttered, "Knew I should have seen a barber before I left. A fright indeed."

"I wouldn't say that," Laura assured him.

"But a shave and haircut will make you feel more like your old self. And perhaps a bath while we're at it."

The plan agreed to, Laura built up the fire, Jago carried in the tub, and Newlyn helped them haul buckets and kettles of hot water to fill the bath.

"We'll replace yer bandages afterward," Miss Chegwin said. "Don't think a soak will harm'ee, but take care getting in and out. You've been on your back for days and are injured besides."

"I shall." The man sat up with effort, stifling a groan.

"Jago could stay and lend a hand, unless you prefer privacy."

Mr. Lucas glanced up at the tall young man with beefy shoulders, broad face, and coarse hair in disarray. Jago looked down, apparently anticipating being sent away.

The patient stood, nightshirt not reaching his knees, the garment shorter on his taller frame than on her uncle. Swaying slightly, he reached out a hand to steady himself.

"If you would be willing to lend a hand, Jago, I would be obliged to you."

Jago nodded, a rare smile on his face. Too few people used his name without derision.

An hour later, they reassembled, bath emptied and taken away, their patient dressed in his own buff pantaloons and shirt, fresh from the laundry. They took the opportunity to change the bed linens as well.

Mr. Lucas sat at the dressing table, a towel wrapped around his shoulders to catch the cuttings. He'd combed his freshly washed hair from his forehead with his fingers, and it remained there in thick glossy waves.

Using the provided tools, including brush, shaving paste, and razor, he lathered up and began to shave himself. Laura was glad not to be asked to do so, sure her hand would nervously shake at performing the domestic service.

He stroked downward on his cheeks, whisked the razor in the basin of water, then went upward on his neck, tilting his chin forward to tighten the skin. Each stroke revealed more of the face beneath—the clear skin, handsome features, the dimples she'd noticed earlier, and a cleft chin.

"I have shaved myself for years," he said, "but confess I have never cut my own hair."

"I can do it," Miss Chegwin offered. "After all, who do'ee think cuts Jago's hair?"

They all turned to look at the big man, whose wiry hair stuck out at all angles. The patient coughed discreetly.

"I could give it a go," Laura said, coming

to his rescue. "I used to cut my uncle's hair before he remarried."

Alexander turned to her. "Thank you, Miss Callaway," he replied before Mary could reiterate her offer.

Laura picked up scissors and comb and stood behind him, his face visible in the dressing table mirror. Sunshine from the window shone on him, lighting his eyes to the color of a turquoise ring she once found. He met her gaze in the mirror, and she looked away first.

She combed his hair, noticing how thick it was, how wavy. Many women would be envious of such tresses. Having straight, rather fine hair, Laura was somewhat covetous herself.

Jago went out with the shaving water, and at some point, Mary slipped out as well. Laura barely noticed, focused on the task at hand, the feel of his hair through her fingers. She gently straightened rich brown locks between the first two fingers of her left hand, and snipped off the ends, which had begun to curl. Again and again, she selected a section and trimmed it, taking her time, enjoying the process, which was somehow far more pleasurable than cutting Uncle Matthew's hair had been. She moved around to the front and snipped the fringe and sides, aware of how strange it felt to stand like this with him sitting, her bodice close to his head.

She bent and brought her face closer instead. Just as dangerous, perhaps, for now she was looking him eye to eye.

She noticed some lather that had strayed behind his ear and wiped it away, showing him a finger of lather as her justification for touching him. "You missed some."

He caught her hand, and she drew in a breath of surprise. Did he mean to stop her, offended at her presumption in touching him? But he held her hand and met her eyes.

"I think I owe you a great debt, Miss Callaway."

"Ha. You haven't seen your hair yet."

"For so much more—for saving my life."

Self-conscious, she diverted his praise. "We all helped. Jago, Newlyn, Miss Chegwin . . ."

"But it was you who saved me. Jago told me about the night of the wreck, the wrecker who wanted to kill me, and you insisting I be carried here for safekeeping."

His warm hand holding hers and his soulful eyes looking deep into her own disoriented Laura, and she felt as unsteady on her feet as he had recently seemed. "Anyone of conscience would have done the same."

"No, they would not."

"I . . . well, you're welcome."

Footfalls sounded in the passage, and he released her hand. She took a step back, under the pretense of surveying her work.

As the steps neared, both turned toward the door.

Eseld came in, eyes widening at the vision before her. "Good heavens. Who are you and what have you done with my pirate?"

Laura flushed. "Don't be silly. He has only had a haircut and shave, as I believe you suggested."

"And a good suggestion it was," Eseld breathed.

Laura whisked the towel from his shoulders. "Eseld, this is Alexander Lucas. Mr. Lucas, my stepcousin, Miss Eseld Mably."

He rose gingerly, favoring his injured ankle. "A pleasure," he murmured, then bowed.

Laura's stomach sank. Of course it was a pleasure. Eseld was the beauty, not her.

Eseld looked similarly struck. "Alexander Lucas, hm? I like it." She curtsied, then glanced up at Laura. "Did I not tell you he would be handsome under all those whiskers? And I was right. A straight aristocratic nose. And a very pleasant-looking mouth."

His thick brows went up at that, and Eseld had the decency to blush. Laura felt embarrassed too.

He looked at Laura, a playful light in his eyes. "And do you agree with your cousin's assessment?"

"I . . ." She shrugged and looked away, ears burning.

Eseld waved a dismissive hand. "Oh, Laura does not notice such things. She only has eyes for clever, learned men. And flotsam."

Again his brows rose, and a grin teased his mouth. "And presumably I am the latter?"

Eseld laughed. "Very true. I had not thought of that. Laura has found another treasure on the beach. Her biggest find by far."

More footsteps approached, and this time Perry Kent appeared in the doorway. Laura was glad for the interruption.

"Speaking of clever, learned men . . ." Eseld said.

Perry looked from Eseld to Laura. "Thank you, I think. What have I missed?" Then his eyes landed on the man behind Laura, who now stood on his own two feet.

"Ah, I see. This is a welcome sight." He stepped forward, hand extended. "Perry Kent."

Alex shook his hand. "Alexander Lucas."

"Dr. Kent is a new physician," Laura

explained. "He helped treat your injuries and fever."

"Oh, I did very little," Perry said modestly. "Laura and Miss Chegwin did the majority of the work."

"Even so, I thank you, sir," Alexander said earnestly.

"Perry. I am not ready for *sir* just yet." He smiled, and Alexander returned the gesture.

While he was there, Perry said he would examine the stitches and the patient's other injuries, shooing Eseld from the room.

"Why can Laura stay but not I? Are we not both ladies?"

Laura took her arm and led her from the room. "Come, my dear, let us fetch tea and biscuits for the gentlemen."

"Do you think he is a gentleman?" Eseld whispered as Laura dragged her to the kitchen. "I was hoping for a pirate. *So* much more romantic!"

*Over the graves of drowned sailors were
planted the figure-heads of wrecked vessels,
and these in the mist might have been taken as
the dead risen and mingling with the living . . .*

—S. BARING-GOULD, *In
THE ROAR OF THE SEA*

Chapter 5

Later that day, the local agent, Mr. Hicks,
returned with Laura's uncle.

As they stepped into the guest room,
Uncle Matthew explained, "I saw Mr. Hicks
in Padstow and happened to mention our survivor had come to his senses. He is eager to
talk with him."

Laura noticed Alexander subtly stiffen.

The agent stepped forward, hat in hand.
"Howard Hicks, wreck agent for the *Kittiwake*."

When Alex remained silent, Laura said,
"This is Alexander Lucas."

"Mr. Lucas. Well, I have written to the

ship's owners for an official list of the cargo and crew, but since yer awake, perhaps you could provide at least some of that information yerself."

"I am afraid not," Alexander replied.

"No? And why not?"

"I was only a passenger. As I've told Miss Callaway, I was traveling with a friend, so I can certainly give you his name—Daniel Marchal—but not all the others."

Uncle Matthew spoke up. "I am sorry for your loss."

"Right, right. Tragic." Hicks wrote in his notebook and then turned a page. "But surely ye met some of the officers or crew. Can ye at least confirm the captain's name?"

He nodded. "Frederick Smythe, I believe. And the mate was Peters—I didn't hear his given name."

"We've traced the owners to Yarmouth. Is that the port ye departed from?"

"Yes."

Hicks wrote it down. "And where were ye bound?"

"Portreath. But heavy seas prevented us from entering that harbour, so we continued on, seeking safe haven. Unfortunately, the sea had other ideas."

"Not surprising," Hicks replied. "Padstow is one of the few safe harbours on the North

Cornwall coast. And what was yer business in Portreath?"

Alexander hesitated. "How inquisitive you are. Do you always question mere passengers about their private business?"

Careful, Mr. Lucas, Laura thought, knowing evasion would only make the agent more dogged. She gently nudged his arm.

"Yer the sole survivor, Mr. Lucas," Hicks said. "There is no one else to question."

Alexander glanced at her and changed tack. "Sadly true. Forgive me, Mr. Hicks, my loss is still fresh."

"Right. I understand."

"The captain planned to deliver his cargo there. I only intended . . . only hoped . . . to go home. We planned to secure passage the rest of the way from there."

"And where is home for ye? Not in Cornwall, I take it?"

"No. I was hoping to reach Jersey. Do you know it?"

Laura's heart lurched at the word. *Jersey* . . .

Hicks nodded. "An island near France."

Eyes glinting, Alexander said, "A British Crown dependency, don't forget."

"Is that where yer from?"

"I have lived in many places. I was educated at Cambridge and on the continent. I have traveled a great deal."

"Suppose that explains yer accent. Haven't heard one exactly like it. Sounds a bit Frenchy to me."

"They still speak French on Jersey, you know," Alexander replied. "As well as traditional Jèrriais. But I've lived in England for years, most recently in Huntingdonshire."

"Heard of it. Never been there." Hicks consulted his notes. "And yer friend, Mr. . . . Marshall?"

"He was also on his way home."

Hicks peered at him over the top of his notebook. "Risky to sail to Jersey while we're at war with France."

"Well do I know it. Yet it was not the French who stopped us, but the sea. Or perhaps more accurately the Doom Bar and Greenaway Rocks."

"They've stopped many a ship before, I can tell ye. Can ye give me the names of any other men?"

Alexander's eyes flashed to Laura's and then away again.

"Miss Callaway showed me her descriptions of the victims. I saw the boy. A cheerful, hardworking lad, but the only name I heard him called was Ginger, on account of his hair. And the cook was a big man named Seymour. Beyond that, I can't help you."

He did not, she noticed, mention the man he believed to be missing from her list.

"Well," Hicks said. "We'll have the official list of passengers and crew soon enough." The agent closed his notebook. "Thank you, Mr. Lucas."

Alexander nodded. "Mr. Hicks."

After the vicar and Mr. Hicks left, the agent's words echoed through Alex's mind, *We'll have the official list of passengers and crew soon enough.*

Dread pulsed through him at the thought.

When the door closed behind them, he turned to Miss Callaway and confessed, "My friend and I won't be on that list."

She eyed him steadily. "Why not?"

"We were not registered passengers. The captain agreed to carry us unofficially, happy to earn extra money."

"I see. And why did you need to be unofficial?"

"The shipowners have policies. No unauthorized passengers allowed. Only duly trained crew. But many a captain has agreed to help a fellow in need of last-minute transportation."

Her expression remained sober. "And why did you need last-minute transportation?

You said you wanted to go home. Why the urgency? Especially knowing the risks?"

He studied her face. Sometimes the pretty young woman seemed so generous and accepting. Other times, like now, she was far too inquisitive. "You have missed your calling, Miss Callaway. You ought to have been a wreck agent like Mr. Hicks. You are a natural."

Her golden brown eyes glinted. "Perhaps. But you, Mr. Lucas, are hiding something."

He decided there was no point in denying it. "Yes, I am. Someday, perhaps, I shall tell you all, but not yet. Not until I know I can trust you."

"And can I trust you?" she asked.

He hesitated. "You are perfectly safe with me. That is all I can promise for now."

Laura returned to her own room, needing to think. She had been jolted with surprise when Mr. Lucas mentioned Jersey. How often she thought of that place, dreamed of visiting that far-off island one day, though she had no idea how she would ever manage it. Years ago, when her parents informed her they were sailing to Jersey, she had begged to go along. Instead, they sent her away to school and traveled without her.

She had felt angry, betrayed, abandoned, and frightened in turns, and as it happened, she'd had every right to feel that way. For after they sailed for Jersey, she never saw either one of them ever again.

That afternoon Laura went with her uncle to the small hamlet of Porthilly to pay calls on a few ailing parishioners. She took a pot of soup to elderly Mr. Carlyon and Wenna's prune-stewed rabbit to the Penberthy family with five children. The youngest two were sick with a fever. Laura hoped it was a teething fever or even croup and nothing more serious. Mrs. Penberthy, a miner's widow, could not afford a doctor even had Dr. Dawe been available, but Laura promised to ask Miss Chegwin and Perran Kent what inexpensive remedies they would suggest.

After their visits, Uncle Matthew went to St. Michael's for a meeting with the church-wardens. Since it was a beautiful autumn day, Laura said she would meet him back at the church in an hour's time. In the meanwhile, she ambled from Porthilly Cove to the nearby village of Black Rock—often shortened to "Rock" in conversation—enjoying the views of larger Padstow across the estuary.

She found herself thinking of baby Charles, her only sibling. She had been so ecstatic when he was born, making her a big sister at last. At nearly nine years of age, she had all but given up hope of siblings and, she'd gathered, her parents had as well. How happy they had all been at his healthy birth. Laura had watched his growth and each new triumph—learning to smile, laugh, crawl, and walk—with nearly a maternal pride of her own.

Then came the week of his second birthday. Papa had been called away to attend an ailing patient.

The nursery maid had brought Charles down to his mother. "Seems too warm to me, Mrs. Callaway. And terrible fussy. Is the doctor at home?"

"No, he is out on a call." Mamma laid a gentle hand on the toddler's forehead. "He has been teething. Perhaps that is all it is."

She went upstairs to the nursery with the boy, and Laura followed, wishing there were something she could do and offering to bring cool cloths to ease his fever.

"Yes, thank you, Laura."

But as the hours passed, the symptoms worsened. Her baby brother's little flushed face tightened into a grimace of pain. His breathing became labored, every inhale sounding raw and hoarse.

Fear began to shadow her mother's expression, and agitation heated her eyes.

"Where did your father go? Do you remember?"

"Mr. Saunder's, near the park."

"Good. Let's send Thomas with a note."

Not wanting to lay down her beloved burden, her mother asked Laura to write the note for her.

A few minutes later, their manservant hurried off to deliver the message, and Laura returned to the nursery. There, she stood beside her mother's chair and took her brother's hand, so small, into hers. How warm and damp it was, far warmer than Laura's own. When he cried, his whimpers were soon followed by dry coughs.

As darkness fell, her father returned from his patient's sickbed tired and drawn. He hurried into the nursery, bag in hand, young partner at his heels. He examined the small dear body, and his expression turned grave. "His throat is swollen."

His young partner suggested bloodletting, but Dr. Callaway did not believe in the procedure for one so young.

"Malignant sore throat, do you think?" the younger man asked.

"God, have mercy," her mother wailed.

With a significant glance at Laura, he stoically replied, "Too early to tell." But Laura saw the ghastly pallor of her father's normally cheerful countenance as he sent her from the room to avoid infection.

Laura had sat on the floor in the corridor, close enough to hear her father's commands and see his partner dart from the room to fetch whatever he asked for. Papa worked tirelessly to save Charles—coating his throat with spirits of sea salt and getting the boy to take small quantities of milk, boiled and allowed to cool. If only she had known to try such remedies earlier.

Hours later, he came out alone. From behind the closed nursery door came the muffled sobs of her mother.

He slumped next to Laura on the corridor floor—dark now. His raspy words escaped a strangled throat. "I am so sorry. I tried to save him but could not. I failed. Oh, my son!"

He pressed his hands to his face as though to hide his sorrow and his shame.

Tears streamed down Laura's face as well. Poor Charles. Poor Mamma and Papa. Poor her to lose her only sibling. She laid her head on her father's shoulder, and together they cried until there were no tears left.

Things with her parents had never been the same after that. Her father seemed to give her more attention, her mother less. Did she resent that Laura had survived instead of Charles? Was she suffering from a depression of spirits? Had she decided to distance herself to avoid the heartrending loss of another child, should something ever happen to her daughter? Laura was never certain. She had played all the scenarios and possible explanations through her mind over the years but had not come to a satisfactory conclusion.

Now, thinking again of the Penberthy children, Laura breathed a prayer, *Please spare them, Lord*, even as her heart doubted God would hear and answer.

While Laura was out walking, she saw a youth she knew from church, the ferryman's son, playing trap ball with a few other boys.

As she walked closer, she saw that he was wearing a man's coat that was too large for him. It was a blue uniform coat with red cuffs, one epaulet almost torn away, hanging by threads.

He ran in her direction in pursuit of a ball, and when he neared, she asked, "Martyn, where did you get that coat?"

The youth shrugged one shoulder, sending the tasseled epaulet swaying. "Where do'ee think? From the sea."

"The night of the wreck?"

"No, miss. Day after. Over in Polzeath."

"I see." Laura thought quickly. She was no expert, but she believed the coat he wore was that of a French officer. Navy, most likely.

British naval officers also wore blue coats, but theirs had white collars and cuffs.

"Well." She summoned a smile for the boy. "I'd be careful wearing that coat. You might be taken for a French spy."

He grinned in reply.

The lads called to Martyn, urging him to hurry back to the game, so he ran off, leaving Laura with more questions than answers.

The following day, Laura attended a christening at St. Menefreda's with the family and, afterward, rode home in the carriage for a quiet dinner at Fern Haven. Uncle Matthew and Laura spoke conspiratorially outside the stable before returning to the house. A short while later, they went to the guest room to invite Mr. Lucas to join them for the meal. Laura lingered in the threshold, awaiting his answer.

"Thank you, sir." Alexander shifted uneasily. "But I'm afraid I would be in stocking feet."

Uncle Matthew looked back at her, eyes twinkling. "Oh, Laura can help with that— can't you, my girl?"

Laura nodded and brought forward a large basket. In it were a pair of boots and two men's shoes that almost matched. She kept all the shoes and boots she found and distributed them to the poor and destitute as needed, and did he not qualify?

"I hope you don't mind, but when you were sleeping, I measured your foot. They are not new, I'm afraid."

"I don't mind. I am grateful."

"Shall we see if they fit?"

She set the shoes before him, and he wiggled in one foot, then the other, wincing on the injured side. "Excellent. You just happened to have these on hand?"

Laura blushed, but her uncle said proudly, "Laura has shod many a poor youth in this parish. Finds them, restores them, and gives them to those in need."

Alexander bent to look at the shoes. Had he noticed they were not a perfect match? He tilted up his head and met her gaze. "I am in your debt."

A few minutes later, he limped into the dining parlour with the help of a walking stick lent to him by Miss Chegwin. Newlyn had added another place at the table, and Alexander joined them for the first time.

Uncle Matthew pulled back his chair with a beaming smile. "You are very welcome, Mr. Lucas."

"Thank you." He bowed to the ladies before taking his seat.

Even Lamorna Bray smiled and said all that was proper, clearly as impressed with the change in his appearance as her daughter had been.

Uncle Matthew asked the blessing, and the meal began.

"My husband tells me you are from Jersey, Mr. Lucas?" Mrs. Bray asked.

He nodded. "My grandparents moved there from England decades ago. It is a beautiful place. Have you ever been?"

"Me? Never. But someone we know went there. . . ." Squinting upward, she searched her memory, then looked to her husband for help. "Who was it, Mr. Bray?"

Laura's heart pounded.

With an apologetic glance at her, Uncle Matthew dipped his head and said gently, "Laura's parents."

"Oh, I quite forgot."

Alexander looked at her, brows high in surprise and perhaps concern. She looked away, pushing a piece of mackerel around her plate.

Noticing her discomfort, Eseld took up the conversation.

"I remember looking for Jersey on a map once. In the English Channel, is it not? Much closer to France than England."

"True." Mr. Lucas nodded. "Only twelve nautical miles."

"What sort of food do they eat there? Not mackerel and turnips, I trust." Eseld wrinkled her nose at her barely touched plate.

"We ate much seafood, as here. Fish and a great deal of crab, lobster, oysters, whelks, and the like, along with many fresh vegetables. Less mutton, perhaps. There were also traditional Jersey dishes like sweet cakes, bean crock, and pickled ormers."

"Ormers?" Eseld asked suspiciously.

"A mollusk. Called *abalone* here, I believe. Most delicious."

This time Laura barely resisted wrinkling her nose. She liked fish but was not fond of snails and other mollusks.

"You were traveling by merchantman, I understand," Mrs. Bray said. "Are you a sailor or a merchant or . . . ?" She let the question dangle and waited expectantly.

He hesitated, sipping from his glass and wiping his table napkin over his mouth before answering. "I am . . . a sailor, yes."

Laura remembered him mentioning being educated at Cambridge and on the continent, and he certainly sounded the part. Was he really a simple sailor?

At his reply, Mrs. Bray's interest dimmed, and she asked her husband to pass the sauce for the fish.

Eseld spoke up again. "What will you do now, Mr. Lucas?"

"Try to get home," he replied, this time without hesitation.

Mrs. Bray nodded and said coolly, "Good idea."

"But first he must fully recover," her uncle interjected, giving the man a kind smile. "There's no hurry."

As they finished the meal, Laura asked, "How about some fresh air, Mr. Lucas? Just out to the garden?"

He smiled in apparent relief. "Thank you, yes."

"I will join you," Eseld said, setting aside her table napkin.

But her mother laid a hand over hers. "Eseld, my dear, there is a chill wind today; perhaps you had better remain indoors and rest."

Eseld's lower lip stuck out in a pout, but she protested no further.

Uncle Matthew insisted Alexander borrow one of his coats.

"One of the older ones, please," Mrs. Bray clarified.

A few minutes later, Laura and Alexander walked outside and slowly around the garden, she in her pelisse and wool shawl, and he in Uncle Matthew's dark brown coat. The garden was fading now but still lovely with its golden mums, dried hydrangeas, Michaelmas daisies, and the leaves of barberry shrubs turning red and bronze.

"Shall we sit a moment?" She gestured to a garden bench sheltered by an arched, vine-clad arbor.

His gaze lingered on it. "We have one like this at home."

They sat quietly for a few moments, then he said, "I would like to visit my friend's grave soon, if you could show me the way."

"Of course. Would tomorrow suit?"

He nodded. "Thank you."

"I should warn you that there is no marker as of yet," she added.

"I understand."

"If the squire, Mr. Sandys, or the ship-owners won't cover the cost, my uncle will likely pay for one himself. He is generous that way."

"Kind of him."

"Yes, he is a good man. Can you walk, do you think? It's about half a mile away. Or should I ask Uncle Matthew for the carriage?"

"Walking would be good for me, I think. Need to regain my strength. With this stick from Miss Chegwin, I think I can manage."

"Very well. Tomorrow after breakfast, then."

She accompanied him back to his room. "Would you like to join us for church some-time? You would be welcome, though I should warn you that you would be stared at and whispered about as a great curiosity."

Laura well remembered this experience from her first service at the main parish church of St. Menefreda's. The prickling awareness of being watched and found want-ing: from her outmoded bonnet and frock to her red hair and her very person. She could still feel the embarrassment of glancing over and finding hard stares and smirks pointed in her direction. And she could still see a young Kayna Roskilly whispering about her to Miss Sandys behind a gloved hand.

"Thank you for the invitation—and the warning," Alexander said. "I don't think I am ready for that just yet, but perhaps you might lend me a Bible so I can read on my own? If you or your uncle have an extra one, that is."

She smiled, pleased he would ask. "We do indeed."

Laura went back to her room and brought him the second Bible she had rescued from the sea—bound in leather and tied tightly with a cord. Very little salt water had gotten in, and she had been able to dry it without lasting damage beyond some minor warping. She had hoped to return it to the family whose marriages and deaths were recorded in the frontispiece, but had not as yet been able to find their direction. So for now, she was glad someone else should have the use of it.

It reminded Laura of the first Bible she found, and one of the more positive results of her letter-writing efforts.

After a shipwreck a few years ago, she'd found a leather-bound New Testament and Psalms in a young soldier's knapsack, still strapped to his back. The owner's name, several generations of his lineage, and even the name of the family estate were written inside. It had taken only one letter in that instance to reach the next of kin, or in this case, several next of kin.

The patriarch of the family, the poor young man's grandfather, had written back, full of all the sadness and grief one might expect, yet with heartfelt gratitude to her for writing to let them know his grandson had been given a Christian burial and that he'd kept the Bible with him. This man and his wife and daughter had traveled to the parish to speak with her. Laura and Uncle Matthew met the family at the inn where they were staying. She restored the treasured book to them, recounted the details of the wreck, and escorted them to the churchyard to show them where their loved one had been buried. Many tears were shed, but Laura was left with the satisfaction of knowing that she had helped them during their time of loss and grief.

It had all been her uncle's idea originally. Not long after they moved to Fern Haven, he'd found a name embroidered in a drowned man's coat, and said, "I really ought to try to get word to his family. I suppose I could track down the owners of the ship, and they in turn might send me the young man's place of birth or next of kin. But sadly, I don't have the time."

He was very busy with three churches to look after, so Laura had offered to write letters of inquiry on his behalf.

Uncle Matthew readily agreed. "Life can be hard, and yours has not been easy. But I can honestly say that serving God and serving others has given me purpose and fills my soul when life is sometimes disappointing. I would love for you to find that same fulfillment."

At the time, Laura had brushed off his encouragement, saying, "Don't make it sound too grand. I am only writing a few letters. Nothing may come of it."

Her words had been fairly accurate. Little had come of her early inquiries. But on that day when they parted company with the young man's family, Laura said to her uncle, "You were right. It isn't an easy or happy task, but it is worthwhile. Thank you for entrusting me with it."

He'd patted her hand. "I am glad to hear it, my dear. But don't thank me. It would have gone undone if not for you. I thank God He is blessing your efforts."

After breakfast the next morning, Laura and Alexander set out together, dressed for the brisk weather, he with walking stick in hand and wearing the tall leather boots she'd given him.

They strolled along a narrow sandy lane toward Daymer Bay. The heath flowers were mostly brown, but here and there dashes of purple remained, and the gorse was still in golden bloom among the fading ferns and reeds.

Soon St. Enodoc came into view, at least those parts that were visible. Because it was set among the dunes stretching up from the estuary, sand had encroached on two sides of the chapel, covering the eastern gable, the low porch roof, and door. At this end, only the slate roof showed. Near the middle stood the squat, crooked spire the winds had twisted over the centuries.

They entered through the lych-gate. At the far end of the churchyard, a mound covered in shaggy vegetation rose to nearly the top of the north transept windows. From there it was possible to lean near the glass and look inside the mostly buried structure.

"This is the north chapel of the parish," Laura explained. "There is also a south chapel in Porthilly. The main church is in the village of St. Minver."

Gesturing toward the sand-covered church, Laura went on, "Some people call it Sinkininny Church or Sinkin' Neddy, for obvious reasons."

"Does your uncle still conduct services here?"

She nodded. "He is required to at least once a year. We lower him down through the roof with a rope—see that hatch there? It covers the skylight made for that purpose. A few stalwart parishioners go down as well, while others gather on the mound to listen to the service."

"How strange," he murmured.

"Yes. He is trying to raise funds to uncover and restore the church, but it is slow going." The Roskillys were hosting a subscription ball soon, which should help his cause.

The lower graveyard was also submerged in sand, but on the higher ground, graves could be seen: Cornish crosses, tomb chests, and headstones.

She led him to a particular section of the graveyard. "These will give you an idea of what the headstone for the crew of the *Kittiwake* may eventually look like."

Together they read a few inscriptions:

SACRED
to the memory of six men and a youth,
names unknown, who were cast ashore
from the wreck of the *Brave I*.
October 21, 1810

DEDICATED
to the unknown dead of the SS *Land Ho*.
November 8, 1811
Remains brought and interred
by volunteer labour.

"Shipwreck victims used to be buried in mass graves near the shore," Laura said. "Most have no markings at all, or perhaps only an anchor or figurehead. My uncle hated the practice. We were so relieved when the law changed, and we were allowed to bury people in the churchyard."

He nodded his agreement, expression thoughtful, even solemn.

As they walked past the listing headstones and Cornish crosses, Laura pointed out a more recent grave of interest:

HERE LIE DEPOSITED
the Remains of the chief mate
and thirteen seamen,
a portion of the crew of the *Price*,
which was wrecked
at the entrance of Padstow Harbour.
September 1813

Finally, she led him to a large rectangle of recently disturbed earth near the lych-gate.

"This is where your friend and the other men lie."

He nodded, staring at the spot. So humble. So wrong. She'd hoped viewing the other headstones and knowing this grave would be properly honored in time might ease the sting of seeing the unmarked patch of sandy dirt. But observing his expression, she doubted anything could ease his present pain.

"I will give you a few minutes alone."

Again he nodded wordlessly, and Laura walked away to give him privacy to grieve. At the corner of the old church, she glanced over her shoulder and saw him lower himself to his knees and press a hand into the dirt.

Seeing him touch that patch of bare ground, fresh grief at her own losses struck her anew. Bare . . . blank . . . that was what she saw in her mind's eye when she tried to imagine her parents' graves on Jersey. Had they even been given a proper burial? A headstone? With her aunt and uncle sick and dying as well, had there been anyone to pay for a memorial? Or had her parents too ended up in an unmarked grave somewhere? She didn't know. She longed to go to Jersey herself and see their final resting place, to be assured that everything had been done properly. It wouldn't fill the gaping hole their absence left in her life, but it would be some comfort.

Glad for a few moments of solitude, Laura blinked away tears. As she walked through a neighboring field, she gathered a humble bouquet of feathery grasses, coneflowers, and harebells. Then she strolled slowly back to the church.

After Miss Callaway left him, Alexander lowered himself to his knees before the grave, hardly able to believe that his dear friend lay lifeless beneath dirt and sand and regrets. He leaned forward and pressed a hand into the soil as if he could reach Daniel. Comfort Daniel. Comfort himself.

I am so sorry, Daniel. Your poor wife! And poor little child, to be born into the world without a father.

Daniel would have been an excellent father. Gentle, patient, and so good with his hands. The family's home would have always been in excellent repair, and there would have been a new toy every Christmas.

Alexander thought of the things Daniel had made during their time in Huntingdonshire—carved boxes and a model ship replicating the dear *Victorine* they had both served on and lost. And most precious of all, an intricate Noah's ark with matched pairs of animals he had crafted for his child to come.

I am so sorry, my friend, Alex thought again. And he wondered how he might get word to Daniel's widow.

If he managed to return home, he would go and see her and relay the news in person. But how likely was that to happen anytime soon? He had almost no money with which to buy passage on another ship. And even if he somehow made arrangements to get there, without the evidence he'd lost to the sea, what was the point? What good could he do Alan without it?

He rose and wiped his hands. Was there

another reason he was reluctant to go home? A reason with beguiling brown eyes and dark red hair? *No*, he told himself. He had learned his lesson where women were concerned. He had already risked his heart—and his life— more than enough.

Then suddenly there she was. Without a word, she reappeared and handed him a simple bouquet of wildflowers. At the thoughtful gesture, his determination to remain aloof flagged.

"Thank you," he murmured. He knelt and placed it on the grave, whispering, "Goodbye, Daniel."

Then the two of them started back toward Fern Haven, Alexander leaning more heavily on the stick, though he tried to hide the strain.

She paused on the seaside path, ostensibly to take in the view, though he guessed she'd stopped to let him rest. Her gaze lingered on the glittering waters of the estuary. The sun lit her fair skin to golden, and strands of dark red hair escaped their pins and danced in the wind around her face. He forced himself to turn from her profile to the distant rocks and waves. Reminded of something, he recited,

> "God moves in a mysterious way,
> His wonders to perform;

He plants his footsteps in the sea,
And rides upon the storm."

He looked over at her and saw her eyebrows lift in surprise. He explained, "You read that to me once."

"I am astonished you remember," she said. "I doubted you heard me."

"I heard you, even before I saw you." He held her gaze, longing to reach out and hold her hand.

For a moment they stood looking at one another, but then a boat on the estuary rang its bell, dissolving the fragile moment.

They continued on their way.

"A rest, I think, when we return," she said. "You've earned it."

As they neared Fern Haven, they heard music coming from Brea Cottage. He and Laura stopped to listen, and Miss Chegwin noticed them and urged them inside.

"Jago is practicing his hurdy-gurdy for Allantide tomorrow."

Alex felt nostalgic as he watched the young man turn the crank of the wheel fiddle with one big hand, while the thick fingers of the other played the keys. His family's orchard keeper had an instrument like it, and Alex had always enjoyed the music, created by a rosined wheel rubbing against the strings.

The wheel functioned much like a violin bow, and the sound was similar as well.

When Jago played the final notes with a flourish, Alex and Laura clapped, and Miss Chegwin beamed from her chair.

"Well done, my friend," Alex praised. "How did you learn to play?"

"An old neighbor taught me."

Miss Chegwin nodded. "Poor Mr. Methyr. I nursed him through his many illnesses. He left that hurdy-gurdy to Jago in his will. Very kind of him."

Alex smiled from her to the young man and said, "He would be pleased to hear you play it. I know I am."

"Come back tomorrow night, and you'll hear more," Miss Chegwin promised. "It's our annual Allantide party. I do hope'ee will join us."

Laura answered for them both. "We would not miss it."

The ancient custom of providing children with a large apple on Allhallows-eve is still observed. [They] would deem it a great misfortune to go to bed on Allan-night without the time-honored Allan apple to hide beneath their pillows.

—ROBERT HUNT, *POPULAR ROMANCES OF THE WEST OF ENGLAND*

Chapter 6

Sparks rose like darts of bright orange light against the darkening sky. The bonfire was an inviting beacon, drawing neighbors to Brea Cottage. Such a large blaze was a luxury. An extravagance. A sure sign of celebration. As people arrived, they added their contributions to the pile nearby: scrap boards, wreck timbers, and fallen branches to keep the fire roaring—and the party as well.

If the bonfire was the invitation, music was the warm welcome.

Jago sat playing his hurdy-gurdy. A neighboring farmer, Mr. Trenean, accompanied him on a flute while one of the man's grown sons played a serpent and another kept time on a small drum.

People sat on rickety chairs dragged outside and a bench made from a plank suspended on two tree stumps. On the makeshift tables sat jack-o'-lanterns carved from large turnips, light from candle stubs within flickering from their ghoulish faces.

Miss Chegwin had made fish pie and rabbit pasties with leeks and turnips. At Uncle Matthew's request, Wenna had contributed an apple cake as big as a barrel head, with a warm sweet glaze. Laura knew Uncle Matthew attended the party out of neighborliness but thought Mrs. Bray and Eseld attended mostly in hopes of seeing Treeve Kent.

There was bee wine, home-brewed ale, and cider sipped from a mismatched assortment of chipped teacups, jars, and tin tankards. It was a harvest dinner and Allan-night all rolled into one.

Bee wine tickling her tummy, Laura was keenly aware of Alex's masculine shoulder against hers as they sat side by side on the bench, reminding her of the night she lay beside him in bed to ease his shivering. She leaned near his ear to be heard over the music.

"Do you celebrate Allantide on Jersey, Mr. Lucas?"

"Not that I recall."

Mr. Dyer and his family mingled with the crowd, and Newlyn came over from Fern Haven to join them. She remained near her parents, but Laura noticed the girl's gaze linger with curious interest on Jago as he drew such sweet music from his instrument.

Uncle Matthew called, "How about a song, Miss Chegwin?"

"Hear, hear!" the others cheered.

Mary Chegwin set aside her cup and rose to oblige, her voice reedy but true. What she lacked in volume, she more than made up for in expression, her arms lifted and hands gesturing with the words.

"We tread upon the golden sand,
   when the waves are rolling in,
The porpoise he comes near to land,
   and to leap he doth begin,
Snorting to the fishy air: prepare,
   (I say) prepare,
Good housewives, keep your fires
   bright,
For your mates come home tonight."

And everyone echoed, "For your mates come home tonight."

The company clapped along as she sang the next verse. Soon an elderly couple rose and began dancing a jig, and a few younger people joined in.

Perran and Treeve Kent arrived on horseback, and Jago momentarily set aside his hurdy-gurdy to take their horses to the lean-to. Miss Chegwin had invited them as thanks for Perry's recent help with their patient.

Eseld brightened at the Kent brothers' arrival, as did Mrs. Bray.

The newcomers were quickly furnished with tankards and generous slices of fish pie. While they'd brought no wood, Treeve untied a jug of rum from his saddle and set it on the table with the other libations, the offering met with a chorus of approval.

"Will you sing for us, Treeve?" Eseld asked with limpid eyes. "You have such a marvelous voice."

"I would have to drink a tankard or two before I'd agree to that," he replied.

But a short while later, he walked over to the musicians and announced, "I will sing if Mr. Dyer will join me in 'The Pirate's Song.'"

This suggestion too was met with approval. Tankard in hand, Newlyn's father came and stood beside Treeve, and the two sang:

> "The ocean is mine, and I take what
>   I can
> Of the wealth that I find on the wave;
> I spurn the control of dominion of
>   man,
> Mine's the life of the free and the
>   brave!
> I sail where I like,
> And never I strike
> My flag to another, d'ye see;
> O'er my billowy home
> Unfetter'd I roam—
> Death or Liberty, boys, for me!"

The crowd enthusiastically clapped along. Laura glanced over at Alexander to see how he would react to such a song and noticed his gaze linger on the singers with speculative interest.

The party continued for several hours. Families with children begged off earliest, followed by the residents of Fern Haven, Uncle Matthew claiming an early morning.

Together they walked up the rise, humming "The Pirate's Song" tune as they went.

When the others dispersed to their rooms,

Eseld darted first into her own bedchamber, then followed Laura into hers.

"Surprise!" Eseld exclaimed. She tried to suppress a grin, which only served to deepen the dimples in her cheeks. In her hands she held two large bright red apples.

"One for you and one for me. Happy Allantide."

Every year it was the same. Laura smiled back. "Thank you, Eseld."

"I know you've refused me before, but this year I insist you sleep with it under your pillow."

"Under my pillow? Why not put a rock there instead!"

"What is some slight discomfort to the chance to dream of your future husband?"

"You know I don't believe in such things. And I doubt Uncle Matthew would approve."

"This is harmless fun, Laura. Don't be a dry stick. Do you not want to see the man of your dreams *in* your dreams? Learn the identity of your future husband?"

"Not particularly."

"Come, it will be diverting. You are too polite to refuse a gift. I bought it at the Allan market especially for you. You can't say no."

Laura accepted the apple. "Very well. I shall do it for you."

Eseld's smile flashed, and her eyes shone

with excitement. "I will be back in the morning for steps two and three."

A few minutes after Eseld left, Newlyn came in to help her undress, still humming a tune. Seeing the apple on Laura's bedside table, the maid said, "You've one too, miss? So have I. Can't wait to see who I dream of."

"Have you done this before, Newlyn?"

"Oh, iss. Ever' year since I were twelve."

"And has it worked?"

"Not yet." She grinned. "But I am *that* sure this will be the year!"

The girl left and Laura climbed under the bedclothes. She blew out her candle and lay in the dark. Moonlight shone on the Allan apple on her side table. She did not believe in such superstitions. Did she even want to dream of a man?

Unbidden, Mr. Lucas's face appeared in her mind's eye.

Oh, why not? After all, she had promised Eseld.

She slipped the apple under her pillow, which caused the feathers to bunch up around her face. *Ah well*, she thought. It was only for one night.

❦

In the morning, Eseld threw open the door and all but ran into Laura's room. Newlyn had not even been in to deliver warm water and fold back the shutters.

"Well?" Eseld asked, all eagerness.

Laura barely resisted the urge to pull the blankets over her head and go back to sleep. "What time is it?"

"Just gone eight."

Laura groaned. She had thought to sleep in after their late night.

"Besides, it's All Saints' Day," Eseld added. "And that means church."

Laura groaned again, threw back the bedclothes, and sat up.

"Did you dream of him?" Eseld asked. "The man you are going to marry?"

Laura reflected. "Actually, I dreamed of several people. The Kents, Jago, you, even that horrid Tom Parsons. And if you tell me I'm to marry him, then I hope this is a *poison* apple."

Eseld watched her closely. "And Mr. Lucas? Was he in your dream as well?"

Laura closed her eyes, remembering. She had dreamed of Tom Parsons leaning over the shipwrecked man again, to her horror and indignation, while others stood there unconcerned, Treeve and Eseld singing "The Pirate's Song" and Perry waiting idly with his medical bag. As Parsons raised his cudgel, Laura tried to reach Mr. Lucas, but her legs were trapped in quicksand, and she could not move. At the memory, Laura shivered. "Yes. The dream was not a romantic one, but he was in it."

"I knew it!"

"And you?" Laura asked. "Who did you dream of?"

Eseld shrugged. "To be honest, when I awoke I could not recall any dreams. So I shut my eyes and daydreamed instead. You know, when you're still half asleep and tipsy-cake drowsy? I imagined Treeve and me riding white horses along the cliff tops, my hair floating in the wind, and him declaring his undying love."

"You don't ride, Eseld."

"What does that signify? I have a vivid imagination."

"You certainly do. Does a daydream count, do you think?"

"I hope so. But let's find out. Come and stand next to me. Bring your apple."

Laura grumbled into her dressing gown and slippers, retrieved the apple, and crossed the room to stand with her before the mirror. Eseld handed her a paring knife. "Careful to keep the paring in one long strip."

Starting near the stems, they began peeling the apples. Around and around, all the way to the bottoms.

Eseld recited, "I pare this pippin round and round, my sweetheart's name to be found." She glanced over to survey Laura's progress. "Good. I shall go first to show you how it's done."

Taking the long peel in one hand, she said, "I fling the unbroken paring free, my true love's initial to see." Then she tossed it over her left shoulder.

She whirled about, eagerly studying the peel, likely hoping to see a certain initial. The peel had spread out, with a small hook at the bottom and a loop at the top.

"I knew it—a *t*!" she exclaimed.

Laura studied the shape with a skeptical eye. "I see a *p*, Eseld. Definitely a *p*."

"I disagree. Now quit stalling. Your turn."

Laura held up her peel, murmured the words as best she remembered them, and tossed it over her shoulder. She turned and found the peel had landed in a tight coil. Her momentary disappointment gave way to amusement. "Seems about right, considering the muddle of my dream. I see an *and* symbol, perhaps, but nothing else."

"Try again. That does not count."

Laura picked up the peel and repeated the steps, flinging the peel with more vigor. This time, the peel spread out in a curvy line of almost cursive appearance.

"My goodness . . ." Eseld breathed. "You have two letters."

"Have I?"

"Yes, see there? A lowercase *e* or perhaps an *a*, not quite closed, and there at the end, a *c*?"

"You do have an imagination."

"It's as plain as the nose on your face."

Someone knocked on the open door. They glanced over and found Mr. Lucas standing in the open doorway, expression taut with concern.

"Pardon the intrusion, ladies, but I was alarmed by the distressing exclamations I heard coming from this room. Is anything amiss?"

Laura instantly flushed with embarrassment, but Eseld brightened.

"Mr. Lucas, you are just in time. Do settle a dispute for us." She gestured to the floor. "What do you see?"

Remaining near the door, he looked down and his eyebrows rose. "Poor housekeeping?"

"Look closer. What initial does each peel form?"

He bent to look closer.

When he remained silent, Eseld tsked. "Don't tell me you have less imagination than Laura has."

He rallied. "I suppose that one looks like a *p*."

Eseld shook her head. "No, it's a *t*."

"If you say so. And the other . . . perhaps *e* and *c*?" He straightened, looking from one to the other. "What does it mean?"

Eseld grinned. "It's an Allantide tradition. It's supposed to tell us the initial of the man we are going to marry."

Laura's face burned. "It's foolishness obviously."

He looked at her, a teasing light in his eyes. "Ah. I am learning so much about your traditions."

"*Your* traditions?" Eseld asked. "Are you not British yourself?"

"I meant Cornish traditions, of course."

Laura echoed vaguely, "Of course." But an apple seed of doubt had been planted.

⁊⁓

After dinner that evening, the family sat talking quietly in the parlour for a time. When the others retired, Laura and Mr. Lucas lingered in front of the fireplace.

"I noticed the family names in the Bible you lent me. Are the Smiths relatives of yours?"

"No. I don't know who they are or where they come from. I wish I did. I found that Bible after a shipwreck. It is a passion of mine, trying to return lost possessions to their rightful homes. Unfortunately, Smith is a very common name, and I've yet to find that specific family, if any survive."

He nodded his understanding. "Thank you again for loaning it to me." With a glance at his feet he added, "And for the shoes and boots. I gather you found them washed ashore as well?"

"Yes."

"Have you found anything else?"

"Many things. I have something of a collection."

Interest brightened his eyes. "Really?"

Laura nodded, self-conscious under his gaze. "I hope you don't think it wrong of me. If I found cargo meant for resale, I would not keep it. But personal items I hold on to for a year and a day per the old decree, in case the owner should come to reclaim them. After that I sometimes sell them to the antique and curiosity dealer in Padstow. I am loath to sell anything that might be important to someone's next of kin, but I also want to contribute to my upkeep here." She did not mention she was also saving money for a hoped-for journey.

"Do the Brays expect you to contribute?"

"My uncle does not. Mrs. Bray . . . Well,

she makes it clear such offerings are welcome and her due. Another mouth to feed and all that."

In the hearth, a log fell and sparks rose from the grate.

"May I ask how you came to live with them?"

"Certainly. It's no secret. My parents left me at a girls' school outside of Oxford when I was twelve, then sailed away to Jersey, never to return."

His eyes widened. "That must have been . . . difficult."

She fingered the trim of her sleeve before answering. "I begged to go with them, but they refused. I felt abandoned when they left me behind."

"Why did they go to Jersey?"

"My mother's sister lived there. It was difficult for Mamma when Aunt Susan married and moved far away. They had always been extraordinarily close, or so it seemed to me, never having a sister of my own. I did have a baby brother, but he died young."

"I am sorry."

"Thank you. When Mamma received a letter informing her that her sister was ill, she panicked and was determined to go and help her at any cost."

Alexander leaned forward, resting his

elbows on his knees. "I can understand that. The desire to help, to save a dear sibling."

She paused, studying his expression. "Can you?"

"Yes, but we were speaking of you."

She continued, "My mother insisted Father close up his practice and travel with her. He was a physician, you see."

"Ah." He smiled at the significance. "No doubt the reason you are an excellent nurse. What took your aunt and her husband to Jersey?"

"Uncle Hilgrove had been stationed there. In charge of one of the British garrisons, I believe, though I was rather young and may not remember the details correctly. Sadly, whatever disease my aunt suffered from claimed my parents as well. Instead of curing her, they apparently both died trying to save her life. Our old housekeeper came to the school to deliver the news in person."

Laura would never forget the day the matron escorted Mrs. Rouncewell into her room at the girls' seminary, a letter from a stranger—some clerk in Jersey—in her hand.

She went on, "After that, the matron reviewed my enrollment records and found that my parents had listed Father's younger sister—Mrs. Anne Bray—as my next of kin after them. The matron wrote to the Brays, and they came to fetch me. Aunt Anne and her husband were preparing to move to Truro, where he had been offered a curacy. They took me with them. I had met Aunt Anne before and liked her, and I quickly became fond of Uncle Matthew as well. They were rather poor but happy, and very kind to me.

"Knowing education was important to my parents, they enrolled me in a girls' school near them in Truro so they could visit me and I could go to them at holidays."

Laura looked off into her memories and found Aunt Anne's lovely, gentle face. "I have never seen two people happier than when my aunt announced she was with child. Sadly, their happiness was short-lived. She died in childbirth." Laura sighed. "After that, I stayed home with my uncle. Truly, he was so low in spirits that I was afraid to leave him. But he eventually rallied. He met Lamorna Mably, a widow herself, and through her connections in this parish, he was offered the living here. We have resided in her home these last eight years."

"Your home now too, surely."

Laura shook her head. "Fern Haven has always seemed like her and Eseld's home, not mine, being no blood relation to anyone under its roof." She raised a palm. "I am not complaining. Mrs. Bray is tetchy but not cruel, and Uncle Matthew is good and loving to me, out of respect for his first wife's memory, I suppose."

"Or perhaps simply because you are lovable."

Her eyes flashed to his.

He looked away first and cleared his throat. "Were you left nothing when your parents died?"

"Nothing to speak of. Thankfully, there was sufficient balance in my school account to pay for that additional year of education in Truro. Our housekeeper brought a few of my belongings, mementos, and letters, but she sold the rest to pay the bills and closed up the house, planning to retire."

"And your father's medical practice?"

"He had a young partner who succeeded to it."

"Did your aunt on Jersey lose her husband as well?"

Laura nodded. "Uncle Matthew wrote to my uncle, Major Hilgrove, via the garrison, but the letter was returned marked *Deceased*. Evidently, both my aunt and uncle died."

"I see."

Yet Laura's thoughts were not on finances or arrangements but on her parents. *Oh, Mamma! Papa! Why did you have to go? Why did you leave me all alone?*

They had very willingly left Laura, their only remaining child, to go to her sister in far off Jersey. Laura had certainly felt cast aside then. She supposed she always would.

That conversation with her parents had broken her heart. They'd called her into the sitting room with a strange formality and shut the door behind her. Her mother, red-haired and bespectacled, had sat on the sofa, gripping a letter, while her father had stood, looking restless and ill at ease.

Her mother began, "Laura, we have something to tell you." Then she turned to her husband and prompted, "My dear . . . ?"

Dr. Callaway cleared his throat. "Your mother and I are traveling to Jersey, one of the Channel Islands. Remember I pointed it out on the map?"

"Yes, Papa, I remember." Since baby Charles had died, her father shifted more of his energies to Laura, educating her and sharing details of his day and his practice as never before.

Laura immediately assumed her parents would take her along. She was only twelve, after all. "I look forward to seeing it with you."

With an apologetic glance, her father said gently, "I am afraid that is not the plan. This is not a holiday. You, my dear, are to go to school. You will like that. Such an intelligent girl and eager learner as you are."

"I don't want to go to school. I want to go with you."

Her mother's grip on the letter tightened. "Laura, it is for your own good. Don't make a fuss. You are a young lady now, and it is time to act like one. I did not cry and throw a tantrum when my parents sent me to school."

Laura felt wrongly accused. A tantrum? She wasn't happy but had not even raised her voice—yet. She defended, "But your parents visited you on Sundays. I remember Grandmamma telling me. And you went home for Christmas. Your family was just up the road in Basingstoke, a mere thirty miles away, not hundreds of miles across the ocean."

Mother glared through her small spectacles. "Jersey is only across the English Channel. Don't exaggerate."

"Why can I not go with you? I am sure travel would be highly educational. And when we get back, if you still want to send me away to school, I shan't complain then. I promise."

Her father sent Mamma a plaintive look. "My dear, if she does not want to go . . ."

Sara Callaway shook her head. "Don't forget why we are going. There are risks. And

I will need to focus on my sister, not worry about Laura's health and safety."

Laura frowned. "I don't understand."

"I have received a letter from your aunt Susan," Mamma explained. "She is ill and needs our help."

"I will gladly help," Laura insisted, turning to her father. "You've always said I was a good helper to you, Papa. Is that not so?"

"Of course you are, my dear. But—"

"Don't give in to her," her mother snapped. "Somehow she always manages to wrap you around her little finger. Now, let us not quarrel about this, especially in front of Laura." Her mother gestured toward the door. "Laura, please go to your room while your father and I discuss this further."

Laura rose and stalked out. As she trudged up the stairs she heard her mother say, "I know you will miss her, but . . ."

The door shut, muffling their voices and leaving Laura to guess at the rest of the sentence. "I know you will miss her, but I won't?" Or "I don't want her underfoot? I want to focus on my sister." Yes, her sister was more important to her than her daughter.

In the end, her parents had remained firm in their resolve to send Laura to school and travel to Jersey without her. A few days later, they drove to the girls' seminary in a post chaise, her baggage stowed in the boot, and theirs as well. They would be traveling on to meet their ship after dropping her off. Laura sat stiffly throughout the journey, staring out the window, avoiding their gazes and answering only in the briefest syllables when necessary. When she glimpsed the sadness in her dear papa's eyes, she was tempted to relent, but then the chaise turned into the drive of the school.

The grey stone edifice looked ancient and formidable, and a shaft of fear joined the bitterness in Laura's heart. The building looked almost . . . gothic . . . like an abandoned abbey or haunted manor in one of the paperback novels from the circulating library. Her pulse beat like a death knell. This was a nightmare. If the door were answered by a hunchbacked giant or wart-nosed witch, she would not be surprised.

The matron who met them was neither of those things. She was in fact a pleasant-looking, plump woman of forty who led them on a tour of the boarding school, pointing out the play yard, classrooms, and dining parlour. They passed a group of pupils, who stared at her, but Laura stiffened her spine and lifted her nose, determined to remain sullen and silent. If her mother wanted her to act the part of a grown-up lady, then she would be as cold and aloof as she imagined a lady could be, punishing her parents the only way she knew how.

It was all over too quickly. She was shown to a room she would share with a few others girls, her trunk was delivered, and the matron left them to say their good-byes in private. Laura was torn, on the verge of crying and longing to beg them one last time to change their minds. But seeing the stony resolve on her mother's face, she did neither of those things.

"I realize you are angry," her mother said. "But I hope you will someday understand that I acted in your best interests, and forgive me."

The moment hung there, Laura's chance to forgive her mother. She said . . . nothing.

Her mother drew a deep breath. "Well, good-bye, Laura. I know you will make us proud."

"Good-bye, my dear," her father added. "We will be praying for you and thinking of you. And we will write to you when we are settled."

Laura nodded, hands primly clasped, but she made no reply.

The moment the door closed behind her parents, however, she ran to the window and watched until the chaise departed, the scene blurred by her tears. She already regretted her silence—regretted the cool farewell, when she had longed to throw her arms around her father, and to feel her mother's kiss one last time upon her brow.

A wine merchant from North Cornwall
wrote repeatedly to the Board of Trade,
pointing out how honest business men could
not compete against smugglers. West In-
dian rum, he said, was available all over
Cornwall at 5 shillings a gallon, whereas
he had to sell it at 8 shillings and 6 pence.

—CAROLYN MARTIN, SMUGGLING RECIPES

Chapter 7

Laura remained restless that night and couldn't seem to fall asleep, her mind filled with memories resurrected earlier that evening when talking to Mr. Lucas. Now that she had lifted the long-shut lid, everything she had locked away boiled to the surface in a stomach-churning stew of sweet, sour, and bitter morsels of her past. Her regrets lingered, as did her desire to travel to Jersey one day.

Some distant sound caught her ear—a door slamming? She climbed from bed and pulled a dressing gown around herself against the chill of the room, the fire having died. She went to the window and looked out. Her room faced the sea, and between it and Fern Haven lay Miss Chegwin's cottage.

Was it her door she'd heard? The night must be unusually calm.

A lantern burning low illuminated two figures in coats, hats, and mufflers. From the relative sizes of the two and the stooping shoulders of the smaller, she recognized them as Jago and Mary Chegwin.

Where were they going so late? It must be nearly midnight. Had Miss Chegwin been called to an ill person's bedside? With Dr. Dawe absent, it seemed likely. Concern filled Laura. She hoped neither of the Penberthy children had taken a turn for the worse.

Laura dreaded going out in the cold but knew she would not sleep thinking someone might be suffering when she could help. She quickly pulled on several layers of warm clothing: wool stockings and petticoat, her thickest gown, pelisse, and half boots.

Hurrying quietly downstairs, she helped herself to her uncle's heavy black greatcoat and a knitted cap. Eseld would be horrified at her ensemble, but she didn't care. To Laura's mind, staying warm trumped fashion any day, and certainly in the dead of night.

Forgoing a lamp of her own, Laura slipped from the house, hoping to catch up with her neighbors before they got too far away. She imagined she would find them in the small lean-to stable, but instead saw their shadowy forms in the donkey cart disappearing over the rise. They were heading not toward Porthilly and the ailing Penberthys but in the opposite direction, toward Polzeath. Laura was relieved but also curious.

She supposed she should have been frightened to be out alone at night, but she was not. She knew these paths as well as the corridors of Fern Haven, and moreover, Jago was within shouting distance, if need be. Yet she was reluctant to call out. The night was strangely still. The ever-present wind . . . absent. Her voice, if she called, would be heard in neighboring cottages and might wake slumbering children. No, she would simply hurry her steps and catch up quietly. After all, the donkey was notoriously slow.

She followed the coast past Greenaways, over the cliff tops, and then down again to sea level as the path neared Polzeath Beach. In the distance, the large crescent of sand shone white by moonlight, and beyond it loomed the dark headland of Pentire Point.

Activity in the water drew her attention. Two ships were moored in the moonlit bay, and several smaller boats were clustered around them like eager bees to dark, bobbing blossoms. Meanwhile on shore, figures carried loads to waiting wagons, and soon Miss Chegwin's donkey cart joined the line.

Shadowy figures carried what looked to be bales of tobacco or tea, wrapped in oilskin to make them as watertight as possible.

She crept closer, wishing again that the area had more trees. She saw ponies and donkeys with half-anker tubs strapped over their backs. Several "tubmen" were similarly burdened with one container on their chests and another on their backs. French brandy, most likely—a favorite currency of the smugglers.

As she had on that long-ago May Day, Laura again felt out of place, observing but not appreciating or participating in a Cornish custom.

Laura guessed Tom Parsons was the ringleader of this late-night haul, and she certainly did not want him to see her spying. With that threat in mind, she backtracked a few yards and ducked into the doorway of a decrepit fish-cleaning shed to continue watching without being seen—or implicated, should the revenue men descend.

At that moment, two men walked off the beach, deep in discussion, their low voices approaching Laura's hiding place. She retreated deeper into the shed, breathing through her mouth to avoid gagging on the lingering stench.

As the footsteps neared, she heard the men talking, or rather negotiating—how much per six-pound weight of tea, and half anker of brandy, and where to store it until all was sold.

She heard the word *Roserrow* and stilled, holding her breath. Were the Kents involved, or was one of their outbuildings to be used without their knowledge? The men stopped walking, pausing near the shed to conclude their arrangements, and without the scrape of footfalls to muffle their conversation, Laura recognized both voices. Tom Parsons, as she had guessed. And the other . . . Treeve Kent.

She raised a hand to her mouth to cover a gasp, and her elbow struck a chain, sending it jangling against the rickety wall. Her heart jangled as well.

"What's that?" Tom asked in a terse voice. "I'll look behind the shed. You look inside."

Footsteps approached the open doorway. Laura backed as far as she could into the shadows of the small, smelly shed.

Would he see her? Call for Tom?

She didn't move, didn't even breathe. By the moonlight outside, she could make out Treeve's outline in the doorway. For a moment she glimpsed the whites of his eyes. It seemed he was looking directly at her.

Tom returned and asked, "Anything?"

"Just a cat," Treeve said. "It ran off."

"Good thing."

The men walked away, and Laura slowly released a long breath.

She crept across the shed only to freeze in terror. A man in a hooded cape stood within the shed beside the door, stick raised over his head like a grim specter. Standing there, he would have been out of sight of Treeve, and had been invisible to her in the darkness, until now.

A scream caught in her throat, while her panicked heart drummed loudly in her ears.

The man slowly lowered the stick. "Shh . . ." he murmured. "It is me. Alexander."

Laura released a second relieved breath in as many moments.

"What are you doing?" she hissed.

"Preparing to strike should either man try to hurt you or detain you."

"How did you get here?"

"I followed you. I saw you leave the house alone at night and was worried about you."

"Th-thank you," she whispered.

"I stepped in here just before you did and was about to make my presence known when those two approached." Alexander limped out of the shed and looked both ways. "The coast is clear."

Walking stick in hand, he turned and offered her his other arm. "May I walk you home, Miss Callaway?"

She managed a tremulous smile. "Yes, please."

They walked in silence for a while, but as they passed an abandoned quarry, a screech owl cried to its mate, and Laura jumped.

Alexander said soothingly, "Why don't you tell me a favorite memory of your childhood while we walk?"

She glanced over at him in surprise, studying his profile by moonlight. Beyond him, the moon shone on the Atlantic below, and with that glimpse of shining water, a memory washed over her like a gentle wave.

"That's easy," Laura began. "Papa took us all to the seaside once. Weymouth." In her mind's eye, she saw the wide sandy bay, the elegant seafront terraces, the colorful umbrellas, bathing costumes, and bathing machines. She recalled the artists with easels and vendors selling cold drinks, confections, and ices.

"What a wonderful time we had," she said. "My whole family all together. I can still see my brother, Charles, as a toddler, sitting on the shore, splashing his chubby feet in the water, giggling with glee. Papa carefree for once, having left his practice in his new partner's hands. Mamma happy and relaxed. It was magical."

Feeling self-conscious, she sent him a shy glance. "Your turn. What is your favorite memory?"

He tilted his head thoughtfully. "You will think me not very original, but mine is also a seaside memory. My family used to rent a house at . . . well, near the sea, and we all stayed there together, my grandparents, parents, me, and my brother, Alan. . . .

"I can still see my parents standing in the surf—her with her skirts tied up, him with his trousers rolled to his knees—holding hands and laughing like children or lovers. Papa wrapped his arms around Mamma's ample waist and gave her a big kiss right there in front of God and for the whole world to see."

Alexander inhaled, then released a long sigh. "They loved each other very much. It was incredibly hard on him when she died. Hard on us all, but he misses her most of all."

"How long ago did she die?" Laura asked softly.

"Sixteen . . . no, seventeen years now. How quickly time passes. I am ashamed to say I cannot recall the exact date, but my father could no doubt tell you to the hour."

They reached Fern Haven, and he held the gate for her.

"Thank you," Laura said. "And thank you again for coming to my aid." In the shadows, she reached for his hand and squeezed his fingers.

"It was my pleasure," he replied, stepping closer.

An unexpected urge to kiss him washed over Laura. She banished the startling impulse and quickly let herself into the house before she could act on it.

As Laura made her way downstairs for breakfast, she saw Mrs. Bray holding Uncle Matthew's black greatcoat—the one Laura had worn the night before—at arm's length. Nose wrinkled and face puckered, she marched into her husband's study and asked, "Why does your best coat smell of rotting fish?"

Laura gave a guilty wince as the door closed behind them and tiptoed into the dining room.

She had taken one bite of toast when Mr. Lucas entered.

"Good morning, Miss Callaway," he said, giving her a fond smile.

A strange warmth spread through her chest at the sight of him. Her rescuer of the

night before was looking especially handsome with his hair combed back and a freshly
shaven face.

"Good morning, Mr. Lucas."

Displeasure flickered over his countenance, and his smile dimmed for some reason. Had she said or done something wrong?
Have marmalade on her face or crumbs in her
teeth? She quickly raised her table napkin and
dabbed at her mouth, just in case.

After helping himself to a plate of eggs
and kipper from the sideboard, he sat across
from her and said, "I have been thinking
about your pastime."

"Oh?"

"Have you received other responses, besides the letter you recently described to me?"

She nodded. "A few. Some have thanked
me for letting them know. A wife wrote that
she had already seen news of the ship's fate
but appreciated the confirmation that her
husband had been properly buried. And one
family came here to retrieve their grandson's
Bible."

He tilted his head. "Are the people who
reply to your letters always thankful? As
Sophocles said, 'No one loves the messenger
who brings bad news.'"

"Good point. And you're right. Not all
have been thankful. I received one very angry

letter." She gave a dry chuckle. "Perhaps it is God's way of keeping me humble."

"Can you tell me what the letter said?"

"If you give me a moment, you can read it yourself." She went upstairs to retrieve the letter from her desk and handed it to him upon her return. Laura stood at his shoulder as he read the words, though she remembered them all too well.

Miss Callaway,

I know you meant well in writing to inform us of Lt. John Hathaway's death. John was my only son, and I loved him, despite his flaws. As long as he was alive, or believed to be alive, his sisters and I could go on living in Hathaway House, safe and provided for. My husband died last year. And since then his will has been held in probate court. The estate is entailed, and goes to our son, John, if living, and if deceased, to the next closest male heir, my husband's nephew. But thanks to your confirmation of my son's death, the wheels of probate are once again turning, and the will is soon to be executed. I am to have a small annuity, barely enough to live on, while my husband's heir is to have the house and all the rest. This nephew demands that we leave, as we have no legal right to stay and he says he has no reason to go on housing and feeding us, insolent devil that he is!

What are my poor girls and I to do with a mere one hundred pounds a year to live on? If one of my daughters does not marry well soon, I fear it will be the workhouse for us, all thanks to you.

Think twice before you meddle again.

Sincerely,
Mrs. Eugenia Hathaway

The words were a blow to Laura's stomach, just as they had been the first time she'd read them. She had wanted to do some good, not make anyone's life worse.

"Do not feel bad. It was not your fault," Mr. Lucas said. "Would the son not eventually have been declared dead?"

"Yes."

He nodded. "The woman was upset and probably regrets writing such a mean-spirited letter."

"I have tried to tell myself that, though sometimes I think I am fooling myself." Laura drew a deep breath. "Well, it was the truth, and is not the truth supposed to set one free? Set free of a comfortable life in this instance . . ."

She glanced over at him, expecting to see

a smile at her little joke, but instead found him looking distracted and ill at ease.

After a pause, he asked, "May I see the collection of items you have found?"

She set down her teacup. "I suppose so. If you are interested."

"I am."

When they finished eating, she retrieved the key from her desk drawer and returned wearing her full-length pelisse and gloves. "You'll want to wear Uncle Matthew's old brown coat again. Where we are going is not warm."

Carrying a lantern, although daylight, she led him behind the house, out of the garden, and up a weedy remnant of drive that now led to nowhere. Here and there a few crumbled foundation stones showed through the brush, and there a toppled chimney.

"A fine house once stood here," she explained. "A wealthy couple from Bath built it high on this hill overlooking the sea. In the summer, all is fair and lovely here. But in the winter, it can be brutally cold and windy. They said the fire was an accident, but I have always wondered."

She pointed out several charred stones before continuing, "At all events, with the wind up here so strong, the fire consumed everything. Only one outbuilding survived.

They did not rebuild but rather sold the property very cheaply to the Mably family and moved back to Somersetshire."

Walking slowly to accommodate Alex's limping gait, Laura led him toward a tall mound amid a line of tamarisk shrubs and a few stunted trees, which grew with a distinct lean, blown by the prevailing winds. From a distance, it might have appeared as if she were leading him to an ordinary earthen mound, but as they neared, a door built into the grassy bank became visible. The icehouse had been built into the earth for insulation, with rubble retaining walls and granite jambs on each side of the doorway, all but covered with encroaching plants. Its plain granite lintel was partially hidden by vines, hanging over it like a fringe of green hair. The sturdy plank door with strap hinges was bolted and locked. The padlock she had bought herself years ago with proceeds from one of her first sales.

"I wonder how long it took them to realize how impractical an icehouse was up here," Laura said. "They probably paid a fortune to have ice carted in from Bodmin or someplace farther north."

She drew out the key and unfastened the padlock. "Eseld thinks it a waste of time, so you are only the second person I've invited inside. Uncle Matthew being the first."

"I am honored."

"Please moderate your expectations. It's not exactly Blackbeard's treasure. Mrs. Bray says I should sell the lot of it, but I am still holding out hope of finding the rightful homes for some things."

Laura pushed open the door, and musty cold air immediately met them, so well insulated was the place, partly above ground, partly subterranean. She raised her lantern high and led Mr. Lucas down the wooden stairs to its flagstone floor with granite roof above.

"Watch your step."

She hung the lantern on a hook to illuminate the cavern-like space. Shelves were built around its circumference, and on those shelves were the things she had found on nearby beaches over the years.

She led him slowly around, giving him a tour of her inventory.

A tea cask. Several Spanish ducaton coins. A tortoiseshell fan. Belt buckles. A sugar bowl. Cloak button and chain. Candlesticks, candle holders, and snuffers. The decorative lid of a lady's cosmetic jar. Lots of clay tobacco pipes. Brushes with bone handles. A carpenter's rule. Medicine vials, sealed in a surgeon's chest and in excellent condition. A hat case. Snuff boxes. A key. Glass beads.

Several chipped china plates and cups, and the ubiquitous seashells.

She pointed to a large instrument that looked like a two-armed compass. "I am not sure what that is called."

"An octant," he supplied. "Used in navigation."

Next they came to a leather shako cap with an eagle badge plate of the French 35th Infantry Regiment of the Line.

"It seems rather small to me," she said.

Alexander nodded. "A drummer boy, perhaps."

She picked up a brooch of gold or gilt in the shape of a salamander with small gem scales. "This is one of my favorites."

He whistled. "Probably worth something too."

She shrugged. "I suppose so, though profit is not my primary aim. I am most interested in things that might help me identify victims who would otherwise go unnamed and unknown."

"That is kind of you," he said.

Another modest shrug. "It was my uncle's idea. He thought it would give me a project, a purpose of my own, and he was right."

Laura did not usually go to the expense of posting items immediately, as there was always a risk the parcel would reach the wrong person, someone unrelated or uninterested. So Laura described the item in the initial letters she sent, sometimes including a sketch and offering to send the object if small, or inviting the person to come and collect larger things at their convenience. In the meantime, she kept the items in the abandoned icehouse for safekeeping.

Laura picked up a narrow, light green bottle. A medicine bottle, perhaps, without a label. Inside was a rolled piece of paper. "You might think a message in a bottle a rare, whimsical thing. But while at sea, they are a practical way of protecting one's final words. More than one officer has written a plea for help or a farewell."

She lifted the bottle. "This one truly touched my heart. I found it the night the *Price* was trapped on the Doom Bar. The first mate must have guessed his fate, for he spent precious minutes of his last hour writing a letter and securing it in this bottle. Perhaps he meant to throw it into the sea but was washed overboard himself before he could do so.

"That night, I saw Tom Parsons bend over him and pull this from one of the man's pockets and his watch from another. Thinking the bottle empty, Tom threw it down in disgust and went off to search his next victim.

"I hurried over and retrieved it. The

bottle contained no rum or whatever Tom was hoping for, but I saw the white ghost of paper within. I tucked the bottle away, then looked closer at the man's face, committing it to memory. He looked so peaceful, green eyes open and wearing a hint of a smile it seemed to me. So much so that I felt for a pulse just to be sure, but no, he was dead.

"I looked for anything else that might identify him but found nothing. So I closed his eyes and waited for my uncle to come and say a blessing over him."

Seeing her listener was transfixed, Laura slid the paper from the bottle. "This is a copy I made for myself." She read it aloud.

"To whoever finds this note,

The waves are beating the ship to splinters. We can't last much longer. If you find this, it likely means I am gone. I hope you will do me a great favor and send this note to my parents to let them know.

It was a foolish and proud young man who left their home four years ago. And an older, wiser, more repentant man who writes these words now.

Father, if you read this, please know I forgive you. You asked me long ago to do so, and I said I never would. That was spiteful and cruel. I do forgive you, and I ask that you forgive me, for the harsh words and for leaving you without a chance to make amends or say good-bye.

I meant to come back this Christmas in hopes of a reconciliation. Would have, had God allowed. But please never doubt that I love you.

Mamma, I am sorry I was not a more attentive, kinder son. You deserved better. I love you too. Forgive me for not telling you in far too long.

May you both find peace in the fact that I have surrendered my soul to God, relying on Jesus' mercy, which as you know I once scoffed at. I scoff no longer. To borrow words from another seafarer, I once was lost but now am found.

> Yours forever,
> James Milton Kirkpatrick III

Please deliver to:
Mr. and Mrs. James Milton Kirkpatrick
The Grange, Bableigh Road
Barnstaple, Devon, England."

Laura paused, affected by the words all over again. "Barnstaple isn't so very far from here. He was so close to home, yet he didn't reach it."

"Sounds like he did."

She tilted her head to regard him. "Are you a man of faith, Mr. Lucas?"

"I am. Though imperfect and prone to wander. Especially at the moment."

"Are not we all?" Laura said softly, then returned her focus to the paper. "I don't usually send the original, in case it should not reach the intended recipient. But in this case, I had such specific direction that I posted the letter, enclosed in another sheet. I wrote a few lines explaining how I came upon it, my sorrow for their loss, and sent it on."

"Have you received any reply?"

"No. I do hope they received it. I like to think it helped, and that his father forgave him. That they reconciled at last."

"Yes, I hope so too." Alexander nodded thoughtfully. "Fathers and sons. Sometimes close, sometimes so easy to let injured pride and disagreements splinter the relationship as surely as rocks and waves splinter ships."

"You speak from experience?" Laura asked.

"I do, unfortunately. I too hope to reconcile with both my father and brother when I return home. Father's health is not good, I've learned. And with the strain of . . . recent events . . . I hope I am in time."

"So do I."

Laura looked around at her collection once more. Had she shown him everything? She thought of her latest finds, still in the Fern Haven scullery. She had soaked the cocked hat in a bucket and set the flask on a shelf for later polishing.

Thinking of those items, and of the uniform coat Martyn had found, she asked, "Were any French officers on board the *Kittiwake*?"

He hesitated. "Why do you ask?"

"I found a *chapeau bras* after the ship foundered."

"I . . . did not see anyone in uniform."

She turned to the door. "Well, shall we go? I am due to help my uncle with his calls."

He looked up, clearly distracted. "Hm? Oh yes. Thank you for showing me your treasures."

The legendary "wrecker of Trevose," Tom Parsons was also credited with luring ships onto the rocks by the use of "false lights." But in truth all the wrecker had to do was wait for the gale to bring home the booty.

—BRIAN FRENCH, *LOST OFF TREVOSE*

Chapter 8

Returning to Fern Haven, Alexander and Miss Callaway parted, her to her uncle's study and him to the guest room. There his thoughts churned, spurred on by the letter she had read to him—the young man's hopes of a reconciliation with his family, which was now never to be.

Alexander too longed to reconcile with his estranged family, the father and brother he loved. He too desired to forgive and be forgiven for the harsh words and arguments. For leaving without making amends or saying good-bye.

Things had not always been turbulent between them. As boys, he and Alan had been good friends, tussling and teasing and roasting one another as brothers do, but looking out for each other as well.

He recalled one small memory among so many fraternal moments. The two brothers swimming together during one of their seaside holidays. Younger Alan had been overwhelmed by the waves, and Alex had lifted him up, supporting him and helping him into shallower water. "I've got you."

When his feet touched sand, Alan pulled from his grasp, glancing toward shore to make sure no one had seen. "I'm all right," he insisted.

"Of course you are." Alexander ruffled his hair, then splashed him. Alan splashed back, the danger soon forgotten.

The pretty girl from next door appeared on the beach in a bathing costume, dark hair in twin plaits.

"Come in," Alexander called to her.

"No!" she called back. "Mamma said one of you was out here shouting like a baby. The water must be freezing."

Alan sent him a pleading look.

"That was me," Alexander lied, covering for him. "Just fooling around. The water is fine—see?"

He splashed at her, and Alan joined in.

When the girl responded with a satisfying squeal, he and his brother shared a pair of smug grins.

"Thank you, Alexander."

Alan had not thanked him for rescuing him from the waves . . . but from embarrassment before a girl? Yes.

Alex winked. "We brothers must stick together."

If only that peaceful bond between them could have lasted.

Alexander paced back and forth across the modest chamber. He had been whiling away the days in Cornwall long enough. It was time to act, to find another ship and return home to help his brother, risky though the endeavor might be. But how could he, without any money and without that flask and the valuable paper it held?

After the Evensong service at St. Michael's in Porthilly that evening, the congregants rose and began greeting neighbors and friends. Laura, as often happened, found herself alone. She was better acquainted with the people at St. Menefreda's, but as Uncle Matthew served all the parish churches, his family accompanied him to all three on occasion as well.

A few awkward solitary minutes later, Eseld approached her, face beaming. "Have you heard the news? Another survivor has been found."

Laura's heart thumped hard. "From the *Kittiwake*? Are you certain?"

Eseld nodded. "Miss Roskilly just told me."

"Where was he found?"

"Near Pentire Point—beyond the Rumps."

"So far?"

Again Eseld nodded. "Come, there's Kayna, no doubt retelling the story to Treeve. She dearly loves an audience."

She took Laura's arm and pulled her through the crowd to join them. "Pardon us, but Laura would like to hear as well."

"Good evening, Miss Callaway," Kayna Roskilly said coolly, and continued her story. "As I was telling Mr. Kent, the man made his escape by strapping himself into one of the *Kittiwake*'s lifeboats."

"Why are we only hearing of a second survivor now?" Laura asked.

"He landed in a secluded cove that was too steep to climb out of. Tom Parsons was out in his lugger and found him sleeping under the overturned boat. He brought him to our house."

Tom Parsons? Laura was surprised the wrecker would help anyone.

Perhaps noticing her dubious expression, Kayna added, "Father gave Tom a generous reward, then fetched Perran Kent to have a look at the survivor. He declared the man bruised and thirsty but otherwise remarkably hale."

Eseld looked around those gathered. "Where is Perry, by the way?"

"Fern Haven, I believe," Treeve replied. "Said something about removing stitches."

"What is the man's name?" Laura asked.

"François LaRoche," Miss Roskilly said, then held up an index finger. "Before you jump to conclusions, let me explain. Yes, he is French. But he is an *émigré* living here legally. You know how many aristocrats fled here to avoid the guillotine during the Terror in France. Even today, Britain harbours many French citizens guilty of nothing more than being titled or wealthy."

"And which is he?" Eseld asked, all hopefulness.

Kayna fluttered her dark lashes. "Both, I imagine, though it would be unladylike to pry." She and Eseld shared a smile.

Doubt creased Treeve's face. "Has he any papers to verify his claim?"

Kayna shook her head. "Lost in the ship-wreck, sadly, along with his other possessions."

"How . . . inconvenient." Treeve looked at Laura. "Perhaps your Mr. Lucas might vouch for him? Might they know one another? Have met on the ship?"

Laura hesitated. "It is . . . possible."

"I did mention to him that there was another survivor," Miss Roskilly said. "But he was too exhausted to take much notice."

"Is he handsome?" Eseld asked, eyes sparkling.

Kayna Roskilly responded with a coy, closed-lip grin. "Rather handsome, yes. But perhaps you would like to judge for yourselves. Would you like to meet him?"

Eseld glanced at Laura. "Yes, of course we would!" she answered for them both.

"Then come to our house on Saturday, say, three o'clock?"

Laura wished she could speak to Mr. Lucas before agreeing, to hear his response to the news and see if he might want to go along.

But Eseld squeezed her arm and hissed in her ear, "Don't spoil this for me. I long to become closer friends with her."

Laura curtsied. "Thank you. We would be delighted to come."

While Eseld and Miss Roskilly continued to chat, Treeve walked Laura out to the Brays' carriage, his eyes glinting with mischief. "I would be happy to take you to Pentire House so you can interrogate the *rather handsome* Frenchman in style."

She smirked at him. "How gallant of you, though I know you only offer as an excuse to see Miss Roskilly again."

"Yes, Kayna Roskilly has many charms—two thousand of them a year, as a matter of fact." He exhaled deeply and turned to her. "If only you were not a poor orphan, Miss Callaway." He tweaked her chin. "I like you much better."

She huffed, torn between offense and amusement. "At least you are honest."

"When I can be, Miss Callaway. When I can be. Though I have my secrets."

"That I can well believe," she replied, thinking of the late-night cargo landing she had witnessed. "Thank you for the offer, but I want to talk to Mr. Lucas first, and—"

Eseld stepped out and, seeing them together, hurried to join them. "What are you two whispering about? Come, no secrets."

"Secrets are exactly what we *were* talking about, Miss Mably," Treeve said.

Eseld looked ready to pout, so Laura deftly reassured her. "Mr. Kent is teasing you. He was just offering to drive us to Pentire House on Saturday."

Eseld sucked in a little breath of surprised pleasure. "How kind. We accept."

Treeve bowed, his gaze holding Laura's. "Until then, ladies."

❦

When they returned to Fern Haven, Laura found Mr. Lucas with Perran Kent, the latter removing his stitches.

The patient winced.

"Am I hurting you?" Perry asked, brows furrowed in concentration.

Alexander gritted his teeth. "Stings a bit—that's all."

Seeing Laura, he managed a smile. "Ah, my angel of mercy." Noticing her tense expression, he said, "Is something amiss?"

"Em, no. Just some news. It will wait until Dr. Kent finishes."

"Ah, I suppose you heard about the second survivor?" Perry asked. "I was just about to mention it to Mr. Lucas."

"Another survivor?" Alexander's face tightened with strain as well as pain.

"A Frenchman," Perry said. "Even so, that is good news, is it not?"

"Of course," Alex replied between stiff lips, his tone not very convincing.

The young doctor finished. Packing up his supplies, he said, "I was surprised to find him in such good health, more than a week after the wreck, cast ashore in a small cove without food or water. But he was remarkably unscathed. I gather he drank rainwater collected in leaves and managed to spear a few fish."

"Very resourceful," Laura murmured.

"Yes, a natural-born survivor." Perry looked from one to the other, as if becoming aware of the tension in the room but not understanding it. "Well, I will leave you." At the sound of Eseld's laughter floating up the stairs, he bowed and quickly departed.

When they were alone, Alexander asked, "What is the man's name?"

"François LaRoche. Says he's a French *émigré* living here legally. Treeve wondered if you might be able to confirm the veracity of his claim."

Alex laughed, but it was not a pleasant sound. "François and veracity do not belong in the same sentence."

"You know him?"

"Yes. We . . . shared a cabin on the ship."

"Do you want to go and see him?"

"Where is he?"

"At the Roskillys' home, a few miles from here. Apparently he escaped in one of the *Kittiwake*'s lifeboats."

Alexander nodded, a bitter twist to his lips. "He helped himself to one of the boats and cut the other loose to keep me from coming after him. Left the rest of us, even the boy, with no way to escape."

Laura swallowed. "Why would you be . . . going after him?"

"Because we fought on the ship." His hand moved to his injured side.

"Why?"

"It's a long story. But he is a dangerous man, Miss Callaway. I don't want you going anywhere near him."

"I would not go alone. Treeve Kent has offered to escort us."

"Mr. Kent shows an avid interest in your affairs."

"Mr. Kent shows an avid interest in Miss Roskilly, not me."

When Alex made no reply, she said, "I have no reason to fear Monsieur LaRoche, and he has no reason to be hostile toward me."

"Does he not?" For a moment he held her gaze, eyes intense.

He looked almost fierce . . . almost like a different man. *What is he hiding?* Laura wondered.

Then Alexander sighed, and the gentleman she had come to know reappeared. "I hope you are right."

Again Laura asked herself, *Who is this man really?* Were they safe harbouring him in Fern Haven?

She went down to her uncle's study and found him bent over the desk, writing a letter. He looked up when she entered. "Yes, my dear?"

"I don't want to disturb you."

"Not at all." He returned his quill to the inkpot. "I always have time for you."

"Thank you. I was just wondering . . . now that you are more acquainted with Mr. Lucas, are you comfortable with him staying here?"

Uncle Matthew interlaced his fingers as he considered. "Yes, I am. He seems a good sort of man. Do you agree?"

Laura nodded in relief. "Yes." It was what she thought as well, but she highly valued her uncle's opinion. Hopefully, they were not both mistaken.

❦

After Miss Callaway left him, Alexander lay thinking about François LaRoche.

As boys, François and Alexander had spent a great deal of time together. They were about the same age, while Alexander's brother, Alan, was a year younger. Their families were from different social spheres—the LaRoches being rather poor—but as youths, they hadn't cared about that. Alexander's father was stern and strict, so as an adolescent chafing under rules and restrictions, he actually envied François, whose parents let him do as he liked. François stayed out late and stole apples and cider and pocket money. When they were young, Alex saw it as harmless fun. But unchecked, François's recklessness only increased.

When Alexander's mother died, François listened to him rail against God for the unfairness of life, then held him as he wept. In those days, they had been as close as brothers.

Other fragments of memory rattled through his mind like links of a chain. Him handing François a loaf of bread when his family was hungry. François too proud to accept. "We don't need it," he'd said, pushing it away. "Don't give me charity."

Alex replied by quoting one of many local proverbs, "Friends do not give, they share everything." After that, François reluctantly accepted the bread and other food as well.

Later, when François offered him his first cigar, Alexander hesitated to try it, but with a sly grin, François challenged him, "Remember, friends share everything."

Alex choked on the thing, and François laughed mercilessly, only to take a smug puff and launch into a coughing fit of his own. Soon they were both laughing.

When François's father died and Alexander came upon the young man weeping, his own tears flowed as well, both for his bereaved friend and for his own dear mamma, who was never far from his mind.

Clearly embarrassed, François tried to hide his tears. Undeterred, Alexander sat beside him and laid a tentative hand on his arm, whispering, "I understand. But remember, friends share everything."

Reclining on the bed in Fern Haven, Alex blinked away those memories. All of that had been a long time ago. He and François La-Roche were friends no longer.

The agent had been busily employed in sav-
ing as much of the cargo as possible, and
in staving off the attacks of the wreckers.
The salvage bills were all honorably paid.
Each wheeled cart was paid one guinea
per twelve hours, the labour men 2/6 a
day. It was a merry day for the men.

—JOHN BRAY, *AN ACCOUNT OF WRECKS*
ON THE NORTH COAST OF CORNWALL

Chapter 9

The next day, Jago came over to visit, bringing Alex one of Miss Chegwin's famous pasties. He thanked the likable young man, and the two sat down to play a game of draughts.

Wenna brought them tea. She swiped the cap from Jago's big head and gave his shaggy hair an affectionate pat. The elderly cook-housekeeper reminded him of Betty, his mother's former maid, and Alex felt another twinge of homesickness.

The wreck agent returned while Jago was there. Mr. Hicks reported the *Kittiwake* had shifted in the sea. For days it had been all but submerged and unreachable, the waves breaking over her. Now that the weather had calmed, the *Kittiwake* lay stranded on a rocky outcropping in the waters beyond Greenaway Beach.

"The cargo that washed ashore initially has already been taken by wreckers," Hicks said with a scowl, "but now I plan to salvage anything else that might be sold at auction to defray the owner's losses. The customs officers will assist me. I anticipate the same wreckers and even tinners may be tempted to interfere, and we'll be outnumbered. May have to call in the militia."

"How can we help?" Alex asked.

"I could use some trustworthy men to assist in the salvaging efforts, if ye would be interested. Pays well."

Hope flared. He could begin earning money toward the journey home. "Count me in. Jago?"

The young man nodded. "I will help too. As long as I can stay on dry land."

Hicks nodded. "Plenty of work loading wagons." He added their names to a list and told them to meet him at the beach at eight the next morning.

Shortly after the agent and Jago left, Miss Callaway came in.

"The agent was here recruiting men to help salvage the wreck," Alex explained, "and I volunteered."

"But with your leg and side, are you sure that is wise?"

"I may be slower than others, but I am still strong, and familiar with ships and seas. Jago is going as well."

"Good. He'll look out for you."

Lips quirked, he said dryly, "Your confidence in me is staggering."

"Forgive me. You are not long recovered."

"I cannot lie about anymore, and I don't like being penniless. I must find a way out of here."

Running a finger over the mantelpiece, she said, "Have we been so inhospitable that you are eager to leave us?"

Her unhappy expression surprised him. "You know that is not the reason. You, Miss Callaway, are everything that is good and right in this world, something I'd almost forgotten existed over the last few years."

"Because of the war, you mean?"

He hesitated. "That too."

She looked at him, eyes wide in question, but he thought it wisest to say no more.

⟨◦⟩

The following morning, Mr. Hicks along with Mr. Tresidder, the engineer, and Mr. Rawlings, the auctioneer, organized the salvage effort.

Hicks ticked off the names of the gathering volunteers, including several tinners from a local mine. "We want no trouble now, boys."

Alexander noticed an older man with reddish-blond hair staring at him through narrowed eyes.

He turned to Jago and said under his breath, "Why is that man scowling at me?"

Jago looked over, and his usually pleasant expression hardened. "That's Tom Parsons, the man our Laura protected you from after the wreck."

Alex turned and stared back at him.

The scowling man approached. "What'ee doin' here?"

Alex lifted his chin. "Same as you, I hope."

"Yer not from here."

"So? The agent said he'd pay any ablebodied person willing to work."

Parsons sent a sly glance toward Alex's leg. "Yer not exactly able-bodied."

"I may not win any races, but you'll find I work harder than most."

The red-haired man jerked a thumb toward Jago. "Then why bring the idiot along?"

Alex clenched his jaw. "He is not an idiot. Being large does not make one slow, any more than having red hair makes one a devil."

Parsons smirked. "I don't know about that. . . ."

Mr. Hicks approached, shaking his head. "Well, well, Tom Parsons. Would have thought you'd already carried off more than enough cargo the night of the wreck. Now you want me to pay you to carry more?"

"That's right. All legal and proper."

"As if you'd know the definition of either word."

Parsons's nostrils flared. "Careful, Hicks. You've got no armed militia standing behind you."

"Not yet. But they are on their way from the Bodmin barracks."

"For yer sake, better hope they arrive soon."

Alex tensed at the thought of the militia joining them. Would they question him? Somehow guess his identity?

Mr. Hicks led the dozen or so volunteers down to Greenaways. When they reached the beach, Alexander saw the customs officials in the Padstow cutter, *Speedwell*, already in the water, and two six-oared Cornish gigs on the beach nearby.

Alex looked around but counted too few oarsmen. Hailing the coxswain, he asked, "Shorthanded, cox'n?"

"Aye," he replied. "Short a hand is right. Moyle broke his in a brawl last night."

"Need another man to row? I've had some experience."

"Suit yerself."

Alex climbed in and looked back at his companion. "Jago?"

The big man shook his head, wild hair flopping forward and back. "Don't like boats. I'll stay here and load carts."

The first gig launched into the surf and moved toward the wreck.

"No catchin' crabs now, boys."

Following their lead, the coxswain commanded, "And row." Alex and the men in the second gig complied.

"Row long!" They did so, Alex pressing hard against his oar.

When they neared the wreck, the coxswain called, "Ease up."

While the men at the oars held the boats as steady as they could against the waves, a man in the prow of each stood and took turns throwing grappling hooks, trying to snag the *Kittiwake*'s rigging, visible between the waves.

After several failed attempts, Alexander spoke up. "Mind if I give it a try?"

"A cocky one, are'ee?" the man nearest him said.

Alex shrugged. He and his men had thrown many a grappling hook over the years. The hooks were used to catch an enemy ship's rigging prior to boarding. He well remembered the dread of hearing the teeth of a grappling hook ensnaring his own ship. It had been the beginning of the loss of his beloved *Victorine*.

Alex carefully moved forward, took the other man's place, coiled, aimed, and threw. His first throw slithered over the wet rigging but failed to catch. Determined, he retrieved the rope and threw the hook again, this time snagging the rigging successfully.

"Proper job," the coxswain commended. "Not yer first time at this, I gather."

"No, sir" was the only explanation Alex offered.

The crew from the *Speedwell* attached a hook as well. Line secured, the boat managed to draw alongside the damaged *Kittiwake*. Mr. Tresidder, engineer and shipbuilder, boarded first, making sure the vessel was relatively stable. Then the others joined him, searching the ship's storerooms and holds for cargo.

The men succeeded in saving the mate's chest and several barrels of salted herring, as well as a good quantity of corn.

The pilot gigs carried the salvaged goods

to shore, where Jago and several other men and even a few bal maidens—women who worked for the mine—carried loads up the steep path to waiting wagons, guarded by a customs official and newly arrived officers of the North Devon Militia.

The Cornish gigs handled the waves with relative ease. If only the pilots had been able to reach the *Kittiwake* the night of the wreck, before Daniel drowned.

"Did you not hear our distress signal?" Alex asked the coxswain.

The man swallowed. "You were on the ship?"

Alex nodded.

"Ah. Yer the survivor. . . ."

The man looked to his mates. "No. Guess we didn't hear it. We were all in our cups."

"A pity. I lost my closest friend that night, and more."

The coxswain ducked his head, avoiding Alexander's eyes. "I'm sorry . . . for yer loss. Would have helped if we . . . could." He sliced a glance toward Tom Parsons and then turned away. "Well, time to call it a day, I reckon."

After dinner that evening, Alex asked Matthew Bray about the pilot gigs, and if he had been surprised they failed to show up the night of the *Kittiwake*'s demise.

The clergyman nodded. "I was. The gigs often carry local pilots out to guide incoming ships into safe harbour. Times are hard for local men, and competition for the pilot fees is usually fierce, so I was surprised none of them tried to reach the *Kittiwake*.

"One theory I overheard whispered in the village shop was that Tom Parsons, hoping for a rich wreck, somehow prevented the pilots from responding, perhaps even bribing them. Most people do not think the brave Padstow pilots would fall to such temptation, while others would not blame them if they had. If Parsons offered to pay each pilot the usual fee, why risk his life for only a *chance* at a reward? But this is only rumor, remember. I can't believe it's true."

Alex, however, recalled the guilty look on the coxswain's face, and his telling glance toward Tom Parsons, and could believe it. Did believe it.

He was preparing for bed that night when a soft knock came to his door. He went to answer it and found Miss Callaway standing there, hair in a long plait over her shoulder. For a moment, he was reminded of his childhood friend, the pretty girl next door who had eventually become his brother's wife.

"I just thought you might want some liniment," she said. "You worked hard today." She handed him a jar. "My own father's recipe. Camphor, comfrey, cayenne, and arnica."

"Thank you. I think. Will I stink to high heaven?"

She shrugged. "I have always found it quite pleasant."

"Well then, that's good enough for me." He pressed her hand. "Very thoughtful of you, Miss Callaway. I suppose I looked like an invalid today, hobbling back?"

"Not at all. You are obviously a very strong man."

His heart thumped. At that moment, he would have given his every worldly possession to have her rub the liniment into his aching back and shoulders. Sadly, he knew he could not ask it of her, much as he might wish to.

Alex awoke feeling more sore than he could ever remember being, despite the aromatic liniment. He was determined not to give up, however, so he joined the other volunteers as they reassembled on the beach. Matthew Bray came down to encourage the men, while a few others watched the proceedings from the point above.

On their second day, they picked up several bales of wool wrapped in jute, as well as the ship's bowsprit, yards, cables, and shrouds.

Soon, every muscle in Alex's body burned. Every pull on the oar seemed more taxing, every trip up the hill more arduous than the one before. He was paying a price for his days lying flat in bed.

Wearily climbing aboard the *Kittiwake* and going below for another search of the ship, he found something light in a dark corner. Something that made the pain and exhaustion all worthwhile.

After Laura finished breakfast and started down the corridor, she heard their cook-housekeeper calling to her, sounding none too happy. "Miss Laura!"

Laura turned and made her way to the scullery. "Yes, Wenna?"

The elderly woman pointed to the shelf with a frown on her lined face. "Could I ask'ee to remove yer *things* from *my* scullery? That hat smells fouler than a wet dog."

"Oh. Sorry. Right away."

Laura sheepishly gathered the hat and flask. After polishing the flask, she had decided it was indeed silver. But she had been so busy with their houseguest that she had not taken the time to clean the hat properly, and it was now in a sad, odiferous state. She had neglected it too long.

With a sigh, Laura carried the two things out to the icehouse and added them to her collection.

After that, she and Eseld walked out to Trebetherick Point together.

From there, the two watched the salvaging efforts below. The volunteers picked up wrapped bales of some kind as well as wooden pieces of the ship and thick coils of rope.

Laura's eyes were continually drawn back to Alexander. He worked hard, straining at the oar, climbing into and out of the *Kittiwake*, loading crates and bales, helping the other men hoist the anchors from the depths, and tossing down sails and cordage into the waiting boats.

Each time they brought a load back to the beach, she studied him. His face gleamed with perspiration, and now and again he rested his hands on slim hips to catch his breath or stretch his back. Knowing of the deep cut in his side and the still-healing ankle, she winced in sympathy, thinking of the pain and exhaustion he must be feeling, though he endeavored to conceal it, determined to earn his wages like everyone else. Determined to get home.

By contrast, Tom Parsons paused often to chat with the other men or to lean against the wagon, smoking a cigar.

Just before the men broke for a noon meal, Alexander waved to her, gesturing for her to come to him. Laura hoped he had not injured himself anew.

As she hurried down the slope, she heard Parsons call, "What have'ee there, man? Not skimming fer yerself, I trust."

Reaching the beach, she saw Alex stride over to the agent, Mr. Hicks, and show him something. From where Laura stood waiting, it looked like some sort of miniature boat.

"May I keep this, sir? My friend made it for his child. I'd like to see it delivered."

Hicks eyed the thing and nodded.

Parsons grumbled, "Well, mebbe I'll see what I can find fer myself too."

"You already did that, Tom," Hicks retorted. "Night of the wreck."

Permission granted, Alex turned and walked toward Laura.

"I found it among a pile of shredded timbers," he said. "Daniel couldn't find his knapsack when the ship ran aground, so he left it behind. It was still there, in the shadows. I thank God I took one more look."

Closer now, she saw he held an intricately carved Noah's ark, with straw marquetry decorating the outside and a few carved animals still contained under its latched roof. "Your friend made this?" she asked in awe.

"Yes. For the unborn child he will never meet. But at least the child can have this, Lord willing. Made by his own father's hands."

Seeing the sweat and tears mingling on his face, Laura felt her heart twist. "I will keep it safe."

"Thank you." Alexander pressed it into her hands. For a moment his rough, warm fingers framed hers as she held the precious relic of a father's love.

After a meal of pasties and cider, the gig crews again rowed out to the unfortunate *Kittiwake*, the partially healed cut in Alex's side crying out with each stroke. But during the interval the wind had intensified, and they discovered that nothing remained of the vessel but the main mast, which had become entangled by the rigging among the rocks and seaweed. This was the last thing they were able to secure.

As Alex climbed back into the gig, his limbs trembled. He wasn't certain he would be able to make the final trip up the hill to deliver the remaining crates.

At last, they returned to shore, exhausted. Seeing Tom Parsons leaning lazily against one of the wagons, an arrogant smirk on his face while the rest of them toiled, sent anger boiling through Alexander. Unable to restrain himself, he stepped near and challenged, "Is it true? Did you prevent the pilots from coming to the *Kittiwake*'s rescue?"

"What's it to'ee? You survived."

"No thanks to you, I understand."

The man's green eyes glinted. "That's right. You wouldn't be standing here in my face were it not for that meddling up-country chit."

Alex pressed closer, nose to nose with the man. "My dearest friend died in that wreck. A married man expecting his first child. His death might have been prevented. He might have been spared."

Parsons shrugged. "Ah well. Life goes on."

Alexander grabbed his collar and pulled tight. "Not for you it doesn't."

Parsons pulled out a knife.

"Alex!" Heavy brows lowered, Jago came charging over like a bull.

Through his fury, Alexander forced himself to think rationally. He didn't want to endanger the young man.

Perhaps having the same thought, Matthew Bray ran over and positioned himself between Jago and the sparring men. "Come now," the vicar said. "This is no way to behave. Be glad you are alive and make the most of each day God gives you."

A militia officer belatedly joined the fray. "Break it up. Unless you want to forfeit yer day's wages."

Alex released the wrecker and stepped back. "He's not worth it."

Parsons jerked away, muttering curses under his breath, and Alex returned to work. All that was left to do was carry the remaining cargo to the wagons. The final load up the steep path threatened to sap Alex's last ounce of strength. He was sweating profusely, and his ankle and side throbbed. Ahead of him, Jago carried twice as many crates as he did, as though the burden weighed nothing. When the men reached the customs clerk, Jago set half his load at Alex's feet and said, "Four crates for him. Two for me."

"Jago, no," Alex hissed in protest.

The big man shrugged. "I have more than enough. Besides, you stood up for me yesterday."

"*Not* to get something from you."

"I know. Today it's my turn."

"Well. Thank you." Alex gave his shoulder a friendly whack.

Jago nodded. "I am glad our Laura saved you."

Alex smiled. "So am I."

He collected his pay and counted the coins. It was a start, though not nearly enough.

The news of the wreck it soon
spread along shore,
And women and men ran for gain;
Thus numbers they harden
each other the more,
That love of curst money may reign.

—RELIGIOUS TRACT BY AN
ANONYMOUS CLERGYMAN

Chapter 10

On Saturday, Treeve, Perry, Eseld, and Laura rode together in the Kent carriage to meet the Roskillys' shipwrecked guest.

"Did Mr. Lucas not wish to come?" Treeve asked.

Laura hesitated. "Mr. Lucas was not invited."

Grinning, Treeve said, "That did not stop us."

As they neared Pentire House, Laura's stomach quivered in a bundle of nerves, and she gripped her hands tightly on her lap.

Perry, ever observant, asked, "Feeling all right?"

Laura forced a smile. "Perfectly well."

She did not tell them the man living with the mineowner's family might be dangerous. She had only Alexander's word for it. For some time, she had known Mr. Lucas was hiding something and suspected he may have lied about his identity. What else might he be lying about? She did not want to besmirch François LaRoche's character before she'd had a chance to talk to the man herself.

When they arrived, they entered the stately stone house and were shown into the drawing room. There, a stranger sat low in an armchair, wearing, she surmised, Mr. Roskilly's long, patterned banyan. His hands, with bruised knuckles, rested on the upholstered arms. He looked like a slouching king on a throne.

Miss Roskilly sat on the sofa near him, one hand on the long narrow bolster. The man raised a languid finger and stroked the back of it. Kayna looked down, blushing. They were the picture of a romantic tête-à-tête.

The butler announced their arrival, startling Kayna. Her guest looked up when Laura and Eseld entered but did not rise. His long dark hair fell back from his face, revealing striking blue eyes and an upper lip much fuller than the bottom. Dark whiskers dotted fair skin, less thick than Alexander's had been. His eyebrows, she noticed, were also sparser. Miss Roskilly had said he was handsome. Laura was not sure she agreed.

The man looked from female to female, eyes alight with interest and perhaps appreciation. He gave a slow, closed-mouth smile. The expression creased his left cheek more deeply than a dimple, revealing a deep scar in the shape of a shepherd's crook.

Recalling Alexander's warning, Laura stopped where she was, going no closer.

Kayna Roskilly began, "Miss Mably and Miss Callaway, please meet François La-Roche."

"*Enchanté*," he said.

"Dr. Kent you already know," she continued. "And this is his brother, Treeve."

The men nodded to one another.

"Do tell us about your experience, *monsieur*," Eseld urged. "Miss Roskilly said you survived by strapping yourself into one of the *Kittiwake*'s lifeboats?"

LaRoche nodded. "That's right. *Le bateau* rolled on the sea like a toy. Laid upon her beam-ends until I was sure to capsize any moment . . ." The Frenchman went on to regale them with the story of his escape, his accent heavier and more foreign than Alexander's.

When he finished his "heroic" tale, Laura thought of what Mr. Lucas had said about this man cutting loose the other lifeboat before anyone else could escape. Was it true? Should she ask?

Hedging, she said, "The others were not so fortunate, *monsieur*. At least eight men and a boy were left on board with no way to escape. Was there only one boat?"

He looked at her, eyes narrowing. "There was one more, but I believe the other men were washed overboard before they could get to it. *Quel dommage*."

Laura held his gaze. "One man survived anyway, thank God."

"The other survivor I mentioned has been recovering at Fern Haven under Miss Callaway's care," Kayna explained.

The Frenchman's blue eyes glinted. "Lucky man."

Laura gestured to Perran and added quickly, "Dr. Kent tended him as well."

Perry nodded, then said, "Perhaps you know each other, though I realize if you were passengers instead of crew, you might not be acquainted."

A line appeared between the man's brows. "A passenger, you say?"

"Yes." Laura felt an unexpected wave of protectiveness wash over her. If Alexander Lucas was not who he'd said he was, did she want this stranger to expose him in front of so many? And he not there to defend himself? She licked dry lips and chose her words carefully. "Though perhaps you are not acquainted, because when he heard *your* name, he said little about you. Only that you two met on the ship."

"Did he?" LaRoche twisted a gold ring on his little finger. "The only passengers I knew were men named Marchal and Carnell."

Marchal had been the name of Alexander's friend, Laura recalled. The latter name sounded familiar as well. Had that been the surname embroidered inside the *chapeau bras* she'd found? She lifted her chin and said evenly, "Several victims were unidentified, but the survivor's name is Mr. Lucas."

He hesitated, eyes glinting. "Lucas, is it? Interesting. Then perhaps he is not the man I thought him. And Marchal?"

"Buried in the churchyard, I'm afraid."

"Well, that is something. And how is this Mr. Lucas? Recovered from our . . . mishap?"

"He is recovering well, thanks to Dr. Kent."

"Then I shall have to pay a call and introduce myself . . . properly."

"Not yet, *monsieur*," Miss Roskilly purred. "You must give yourself time to recover. You've been through an ordeal. Rest and good food are what the doctor prescribes. Is that not right, Perry?"

Perry looked from her to Laura to the patient and, taking the hint, said, "Yes. Exactly. Too soon to go gallivanting across the parish."

LaRoche watched this exchange with an ironic tilt to his lip, which curled into a smile when he looked at Kayna. "*D'accord.* I am in no hurry to leave my lovely hostess and such charming accommodations." He turned back to Laura. "But the time will come, never fear."

"You may meet him in two days' time, right here." Miss Roskilly said, then looked up at Laura. "Mr. Lucas is coming to the ball, is he not? I do hope you've invited him. We could use more men to make up our numbers, otherwise we shall be sadly lacking in dance partners."

"I don't know that with his recent injuries, Mr. Lucas will be equal to dancing," Laura replied. Considering his salvage work, it was a weak excuse, but she did not want to divulge the real reason Alexander might hesitate to attend.

"Bring him anyway," Kayna said. "The more the merrier. And what about you, *monsieur*? Will you dance?"

"*Bien sûr.*" LaRoche grinned. "Others may make excuses like a whiny little boy, but I would not miss my chance to dance with such *belles femme* for all the world."

Miss Roskilly smiled at the Frenchman. "Good. I shall hold you to that."

LaRoche held her gaze, wearing the self-satisfied expression of a cat. A cat with a mouse under its paw.

"We are hosting a subscription ball to help raise funds to uncover St. Enodoc and see to its restoration," Kayna explained.

"I have a new dress for the occasion," Eseld added.

Eyes twinkling, Miss Roskilly said, "And now I see why Mr. Bray struggles to pay for renovations."

Eseld blushed, and Miss Roskilly touched her arm. "Only teasing you, pet. I have a new dress too."

Laura had no new dress but said sincerely, "My uncle is very appreciative, I know. He has been trying without success to make headway on the problem since he moved here."

"We are happy to help."

LaRoche's blue eyes glinted. "How noble. I shall look forward to doing my part as well."

On the drive back, Laura decided she did not like François LaRoche, nor did she trust him.

She knew she was not objective in her assessment, and that she was already prejudiced in
Alexander's favor. Even so, there was something about LaRoche she wouldn't like even
had she no prior knowledge of his character.
He struck her as arrogant and insolent. And
there was something rather oily—unctuous—
about the man.

When she returned to Fern Haven, she
thanked the Kent brothers for the ride and
went to find Mr. Lucas, knowing he would
be anxious to hear her account of the visit.

She found him in the parlour, reading war
reports in the newspaper.

He looked up when she entered. "How
did it go?"

Laura described LaRoche's account of
his escape and the Roskillys' kind offices to
their guest.

"Perry asked him if he knew you. And
LaRoche said the only passengers he knew
were men named Marchal and Carnell."

She watched his face as she said the
names, but his expression remained inscru-
table. When he didn't respond, she added,
"I remembered your friend's surname was
Marchal, though I reiterated that yours is
Lucas."

He nodded vaguely.

She studied him. "Do you wish to explain

why this man whose name you knew and with whom you shared a cabin does not know a Mr. Lucas?"

"I . . . cannot say."

"Cannot or will not?"

"As I said before, I will tell you all when I know I can trust you."

"And how can I trust *you*?" She thought again of the *T.O.* she had seen in his friend's clothing. Garments issued by the Transport Office carried this mark—garments issued to prisoners of war. "How do I know you are not the dangerous one?"

Pain creased his face. "Do you really think that?"

Did she? Laura considered. He might not be who he claimed to be, but no, she did not think he posed any danger. At least . . . she hoped not.

Laura decided to let the issue of names drop for the time being. "He asked if you had recovered from your mishap."

"How kind," Alexander murmured, his tone acerbic.

"He also said he will pay a call here to introduce himself. Perry and Miss Roskilly insisted he wait until he has more fully recovered, though he looked quite healthy to me."

Laura hesitated to bring up the ball but

forced herself to do so. "In the meantime, Miss Roskilly has invited you to attend the subscription ball her parents are hosting to help raise funds for St. Enodoc. I told her you might not feel equal to it."

"Because of my ankle or LaRoche?"

"I was not sure that with your injuries, you would wish to dance," Laura replied. "Though Miss Roskilly is most adamant that you attend anyway. However, I won't press you if you don't want to go."

"LaRoche will be there?"

"Yes, he promises to dance with all the *belles femmes*."

"Of course he does. And charm them all, no doubt."

Again the bitterness crept into Alexander's tone. What was the real history between the two men? She guessed they had known one another long before boarding the *Kittiwake*.

He said slowly, "If I attend, scenes may arise unpleasant to more than myself. Though I would endeavor to be on my best behavior."

"I understand."

He looked off into the distance, considering. "What would I wear? I don't suppose you have evening clothes my size in that collection of yours?" He managed a small smile.

"I'm afraid not, though Uncle Matthew

is sure to have something suitable you could borrow for the occasion."

"Let me think about it. I will let you know in the morning."

"Very well."

When Laura left him, Alexander remained where he was, considering the situation from all angles. He did not like the idea of hiding from LaRoche as though he were afraid of him. He was not. Would LaRoche reveal his identity and where they had come from, considering the revelation would implicate *him* as well? Or would he produce the papers he counted on for impunity?

If LaRoche accused him in front of the assembly, Alexander would have no choice but to flee. He could not risk anything that would keep him from his mission to return home and save his brother—if such a feat was possible.

But better to face LaRoche like a man than to hide in Fern Haven like a capon in a cage, awaiting his fate. Better to meet him in a public place, where LaRoche would have to be civilized and watch his tongue if he didn't want to risk arrest himself. That possibility might restrain him, although François had never been one to think before he spoke.

Either way, Alexander decided he would go.

He would appeal to his former friend to avoid a scene that would embarrass his generous hosts and endanger them both. But there was no guarantee François would listen.

Alex folded the newspaper he'd been reading and thought back.

He, Alan, and François had been mere children during their country's revolution. With hostility toward the upper classes escalating, François began to resent Alexander and his wealthier family. As the two grew into manhood, they spent less and less time together. During the Peace of Amiens, Alexander studied in Cambridge for a few terms, then returned home and enlisted. François, meanwhile, became involved with a band of counterrevolutionaries who fought against the new regime. Many of those men lost their lives.

Alan had always looked up to François, who was confident, daring, and charming, and once Alexander went to sea, Alan apparently followed in LaRoche's footsteps.

Alex recalled with regret the night he had last seen Alan.

Returning home on leave, Alex had been heartsick and angry to learn of Alan's clandestine activities—his involvement with the royalist counterrevolutionaries, rumored to be partially financed by the British government.

One night he heard something and went downstairs to investigate, sword drawn, on guard against an intruder. Instead, the brother he had not seen in more than a year stood in the shadowy entry hall. Alan's hair was long and his clothes coarse—hobnail shoes, knee-high leather gaiters, and a broad-brimmed hat. Rawboned and weary, he looked like a peasant, or at least like the Breton insurgent he was.

For a moment, Alexander watched him pawing through the postbox, pocketing the coins kept there to pay messengers who arrived at the door. He then said dryly, "Come to steal from your own family?"

Alan turned to glare at him. "I need to buy food for our people, some who are severely wounded. Is it stealing to keep men from starving? To keep myself from starving?"

"It is still wrong. LaRoche must have put you up to this."

"He has nothing to do with it. Not . . . anymore."

Their father emerged from the servants' area, a burlap sack of apples in one hand, potatoes in the other.

Indignation shook Alexander. "You are aiding him? Knowing the penalty?"

Alan scowled. "Will you report your own father? Your own flesh and blood?"

"You endanger your own family by coming here!" Alex shouted, then turned to his father. "Don't you know the longer you support these brigands, the longer the bloodshed will last?"

He gestured toward Alan. "They have degenerated into a band of vandals, thieves, and killers. Did the Vendée teach you nothing? The failed assassination attempts? The death of the *Chouannerie* leaders?"

"We are not dead," Alan insisted. "*La petite Chouannerie* lives on."

"For how long?" Alexander asked. "Until you are dead too?"

Alan shook his head. "The *Royalistes* will prevail. But I agree the old methods are no longer effective. That is why I am considering a new course."

Fear tightened their father's face. "What course?"

"I cannot tell you."

"Because you are ashamed?" Alexander challenged.

"Because my brother would report me to the usurper or at least his henchmen."

"Alan, what are you involving yourself in?" their father asked again.

Wariness gripped Alexander's gut. He had heard rumors of local men aiding *les rosbifs*. "Tell me you are not helping the British."

"I am not. But since when is our mother's country the enemy?"

Angered by this justification, Alexander thundered, "Alan!"

His brother raised his hand. "I will do nothing she would disapprove of. Nothing my conscience would disapprove of. That should be enough for you."

"It's not. You seem determined to destroy yourself and this family. And what of Léonie? What has she to say to all this?"

Eyes hot with fury, Alan grabbed Alex's lapel. "You leave her out of this. You had your chance with her and gave it up. Your right to say anything about her, about us, is gone too."

"Alan, let him go," their father pleaded. "He is your brother. He loves you and is concerned for you. We both are."

Alan scoffed but released his hold. "Ha. He has chosen his allegiance, and I have chosen mine. He doesn't love me. If he did, he would support me."

Alexander shook his head. "That is not how love works. It is not blind to faults, nor must it accept the wrongdoing of those dear to us."

"Nor do I accept your wrongdoing," Alan retorted. "Off conquering foreign lands while our countrymen bleed and die and tear each other apart?"

"You forget how bad things were under the monarchy you dream of restoring. You were too young. We both were. The nobles lived in luxury, the common man starved."

"And this regime is better? Executing all who speak against them, who resist their conscriptions and tyranny?"

"My sons, please," their father begged. "Do not fight. Alexander must return to duty soon, and . . ."

"And I must rejoin my men before my brother has me arrested or shoots me himself."

"I would not shoot you."

"Ah. How generous." Alan turned to their father. "*Alors. Dernier adieu, mon père.* I shall not trouble you again."

"Don't say that," his father urged, pressing the sacks of produce into his arms. "You are always welcome, Alan. This is your home."

"Not anymore."

His brother stalked out. When the door slammed behind him, his father turned on Alex. "Did you have to provoke him? Now I may never see him again!"

"He has brought this on himself."

"How easy for you to sit in judgment of him. Are you so sure you are right? That the emperor is just and has our country's best interest at heart? Or are you blinded by ambition and lust for power as well?"

Alex gasped for breath, shocked and hurt as though his father had struck him. "Are you not the one who encouraged me to enlist?"

"If I could have seen into the future— seen my homeland in tatters, my sons at each other's throats . . ." He shook his head. "I would have kept silent."

As the memory of that horrible night faded, Alexander sighed. He believed his brother's devotion to the *Royalistes* was misguided but selfless. François, however, was loyal only to himself, to whichever group or side could benefit him the most.

Alexander had told Laura he would be on his best behavior. He would also have to be on his guard.

Long live the rose.
—FRENCH FOLK SONG

Chapter 11

Uncle Matthew loaned Alex evening clothes, and Laura brought out a beaver hat from her collection, brushing it until it looked like new.

She had planned to wear her best dress, a simple white gown with a bit of embroidery on the bodice, but Mrs. Bray protested.

"Come, we can't have you looking like a neglected orphan. Borrow one of Eseld's gowns. Or one of mine."

Eseld's frocks would likely be too short and Mrs. Bray's too large. Laura said, "That's all right. I don't mind. The event is for charity, after all."

Eseld tipped her head to one side. "Actually, if you wore Mamm's petticoat with the ruffles at the bottom under my green silk, and added a white ribbon at your waist and white gloves, you would look charming."

Laura agreed to at least try on the ensemble.

Eseld was right. The girl might be silly in some ways, but she had a good eye for fashion. She even arranged Laura's hair for her and added a string of paste pearls and a small green silk flower.

"Perfect. You really are lovely, Laura."

The sincere compliment gave her more pleasure than any of Treeve's flattery ever had. "Thank you, Eseld."

The gentlemen were waiting downstairs. Mr. Lucas looked up as she descended into the hall. The slow softening of his features, shining eyes, and parting of his lips seemed to echo Eseld's praise.

Uncle Matthew glanced at the man. Alexander said nothing, so he filled the gap, saying, "You look beautiful, my girl."

"Thank you. Eseld deserves the credit."

He gave her hand a reassuring squeeze. "I think you own the lion's share."

When they arrived at the Roskillys' fine house, a footman helped the ladies alight, while a groom took charge of their horses and carriage. In the entry hall, one of the churchwardens sat at a table accepting subscription fees and any additional donations.

Uncle Matthew paid their dues, and Laura donated two guineas from recent sales of her collection. Then they followed the crowd into the drawing room. The event was well attended by local gentry and merchants as well as a magistrate, constable, and a few officers of the North Devon Militia who were stationed in Cornwall to assist revenue officers in the suppression of smuggling.

Laura looked across the room and spied François LaRoche. Beside her Alexander stiffened, clearly also seeing the man over the heads of the assembled guests.

"Pardon me a moment."

Alexander made his way through the crowd to the man, hands raised as though in entreaty or surrender.

Laura followed more slowly and overheard part of their conversation.

"Let us avoid an unpleasant scene for the sake of the ladies and the church, all right?"

LaRoche hesitated, eyes glinting. "For the ladies, perhaps. I don't care about the church. Or you."

"Fair enough."

Miss Roskilly came and took LaRoche's arm. "Come, *monsieur*. It is time to take our places."

He allowed the young woman to lead him away.

Alexander returned to Laura's side, still looking wary and uneasy.

The evening began with a concert. The Roskillys had engaged a singer for the occasion who regularly performed in Bath and Exeter.

She sang beautifully. The first half of her repertoire included a few songs in English and one in Italian.

During the interval, François approached her, flashed his charming smile, and asked something of her. She nodded her agreement, and he touched his fingertips to his heart with a small bow of gratitude. Laura wondered what he had said. She doubted he'd been flirting with the singer, as the woman was probably a decade older than he was, but couldn't be certain.

When the singer returned to the front of the room to continue her program, she said, "I have received a special request. One among us is from France, as you may know. So for a few minutes at least, I hope you will set aside thoughts of war and enjoy a French folk song, 'Vive La Rose.'"

She began singing:

"Mon ami me délaisse
Ô gué, vive la rose
Je ne sais pas pourquoi . . ."

Laura had studied French in school and on her own for a time afterward, but while she recognized many words, she struggled to understand the gist of the song.

In the row ahead of her, Miss Roskilly leaned near Monsieur LaRoche and asked softly, "What does it mean?"

"It is a song of, how do you say, unreturned love?"

"Unrequited love?"

"*C'est ça.*"

As the singer continued, LaRoche quietly translated:

> "My friend is leaving me. I do not
>   know why.
> He's going to see another, who is
>   richer than me.
> They say she is more beautiful; I do
>   not disagree.
> Long live the rose.
>
> They say that she is sick. Perhaps she
>   will die.
> If she dies . . . he will come back to
>   me.
> But I won't want him anymore.
> Long live the rose."

"Not a very cheery song," Miss Roskilly observed. "Why did you request it?"

"I thought Mr. Lucas would enjoy it."

Miss Roskilly glanced in his direction. "It does not appear that way."

Laura looked over as well, and was stunned to see tears in Alexander's eyes and his jaw clenched.

François smirked and crossed his arms. "Ah well."

It took all of Alexander's self-possession not to leap across the seat back and knock François to the floor. How dare he request that song, knowing the words would stab his heart and his pride? Alex knew what the man was doing. Goading him with the knowledge that his love for Enora had not been returned. The gender of the lyrics might be reversed, but the meaning was perfectly clear.

And then to give the knife a final twist, the woman sang, "'They say that she is sick. Perhaps she will die.'" Enora had died, after bearing another man's child. *Long live the rose, indeed.*

Soon the concert ended, followed by hearty applause. Alexander did not join in.

Laura leaned near and whispered, "Are you all right?"

He forced a dishonest nod.

"Did that song mean something to you? Monsieur LaRoche said he chose it for you."

"LaRoche enjoys baiting me." He turned to her, his cold, bitter heart melting as he looked into Miss Callaway's face. "But I promised to be on my best behavior, remember?" He managed a small smile. Oh, but it was costing him.

"You are being the perfect gentleman, and I appreciate it." She touched his arm. "Miss Roskilly would as well, if she knew."

He relished the warm pressure of Laura's hand on his sleeve. Too fleeting. "If you are pleased, that is enough for me."

The servants moved aside the chairs and rolled up the carpet for those who wished to dance. A hired musician sat down at the pianoforte and arranged sheets of music. Meanwhile, Treeve came over and stood beside Laura, asking how she had liked the music and if it measured up to her Town tastes. She assured him it had.

Eagerly moving to the center of the room, Miss Roskilly called for a country dance, the Rakes of Rochester. Thinking of François LaRoche, Laura thought, *A rake to be sure.*

She looked around but did not see the Frenchman anywhere. Miss Roskilly too seemed to search the room in vain. Laura wondered where he had disappeared to—he who had blustered that he would not miss his chance to dance with all the *belles femmes*. So where was he?

Looking self-conscious, Miss Roskilly turned to find Treeve. Seeing him talking with Laura, she asked Perry to lead the dance with her instead.

Perry agreed, all politeness, though he was clearly ill at ease with so many eyes upon them. He and Kayna stood facing one another at the top of the set, while other couples joined them, forming groups of six.

Treeve, receiving a pointed nudge from Mrs. Bray, asked Eseld to dance. Eseld blushed and tried not to look as pleased as she clearly felt. Even Uncle Matthew participated, asking his wife to dance. Mrs. Bray accepted with a girlish smile.

As Laura stood there awkward and alone, Alexander pushed himself off the wall, limped forward, and bowed to her. "May I have this dance?"

"Yes, if you feel equal to it."

"To dance with you, Miss Callaway, I would endure far more than a sore ankle."

The musician played the introduction, and the dance began.

The first man turned the second lady with one hand, then his partner with the other. Then the first lady performed the same sequence.

After this, Perry and Miss Roskilly held hands and skipped down the line, and back up, before casting to second place.

The couples danced four changes of left and right hands in a circle, then they all repeated the figures from their new positions.

Perry danced methodically and stiffly, clearly concentrating on the steps. Treeve danced with effortless skill, grinning at Laura whenever he caught her eye.

Mrs. Bray too moved gracefully, and it was easy for Laura to imagine her the lithe young woman she had once been.

Alexander managed to keep up better than Laura had expected. Surprisingly, his ankle did not seem to much hinder him.

Eventually, François LaRoche appeared from wherever he'd been and stood on along the side, watching the dancers, arms crossed and smirking at Alexander's imperfect performance. Laura barely noticed. To her, Alexander seemed to dance competently beside her, step for step, hand in hand. There was no one she would rather dance with, secrets or not.

Alex enjoyed the feeling of Miss Callaway's smaller hands in his, and the warmth of her smile as they skipped down the line and back again. He gazed into her lovely face and shining brown eyes, relishing being so near to her. Looking at her, touching her, talking with her, he felt smitten and happy, the dark days of fighting and betrayal seeming so far behind him. He was already dreading having to leave her.

After the set ended, he escorted Laura to the punch table for refreshments. François joined them, apologizing to Miss Roskilly for missing the promised dance.

François drank his punch with his little finger raised, candlelight glinting on the gold ring he wore. Seeing it, anger again simmered in Alexander's soul.

When François set aside his glass, Miss Roskilly took his hand and raised it, studying the ring.

"Is this your family crest?" she asked.

"Ah, you notice my ring. You flatter me. I was hoping someone would notice."

He held up the back of his hand toward Alex, fluttering his fingers.

Alexander clenched his jaw.

"This is the crest of an old family in France," François said. "It belonged to a friend of mine, Capitaine Carnell. I don't suppose you, Mr. Lucas, were acquainted with this family? No, I did not think so. The ring of a French naval captain could hold no interest for you." He gave a melodramatic sigh. "Sadly, the Carnells are becoming extinct, the line dying out."

Miss Roskilly clucked sympathetically. "Why?"

"The elderly father is sick, and his two sons in mortal danger."

"Oh no," Eseld said, eyes wide. "Because of the war?"

"Perhaps."

Alex fisted his hands, every muscle tense. He longed to reel back and punch François, decrying him as the thief he was. But to claim the ring would be to reveal his identity in front of everyone, including several militia officers. François knew that as well, which was precisely why he taunted him in this blatant manner.

Oh, but he was tempted to rip the ring from LaRoche's finger. To wipe that smirk from his face . . .

Calm down, he told himself, summoning all his self-control. Now was not the time or place. But soon, he would take back his ring and his name, and do whatever it took to save his brother. Enora, however, was lost to him forever.

⧉

After the party, they returned to Fern Haven and bid one another good night. Miss

Callaway and her cousin went up to their bed-chambers, and Mr. and Mrs. Bray retreated into the parlour to dissect the evening over small glasses of sherry. Alexander, however, was too agitated to sleep or engage in polite small talk.

Receiving permission to borrow the vicar's horse, he set out for the Fourways Inn, known to be frequented by smugglers, according to Jago. As he rode along, thoughts of François and the past filled his mind.

Alan had not been the only young person to admire François LaRoche. Young women were drawn to him too. Enora Le Gall had been one of them. Enora was exception-ally beautiful, and she knew it. Sensual and flirtatious, she could have had any man she wanted, and she wanted François. Even so, Alexander fell under her spell. He admired her from afar but kept his distance, knowing she preferred François above all others and believing he had little chance with her.

The only other woman he had ever cared for with a flicker of romantic love was Léonie. They had grown up together. Their families had even rented neighboring houses for their seaside holidays. Léonie was beautiful too. She had not Enora's sensual appeal but rather a ladylike elegance, though she was not afraid to deliver a well-deserved setdown when he or Alan teased her too much.

As she matured, Léonie became everything good, lovely, and noble. And she was fond of Alex. Léonie might have accepted him, had he asked for her hand. He had, in fact, considered a proposal during his long days at sea. But when he returned home on leave, things changed.

François had left. No one seemed to know where he'd gone, though some speculated he'd taken refuge on Jersey with one of the defeated rebel leaders to avoid arrest. There were rumors he made clandestine visits to Brittany, trying to foment actions against the "usurper," as they saw Napoleon. But he had not returned to their village to see Enora.

Shortly after Alex came home, Enora turned her attentions to him, leaving Alex to assume she had become disillusioned with François and his prospects. Whatever the reason, he rejoiced in what he foolishly thought was his good fortune. Enora assured Alex that she and François were through and he would not be returning to her. He believed her and asked her to marry him before he left on his next commission. Everyone was surprised when she accepted. Perhaps it was disloyal of him—to François and Léonie—

but Alex let his desire for Enora overwhelm his better sense and higher principles.

When he became engaged to Enora, Léonie accepted his choice with warm, dignified congratulations. Alan saw his chance and swept Léonie off her feet. Alexander sincerely wished them both happy.

But in the days leading up to his wedding, Alex knew something was not right. He sensed Enora's uncertainty and wondered if she harboured lingering feelings for François. He also wondered if she'd accepted him only because her family had persuaded her to, reminding her that Alexander was heir to his family's estate and that her life with him would be far more comfortable than if she married a rebel like François. Either way, Alexander could see Enora was having second thoughts. But when he broached the subject, she declared all was well and insisted they go through with the wedding.

Alexander's father attended their small, quickly arranged wedding, as did Léonie and Daniel—his friend from *la Marine Royale* who'd grown up in a neighboring village— but Alan did not.

After the wedding, Léonie said, "I am sorry, Alexander. I thought he would be here."

He pressed her hand. "That's all right. I am glad you are here. Thank you for coming."

Alex gave her a brave smile, but his bravado was shaken when he stepped out of the church.

Enora had been delayed inside by many aunts stopping to kiss her, so Alexander stepped outside alone.

There stood François, hand pressed to his face, weeping. Alexander's heart sank. Guilt swamped him, and he could barely breathe. He was instantly taken back to the day Monsieur LaRoche died, and saw his old friend not as a man of twenty-something, but as a boy. Hurt, alone, grief-stricken.

"Fañch, I . . ."

François looked up, tears evaporating in a flash of fury.

Even so, Alexander tentatively approached him. He pressed a hand to his shoulder in camaraderie and comfort, as he had all those years ago.

François shoved it away. "Friends share everything—is that it?"

Alexander hesitated, then spoke over a thick lump in his throat. "You left. We thought you were not returning."

"And you lost no time taking what was mine. Why am I surprised? One who serves the usurper would not scruple to take another man's love."

Alexander stood frozen with remorse, knowing he had deeply injured his old friend.

Enora stepped outside then, wearing the white lace cap of a Breton bride. Her bright smile fell away upon seeing the man at the bottom of the steps. "François . . ." she breathed, her face turning ashen, her eyes large and dark and . . . desolate.

"*Bonjour*, Madame Carnell." He spat out the surname as if it were spoiled meat, lip curled in contempt.

Tears instantly filled those dark eyes. "You left me, without a word. Without a promise. You loved the *Chouans* more than me."

Seeing her tears, her pale trembling form, François changed tack, lifting his chin and feigning indifference. "I love no one—except myself. Now I wish you both *bonne chance*. You shall need it." He turned and strode away.

In his heart, Alexander bid his old friend a regretful Breton farewell. *Ma digarez, breur kozh*.

Beside him, Enora watched him go, her longing look directed not at her groom, but at the man she loved.

When Alex reached St. Minver, he left the horse at the livery and walked to the Fourways Inn. There he ordered a pint, using one of his prized coins, hoping the purchase would loosen the publican's tongue.

"Anything else, friend?" the aproned man asked, wiping the counter.

"Actually, I'm searching for a ship to take me across the Channel."

The rag on the counter halted. The man looked up at him, friendly gaze evaporating, eyes narrowed. "Who are ye? Never saw'ee in here before."

"One of the survivors of the *Kittiwake*."

"Ah. And why'd'ee think anyone here might be sailing so far? I serve fishermen here. Shipbuilders and farmers and the like. We don't stray so far from home."

True or not, Alexander knew there was no point in arguing.

"I see. Well, thank you anyway."

He hid his disappointment behind a sip of ale.

Glancing around the taproom, he noticed Treeve Kent sitting at a table with three unlikely men. Seafarers, he guessed, by their beards, slouch hats or kerchiefs, salty language and saltier smell. One of them he recognized as the housemaid's father, Mr. Dyer, whom he'd met at Miss Chegwin's party. Poring over a map as they were, the men did not notice him.

Treeve Kent looked out of place there still dressed in evening attire: tailored coat, patterned waistcoat and cravat, his beaver hat sitting primly on the window ledge behind him. Even so, the young man seemed at his ease with the sailors and bought the men another round.

Alex decided he ought to become better acquainted with Treeve Kent at his next opportunity.

For centuries sailors on board doomed ships have sealed messages, along with notes to their loved ones, inside empty bottles and cast them overboard, in the vain hope that someday, someone, somewhere in the world would discover them.

—CAROLINE ROCHFORD, *FORGOTTEN SONGS AND STORIES OF THE SEA*

Chapter 12

Laura slept in to make up for the late night at the ball. But that afternoon, she went back to the Penberthys' cottage in Porthilly to check on the children with fever. Perry drove her and Miss Chegwin in his family's carriage. When they arrived, they learned all five of the children were now ill. Laura was glad she'd asked Perry to accompany them—the suffering children and worried mamma needed all the help they could get. Since the Penberthys could not afford to go to the apothecary in Padstow for leeching or fever powder, Perry prescribed honey in hot water instead. Laura hoped it would be effective.

When she returned to Fern Haven an hour or so later, Laura removed her outer garments and went to find Alex. He was not in his room—yes, she had begun to think of the guest room as *his*—nor was he in the parlour.

That was strange. A shaft of foreboding sliced through her. Had he left, to avoid another confrontation with François LaRoche, or something else . . . something worse? She couldn't imagine him getting far with three guineas and a few days' wages.

A worrisome thought came to her. Had he recalled the collection of "treasures" she'd shown him? Thought of another way to raise money quickly?

She hurried to her desk drawer and opened it, then breathed a sigh of relief. Her key was still there.

Then where was he? In the garden or with Jago at Brea Cottage, perhaps? She looked out her window, then crossed the hall to look out Eseld's. From there, she saw the back of a man disappear up the lane that led to the abandoned icehouse. Concern flickered over her. Why would anyone go up there, unless . . . ?

Laura put her cape and bonnet back on and, taking a lantern with her, went out to investigate. She walked up the old gravel drive, her gaze trained on the icehouse door. As she neared, her heart began to pound.

The door was ajar, the padlock unlatched. Someone had picked or broken the lock. Alexander?

She sucked in a breath at the thought, betrayal rising up in her, squeezing her throat.

Moving forward like an automaton, Laura hoped she was mistaken, and wished she would find someone else inside—even a stranger. As frightening as that prospect would be, the betrayal would not hurt as bad.

Slipping inside, she tiptoed down the stairs. She knew it was probably foolish to put herself in harm's way, but righteous indignation fueled her steps.

There he was, in a pool of lantern light—in her private place—hands full. Nausea swirled in her stomach, but she raised her chin and said briskly, "What are you doing in here?"

The man turned. Not Alexander, as she'd feared, but Tom Parsons. Relief filled her, quickly followed by dread.

"Just seeing what'ee gathered. I said I would be watchin'ee, up-country lass. Found quite a few things, I see."

"How did you get in here? Did you break my lock?"

"No, it's as good as ever, which ain't saying much. Suppose'ee bought it at the Trebetherick village store?"

Laura had but did not admit it. She glanced around, quickly surveying her collection. The most valuable item, the salamander brooch, was still there. She stepped between him and the shelf where it lay. Then she looked more closely at the objects in his hands. A fistful of Spanish coins in one and the silver flask in the other.

Pointing toward them, she said, "Those are mine."

Parsons smirked. "Are they, now? I imagine the duchy agent or customs man might have somethin' to say about that."

"Those are not taxable goods."

"What about these coins?"

"Those are old ducatons. No longer legal tender, as far as I know."

"Could be melted down for the silver. It's a waste to let them sit here."

"I found them."

"And now *I* found them." He took a menacing step toward her.

Boots scraped the flagstones behind her. Laura whirled.

Alexander appeared at the bottom of the

stairs, wary eyes shifting from her face to the man standing near her. "Good day, Miss Callaway. Showing Mr. Parsons your collection?"

The man smirked. "Somethin' like that." He stepped toward Alexander. "Now I've seen what I come fer, I'll be on my way."

Alexander's focus landed on the silver in the man's hand, glinting by lantern light. "Give the lady back her things."

"Stay out of this, man. It don't concern'ee."

"Actually it does." Alex jerked the flask from Parsons's hand. Parsons swore and reeled back a fist.

"Stop it!" Laura called, stepping between them. "Mr. Parsons, if you want those coins so badly, then take them and go. But I don't ever want to see you in here again. Understand? Next time, I will report you to the constable."

Parsons pocketed the coins and took a last glance around the cellar. "Very well. Most of this stuff looks like rubbish anyway." He picked up his lantern and sauntered up the stairs.

Alexander frowned after him, then turned back to her. "Why did you let him take those?"

"I don't want him to have any reason to return. He thinks the rest of this is worthless, and that's for the best." With that thought, she decided to take the salamander brooch back to the house.

Apparently, Alexander had a similar thought about the flask, for he kept it in his hand and started for the stairs. A moment later, he slipped it into his pocket.

Bile soured her mouth. Was he thinking if Tom Parsons could get away with it, why not him?

"The flask . . . ?" she prompted.

He turned, guilt written on his features. "You found it after the wreck of the *Kittiwake*, did you not?"

She nodded. "Is it yours?"

He hesitated, clearly conflicted. "No."

"Then why on earth would you take an empty flask? It cannot be worth that much. If you need money, I—"

"It is not empty—at least I hope it's not. I apologize, but please, let me explain."

Setting down her lantern, she crossed her arms tightly across her chest. "Very well, I am listening." Was she a fool to do so?

Releasing a relieved sigh, he began, "When the gale blew up and we realized the ship was in trouble, I saw François roll up a letter and shove it inside a silver flask. I tried to take it from him."

"Why?"

"Because he led me to believe the contents could save my brother. François and I fought for the flask, but the ship heeled and I fell. When he escaped by boat, I assumed he took the flask with him, and all my hopes of saving my brother with it. Imagine my shock and elation to see it again."

"My goodness," she breathed. "You might have said so instead of trying to sneak it out."

"Yes, in hindsight I should have. But I wasn't sure you would be willing to part with it."

She lifted her chin. "If that flask belongs to Monsieur LaRoche, then your taking it is stealing. He claims to be here in our country legally. Can you say the same?"

He opened his mouth, hesitated, then said, "It is . . . complicated. But if it absolves me at all, François stole that flask from a crewman."

"And the letter?"

"No, that was his."

Incredulity swamped her. "How could his letter save your brother?"

"I . . . would rather not say."

She shook her head. "You had better tell me everything, and it had better be true, or I will report you to the militia myself."

He ran a hand through his hair. "I will tell you everything, I promise. But—"

A voice called from above. "Our Laura?" It was Jago, sounding concerned.

"We're coming," Laura called up the stairs. She turned back to Alex, held out her hand for the flask, and whispered, "I will hold on to it for now. We can look at the contents together, and then I will decide whether to restore it to you or to Monsieur LaRoche."

His eyes glinted, and he pressed his lips together tightly. "Very well," he acquiesced, though obviously not pleased.

Retrieving her lantern, she went up the stairs, thoughts whirling, Alexander close behind her. Had she relinquished the flask to him, would he have disappeared forever then and there?

Above them, the big man stood at the ice-house door, brows drawn low. "You all right? Saw Tom Parsons leaving."

"Yes. All is well, thank you."

"Good." Jago looked from one to the other. "Alex, can you come to the cottage a minute? I need help restringing the hurdy-gurdy. My fingers are too big."

"Very well." Alexander turned back to Laura. "I will be in shortly, and we'll talk more then."

Laura nodded and returned to Fern Haven, entering the back door alone. As she passed through the kitchen, someone pounded on the front door, and Laura stiffened. Had François LaRoche come to call as he'd promised? She slipped the flask into her pelisse pocket, just in case.

Laura peeked into the entry hall just as Newlyn opened the front door to a tall, grey-haired, intense-looking man.

"Miss Callaway?" he asked sternly.

"No, sir," Newlyn timidly replied. "I-I'll see if she's at home. If you will wait here . . . ?"

"Dash and blast, girl. Don't fob us off. We've traveled more than fifty miles."

The man was intimidating but not, thankfully, François LaRoche. Was he some authority come searching for Alexander?

Laura forced her feet to the door. "It's all right, Newlyn. I'm here."

The man's bristly grey eyebrows dipped as low as storm clouds. "Laura Callaway?"

"That's right, Mr. . . . ?"

The man lurched forward, arms spread wide, and grabbed hold of her, the folds of his cape enveloping her like bat's wings.

Laura panicked. Did he mean to abduct her? Crush her to death? Grasped in his steely arms, she struggled to draw breath. Then she slowly realized he was shaking with emotion and . . . embracing her. Unease and uncertainty roiled within her. The man was a complete stranger. Should she call for help? Or pat his back and ask what the matter was?

A gentler voice from behind urged, "My

dear, take care, or you will suffocate her. You must forgive my husband, Miss Callaway. He is overcome to meet you."

The man released her and stepped back, pressing a handkerchief to his face.

The woman, still in the doorway, said, "We both are, truth be told." Her eyes filled with tears. Green eyes, and somehow familiar.

Laura looked from one to the other. "Who are you?"

"Pray, forgive me," the man said. "I am as surprised as you are by my outburst." He bowed. "James Kirkpatrick."

James Kirkpatrick. The name struck a chord. *James Milton Kirkpatrick III*—the young man who'd left a message in the bottle she'd found and sent on to his parents.

Relief flooded in. "Oh! Mr. and Mrs. Kirkpatrick. You must have received my letter."

"We did. It was misdirected at first. But we received it several days ago and made plans to come to see you as soon as we could manage it."

"I am glad. And so sorry for your loss."

The older woman nodded. "A bitter loss indeed, or it would have been save for you."

The back door slammed. Alexander bolted inside, face tense. "Are you all right? Newlyn said a big angry man had come for you."

"I am perfectly well. Newlyn exaggerates."

Mrs. Kirkpatrick laughed. "Oh, my dear. You must have frightened that poor maid half to death. Please forgive my husband. He does look scary when agitated."

"I can't help my face," the man defended. "I was too overwrought to feign politeness."

"Mr. Lucas, these are the parents of James Kirkpatrick," Laura explained. "I told you I wrote to them about their son?"

"Ah, the message in the bottle."

"Yes." She turned to the older couple. "Mr. Lucas recently survived another shipwreck here on our coast."

"Miss Callaway saved me," Alexander added simply.

Laura clasped her hands. "I wish I could have saved your son, but he was already gone when I got to him. If it helps, he was not battered. He was whole and peaceful looking. He had such a pleasant expression. Almost a smile, as though he'd seen his Maker. He was lying on the beach, looking up at the heavens. And I thought, he's already there. In heaven, I mean. I remember he had a handsome face, and eyes so green. Like yours, ma'am."

At that, those green eyes again filled with tears.

The man nodded, voice tight. "That's our Jamie. Always said he was too pretty for a lad." He shook his head. "That's not true. He was a beautiful boy, inside and out."

"We read in the paper about the *Price* going down before we got your letter," Mrs. Kirkpatrick continued. "We feared the worst. That our boy was gone, never knowing if he thought of us, or loved us, or . . ."

"Or if he was still angry with me and with God," her husband finished.

The woman nodded. "You don't know what receiving your letter meant to us both."

"I almost didn't believe it at first," her husband said. "It looked like our Jamie's handwriting, but we'd not seen it in so long. How I wanted to believe he forgave me in the end. And reconciled with his Maker. And thanks to you, I know he did."

Laura smiled gently. "I am so glad."

Then she asked Wenna for refreshments, and the four sat down and talked longer over tea and a plate of cold meat, bread, and cheeses. Laura decided not to tell them about Tom Parsons taking their son's watch. No good could come of it, and it would only upset them.

Her uncle and Mrs. Bray joined them for tea, their curiosity piqued. Laura explained why they'd come, and both were suitably sympathetic.

Mr. Kirkpatrick gestured to Laura. "That's quite a girl you have there. A treasure."

"I agree wholeheartedly," Uncle Matthew replied.

Mrs. Bray smiled at them, then turned to give Laura an appraising look, her expression softening. And she said nothing disparaging.

Later, Laura walked the couple to the churchyard and showed them the grave.

Before the Kirkpatricks departed, she fetched the bottle from the icehouse and gave it to them. "It isn't much, but James did touch this, and had it in his pocket. You might like to keep it. Maybe put a few flowers in it to remember him by."

Mrs. Kirkpatrick smiled. "A good notion, my dear. I shall."

Again the couple thanked her and took their leave, planning to stay the night at an inn before beginning their journey north in the morning.

Laura returned to the Fern Haven parlour, weary but satisfied.

"I am proud of you, my dear," her uncle said.

"Thank you."

The tears came then, tears of loss and confusion and uncertainty. Uncle Matthew held her as he had not done since she was a young girl. He no doubt believed she cried for the bereaved parents alone. She didn't explain that her emotions were far more complicated.

⁓

With the unexpected visit by the Kirkpatricks, the night had grown late, and Laura and Alexander had not had time to continue their conversation begun in the ice cellar. So the next morning, after she dressed and ate a small breakfast, Laura went to the guest room. Alexander was not there.

Newlyn passed by with a laundry basket. She told Laura he'd gone out early, but she didn't know where. Had he gone to Padstow's harbour, hoping to find a shipmaster willing to take him to Jersey or wherever his home was?

Mrs. Bray called up the stairs, vexation evident in her tone. "Laura? Mr. Kent is here and wishes to speak with you. Alone."

Surprise and foreboding flaring, Laura went downstairs. Treeve stood near the parlour hearth, a folded paper in his hand. When the door closed behind them, she glanced around the room. "Perry is not with you?"

"He has gone to visit some ailing miner's children. I hope you are not disappointed it is only me?"

"No, I . . ." She clasped damp hands. Surely this was not a courting call.

His next words soon put those concerns to rest . . . while raising others.

"Perry and I visited the Wadebridge coffee house this morning—the best place to learn the latest news and war reports, you know. They bring in many newspapers from around the country, to serve the interests of their varied clientele. At all events, we saw a notice I thought you might find . . . interesting."

"Oh?"

He handed a recent issue to her, then watched her face as she read.

Escaped from Norman Cross
Three French prisoners:
Capt. A. Carnell
D. Marchal
F. LaRoche
Dangerous. Also suspected of theft.
Reward for successful recapture.
Superintending Prison Agent,
Capt. Wm Hanwell.
Huntingdonshire.

Dangerous? Did the insertion of the word refer to the name listed directly before it, or to all three men? The notice was not perfectly clear.

She thought again of the bicorn hat she'd found with *A. Carnell* embroidered within. She also thought of François LaRoche, staying with the Roskillys.

She looked up at Treeve. "You don't think . . . ?"

"Think? Me? You know me better than that." His chuckle sounded forced. "My brother, however, wondered if we ought to go to the authorities. I prefer to avoid authorities myself, so I talked him out of it.

"I did, however, go to Pentire House and confront Monsieur LaRoche with this, since we recognized his name. I've just come from there. LaRoche explained it away. He says he was an informant in that prisoner-of-war camp, actually working for the British among all the Frenchmen being held there. Said he followed two escaped prisoners here and plans to report their whereabouts to the authorities. He accuses your Mr. Lucas of being this Captain Carnell."

Laura's stomach knotted. "And did you believe his claims? First saying he is here legally, and now, what . . . a spy?"

"Mr. Roskilly certainly believed him. I must say he is very convincing, throwing out dates of battles and names of British commanders he has supposedly worked for."

"If that is true, why would British authorities list his name with the escaped prisoners?"

"To maintain his disguise, he says. Apparently, the Frenchmen he sailed with believed him a fellow prisoner."

"I don't know . . ." Laura murmured. "I have my doubts about LaRoche."

"I do as well." He hesitated. "I did want to caution you, though. Because of your . . . houseguest."

"Thank you, Treeve. And thank you for telling me in person instead of jumping to conclusions and going to the authorities."

"Do you want me to do anything about it? Talk to him? Or to the constable?"

She shook her head. "Leave it to me."

"As you wish." Treeve pressed her hand and took his leave, only to be accosted by Eseld in the hall, peppering him with questions and flirtation.

Alone in the parlour, Laura had already jumped to her own conclusions. She thought back again to finding the initials *T.O.* in the clothing of the shipwreck victim with the strawberry birthmark. Alexander had no such markings in his garments, but if his friend, *D. Marchal,* was an escaped prisoner, that was very incriminating for Alexander as well.

What should she do? Confide in her uncle?

He might insist Alexander leave immediately or even report him to the militia or local constable. And if the agent saw this notice, he might recall the name Daniel Marchal as being among the dead identified by the survivor, Alexander Lucas. Or was it Alexander Carnell?

Chapter 13

Alexander had left Fern Haven early to take the ferry to Padstow before the tide went out, hoping to find Treeve Kent or a ship's crew willing to take him home.

As the ferry crossed the estuary, he thought back to the night before. Miss Callaway had found a silver flask. It might not be the same flask, he cautioned himself. But found on a nearby beach shortly after the demise of the *Kittiwake*? It had to be. . . .

Slowed by injuries and discouraged by his circumstances, Alex's urgency to pursue his plan had dimmed over recent days. He had allowed himself to be lulled into a stupor of inaction, telling himself even had he the means or connections to find another way home, it was unlikely his return would do any good. For he had lost the only evidence he knew of that might exonerate his brother and free him from prison and impending execution. He'd thought it had slipped from his grasp forever, consigned to Davy Jones's locker, never to be seen again.

But now?

If Laura Callaway had rescued the letter that could save Alan, he might be tempted to believe God had orchestrated their meeting.

How stunned he'd been to see the flask in the hand of Tom Parsons. Even if it was the same flask, however, would the paper still be inside and intact, or had the flask leaked and ruined the letter and his hopes with it?

He'd been tempted to demand its return then and there but worried Miss Callaway might refuse, because in all truth, it did not belong to him. Or she might hold fast to her "year and a day" principle, and he did not have that long to wait.

Reaching the harbour, he walked along the quay and soon found John Dyer, Newlyn's father, in a substantial vessel at least forty-five feet long moored nearby.

"Impressive ship," he called.

The man raised a hand in greeting. "Aye."

He walked closer. "May I ask where you're bound on your next journey?"

"Not sure. Guernsey, mayhap."

Hope rose. "Would you be willing to take me across the Channel?"

The older man frowned. "Why? What's yer business there?"

"I . . . simply wish to return home," he replied. "To see my brother and ailing father."

The man's expression eased but still he shook his head. "Not up to me. You mistake the matter—this ain't my ship. I just signed on because my fishing boat needs repairs. A decision like that would be up to the owner."

"Who is he?"

Dyer hesitated. "Not my place to say."

"Then would you ask him for me?"

He shrugged. "Very well. I'll send a reply through Newlyn."

"Thank you, Mr. Dyer. The sooner the better."

Alex waved and walked away. He stopped to speak to two old salts bent over a newspaper. "Good day, gentlemen. . . ." He went on to describe his predicament and goal. In his urgency to secure passage, his voice wavered, and he heard the accent he tried so hard to curtail.

The men seemed to hear it as well, for they

scowled and turned away, muttering the word *foreigner* under their breaths.

Determined not to give up, Alex continued down the quay, looking for another likely vessel. But he was distracted from his purpose by an unexpected sight: François talking with Tom Parsons, who was gesturing to a smaller sailboat in the harbour. François handed the smuggler something and the two shook hands.

Alexander's suspicion was instantly aroused. He hailed, "François!"

LaRoche walked toward him, leaving Parsons watching from behind.

When he neared, Alex lowered his voice. "What is your business with Tom Parsons?"

François began replying in French, but Alex forestalled him with a raised palm. "English. To be safe."

"Very well. Just arranging transport to Jersey." He glared at Alex. "I paid extra to guarantee Parsons would not carry you as well."

Little chance of that, Alexander thought. In any case, he wondered where François had gotten the money. Or had he not lost his purse along with his papers?

Alex lifted his chin. "I will have my ring back now."

"Too late." The man stepped forward,

toe-to-toe with Alex. "You should have claimed it the other night."

"You know why I did not. I didn't want to ruin the party and embarrass our hosts."

"*Très galant*. But we both know the real reason. Too many witnesses, not to mention authorities who would love to capture an escaped Frenchman."

"*Two* Frenchmen."

LaRoche shrugged. "I would not be imprisoned for long. Thanks to you, I lost my papers. But it would only take one letter sent to Jersey and I would be freed. You, however, would be sent back, or worse."

"If the paper you lost held so much power, why did you remain in Norman Cross so long?"

"The superintendent found me useful, and in turn my time there was quite profitable, not to mention diverting—that is, until you and Marchal left."

Alex extended his hand. "My ring."

LaRoche's eyes glinted. "Better tuck that into your pocket, unless you want to draw back a bloody stump."

François's hand moved to his waist, where he kept a knife. Alex sprang and jumped him before he could pull it, knocking him to the ground. He sat on his chest, pinning his arms to the stone quay.

Some of the fishermen and workers who had been unloading a sloop gathered around, John Dyer among them. The men exclaimed among themselves, surprised to find two strangers fighting. Two survivors. Alex imagined it made it dashed difficult to know which man to cheer for.

"Alex?" Jago's voice. The young man appeared among the others, eyes wide.

"No helping him now, big 'un," someone said. "Let 'em fight fair."

"This man stole my ring," Alex said. "I just want it back."

"That is not all I stole. Took his wife too."

Fury pounded in Alex's veins. Momentarily distracted, he slackened his grip, and François managed to free one arm and strike him in the eye. Alex punched François on his bony nose. He returned the favor with a blow to the mouth followed by a hard shove. The two men tumbled across the quay and rolled to their feet, a flash of metal in LaRoche's hand.

"He's got a knife!" Jago warned.

François slashed. Alex dove. Again he rolled to his feet, just as François advanced, knife at the ready.

"Mr. Lucas, catch." John Dyer tossed him his own knife. "Let's keep it fair, lads."

Alex wished for a sword instead. Then he

would have easily bested François. But he was less experienced with a short blade.

They circled one another, François slashing, Alex blocking and evading.

"Just give me the ring. It's not worth dying over."

"I have no intention of dying. Certainly not by your hand."

Someone shoved a crate behind Alex, tripping him. He caught a glimpse of the interloper—Tom Parsons. Alex fell back, and François lunged. John Dyer stuck out his boot, tripping him in turn.

François dropped to his knees with a curse.

"You lot! Break it up." Two militia officers appeared up the street and turned their steps toward the harbour.

The crowd quickly dispersed, some men to their own boats or back to work on the sloop.

François glanced at the approaching officers, then pulled off the ring. "See how it feels."

He reeled back and threw it toward open water.

Shock thundered through Alex as a flash of gold flew over his head. "No!"

Suddenly Jago jumped, long arm outstretched, big palm extended, and caught the ring. He landed on the edge of the quay, teetered, then regained his balance.

Jago handed over the treasured possession, then gestured toward the Black Rock ferry, about to depart. "Better get out of here."

Alex nodded and stood, returning Dyer's knife.

Tom Parsons helped François up and slung a casual arm around the man's shoulder, as though the two were old friends. He handed him a rag for his bloody nose and led him toward the nearby inn. "Come on, mate. Let's celebrate our bargain with an early drink."

Seeing the crowd disperse and the fight break up, the officers retreated, turning toward the custom house instead. But Alex guessed he had not seen the last of them.

As he stepped aboard the ferry, the ferryman took one look at him and winced, and the few other passengers gave Alex a wide berth. He no doubt looked like a ruffian or the lowest *raffalé* with his rumpled clothing and bleeding lip.

After the ferry crossed the estuary and landed in Black Rock, Alexander began the walk to Trebetherick, his eye swelling, knuckles bleeding, and whole body sore from the fight. As he trudged along the sandy track, he muttered an unflattering epithet about

François. He'd been surprised to see his old nemesis in Padstow with Parsons, and Alex remembered feeling a similar jolt upon finding François in the same prisoner-of-war camp more than a year before.

The British frigate that captured the *Victorine* had carried Alexander and his crew to northern England. In Norfolk, at the port of King's Lynn, they disembarked and were transported inland on barges and lighters, escorted by armed militia. Hour by hour, they moved farther from France and freedom—and in Alexander's case, closer to Cambridge, where he had briefly been a student not so many years before. He did not mention this to his men, knowing it would serve only to alienate him from his crew at a time when morale had already plummeted.

But Daniel stood near him and asked in quiet French, "Are you familiar with this area?"

Alexander nodded, wondering if that familiarity might aid them in a future escape.

From the town of Peterborough, the captives were marched to their final destination. When they filed through the gate of the Norman Cross prison, Alex surveyed what seemed like a bustling city of some forty acres. In the center stood an octagonal block house, mounted with cannons and manned by soldiers.

Guards ordered the prisoners to line up in front of several desks, where clerks registered their names and ranks. When Alex's turn came, he quietly stated his identity and handed over his papers.

The clerk looked up, quill suspended. "Captain, ey? That qualifies you for lodging in separate officer's quarters, with the possibility of parole."

Alexander glanced at Daniel, then demurred in polite English. "I prefer to remain with my men."

"Suit yourself." The clerk shrugged and made a notation in his register.

Then Alex and Daniel moved on, gathering their provisions. First there was clothing—coat, pantaloons, shirts, stockings—all in either bright yellow or blue and stamped with the letters *T.O.* for Transport Office. Each man was also issued a hammock, straw mattress, blanket, tin mug, bowl, platter, and spoon. Arms full of new requisitions, the prisoners found their way to the assigned barracks. Inside, Alex and Daniel found empty hooks and hung up their hammocks. Exhausted from their ordeal, they quickly fell asleep.

At sunrise, the turnkey gave the signal for the prisoners to rise, fold up their bedding, and hang their hammocks against the wall to allow more space for general use during the day. After a breakfast of bread and cheese, they gathered in the graveled exercise yard where, they'd been told, they would spend the greater portion of their waking hours.

There, Alexander was shocked to see François LaRoche among the hundreds of milling men, some fencing with wooden swords, others playing skittles, carving, smoking, or talking.

When he noticed him, François's lip instantly curled. He said in French, "*Eh bien.* If it isn't the spoiled rich boy, come to wallow with the peasants."

Beside him, Daniel stiffened, retorting, "This is a *capitaine* in our emperor's navy, deserving of your respect."

"*Capitaine*, is it?" François smirked. "Not a very good one, obviously, or he wouldn't be here."

Alexander lifted his chin. "And what about you? I am surprised to see you, François. Though there are other civilians here, I gather."

"Not exactly an ordinary cit, now, am I? I was en route from Jersey when our ship was commandeered." He shrugged. "I could leave this place any time I want, yet I have my reasons to stay. How much more so, now that you are here. What *amusement* we will have. I shall enjoy showing you the ropes and watching you trip over them."

Alexander's hand fisted, but Daniel held him back, murmuring under his breath, "Remember rule number five."

Right. *Fighting, quarreling, or exciting the least disorder is strictly forbidden*. He forced himself to remain calm and walk away, joining his men.

After that initial encounter, the next few weeks passed quickly and uneventfully. Conditions in the prison were fair overall, and Alex's men were well treated and in reasonably good spirits, though François seemed to delight in tormenting Daniel whenever he could.

The authorities encouraged prisoners to use their skills and time wisely, and provided them with animal bone, wood, and straw to work with. On market days, local people flocked to Norman Cross to peruse the prisoners' crafts offered for sale—items that displayed French dexterity, ingenuity, and taste: toys, domino sets, model ships, spinning jennys, and more.

Visitors remained on one side of a wooden fence while the prisoners stood behind, the slats spaced far enough apart to allow items, payment, and conversation to pass back and forth. Guards kept a watchful eye on the proceedings to make sure no clandestine correspondence or prohibited items like spirituous liquors changed hands.

Despite these restrictions, market days took on a fair-like quality. In addition to wares offered for sale, some industrious inmates put on Mr. Punch puppet shows, while others played French tunes on homemade flutes in hopes of earning a few spare coins.

Not all of the inmates were allowed into the market. Representatives of each barracks manned the stalls. Daniel was one of those. He worked one store, while François manned the next. LaRoche's English was far better than most others', and he did much of the negotiating for the nearby stores. Alexander wondered if he took advantage of Daniel and other craftsmen like him.

As he watched the goings-on through the grill of the prison gate, Alexander came to realize that some visitors viewed the inmates as little better than caged animals, while others looked upon them with decency or even sympathy.

One day two pretty young women stopped near François's table. One of them smiled at him. "What a very handsome straw box. Did you make it?"

"*Ma chère mademoiselle*, you flatter me."

He humbly dipped his head, fingers to his heart.

Alexander knew full well he had not made the box but was simply selling it for another man, but that did not stop him from taking credit. François was a good salesman, Alex had to give him that.

Napoleon had reportedly paraphrased Adam Smith when he said of England, *"L'Angleterre est une nation de boutiquiers."* But François LaRoche could outsell a whole nation of shopkeepers, charming devil that he was.

Daniel's skills in carving and carpentry, which had served him well in his role as ship's carpenter, also well prepared him for industry while in prison. The talented man began building model ships and Noah's arks along with matched sets of animals.

One day, another pretty young woman in the company of her stately mamma stopped to admire Daniel's creations.

"What a darling Noah's ark," the older woman said. "Such detailed animals."

François spoke up. *"Merci, madame."*

"Oh and look, Noah's wife in her pretty yellow dress and hat!" The young woman looked up coyly into LaRoche's face. "Did you model her after your own wife, *monsieur?*"

He smiled down at her. "Alas, I am not blessed with a wife. But had I one as beautiful as you, *mademoiselle*, I could die a happy man."

The women tittered between themselves and bought the Noah's ark set for a nephew. François pocketed the coins while Daniel sat there helplessly.

Daniel's work was popular and sold quickly, yet he never seemed to have any money, while François got richer though he created little of value and far more trouble.

As the autumn passed and winter weather descended, illness—always a problem in crowded conditions—became more rampant in the camp. Alexander remained hale, but Daniel, with his weaker constitution, developed a rattling cough. In the new year, many died of respiratory complaints in the prison hospital, and Alex began to fear his good friend would follow suit.

On one blustery market day, Alex saw Daniel outside without coat or hat. Concerned, he chided his friend, "Daniel, where is your coat? You'll freeze."

"I've got to get to the market."

"You've got to put on your coat. If you are caught without, they'll accuse you of selling your provisions for gaming."

Some prisoners did sell their clothing and

rations to obtain money for gambling or tobacco. Now that the weather had turned bitterly cold, it was becoming a real problem.

Daniel frowned. "I did not!"

"Well then?"

His friend sliced a look at François across the yard but said only, "It's . . . gone. I lost it."

"Lost it? Where? In the laundry? Or did someone take it?"

Daniel refused to say.

Soon Alexander pieced together the truth from observation and overheard whispers. François had set himself up as a "provisions buyer," making money by preying on the weaker men among them. He even took prison-supplied hammocks from new arrivals and rented them back to the men for a half-penny per night, contributing to the suffering of many who went without adequate clothing and bedding on frigid nights.

The prison surgeons reported that increasing numbers of men were becoming ill from exposure to the cold without proper clothing or from going without rations. More than one death certificate recorded the cause of death as "debility due to selling his provisions."

When newcomers complained of deprivation, the militia guarding the barracks tried to ferret out those responsible. But no one would name names. Alexander wished he had evidence against the man, but he had none, as François had wisely left him alone.

"Why will no one say anything?" Alexander asked in frustration.

"They are afraid of LaRoche," another prisoner answered. "He wields power here."

Alexander couldn't speak for the others, but he could guess why Daniel remained silent. He was afraid Alex would fight François and both would be sent to the Black Hole or, worse, to one of the hellish hulks instead of this relatively comfortable inland prison.

To get to the bottom of it, the prison officials eventually closed down the market. Their source of funds cut off, two of François's victims finally stepped forward and named LaRoche as the provisions dealer. Guards immediately put him in the Black Hole, a windowless block of cells where prisoners were kept shackled on half rations as punishment for gross offenses.

Alexander's relief at this justice was short-lived. The superintendent learned of it and had François released by morning, supposedly believing his claims that the men had sold their own provisions to fund their lust for gaming and blamed him as a scapegoat.

Witnessing François's power in the prison, and concerned over Daniel's growing fear and worsening health, Alexander changed his mind about parole. He signed a parole certificate, requested Daniel accompany him as his servant, and left Norman Cross for parole in Peterborough.

He'd hoped they'd seen the last of François LaRoche.

He'd been wrong.

Laura was on her way out the door to find out where Alexander had disappeared to when Eseld stopped her. "Miss Roskilly has invited us to go shopping with her in Padstow this afternoon. Will you join us?"

It was rare for Miss Roskilly to include her. Laura realized she should have been gratified but was instead distracted by more important matters. "I don't think so, Eseld. But thank her for me."

Eseld shrugged. "Suit yourself."

Laura was just stepping through the garden gate when Alexander returned, head hung low.

He glanced up, and she got a better look at his face. Seeing his swollen eye and cracked lip, alarm shot through her.

"What happened?"

"I went to Padstow to find a ship. Instead I found François and Tom Parsons."

"Oh no. Are you all right?"

"I will be."

"No luck finding passage?"

He shook his head. "Not yet. The sailors I spoke to seemed suspicious of me for some reason."

"Perhaps because of this." She handed him the newspaper and waited while he read it.

He looked up at her dully and handed the paper back without a word.

"I think it is time you told me the truth, Alexander. If that is your real name."

He looked around and lowered his voice. "I am sorry I didn't tell you earlier. As I mentioned, I have learned not to trust others."

She huffed. "I have given you every reason to trust me, and I can prove it."

"How?"

She led him away from the house so they would not be overheard by Wenna or Newlyn. "I have had ample opportunity to report what I suspected to the agent or customs officer, but I have said nothing to contradict you."

His eyes hardened. "And what is it you might have reported were you *less* trustworthy?"

"I might have told them that I saw the initials *T.O.* in the collar of your friend's shirt and smallclothes. I am well read and know what those initials mean and where those clothes came from."

His jaw tightened. "Do you indeed?"

She nodded. "The Transport Office. This newspaper was not my first indication that you and your friend might be prisoners of war. I am also fairly certain that your name is not Lucas. Am I right, Captain Carnell?"

*Breton vessels were [once] a regular feature
of Cornish ports, as were the Breton residents in many port towns. A common language and their status as semi-autonomous
states linked Brittany and Cornwall.*

—HELEN DOE, *THE MARITIME HISTORY
OF CORNWALL: AN INTRODUCTION*

Chapter 14

A tense moment followed Laura's chal-
lenge. Alexander grimaced and looked
around. "Where can we talk privately?"
Without a word, she led him to Miss
Chegwin's cottage, knowing the older woman
would not mind and that she and Jago had
gone to take a meal to the Penberthy family. Laura supposed she should not risk being
alone with the man now that she knew he was
a French prisoner of war, but logical or not,
she was not afraid of him.

They sat together in the quiet sitting room,
early-afternoon sunlight and a chilly draft

coming in through the small windows. Brea Cottage was damp and cold, but at least they were out of the biting wind.

Looking grim yet resolute, he began, "You are right. My name is Capitaine Alexander Lucas Carnell."

Laura had guessed as much but still flinched to hear him say the words, the name, with a decidedly French pronunciation . . . She drew a shaky breath and asked, "A captain of . . . ?"

"The French navy."

Just as LaRoche had intimated. A lump of betrayal lodged in her throat. "But you told us you were from Jersey and had been educated in Cambridge. Were those lies too?"

He shook his head. "I concealed my nationality to avoid recapture, but most of what I told you is true. I spent many happy summers with my grandparents who lived on Jersey. And yes, I was educated in England as well as in France. My mother was a British diplomat's daughter. That is how she met my father, who is from Cornouaille."

He pronounced it *Corn-uh-way*, which sounded a bit like *Cornwall*.

"In the Breton language, we say *Kernev*," he explained. "It is a region of Bretagne, in France. You call it Brittany."

"Brittany . . ." Realization flared. "Miss

Chegwin said something about that. Is that why you understand Cornish?"

He nodded. "I had always heard there were ancient ties between our region and Cornwall, and that Breton is quite similar to the old Cornish language, though I'd never heard it till I met your Miss Chegwin."

"I see." Noticing his eyebrow and lip were still bleeding, as well as his hand, Laura retrieved a cloth and Mary's medicine case and began cleaning his wounds with one of her fragrant salves.

Barely hiding a grimace, he explained, "After a few terms at Cambridge, I returned home and enlisted in the navy. About a year and a half ago, my ship, the *Victorine*, was captured during a battle, and I was taken prisoner along with my men. We were transported to the Norman Cross prison, north of Cambridge." He added wryly, "Not exactly how I imagined returning to my alma mater."

She dabbed the ointment on his cut eyebrow as he continued.

"I was surprised to find François also in the prison. He was from my home village. I had known him since boyhood and heard he'd begun spying for the British. At first I did not believe those rumors. I reasoned that if he *was* working for the British, they would not leave him locked up in that remote prison. They would covertly have him released, perhaps in a prisoner exchange. But no.

"I saw him talking to the prison superintendent more than once, and it made me wonder. . . . With that many captive French officers, not to mention the Dutch and other French allies from Spain, Italy, and some German states, there was plenty of information to be had at Norman Cross. And although clandestine correspondence was prohibited, some sneaked through, especially among the paroled officers. François hinted that this was why he stayed."

She moved on to his injured mouth, lingering there, noticing again that his lips were fuller at the center.

"For some time I lived in the barracks with my men. The place was overcrowded, but being an officer, I was eligible for parole in a neighboring town. When . . . conditions in the prison worsened, I accepted. It was not true freedom, as we were required to remain within the town limits and observe a strict curfew, but once on parole, I was able to send and receive a few clandestine letters of my own. Through one of these, I learned Daniel's wife was expecting a child and my father was ill, and through another, that my brother, Alan, had been arrested as a spy and was being held in a French prison. I feared every day would be his last. So many royalists had already been executed."

Compassion swept over Laura. She longed to comfort him but—still stung by his deception—concentrated on treating his wounds instead.

Alexander went on, "They allowed me to have one of my men live with me as a servant, providing I would vouch for his character. I requested Daniel. Once I learned of Alan's imprisonment, I determined to try to get home to help him, but I never should have asked Daniel to escape with me. He might have lived out the rest of the war in prison and then gone home to his wife and child. At the time, I felt justified because Daniel was sickly. I thought I was helping him. I did not think through the possible consequences. It's my fault he's dead."

Laura's heart squeezed. "You were trying to help a friend. You could not have predicted shipwreck."

"True. Still, I knew the risks, though we were both eager to return home. Him for the birth of his child and me to help Alan. We disagree politically, but he is my brother, and I love him."

"That's why you said you could understand my mother's urgency to go to Jersey and try to save her sibling," Laura observed.

"*Exactement.*"

Laura blinked. It was the first time he had spoken French to her.

He went on. "While on parole, I formed a relationship with a neighbor woman."

Her wariness must have shown on her face, for he raised his hand. "Not that sort of relationship. She was a widow far older than I. We were friends, and she was eager to help. She gave me her late husband's clothes. Daniel wore the blue trousers and shirt from the depot under a civilian coat, thinking no one would be any the wiser."

Laura nodded her understanding. She took his hand, glad for an excuse to do so, and began treating his bloody knuckles.

"Before I left on parole, François boasted that he had an important letter hidden safely away, his ticket to freedom whenever he wanted it." Alexander shrugged. "At first, I doubted his boast was true. I assumed he simply enjoyed provoking me."

Laura stopped her work to look up at him. "Why? Why does he hate you?"

"Among other things, because we loved the same woman."

Laura's breath caught to hear him say those words. "Honora?"

His head snapped toward her, eyes blazing. "How did you know? Did François have the gall to mention her name?"

"No, nothing like that. When you had the fever, you muttered the name."

For a moment longer he stared hard. Then his ire faded. "Enora, the French version of Honora. Sadly, she did not live up to her name. Although I didn't realize until it was too late and she was my wife."

Laura's throat tightened, and she felt light-headed. "You have . . . a wife?"

"I *had* a wife. When Enora married me, I thought she had chosen me over François. But no. After we wed, she saw no reason to stop seeing him. I had to ship out, but François stayed in the area. When I received Enora's letter and read that she was with child, my momentary joy quickly faded as I counted back the months. I knew it could not be mine. I had been gone more than a year by that point, and I am not an imbecile. The humiliation and betrayal are forever with me."

Seeing the anguish on his face, Laura whispered, "I am sorry."

"So was I. Despite her infidelity, I felt no satisfaction when I learned the child was stillborn and Enora died from childbed fever a few weeks later."

Pity washed over Laura. She thought of her poor aunt Anne, who had died in similar circumstances.

"At all events," he continued, "I was determined to help Alan and see my ailing father, and to return Daniel to his beloved wife. So he and I made our plans."

His wounds tended, Laura repacked Miss Chegwin's supplies.

Alexander rose and began pacing the room. "We broke curfew, and my neighbor sneaked us out of Peterborough in her coach. We made our way to Yarmouth. There, we hoped to find a ship to take us to the south coast or even farther, but the only southbound ship we were able to find that day was the *Kittiwake*. We didn't want to wait around and increase our risk of recapture. We knew the *Kittiwake* wouldn't take us to France, but it would get us far away from the local militia pursuing us and to the southwest coast, where we thought we'd find plenty of ships crossing the Channel. The captain welcomed us and our money and gave us a small cabin, and we went in, praising God we'd made it.

"But moments later our cabin door burst open and there stood François, triumphant. He said if we objected to sharing the cabin, he would tell the captain we were escaped prisoners of war, and I believed he would have, even if it meant implicating himself."

Alexander slowly shook his head. "Such uncanny bravado. He didn't seem to worry about being caught. It convinced me he really did have British connections who would come to his aid if worse came to worst."

"He stayed in that small cabin with us throughout the journey. Shared our food and sprawled across one of the two bunks, leaving Daniel and me to take turns on the second.

"One day he again boasted about the important letter in his possession. . . ."

In their small cabin, François pulled a folded page from his pocket with a flourish. "You, Alexandre, would find this especially *intéressante*. If only your brother possessed such a letter. *Mais, non. Tant pis pour lui.*" Too bad for him.

With a self-satisfied grin, François tucked the letter into his pocket, out of sight.

Might that paper, whatever it was, truly exonerate Alan? Alexander wondered. Or was François merely taunting him to provoke a fight? Alexander's fingers curled into a fist, ready to oblige him. But remembering how François had tormented Daniel in the prison camp, he feared his smaller friend would end up being hurt if violence broke out in that confined space. Alexander clenched his teeth until his jaw ached and he'd mastered his anger.

"What is your plan once we reach Portreath?" Alexander asked him. "If you think we will take you with us to France, you are badly mistaken."

François shrugged. "I have no wish to go to France. Jersey is my goal." Again he patted the letter in his pocket.

A crewman delivered a simple dinner of boiled salt beef and biscuits, his expression more harried than usual.

"Anything amiss?" Alex asked.

"Heavy seas, sir. Captain says it ain't safe to enter the harbour at Portreath. We have to go farther. Sure to be a long night."

Alex sent Daniel a concerned look, wondering how this delay would affect their onward travel plans. Unwilling to discuss it with François present, the men settled into tense silence broken only by idle conversation.

Hours later, François restlessly stood. "*Excusez-moi, garçons.* I think I will go on deck to speak with the captain." He opened the door and, before he closed it, smirked, saying, "Don't talk about me while I'm gone."

When his boot steps faded, Alex sat on a low stool facing Daniel on the bunk. The two shared a long, sober look.

In a low voice, Daniel asked in French, "What should we do about François?"

"I don't know."

"Do you think he will betray us to the authorities when we land in Cornwall, him with his powerful letter and us with nothing?"

"It is a possibility."

"He is up there ingratiating himself no doubt to the captain and crew."

Alexander had not thought of that. "What can we do? It will be our word against his."

"But you sound like an Englishman. He does not."

"Nor do you, *mon ami*," Alexander reminded him. He might be able to talk his way out of arrest, but his friend with limited English and no passport could not.

"True." Daniel winced in concentration. He glanced at the coil of rope on the floor and asked, "Could we restrain him here in the cabin? Just to give us time to put some distance between us?"

"Not if a storm is—"

The door flew open, and they both started. François stood on its threshold, knife drawn and a look of triumph on his face, even as his blue eyes sparked with fury.

"I knew it! I knew it was only a matter of time until you two plotted against me. Now I shall do to you what you planned to do to me. *Merci* for the excellent idea."

He turned a flintlike face toward Alexander while he pointed his knife at Daniel. "Resist and your weak little friend will pay the price. You used to have much better taste in friends. But beggars cannot be choosers, I suppose."

Gesturing with his knife, he kicked the rope toward Daniel and commanded, "Tie his wrists and ankles securely. No tricks or you both die. I know you are a sailor who is trained in tying knots."

Daniel glanced at Alex, brows high with fear and uncertainty. Alexander nodded back. Daniel proceeded to tie him up as directed— and he was indeed proficient in tying knots. Once Alexander was restrained, François cut off a length of rope and tied Daniel's wrists to a bunk chain.

Over his pounding heart and swirling thoughts of escape, Alexander became aware of other noises. Howling wind. Lashing waves. The cabin, he belatedly realized, had begun rolling and pitching. He knew the sounds and sensations too well. The storm had intensified.

From above came barked commands and shouts of confusion. The crew and ship were struggling. Everything in Alexander wanted to assist them.

"François, release me so I can go and help," he urged. "It's a storm. A violent one by the sounds of it."

"Nice try."

"I am in earnest. You can tie me up again

if and when we reach safe harbour, but let me help now."

Another smirk. "Not afraid of a little rough water, are you, *Capitaine*?"

François gathered his few belongings, then turned back. "Before I go, there is one more thing I need from you." He squatted behind Alex and wrenched the ring from his finger, whispering slyly in his ear, "I have taken your wife and your brother, why not this too?"

Then François straightened and strode from the cabin, slamming the door shut behind him.

When the echoing slam faded, the sound of the wind, waves, and shouts of alarm seemed to fill the cabin. Alexander realized the possible threat of authorities was secondary to the imminent threat to their lives.

Suddenly the ship struck something, lurching violently. Alexander flew across the cabin and, with no way to stop his fall, landed hard on his shoulder and side. Daniel, tied to a bunk chain, was lifted from his perch but fell back against the rails.

"Are you all right?" Alexander asked.

"Yes. You?"

Breathless, Alex nodded and awkwardly rose to a sitting position, which was dashed difficult with ankles bound and hands behind his back.

Above them, he heard more panicked shouts and the captain trying in vain to keep his men on task. "Remain calm! Stay at your posts. Down helm. Sheets up. We've got to lift her off."

Alexander had experienced similar chaos when the *Victorine* was captured. And from the keening sounds the ship was making, he knew they were in serious danger.

He struggled against the ropes to no avail. *God help us*, he prayed. Then, with a battle cry, he yanked at his bonds with all his might, not caring if he scraped off every layer of skin or dislocated his wrists. He managed to wrench free his hands, his skin flaming, but at least he did not dislocate or break any bones.

Then he untied his ankles.

From the bunk, Daniel urged, "Go. Save yourself."

"I will not leave until you are free."

François had tied a proper knot on Daniel, and the more he struggled the tighter it became.

"My carving tools," Daniel shouted. "In my pocket!"

Alexander found a likely tool and began cutting away at the rope. Water flowed beneath the cabin door, and Alex sawed all the faster. If François had realized the danger, would he still have trapped them? Surely his intention had been to detain them and perhaps turn them over to the authorities, not see them drowned. Either way, anger seared Alex, burning hotter than his blazing wrists.

Finally, Daniel's hands were free. Thankfully, François had not bothered to tie Daniel's ankles as well, for by then water was gushing into the cabin.

Alexander sloshed to the door. "I am going after François."

"Be careful. I will join you as soon as I find my knapsack." Daniel frantically searched the small cabin.

"Don't be long."

Alexander pushed open the door against the flow of water and bolted up the narrow stairs as though climbing a waterfall.

When he reached the deck, he saw François roll up the folded paper he had taunted Alex with and shove it inside a silver flask. Alexander guessed he'd stolen the flask from among the crew's belongings to protect his prized letter. The crew had no doubt been too busy trying to save the ship to notice the theft. Nor did they seem to notice the passengers now, clustered as they were on the elevated quarterdeck, with one terrified youth perched in the rigging above.

Remembering LaRoche's hints that the letter might help and perhaps even save Alan, fierce determination swept over Alex. He charged across the deck and grabbed at the flask, trying to wrench it from his clutch. François took a swing at his head. Alex ducked and kicked the man's legs out from under him. With the two still gripping hands over the flask, they fell hard to the deck, which tilted at a precarious angle, water rushing over its rails. They wrestled through the icy flow. Alex managed to jerk the flask free, but François drew his knife and shoved it into Alex's side. Pain flared. Flask in one hand, Alex pressed the other to his wound and made one final lunge at his foe, but injured as he was, he fell short, and the flask went sliding across the deck.

For a few moments, Alex lay there in the water and his own blood, stunned and winded. Then Daniel knelt at his side.

"*Capitaine*, are you all right?"

"Been better," he muttered. "Find your knapsack?"

"No, but that's hardly important now."

"We . . . must . . . stop . . . François," Alex panted.

His friend helped him to his feet, and together they moved to the rail in time to see François rowing away in one of the *Kittiwake*'s lifeboats. The second was floating away, empty and useless.

"The devil!" Daniel cursed.

They were too late. Alex did not see the flask anywhere and assumed François had taken it with him—and all his hopes of saving his brother with it.

As he finished describing that awful night, Laura murmured, "That's why you were injured and your wrists rope burned." Taking one of his hands in hers, she turned the wrist up and gently stroked the newly healed skin.

He nodded, mouth dry. The sensation was most pleasurable, and soon the terrible scenes in his mind faded. "Thank you again for saving me, Miss Callaway. I am sorry I repaid you with less than the absolute truth. Can you understand now why I want that flask?"

"Yes."

Then he noticed her shiver and began rubbing both arms to warm her. "You are cold, and Miss Chegwin is out of firewood. Let's get you home."

The escapes of French prisoners-of-war in this country, and especially those on parole, having of late become exceedingly frequent, and such prisoners being in the practice of proceeding to [the] coast and seizing upon any vessel which they may not find properly guarded, a caution is hereby given to all owners of boats.

—WEST BRITON, NOVEMBER 1810

Chapter 15

Together, they walked back to Fern Haven. There, they stood warming themselves by the kitchen fire, quiet at this time of day, when Wenna rested between meals. After a few moments of silence, Alexander asked, "Will you give me the flask and a few minutes of privacy to read the letter—assuming it's still there? I have been waiting a long time to discover what it contains."

Laura considered. "No."

"No?" His brow furrowed.

"You have lied, and I have corroborated

your lies to protect you. We are in this together. For better or worse."

"Be careful, *ma chère*. I said those words once and lived to regret them."

She met his gaze. "Even so. I will read it with you."

"Very well. I will trust you."

"Will you?"

"It seems I must."

She retrieved the flask from where she had hidden it and, when she returned, said, "I still don't see how one letter might exonerate your brother."

"I'll explain. Officials learned that information was traveling from Brittany to the British. They had traced the source to a port near our home and began searching for an informant. François fell under suspicion, and I believe he pointed a finger at Alan to save his own neck."

She handed him the flask. He removed the cap and set it aside while she lit a candle from the kitchen fire and trained its light on the mouth.

"I don't see anything," she said.

He reached up and directed her hand. "Bring the light a little closer."

She did so and glimpsed paper curled around the interior. "There is something."

With his finger, he drew out a rolled letter.

Straightening it, he began reading and soon grimaced. "So the rumors about François were true. This is a letter to him from the British officer Philippe d'Auvergne."

The name didn't sound British to Laura, though it did seem vaguely familiar. "I believe I have seen his name in the newspapers."

Alexander nodded. "D'Auvergne is stationed on Jersey. He sends men into France to gather information to help the British. Our government knows of him, has even contemplated another invasion of Jersey to stop him, but it has not yet transpired."

He raised the letter. "This proves François is working for the British. Or was. It does not directly exonerate Alan, but hopefully with this evidence that the local informant they were seeking was LaRoche, they might release Alan."

He looked toward the door. "I have to take this to France. The longer I remain here, the more I endanger you and your family. If François comes to Fern Haven it will not be a pleasant reunion, and I don't want you or your loved ones in harm's way."

"Do you really think we are at risk?"

"If you are sheltering me, you might be. I need to find a ship to take me to Brittany, or at least the Channel Islands. Do you know anyone who might be persuaded?"

"Most of the vessels here are simple fishing boats or, in all honesty, smugglers' ships. Surely you don't want to—"

"That would be perfect, actually. They go regularly to the Channel Islands to trade, do they not?"

"I believe so." She added dryly, "Unfortunately, I am not personally acquainted with many smugglers."

He cocked one eyebrow. "Are you sure? What about Treeve Kent?"

Laura paused, recalling seeing Treeve with Tom Parsons the night of the wreck and during the late-night landing of smuggled goods. Yes, Treeve had connections all right, but would he be willing to help a French prisoner of war?

Alexander's frown pulled Laura from her thoughts as he once again peered inside the flask. "Hold on. What's this?"

She held the candle to the neck while he again inserted a finger and, with effort, drew out a thin rectangle of paper that had been coiled beneath the letter. He flattened it, and they looked at its face. It was a bank note for fifty pounds, drawn on Mortlock's Cambridge bank and signed by banker John Mortlock himself.

Alexander drew a long breath. "So it was François who stole from the superintendent's office. My parole agent mentioned the theft to me." He shook his head. "I cannot be caught with this. The militia would no doubt assume that I was the thief, if François has not already accused me."

Laura held out her palm. "I will take it to the custom and excise office. It may not go back to the prison directly, but it will go back to our government, which is better than nothing."

"I agree." He relinquished the bank note with obvious relief.

Loud pounding shook the front door.

Startled, Laura impulsively grasped Alexander's arm, her fingers curling partway around his sturdy bicep.

Had François come as he'd threatened to do?

She heard Newlyn's timid tread, followed by the front door opening and an official-sounding voice announcing, "Lieutenant Moore and Ensign Rogers of the North Devon Militia, here to question yer houseguest."

She didn't recognize the officers' names. Militia regiments were usually required to serve away from home, and were frequently moved to reduce the risk of them sympathizing with locals during times of civil unrest.

Alexander stepped forward, but Laura held him back, whispering, "Not yet. Not while we have the bank note. Go out the kitchen door and back to Miss Chegwin's. Stay out of sight."

"I don't like the thought of running."

"And I don't like the thought of you returning to prison."

He ran a hand over his face. "Very well." He slipped out, and she gingerly closed the door behind him. Hopefully, no one would see him from the windows.

She tiptoed into the passage and from there heard voices in the parlour. Uncle Matthew, Mrs. Bray, and the two militia officers.

"He has been gone since early this morning, I believe," Mrs. Bray said. "I don't know if he plans to return, though I assumed so."

Her uncle added, "He would not leave without saying good-bye."

The parlour door closed, muffling their voices.

Laura wished she could hear what they were saying but did not want to be caught eavesdropping.

The officers must have asked to see the room where their guest had been staying, for a few minutes later the parlour door opened again and Mrs. Bray led them upstairs. Laura ducked back into the kitchen, unnoticed.

What conclusions would they draw from his few possessions, a borrowed Bible, and pair of shoes? Had he left his watch? Would they open the back as she had done and see it had been made by a French watchmaker? Unlikely. Thankfully, he possessed little else to give away his nationality.

While Laura considered her next move, Eseld arrived home, sneaking through the kitchen door as Laura and Alexander had done, looking a little guilty.

Seeing her, Eseld pressed a hand to her heart. "Oh, good. It's only you."

Laura vaguely wondered where she had been but let the comment pass. She asked, "Are you still going to Padstow with Miss Roskilly this afternoon?"

"Yes. Have you changed your mind?"

"I think I will go with you."

Eseld's face brightened. "Excellent. I am meeting her at the ferry in an hour's time. Your uncle has offered to drive me."

The girl was always eager to visit the shops of larger Padstow. Laura did not tell her shopping was not why she wanted to go to town that day.

At the kitchen door, Eseld turned back. "Have you any spending money?"

Laura nodded. "I plan to leave Padstow with a lighter purse."

Eseld grinned. "That's the spirit!"

After the officers departed and the Brays

returned to the parlour, Laura waited a few minutes, then, taking a deep breath to calm her nerves, casually entered the room.

"Laura," her uncle exclaimed. "Where have you been? Is Alexander with you?"

"No, he isn't here. I was in the kitchen with Eseld. What did those men want?"

"They were the militia, Laura," Mrs. Bray explained. "They want to question our guest. Apparently, they have reason to believe he is an escaped French prisoner of war."

Laura's stomach clenched, but she feigned surprise. "Really?"

Her uncle nodded. "I told them he was from Jersey, but I am not sure they went away satisfied."

"They were not," Mrs. Bray snapped. "They will be back. Mark my words."

Uncle Matthew said gently, "I am sure Mr. Lucas will return soon, answer their questions, and settle the matter." He rose and said, "Well, I had better change. I am headed to Porthilly for a churching. I promised to drop Eseld at the ferry. She and Miss Roskilly are going into Padstow."

"May I ride along?" Laura asked.

"Of course. But you'll have to be ready to leave in ten minutes."

Laura excused herself, going to her room for her reticule and warmest pelisse. From her window, she saw Uncle Matthew and Eseld chatting companionably as they headed to the stables together. Laura hurried downstairs, eager to get the stolen bank note to the custom house. The front door was closer, so she went out that way, slipping the silver flask into her reticule as she hurried down the walk.

She drew up short with a gasp.

François LaRoche stood there, his blue eyes riveted on her reticule. Had he seen what she'd slipped inside? Recognized the flask?

She pulled the drawstrings tight and her wits with them.

"*Bonjour, mademoiselle*," he purred in his unctuous voice.

"Monsieur LaRoche, you startled me."

"Did I? I said I would pay a call. And what, Miss Callaway, did I see you hide in your bag?"

"Hide? I am merely gathering everything I need for an afternoon's shopping."

"I saw a flash of silver."

"I should hope so. The ferry is not free." Oh. She'd not meant to tell him they planned to take the ferry.

"May I see?"

"Into my reticule?" Laura lifted her nose in exaggerated offense. "A woman's reticule is a private, mysterious place, *monsieur*. An Englishman would not make such a request."

"But I am not an Englishman." Smirking, he walked toward her, his hook of a scar mocking her like a leer.

"Pray excuse me. I don't wish to keep my uncle waiting." She moved to walk around him, but he grabbed her arm.

Thank heaven, there came Uncle Matthew and Eseld in the carriage. Hearing the jingling tack, LaRoche loosened his grip. Laura jerked free and walked briskly toward them.

"Come on, slow molasses," Eseld called. "We had better hurry or we shall miss the ferry!"

Uncle Matthew, reins and whip in hand, turned a hard stare on the man. François stopped where he was.

"Farewell, *monsieur*," Laura dismissed him, hoping he would not follow.

"*À très bientôt*," he replied. *See you very soon.*

Laura prayed not.

Her uncle gave her a hand up, and the three of them departed.

As they topped the rise, Laura risked a glance over her shoulder, but LaRoche had already disappeared.

Reaching Black Rock a short while later, Eseld and Laura alighted at the quay to meet Miss Roskilly. They waited for nearly a quarter of an hour, but there was no sign of her. The ferryman signaled it was time to depart.

"Do you want to keep waiting?" Laura asked.

Eseld shook her head. "Something must have happened to prevent her coming. The tide is high now. Let's go while we can."

They paid their pence and climbed aboard, greeting the ferryman, whom they'd known for years.

Just as his son Martyn untied the rope and was about to cast off, a man jumped aboard. François LaRoche.

Laura's stomach clenched and her pulse pounded. She felt trapped.

"Miss Callaway. *Enchanté*." He turned his wolfish smile on her companion. "And Miss . . . ? *Excusez-moi*, I forget your name. A friend of Miss Roskilly's, I know."

"Mably," Laura answered in Eseld's stead.

Something about the man put even the usually flirtatious young woman on her guard. Eseld murmured, "*Monsieur*," but did not smile or engage him in conversation.

LaRoche sidled up beside Laura. "What business have you in Padstow?"

"None of yours, I assure you." The lie smote her. "And you?"

Perhaps she should like him better now that she knew he was a spy for the British, but she did not. Nor did she trust him.

"I wonder if you have something of mine,"

he said. "Something I would very much like returned."

"Do you accuse me of theft, *monsieur*?"

"Not you. But perhaps your guest?"

Laura took Eseld's arm, and the two moved closer to the ferryman, but to her dismay LaRoche moved closer too.

"How are you, Mr. Wilkes?" she asked in a neighborly manner, seeking his protection, even if he was unaware of it.

The man looked a little bleary-eyed and smelled of ale. Hopefully, he was fit to navigate the estuary, and to intervene if LaRoche tried to harm her.

As they neared Padstow, Laura sneaked a small item from her reticule into one of her kid gloves, just in case. Then she turned to LaRoche. "I am going to speak to one of the customs officers now, if you will excuse me."

She hoped mentioning her plan to meet with a British official would dissuade François from following her.

When they docked in Padstow, Laura and Eseld walked around the quay, following the strand to the tall custom house and warehouse. The rubblestone-and-brick building had white frame windows and stood close to the water's edge, overlooking the harbour.

"Must I go in with you," Eseld moaned,

"when there is a perfectly good milliner's shop right up the street?"

Laura hesitated. "Oh, very well. But meet me back here. Don't wander off. I may need you."

"Need me for what?"

"Never mind—just don't be long."

No sooner had Eseld entered the milliner's shop than François stepped in front of Laura, blocking her entrance to the custom house.

"Again, *mademoiselle*, I must ask if you have something that belongs to me."

The door opened, and a man in a dark, unpretentious uniform stepped out, drawing up short at finding two persons in his way.

"May I see the officer in charge?" Laura asked him.

"Certainly. Right this way, miss."

He held the door for her.

François followed her inside.

Surprised, Laura hissed under her breath, "Are you sure you want to be here?"

Looking bored, the man at the desk asked, "Yes, what is it?"

Laura glanced at his nameplate. "Officer Prisk, I am here to turn in something I found washed ashore on Polzeath Beach after the wreck of the *Kittiwake*."

"Oh? Have you reported it to the ship's agent, Mr. Hicks?"

"No. I came right to you." She loosened her reticule and drew out the flask. The silver gleamed in the desk's lamplight.

She risked a glance at François and saw that he stared at it with palpable longing.

"Miss, we deal primarily with significant shipments of taxable goods, tea, brandy, and the like. This flask is not—"

"It's mine," François spoke up. "I lost it in the wreck. I am one of the survivors."

"Is that so?" The man's eyes narrowed. "A Frenchman, are you?"

"Yes. But I am here legally."

"Really?" The officer turned to Laura. "Do you know this man, miss?"

"I have met him, but I cannot vouch for his character."

François gestured toward the flask. "I lost it in the shipwreck. I only want it back. I would be happy to offer a modest reward for its return. . . ."

Laura said to the officer, "You might wish to examine its contents before you decide."

"Is that right?"

François's eyes hardened. "I repeat, it is mine. The flask and its contents."

The officer began unscrewing the cap. Beside her, LaRoche tensed.

Officer Prisk extracted the rolled bank note as Alexander had done and studied it. "Know what's interesting?" He leaned back in his chair. "A report circulated recently among the militia, customs, and excise offices. A report about prisoners of war escaping from Norman Cross and a theft of bank notes. Bank notes drawn on Mortlock's Cambridge bank very much like this one." He looked up at François. "And you say this is yours?"

François hesitated, seeing the trap and sidestepping. "I know nothing of a theft. That was payment for services I rendered to the superintendent. Write to him if you don't believe me."

"I shall."

"In the meantime," LaRoche continued, "if you are looking for an escaped prisoner of war, you need look no further than the man lodging in this woman's house, Captain Carnell—though he has been using the name Lucas to avoid detection."

The officer waved his hand. "That is a job for the militia. Where is this French captain now?"

"I don't know," Laura said. "He left Fern Haven this morning."

"Hm. Well, I had better lock up this bank note for the time being. I'll write to the Norman Cross superintendent for confirmation. In the meantime, I'd like your name, sir. And your papers."

LaRoche's eyes glinted. "I want my papers as well. That is what should have been in the flask. I lost them in the wreck."

The customs officer held out the empty flask to Laura. "You ought to have some reward for turning in the bank note."

Unsure what else to do, she accepted it.

François gave his name to the officer and told him where he was staying. Hearing the name Roskilly—a prominent local family—the officer decided not to detain François but to release him on his own recognizance until he heard back from Norman Cross. LaRoche then followed Laura outside. She looked for Eseld but did not see her, so she started toward the millinery shop.

LaRoche called after her. "You have something of mine, and I'll have it back."

She turned to him. "If the flask means so much to you, take it." She tossed it to him, or rather, at him, and walked briskly on. She vaguely heard the unscrewing of the cap but soon moved out of earshot.

She had almost reached the milliner's door when a rough hand grasped her arm and whirled her about.

Outrage and offense shot through her. "Unhand me."

Seeing François's murderous look, fear overcame her anger.

"My letter is not in here. That means either you or Carnell have it, and I want it back."

She didn't have it, but she didn't want him to go after Alex either. Seeing her waver, he jerked the reticule from her wrist, which went flying to the ground, its contents spilling out.

"Stop that!" Laura cried.

He knelt and pawed through the contents—a small comb, handkerchief, and a few hairpins—grumbling under his breath as he did so.

Footsteps crossed the street toward them. A man's voice called, "Everything all right, miss?"

She turned and looked, relief filling her. Two militia officers crossed the street toward them, one short and one tall.

Before she could speak, LaRoche said, "Miss Callaway dropped her purse. I simply stopped to help her."

She shook her head. "That is not true."

The shorter officer speared LaRoche with a probing look. "Yer accent. Yer a Frenchie, if I don't miss my guess."

His voice sounded familiar. Were these the same officers who had come to the house looking for Alexander?

LaRoche lifted his chin. "I am here legally, as are many of my countrymen who fled France during the revolution."

"Let us see yer passport."

He extended both hands. "I'm a ship-wreck victim. I have lost everything."

The officers looked at her. "That true, Miss Callaway?"

Laura could not deny it. "Yes, from the *Kittiwake*."

The shorter officer turned to his com-rade. "You have that list from the Transport Office?"

His partner pulled a paper from his pocket and unfolded it.

"What'd you say yer name was?"

"I didn't."

"François LaRoche," Laura said helpfully.

The officer read from his list. "F. La-Roche. Dark hair, blue eyes. Thirty years of age. Scar on left cheek."

His partner drew his gun.

"I have the right to be here," François in-sisted. "Ask Philippe d'Auvergne. He'll vouch for me. I work for him."

"Don't know him. Sounds like another frog to me."

François scowled. "He's a British officer stationed on Jersey."

"Come with us, and we'll investigate yer claim."

François threw up his hands in protest. "What about Carnell? He is not here legally. He's an escaped prisoner of war. Worse, a thief. You find Capitaine Carnell, and there will be a grand reward for you."

"I don't suppose you know where he is?" the tall officer asked.

"*Non.* But watch her house"—he jerked a thumb toward Laura—"and you are sure to find him."

"I told you, he's gone," Laura said.

"Oh, he'll be back. You saved his life, after all."

"I may have helped, but I am not his keeper."

François smirked, the expression emphasizing the scar on his cheek. "You underestimate your charms, *mademoiselle.*"

"We have been looking for him without success," the tall officer admitted.

"I shall help you," François said. "I know just what he looks like."

"We shall see. For now, come with us." Gesturing with the gun, the men led LaRoche away, to Laura's relief, though she feared the militia would now redouble their efforts to find Alexander. She prayed she had not just doomed him to recapture . . . or death.

Half-buried in the loose sand of the east shore of the estuary stands the ancient church of St. Enodoc.

—BLACK'S GUIDE TO THE DUCHY OF CORNWALL, 1876

Chapter 16

Before returning to the ferry, Laura visited the antique and curiosity dealer in Padstow.

The proprietor's face lit upon seeing her. "Ah, Miss Callaway. What have you brought in for me today?"

Laura reached into her glove, where she had hidden her treasure, then placed the gold salamander brooch on the counter.

A short while later, errand completed, Laura walked to the milliner's and all but dragged Eseld from the displays of bonnets, ribbons, and lace. Together, they returned to the harbour to await the ferry.

They reached Black Rock as evening fell,

and Uncle Matthew was waiting for them at the ferry landing. There was still no sign or message from Kayna Roskilly. Eseld was quite worried about her friend by this time and pleaded with Matthew to drive to their house.

He eventually relented and turned the horse toward Pentireglaze, though doing so would add a few miles to their journey.

"I do hope she hasn't fallen ill or something," Eseld said. "It isn't like her to not keep her appointments without at least sending word."

Laura could not blame Eseld for her concern, but she was even more concerned about Alexander. Would he still be at Miss Chegwin's? She longed to confide in her uncle but thought it best to hold her tongue.

When they reached the Roskillys' drive, a groom helped Eseld alight, and she hurried into the house while Laura and her uncle waited outside. Eseld returned a few minutes later with Dr. Kent.

"The family is upset," Perry explained. "There has been a theft. The money raised at the charity ball is missing, as well as a pair of Kayna's earrings."

Uncle Matthew's expression fell. "I am very sorry to hear it."

"I know you are." Eseld squeezed his hand.

"I am going to stay with Kayna for a while. Her father has gone for the constable."

Uncle Matthew nodded, eyes troubled. "Kind of you. I'd stay too, but Mrs. Bray is expecting me."

"I will make sure Eseld gets home safely, sir," the young man offered.

"Thank you, Perran."

Offering his arm, Perry led Eseld into the house, and Laura and her uncle started back toward Fern Haven.

"I am sorry, Uncle Matthew," Laura said. "I know you have your heart set on restoring St. Enodoc."

He nodded again but said little, clearly distracted and disheartened by the setback.

She decided not to add to his woes by sharing what had happened in Padstow, nor what she had learned about their guest.

When they returned to Fern Haven, Laura helped her uncle with the horse, and then the two walked into the house together. He went into the parlour to speak to his wife, while Laura went upstairs. She planned to walk over to Miss Chegwin's but first went up to her room for a small coin purse to give to Alexander. Seeing a man sitting in the passage outside her room, she jumped, then whispered, "What are you doing here?"

Alexander rose, a vulnerable smile on his lips. "Not the greeting I hoped for."

"You shouldn't be here. The militia are looking for you and will soon come here again. They're questioning Monsieur La-Roche now."

She told him about the encounter outside the custom house.

He stepped nearer, searching her face in concern. "Are you all right?"

"Yes. Shaken but well."

"Good." He pressed her hands, then his eyes hardened. "That man . . . he will be the death of me yet."

Alexander took a deep breath and drew back his broad shoulders. "Any progress in finding a ship to take me across the Channel?"

"Not yet. I'm sorry."

"Don't you dare be sorry, *ma chère*. I should never have asked it of you."

"I will try, but in the meantime, this should help." She extended the money from the sale of the jeweled salamander. He'd been right; it was worth a good deal.

He shook his head. "No, Miss Callaway. I cannot accept it, but thank you."

The sound of distant men's voices came from outside. Laura looked out a dormer window and saw figures with lanterns approaching—two in uniform and a third man. LaRoche?

"Shh. They're coming!" She pressed a finger to her lips, then turned him by the shoulder. "Go out the back again. Run. Hide. If you are captured, you will be sent back to prison or even shot."

His mouth tightened. "I don't like to run like a frightened rabbit searching for a burrow to hide in."

"I know," she said. "But remember, if you are caught, you won't get home to your brother."

He winced, then sighed. "So be it. For Alan and his family, I will go."

He started toward the stairs, then turned back. "I have to tell you something before I leave."

"What is i—"

He pressed his lips to hers, silencing her with his mouth.

For a moment she stilled in surprise, then kissed him back, wishing it were not a kiss good-bye.

He broke away and smiled into her eyes. "That is what I had to tell you."

She managed a wobbly grin. "I am glad to hear it." Quickly sobering, she all but pushed him toward the stairs. "Now go."

He slipped quietly down them and out the

back door as two militia officers and LaRoche came through the front gate.

Laura paused where she stood. Alexander saying the word *burrow* belatedly gave her an idea of where he might hide. Grabbing her cape and gloves, she hurried out after him, catching up with him in the back garden.

"What are you doing?" he hissed.

"Going with you. I know where you can hide, and you'll need me to help you."

She led the way up the track, past the abandoned drive.

"The ice cellar?" he asked.

She shook her head. "Too risky. My uncle and Eseld know about it. They might guess I would hide you there and tell the militia."

They stayed in the shadows as much as possible, following a line of scrubby tamarisk bushes to the nearest dune. The wind gusted, stirring sand into their eyes as they went. Finally, the narrow track led them to St. Enodoc, the partially buried church.

Laura retrieved the rope from the sexton's shed. Then they continued through the lych-gate into the churchyard. She scurried up the grassy mound and onto the roof, and Alexander followed.

"Are you sure about this?" he asked.

"Have you a better idea?"

"Just keep running?"

"Then how would I get word to you about a ship captain willing to take you across the Channel?"

"Good point. Very well. I'll go down, but if they find me here it will be like shooting fish in a barrel."

"The officers are not local men. Let's hope they don't know about the hatch in the roof. It's the only way in."

As she had seen done every year since arriving in Cornwall, she secured a noose of rope around a Cornish cross on the mound and pried opened the hatch.

Tossing down the other end of the rope, she said, "God be with you."

"And with you, *ma chère.*" He pressed another firm kiss to her mouth, then lowered himself, sliding down the rope into the chancel, his feet hitting the paving stones between the altar and rood screen.

"If anyone comes searching, hide behind something," she called down, then added, "I wish I had thought to bring you something to eat."

"I'll manage. I have been eating well lately."

"I will bring you something as soon as I can. As soon as it's safe."

"Thank you, Miss Callaway."

She pulled up the rope, shut and secured

the hatch, and hurried off the roof. If they caught her up there, it would surely give away his hiding place.

Instead of returning the rope to the shed, she hid it in the shadows between a nearby tomb chest and the church wall. She didn't want to give his pursuers the means to enter the church themselves if by chance one of them knew of the hatch. Hopefully the militia officers had not recruited the local parish constable to aid in their search.

Hearing footsteps coming fast, she darted through the lych-gate and crept along the hawthorn hedge. She prayed she could get far enough away that, if they found her, they would not automatically guess she had been at the church. She rounded the sexton's shed, planning to stop and catch her breath, only to gasp in surprise. Two people stood there in the shadows, clutched in a fond embrace. By the dim twilight, she recognized Eseld and Perry.

He stepped back sheepishly, clearing his throat, but Eseld seemed too transfixed to do more than smile softly up at him. The young doctor had told Uncle Matthew he would see Eseld home safely. He must have decided a leisurely moonlit walk would be more romantic than a brief carriage ride.

Perry opened his mouth to speak, but

Laura shook her head and put a finger to her lips in warning.

Footsteps passed nearby and entered the churchyard.

"Let's search the church," a familiar masculine voice called.

The militia officers she'd met in Padstow, Laura guessed. Was François still with them? Her heart beat hard, and her palms perspired. She drew in shallow breaths, straining to hear, and caught the sounds of scraping footfalls and a muttered oath.

"Cursed sand is covering the door."

And it would be difficult for them to see inside, Laura reassured herself, assuming Alex hadn't done something foolish like find a flint and light a candle.

She whispered to the others, "The militia are searching for Alexander."

Eseld's mouth formed an *O*, and Perry stepped nearer to reply without being heard by the others. "Do you know where he is?"

Laura hesitated. Both he and Eseld could be trusted, she believed, but neither were known for discretion. She made do with a nod.

The closure of the hatch had echoed through the church, then faded away, followed by Laura's retreating footsteps before silence descended. Alexander stood in the cool grey-blue silence of St. Enodoc until his eyes adjusted to the dim light. Then he looked around the chancel, nave, side chapel, and entry porch—buried by sand and unusable. He walked slowly down the central aisle, past the transept leading to the tower, his boots clapping against the smooth slate floor, past rows of wooden pews to a granite font toward the rear. The font and rood screen seemed particularly ancient.

Walking back toward the altar, he sat in the front pew and looked up at the angled ceiling, the black arms of the wrought-iron chandelier holding ghostly white candle stubs. Soft twilight filtered through the modest green-glazed windows—one three-light window above the altar and another in the adjoining side chapel.

In that quiet, reverent place, prayer seemed natural. "Please protect Laura, Father. Let no harm come to her because of me. And in your mercy, please help me get home in time to help Alan."

Alex then sat back to rest in the sanctuary's peace . . . but that peace was short-lived. Rapid footsteps approached—at least two or three people. The flash of torchlight flared through the glazed windows like a beacon.

"Let's search the church," a voice called.

Alexander's pulse quickened. Remembering Laura's warning, he tiptoed farther back and slipped into the entrance porch shrouded in sand. He stood still, straining to listen over his pounding heart. He heard the scraping of boots and a muttered epithet.

"Cursed sand is covering the door."

"Is there another way in?"

Torchlight chased its way around the church, flashing on and off as it passed the high windows of the tower and transept. Alex dared a peek into the chancel. Ghoulish faces pressed to the glass, trying to see inside. He ducked back into the porch, behind the arched doorway, breathing hard. Could they see him? He doubted it, but better safe than sorry.

What should he do if the hatch opened and a searcher descended? Give himself up before violence might be done on either side? Hide in that ancient chest near the font? Try to escape out a high tower window? He hoped it wouldn't come to that.

Again he prayed, this time silently and more desperately. *Have mercy, Father!*

Did he believe God would hear him? Answer him? After all, God had not prevented his ship's capture, his imprisonment, or the shipwreck. But He *had* spared his life. Alexander hoped that meant God had a purpose for his remaining days beyond recapture.

Yes, he realized. He did believe the Almighty heard his prayers, although God had not promised he would not suffer. If the Father had allowed his beloved Son to suffer and die on this earth, why should a mere mortal like him expect a carefree life?

Your will be done, almighty God.

He heard an unexpected voice outside. A female voice but not Laura's. The torches moved away from the windows, and darkness descended once more.

Alex closed his eyes in silent relief.

Laura was surprised to hear Kayna Roskilly's voice. "I don't think they use that church anymore, for obvious reasons."

"And who are you, madam?" an officer asked.

"Miss Roskilly. My father is one of the owners of Pentireglaze mine."

What is she doing here? Laura wondered. The Roskillys lived a few miles away, but surely she knew the vicar entered the church once a year—that there *was* a way in. Was Kayna helping them, helping Alex, for some reason?

Laura whispered to Eseld, "What are you three doing out here? Last I saw you, you were at Miss Roskilly's house."

"When the constable arrived, Perry drove

Kayna and me to his house to avoid the un-pleasantness," Eseld whispered back. "She is staying the night with me, says she'll feel safer there after the theft. Since Roserrow is only a mile or so from Fern Haven, we decided to walk back, and Perry offered to escort us."

When had Eseld and Miss Roskilly become such bosom friends? Laura wondered. Clearly while she had been preoccupied with Alexander.

"How nice," Laura murmured and found she meant it. She was glad Eseld had a good friend, and that Perry had earned the girl's affection at last. She hoped Eseld would endeavor to deserve him.

In the distance, the same officer asked, "What are you doing out here alone, miss? Or are you not alone, but with a certain Frenchman?"

"Certainly not. I don't trust Frenchmen. I am out for a stroll with two friends. They shall rejoin me any time, I'm sure."

Laura whispered a plan, and a few moments later the three walked casually through the lych-gate. At Laura's nod, they began chatting of nonsense and of the temperate evening, hoping to be heard and avoid any panicked gunshots. As she'd guessed, two officers and François LaRoche stood in the churchyard near Kayna Roskilly.

"Ah, Miss Roskilly," Eseld began. "There you are. We wondered where you got to." Eseld clearly relished her acting debut.

Miss Roskilly looked from person to person, no doubt thinking quickly. "And here are my friends now." She gestured toward the trio, then explained to them, "I heard voices in the churchyard and walked over to investigate. These men were looking for a way in, but naturally I told them there isn't one."

"Well, there is—" Perry began, but Laura silenced him with a quick elbow to the side. He might be a learned doctor, but his ability to read female cues was certainly lacking.

"Well, there it is," Eseld finished for him, smiling from man to man. Laura was glad at the moment for her cousin's feminine appeal. She really had the most charming smile.

The taller officer smiled back, while the other remained aloof. LaRoche scowled.

The stern shorter officer asked, "Did you see a Frenchman—a Captain Carnell—out here somewhere? We thought he'd be with Miss Callaway there." The officer nodded toward Laura.

"Miss Callaway is with us," Eseld said, sliding a protective arm around her.

The shorter officer frowned at Miss Roskilly. "I thought you said *two* friends."

"Well, yes, but I didn't want to mention the gentleman. I wouldn't malign my friends' reputations for the world." Kayna spoke imperiously, as though greatly insulted, and Laura realized she was the best actress of them all, and more intelligent than Laura had credited.

LaRoche spoke up, disgust on his face. "They are all in on it together. It's obvious. Where did you hide him? Must we search each of your houses?"

"You gallant officers are welcome to visit, of course," Kayna said. "But do not bring *that* man." She pointed at François. "And don't trust anything he says. We took him in after he was shipwrecked, and how does he repay us? By stealing from us and seducing my lady's maid."

François smirked. "Jealous? Angry I turned my attentions to your French maid, once I realized what a cold witch you are?"

"Whatever the reason, I can only be grateful you left our home. Don't come back."

"What did he steal?" the officer asked.

"Nothing," François insisted.

"Liar. He stole the money we'd raised at the charity ball and a pair of garnet earrings my maid had taken to clean. Perhaps more. My father is meeting with the constable now. In the meantime, I would lock him up and

search him if I were you. Take him to Bodmin Gaol and save yourself the trouble of
recapturing him for arrest."

Hell hath no fury like a woman scorned,
Laura thought. She was certainly grateful for
the brave young woman's assistance, but she
hoped LaRoche would not take revenge for
her sharp tongue.

The Frenchman said, "If anyone is a thief,
it is Captain Carnell, the man who calls himself Alexander Lucas. He stole my papers.
Probably stole your money as well."

One of the officers asked Miss Roskilly,
"Have you seen this Captain Carnell?"

The young woman shrugged. "I have
seen him once or twice during his stay, but
not recently. Nor do I know where he might
be bound. Perhaps Padstow? I honestly don't
know his plans. I doubt any of us do."

She looked at the trio, who all dutifully
shook their heads.

"Look around you," the young woman
added. "There are not many places to hide
out here, except perhaps the sexton's shed.
Busy Padstow would be a far better place to
conceal oneself."

Laura almost wished she would not keep
mentioning Padstow. For if Laura was successful in finding a ship to take Alex away, it
would most likely be harboured there.

"We had better be heading back," Miss Roskilly said. She took Laura's arm companionably and started the walk back to Fern Haven. Perry and Eseld followed.

The officers made no protest as they left. Laura looked back and saw that one man kept a gun trained on LaRoche while the other searched the shed.

Laura wasn't sure the officers believed their protestations of ignorance, but she knew for certain François LaRoche had not.

When they reached Fern Haven, Eseld and Perry continued into the parlour, but Laura talked quietly to Miss Roskilly in the passage.

"Thank you. I don't know why you helped us, but thank you."

"Do you not?" Her dark eyes glinted. "That is easy. I have always had a soft spot for true love. Just look at how I maneuvered Perry and Eseld into each other's arms."

They both glanced through the open parlour door, where the couple stood near the hearth, faces shining by firelight as they gazed at each other.

Kayna said, "You know she initially admired Treeve, while he clearly admired you. I was able to show her the error of her ways and the futility of pining for him. Now that you have made your interest in another so plain, hopefully Treeve can be swayed in time as well."

"I don't want Treeve," Laura insisted. "I never have."

"I know you don't. Why do you think he wants to win you over? Men are so proud. Can't stand it when a woman doesn't think they're God's gift. That was the mistake I made—letting Treeve know I admired him. So he has given up the chase, unless it is the chase for my dowry." She sighed.

"And Monsieur LaRoche?"

A frown flickered over her pretty face. "I admit I briefly admired him—the mysterious Frenchman under my own roof. Surely you can understand that. He can be charming when he wishes to be, when he wants something. But refuse him, and you see the real man. The selfish, scheming, dangerous man."

"You were very brave tonight, the way you spoke to him."

She shrugged. "He was being escorted by armed militia. I had nothing to fear at the time."

"And now?"

"And now . . . let us hope the officers take my advice and keep him under lock and key." A tremor passed over the slight woman.

Laura pressed her hand. "How can I help?"

Miss Roskilly held her gaze with intense, glittering eyes. "You can help by taking your French captain and leaving this place. François will continue to pursue him, and hopefully, we will have seen the last of him here."

"You think I should leave with a man I barely know? Leave my uncle and just . . . run off with him in secret?"

The woman shrugged. "Come. I saw him kiss you on the roof. Besides, you have made no secret of wishing to be anywhere but here since you arrived. Why do you think you were never fully accepted? Well, now you have your chance."

Was it true? Had her own disdain of the place and its people been the real reason she'd never belonged? Laura swallowed a hard lump, then said, "No one is going anywhere until we find a ship to take Alexander across the Channel."

"Then you need look no further than Treeve Kent."

"Treeve?"

Kayna nodded. "I had been curious about his clandestine nighttime activities, so I had our manservant follow him. I feared he might have a lover in Padstow. He does in a sense. Her name is the *Merry Mary*."

Laura blinked in surprise.

"If you hurry, you can probably find him at the Fourways Inn with his new friends."

Mrs. Bray came stalking out of her husband's study. "Laura . . ." Seeing Kayna, she hesitated and greeted her politely. "Good evening, Miss Roskilly. Welcome. May I have a private word with Miss Callaway?"

"Of course." The young woman joined Eseld and Perry in the parlour, while Mrs. Bray led Laura into the study and shut the door. Uncle Matthew sat there, looking ill at ease.

Mrs. Bray hissed, "The militia were here again. I told you they'd be back. They had the other survivor with them. The Frenchman. He told us that your 'Mr. Lucas' is in fact a French naval captain. An enemy officer! Did you know it?"

Laura shifted awkwardly, feeling guilty for keeping her suspicions to herself. "I have wondered where he came from but knew nothing for certain. . . ."

Kindhearted Uncle Matthew said, "We still don't know that he meant any harm."

Mrs. Bray ignored him, keeping her gaze on Laura, eyes snapping with anger. "You brought that man into my house. I never wanted him here. If he endangers us all, it will be on your head."

Uncle Matthew tried to intervene. "My dear, please . . ."

But Mrs. Bray held her ground, pinning Laura with a hard stare. "Do you hear me?"

Feeling ill, Laura nodded and turned to go. "Yes, I understand."

⁀∽

Laura walked over to Brea Cottage to ask a favor. With Miss Chegwin's approval, Jago accompanied Laura on her errand to St. Minver, driving her in the donkey cart.

When they reached the Fourways Inn a short while later, Jago tied the reins and walked around the cart. As he helped her down, Laura saw Treeve Kent coming out with a few men she did not recognize.

"Miss Callaway," Treeve called. "What are you doing here?"

Noticing Jago, the other men hung back, but Treeve walked toward them, a smile on his handsome face.

When he neared, she began, "I understand you own a ship."

He tucked his chin in surprise. "Who told you that?"

"Miss Roskilly mentioned it."

His golden eyebrows rose high. "Did she indeed?"

Laura nodded. "Is it true?"

"Yes, as a matter of fact."

"Do you captain the ship as well?"

"No, I leave the navigation to those more expert than myself."

"May I ask what you use her for? Or am I better off not knowing?"

"Oh, family business and the like."

She let the dubious reply pass. "I wonder if you might do something for me?"

"Anything for you, Miss Callaway. You know that."

"You may reconsider once you hear what I want."

He stepped closer. "Sounds intriguing."

"I wonder if you . . . or someone you know, might be willing to take a passenger on his next voyage to trade in the Channel Islands."

Several emotions passed over Treeve's face. Surprise. Suspicion. Admiration?

"Always knew you were clever. Clever and pretty. What a captivating combination."

"Miss Roskilly surpasses me on both counts, actually. She is more clever than I realized. I have a new appreciation for her, after tonight."

"Oh?"

"I'll explain later. Can you help me?"

"Help your Frenchman, I believe you mean?"

"Well, yes."

"I would be only too happy to see him

sail away, Miss Callaway, if I did not know it would make you sad."

"Seeing him recaptured or shot would make me far sadder. It's only fair to tell you the militia are searching for him. So my request is not without its risks."

"As are most worthwhile endeavors—even the less noble ones."

He considered, then drew himself up. "Yes, I know someone. Reliable, respectable. Some might even say devilishly handsome." He winked at her. "But can I trust you to keep all of this to yourself?"

"Absolutely. I have lived here long enough to understand things like free trading are sometimes necessary in the face of hard lives and poverty. But for you to be involved—a Kent of Roserrow?"

"Poverty is no respecter of persons, Miss Callaway. And when one of the leading families of the parish struggles to pay their bills, they cannot fall on the mercy of the parish poor fund as others might. We must protect the family name and save face." He gave her a mischievous grin. "And you must admit, it's a face worth saving."

She shook her head, giving him a tolerant smile. "Yes, Treeve. You are good-looking, as you well know."

"Thank you, my sweet." His grin faded. "If only I did not have to pull it from you."

He inhaled. "These days it's up to me to bolster the family fortunes. My father has his head in the sand, and my mother, if she has a clue, has turned a purposeful blind eye. Perry is too busy lancing boils and handing out laudanum to notice what I do. Most assume I am a lazy ne'er-do-well. But I do pretty well, I must say. I've taken to it like a duck to water, as the saying goes. Tea, brandy—terribly taxed. A little trip to Guernsey or Jersey, and . . . *voilà*. Saves my family money on what we consume ourselves, and the rest I distribute through profitable channels. Discreetly, of course."

He squared his shoulders. "How soon can your Frenchman be ready?"

"Anytime. The sooner the better. Though beware the preventive men."

"I am always aware of them. Hazards of the trade. We'll leave late and won't chance the quay. Have him meet me at St. Saviour's Point at two in the morning. Should be half tide by then."

"But the ferry doesn't run in the middle of the night."

"Come, Miss Callaway. I'm sure a clever, resourceful female like you will work out something. Also, outfit him with dark clothes, and don't tell a soul where we're going. Promise?"

"You have my word."

"Shall we shake on it?" He offered his hand, and she put her fingers in his.

His eyes glimmered with surprising sadness. "Ah, how I have longed to hold Miss Callaway's hand. And hopefully not for the last time."

From Padstow Point to Lundy Light,
Is a watery grave by day or night.
—TRADITIONAL CORNISH SAYING

Chapter 17

Before leaving the Fourways Inn, Laura gave Jago money to go in and buy two pasties—one for him and the other for Alex. On the way back, Laura asked him to drive to Black Rock. When they reached the ferryman's house and knocked, Martyn came to the door. By that time of night, the boy's eyes were heavy, clearly eager for his bed, but she handed him a gold coin and his eyes snapped awake.

"Sorry to ask, Martyn, but could I trouble you for a private, late-night crossing?"

"At that price? Indeed you may." The youth often took the helm, especially in the evenings when his father had too much to drink.

"There is something else I'd like from you as well."

They talked for a few minutes about arrangements, and then Laura left him.

Finally, she and Jago drove to neighboring Porthilly. There, she let herself into the St. Michael's vestry, where a pile of donated clothing awaited to be distributed on Boxing Day. She picked a suitable garment, folded it tightly, and tucked it under her arm before rejoining Jago for the drive back by the light of the moon and stars. Laura was glad for Jago's company. It would have been a little frightening to walk alone after dark on less familiar roads.

Reaching the tall sand dune, she directed Jago to park near the sexton's shed and surveyed St. Enodoc from there, making sure no one was near. Then she approached the church, climbing up the mound and onto the roof. She opened the hatch, nerves pulsing in her stomach, hoping she would find Alexander well.

"Are you there?" she called down in a strained whisper.

"Laura?"

Her heart hitched to hear him say her given name.

The half moon of his face appeared in the dim light from the transept windows. "Are you all right?" she asked.

"Restless and anxious about you."

"I am well. Here, catch."

She tossed down the pasty, which he deftly caught.

"Eat that. And put this on."

He set the pasty aside and extended his hands to catch the bulky garment.

"I have to go to Fern Haven before they send up an alarm, but I will be back to get you out as soon as I can. We are meeting a ship tonight."

"I'll be ready."

Saying the words aloud solidified the conclusion that had gradually been forming in Laura's mind. We *are meeting a ship tonight.* . . .

This, she realized, was her opportunity to go to Jersey, as she had long wished. To learn the final fate of her loved ones as she had helped so many others do. Was it so wrong to want that knowledge, that peace, for herself? And when would she ever have another chance?

When they returned to Brea Cottage, Laura went inside to speak with Miss Chegwin.

"May I borrow a dark dress?" she asked.

Miss Chegwin reared her head back in surprise but then agreed. "Certainly, my dear." She retrieved an old gown of black crepe and handed it to her. She did not ask

why, but her wide eyes shone with questions
and concerns.

"*Meur ras, Mamm-wynn,*" Laura said in
trembling Cornish, then quickly embraced the
woman. Thanking Jago as well, she departed.

Laura stopped at the ice cellar to gather
a few more things, then returned to Fern
Haven. Setting the items aside, she greeted
her uncle and Mrs. Bray, and then made a
pretense of going to bed. Newlyn came in as
usual to help her undress.

"I am going out again," Laura said to the
girl. "I don't want you to worry if you come
back in and find me gone. Nor to raise any
alarm, all right?"

Newlyn's eyes rounded like an owl's.
"Are'ee meeting that Frenchie?"

"I will be in the company of two respectable persons known and trusted by Mr. and
Mrs. Bray. I'd rather not say more."

"Are'ee elopin', miss?"

"No. Not that . . . exactly."

"Oh, miss . . ." Wariness glimmered in
the girl's eyes.

"Not another word, all right?"

Newlyn nodded. Her expression remained
troubled as she brushed out Laura's hair and
helped her into Miss Chegwin's mourning
gown, but she asked no more questions and
bid her good night and . . . good-bye.

Laura hoped what she was about to do wouldn't harm Eseld's reputation. For the first time, she was glad they were not really cousins. Knowing how much Perry adored Eseld, Laura doubted anything she did could change his affections.

When Newlyn had gone, Laura packed the ark and a few other things into an old leather knapsack she'd found, wrote a letter to her uncle, and then blew out her candle. She prayed he would not be too worried. Considering her recent angry outburst, Mrs. Bray might actually be relieved.

Laura waited until the house was quiet, then tiptoed to her uncle's study and tucked the note six chapters ahead in his Bible. Then, taking the knapsack for Alex and a lightweight fabric traveling bag for herself, she slipped out of the house. She didn't ask Jago to accompany her this time. She had decided she must go alone.

She walked briskly to St. Enodoc. Reaching the chapel, she set down the bags, retrieved the hidden rope, and secured it as before. Again making sure no one was near, she climbed onto the roof and opened the hatch, feeding the rope down through its mouth.

She glimpsed Alexander reclining on a pew, head pillowed on a kneeling cushion. He rose immediately and crossed the chancel.

"Ready?" he asked.

"Ready."

He grasped the rope and pulled himself up with hands and knees as she had seen sailors climb on rigging. It was an impressive display of strength.

With awkward effort, he gained the roof and stood hands on knees to catch his breath.

"I don't know how your uncle does that every year."

Laura retrieved and coiled the rope. "Three men stand here to pull him out. I'm afraid you have only me."

"For which I am deeply grateful."

With a final glance into the murky depths of the tomb-like church, Laura closed the hatch. "Let's go."

She returned the rope to the sexton's shed. There she handed him the knapsack. Seeing his friend's creation inside, Alex thanked her with enthusiasm—enthusiasm that quickly faded when she handed him the rest of his disguise.

He had already put on the old watch coat she'd tossed down earlier but now looked askance at the powdered wig. "You're joking."

She didn't blame him. Mostly old men, judges, and barristers wore wigs. "I am not. The militia are looking for you. Not to mention François, if he managed to escape custody."

"It's not very dignified."

Laura put on an old pair of spectacles, a mobcap, and a shawl around her shoulders. She turned to look at him over the top of the small frames. "We can trade disguises if you prefer."

"Ha-ha." He put on the wig, followed by a hat. "Where did you get all this?"

"From my collection and the poor box, and this black dress from Miss Chegwin."

"*Quelle folie!* I can understand why I should disguise myself, but why you?"

"More people here know me than know you. And while they may be accustomed to seeing me wander the beaches alone most every day, seeing me with a man after midnight would certainly raise questions."

"You should stay here, Laura. I'll go alone."

She hesitated to tell him just how far she planned to go. Swallowing, she said, "How will you know which door to knock at to fetch the ferryman's son who's agreed to take us across at such an hour? And how would you find the rendezvous point?"

"You could draw me a map."

"It's more than that. The militia are looking for a man of your description. They are not looking for an elderly couple making their way home after having a few too many at the Fourways Inn."

One dark brow rose. "That's to be the way of it, is it?"

"Unless you have a better idea."

"None as . . . creative as yours, no."

"Then let's go."

They avoided the road, and walked along the blustery seaside path, wind blowing sand in their faces. Laura tasted the salty tang of the sea on her lips. Glad for the protective shawl, she raised it over her face.

In the long, salt-stained coat and powdered wig, Alexander looked a bit strange, but still handsome and virile, like some aristocratic ancestor in the framed portraits at grand Prideaux Place, on the outskirts of Padstow.

"If we pass anyone," she admonished, "you'll have to affect an older person's gait."

He nodded his understanding.

Reaching Black Rock, Laura led the way to the ferryman's cottage, where Martyn's father was likely sleeping off one too many. For once, Laura almost hoped so. At her tentative knock, a sleepy Martyn came to the door. "Who are . . . ? Oh . . . it be you, miss. Strange to see you like that. 'Bout gave up on you."

"Sorry, everything took a bit longer than I expected." She turned to Alexander. "And this is . . . my friend."

The boy nodded but didn't look too close. For one so young, he'd already learned the sometimes cagey ways of the Cornish. A wise seafarer could look an excise man in the eye and say he couldn't describe whomever it was they were looking for, be it for wrecking, smuggling, or anything else.

"And here's the other you wanted." He handed her a wad of something, and Laura stuffed it into her bag, then handed the youth another coin.

They made their way to the village quay, where the ferry was moored, and a few fishing boats besides. As Treeve had predicted, the tide was rising.

"All right if we take my uncle's fishing boat instead?" Martyn asked. "Easier to row and will draw less notice this time o' night."

"Sounds like a wise plan."

While the youth untied the mooring lines, Alexander gave Laura a hand in, then helped the lad push the boat over the sand and out into the water.

"I'll row," Alex offered.

"No," Laura said. "Someone might see you. Martyn is strong enough. Aren't you, Martyn?"

"Aye. I row regular-like for Pa."

Alex frowned. "Very well, but I don't like it."

When they reached the Padstow harbour a short while later, Martyn hopped out, very fleet of foot, and secured the rope.

Laura was not happy to see a few men loitering about. Did they never sleep? She said under her breath, "Time for your acting debut, Captain."

He rose to step from the boat to the quay, swayed, and nearly fell backward. She braced his back and gave him a shove forward, and in her best impression of Wenna said, "Out with'ee, old man. Ye be *that* blind."

Alex mumbled something incoherent, or perhaps stifled a laugh.

She kept her face down, back stooped, and stepped out after him, Martyn reaching down to offer her a hand. "Thank'ee, lad."

Martyn quickly climbed back into the boat, apparently eager to return to his warm bed.

Laura put her arm through Alex's, oddly glad for the chance to do so. The two leaned on each other, walking up the quay in a stuttering gait that hopefully passed for the aged or intoxicated or both.

One of the seafarers stared at them through bleary eyes.

"What'ee doing out so late, old maids?"

She felt Alex stiffen beside her, but he surprised her, singing a few bars of an old sailor's ditty in a warbling tone. "'Of all the wives as e'er you know, Yeo ho! Lads, ho! There's none like Nancy Lee, I trow—'"

"Hush, man," she chastised. "Ye'll wake the dead."

Back of her neck prickling, Laura resisted the urge to look over her shoulder as she led Alex around the harbour, past the custom house and the shipwright's, then along the coast out of town. She was relieved to hear no footsteps following them.

Continuing along the bank of the Camel Estuary, they made their way to secluded St. Saviour's Point, half a mile away.

"How much farther?" he whispered.

"Just down there." She pointed to a moon-lit cove visible between the scrubby trees and rocks. "See?"

"All right. I can go the rest of the way on my own."

Her heart pounded. "No. They don't know you. That is, I made the arrangements, so I—"

"I will explain," Alex assured her. "I met Perry's brother on several occasions, remember."

"No. I—"

"Laura, I don't want to put you in more danger than I already have. Crossing the river was one thing, but meeting known smugglers when the militia are nearby?" He shook his head. "It's too risky. I don't like that you'll have to walk back alone, but—"

"I can't go back. Martyn has already gone."

His brows lowered. "Thunder and turf. Why didn't we tell the boy to wait?"

"Because I didn't want him to wait. I am going with you."

He frowned. "Laura, you can't go off on a ship with rough men. It isn't seemly."

"Seemly? I don't care about that. Besides, my uncle trusts Treeve. He doesn't know what he's involved in, but Treeve is not rough nor a stranger. He won't let any harm come to me."

"He can't promise that. No one can. You know better than most how merciless the sea can be. How it breaks hulls and bodies and lays them to waste."

"I want to go."

"What are you saying? You want to go as far as the smugglers take me and then you'll return with this Treeve of yours?"

"He is not mine. A friend at most. But yes, I want to go to Jersey. And I want to know you've been restored to your family."

"Laura, I am not some . . . message in a bottle or a lost locket."

"I know. But you are important to me. And I have long wished to go to Jersey for myself. To see my parents' grave, if there is one."

He looked away, clearly torn, then ran an agitated hand over his face. "What about your poor uncle? He'll be sick with worry."

"I left him a note in his Bible. I know his habits well. He reads two chapters every morning. He'll find it after we are safely gone."

Alex shook his head. "What on earth did you tell him?"

"That I had something I had to do and not to worry about me. That I was safe in the company of two people he trusts and respects."

"He'll still worry."

"Yes, and I am sorry for it. But what else could I do?"

"Stay home."

She shook her head. "Fern Haven is not my home."

He sighed deeply. "Oh, very well. Let's go and see what your smuggler-friend has to say about a woman coming along. Many seafarers are superstitious about females on board."

Treeve, she knew, liked females. Liked *her*. But the ship's captain and crew? That could be a far different story.

They continued through the scrubby trees down a steep path to a moonlit point.

A crescent of lighter sand shone between the darker water and shadows.

At first she saw nothing. Had Treeve deceived her? Then at the far side of the landing, she made out a small boat beside the rocks. She'd been beached stern first, bow out, ready to make a hasty departure.

"Is there a signal?" Alex whispered.

"Not that he mentioned."

Laura raised her voice slightly. "Treeve? It's us."

"Us?" Treeve appeared from the shadows as if by magic. Dressed in tall boots, caped carrick coat, and wool cap, he looked less like the polished gentleman she knew.

He frowned and walked closer. "What are you wearing? I took you for strangers. Miss Callaway, I am surprised to see you. I know I encouraged you to find a way across the river, but I didn't think you'd come so far."

Laura licked dry lips. "I want to see him carried to safety, and I—"

"And here I thought you missed me. Ah well." He tipped his head back. "Wait . . . are you saying you plan to sail with us? I don't know that my crew will accept a female passenger. . . ."

"Treeve, please. I want to go to Jersey. I want to visit my parents' grave in St. Helier."

"Oh." He shifted from foot to foot. "Are you truly determined to come?"

"I am."

Treeve huffed. "Very well." He peered into the darkness behind them. "Are you certain no one followed you out here?"

"As certain as I can be. I checked behind us several times."

"Good." He turned to a man lingering near the boat. "Let's go."

Together the men pushed the tender into shallow water. Then Alexander turned to her and held out his hands. "May I?"

She nodded, mouth dry.

He lifted her into his arms, carried her to the boat, and set her down. Then the men scrambled in after her.

Propelled by both the current and oars, they rowed to the mouth of the estuary to meet the waiting lugger. By moonlight, the anchored vessel appeared a greyish black, its dark sails stowed. The ship was larger than most of the Cornish luggers she saw along their coast, with three masts rather than two. The bowsprit, a long wooden spar projecting upward from its prow, put her in mind of a bottlenose dolphin.

Reaching the ship, Treeve whistled, and they drew up alongside.

The dim shapes of a few other men appeared on deck.

Treeve called, "Seems we shall have two passengers instead of one."

One of the men sputtered, incredulous. "A w-woman, sir?"

"Yes. Wonders never cease. Perhaps she will bring us luck."

"Or doom."

Despite the protests, the crew helped them into the ship and then stowed the small landing craft.

Only after they had cleared Stepper Point and were out on open water did one of the men bring up a lit lantern from below.

By its light, Laura saw three men dressed in loose trousers, dingy striped shirts, and short jackets with handkerchiefs around their necks. A stout fourth man in boots, caped coat, and cocked hat she identified as the captain.

Then she looked closer and recognized him as Newlyn's father.

He returned her stare, his spidery eyebrows rising almost to his hairline. "Miss Callaway?"

"Mr. Dyer, you are the captain? I thought you were a fisherman."

"I was, till my boat was damaged. But I sailed a cutter in my younger days. Gave up free trading for the missus years back. But, well, times is hard. Since my boat is in for repairs, and Mr. Kent here was in need of a skipper . . ."

"I see."

No formal introductions were made, but over the next several minutes, Laura gleaned the names, or at least nicknames, of all the crewmen.

Archie, a tall, wiry fellow, was first mate; Pucky was sometimes carpenter and all-around sailor; Jackson was chief net mender and reluctant cook; while John Dyer—cap'n or skipper, in turns—oversaw everything as he smoked his pipe.

At his command, the crew began hoisting the main sail, two men pulling hard on the lines like eager bell ringers, the cross bar rising, the dark cloth unfurling. The sails were a deep burgundy, perhaps better than white for hiding from revenue men in shadowy coves.

Laura watched, noting the intricate web of pulleys, lines, chains, and coils of rope like giant embroidery floss.

The wind immediately began filling the sails, while the waves played percussion on the hull planking.

The captain stood at the helm, now and again relinquishing it to the first mate to look through the glass or to converse with Mr. Kent.

Surveying the deck, masts, and sails, Alex asked, "A lugger, yes?"

Treeve nodded. "A south coast lugger, to be precise. Narrow beam, and drawing only four feet."

Alexander nodded. "I suppose her low draft helps navigate the estuary and avoid the hidden sands of the Doom Bar."

"Indeed."

"And the narrow beam?"

"Allows us to get in and out of smaller coves and landing places."

"I see."

Treeve cocked his head to the side. "Have some sailing experience, do you?"

Alexander flashed an ironic smile. "A bit."

As they sailed south, the lugger moved easily through the swell without taking on water or broaching. Thankfully, the breeze was steady and the sea mild.

"Coming about," the skipper called. "Watch the boom."

Finally, when they safely passed Gulland Rock and Trevose Head, Laura released her first easy breath.

She felt Treeve studying her profile. "You look exhausted," he said. "Why don't you go below and get some sleep? The cabin is small, but there are bunks and a mess." He pointed to the deck doors in the bulkhead. "I'll show you. It's a little tricky."

Sliding back the cabin hatch, the smells of damp nets, fish, smoke, and sweat assailed her.

"Sorry. Still smells like pilchards, I know. Though nowadays, she carries less odoriferous cargo. Watch your head."

She knew he referred to smuggling cargo, likely tobacco, brandy, and the like.

Going below, he lit a candle lamp from the embers in the stove and set it on the shelf. She saw the cabin had five bunks, three across the transom and two on either side. Oilskin hats and coats swung gently from nails beside each. A miniature black lead range was bolted to the floor, while lockers on either side held coal for the fire.

"We use that for cooking fish or heating pasties," Treeve explained. "We eat simply while on board."

There was also a small enclosure in the fore of the cabin: a bunk with walls on three sides that offered a bit more privacy than the others.

Treeve gestured to it. "You may have my bunk. Probably the cleanest and most comfortable."

Laura hesitated. "I don't know that I should."

He gave her a sidelong glance. "Miss Callaway, you are a single female on a ship of men. I fear it is futile to worry about propriety at this point."

She sighed ruefully. "True."

He pointed to a crate near the stove. "There are potatoes and bread, along with butter and cheese. You can heat water for tea on the stove."

"I think I'll just lie down for a while, if that's all right."

"Of course." He gestured to his bunk. "My castle is your castle."

"Won't you need to sleep?"

"I may come back and join you later."

Her mouth fell open. "Treeve!"

He grinned. "Teasing. Mostly."

"Just wake me in a few hours, and I'll get up so you can sleep."

"Very well. If the night remains quiet, I may. Take care with that candle. Don't want to start a fire."

"I shall."

Treeve paused, then said, "I suppose your Frenchman should stay out of sight as much as possible. Do you mind if I send him down? He can take one of the other bunks, assuming you trust him in such close quarters?"

"I do. And you are kind to think of him."

"I am not so selfless. If the militia or one

of the revenue ships is searching for him, I don't want to give them any reason to stop us."

"Good point."

For a moment he hesitated, then he turned and climbed out of the hold without another word.

A few minutes later, Alexander descended, pulling off his hat and wig. "Mr. Kent said you wished me to join you?"

The words were uttered innocently, yet Laura's face heated at the implication.

She hurried to clarify. "He says you should stay out of sight as much as possible."

He studied her closely. "You don't mind the sea? Feel sick?"

"Not at all. I find it exhilarating."

"I am glad to hear it."

He crossed the cabin, lifting both hands toward her. "May I?"

May I what? she wondered but could form no words because his hands touched her face. She made do with a vague nod.

She held her breath as he gently unhooked the spectacles from her ears and lifted them from her nose. He set them aside and returned his gaze to her. She sank into his sea-storm eyes.

Then his fingertips slowly tugged the mobcap off her head. He looked at her by the light of the flickering candle. "Much better. Your hair is far too pretty to cover."

He set the cap aside, his eyes lingering on hers. "Thank you, Miss Callaway. Because of you, I have hope for the first time in a long time."

Her heart thumped at his warm words. He reached up, stroking a tendril of hair that had come free when he'd pulled the cap away.

Then Alexander cupped her jawline. He dipped his head, lowering his face toward hers, and his sweet peppermint breath and shaving soap were a pleasant haven amid the dank cabin.

She breathed in the smell of him, feeling flushed. He leaned nearer yet, and his lips touched hers, softly, tentatively. She stood on tiptoes and pressed her mouth more tightly to his. In a second, his arms were around her, holding her in an embrace that stole her breath.

He abruptly pulled away, grasped her shoulders, and took a half step back. "Forgive me, I got carried away."

"Me too."

He cleared his throat and retreated a few more steps. "Get some sleep, Laura. I'll watch over you."

Laura drew a steadying breath, then said,

"Perhaps you should sleep too. Before one of the crewmen wants his bunk."

He lay atop one of the low bunks, fully dressed, boots on the floor.

Laura unlaced her half boots, removed them, and crawled into Treeve's bunk, pulling the bedclothes up to her chin.

She would just rest for a few minutes, she told herself. But the berth was like a cradle, rocking her gently side to side. From above came the sounds of occasional footsteps on deck, men on the watch, which assured her they were in good hands. The rigging softly strumming against the wooden masts soon lulled her to sleep.

*The ship that will not obey the
helm must obey the rocks.*

—Cornish proverb

Chapter 18

When Laura awoke, sunlight shone through the cracks of the cabin door.

Alexander sat near the stove, watching her. He smiled. "Did you sleep well?"

"I did, though I did not intend to sleep all night. Poor Treeve."

"Oh, he and the others slept in shifts, as did I."

She sat up. "I have been a poor example of the fortitude of my sex, I'm afraid."

"Not at all. I am already convinced of your strength, Laura Callaway. Who could not be who knows you?"

Pleasure washed over her at his words.

He rose. "I will leave you. Come up when you're ready."

Laura nodded. She tidied her hair as best she could and put on her shoes. Then she went up on deck, feeling embarrassed for sleeping so long while the others worked, but the men respectfully tipped their caps or wished her a mumbled "Morning, miss."

For a time, she watched Jackson at work with a needle, mending tears in the nets. And soon Laura was taking a turn, learning to mend "bars" and "three-ers."

Now and again, the captain called out a port or landmark as they passed. Parran-porth, Portreath, and others. As the hours lapsed, Laura began to relax and enjoy the journey, to believe they would make it. She tried not to think about the fact that war still waged, and they might encounter a warship or blockade. Treeve, however, seemed more concerned about the preventive men.

Alexander made himself useful by fishing as they went, hand-lining for hake and employing the nets to bring in herring or mackerel.

Laura had helped in the kitchen during those years when it had just been her and Uncle Matthew. So she happily peeled and sliced potatoes, fried the fish Alex caught, made tea, and poured ale. They ate in shifts, and food had rarely tasted so good.

As evening fell, they passed St. Ives, and

the mood became jovial, perhaps helped along by the ale served with supper.

Behind them, a ship slipped out of the harbour and seemed to follow their course from a distance. John Dyer snapped to attention, eyes narrowed and jaw tight.

"What is it?" Treeve asked.

"A revenue cutter is stationed at the Port of St. Ives. I thought we were far enough out not to attract attention, but now I wonder."

Treeve turned to study the distant vessel. He took up a glass. "I can't tell for certain, but she's bigger than we are. Probably just out cruising on patrol."

"Let's hope."

They continued on, but as the breeze freshened, the cutter gradually drew nearer.

"Let's alter our course and see what she does."

They did so, but the other ship altered its course as well and soon began to gain on them.

"The wind is blowing a solid twenty knots straight out of the north," the captain said, then ordered all to go about on another tack.

The cutter, running with the wind on her quarter, came up fast.

"She's carrying a smart press of canvas— that's for sure," Dyer said. "She must be doing eight knots to our five."

Treeve grimaced. "We can't let them get close enough to order us to heave to. Or be in range of their guns."

Dyer nodded. "Set the topsail, men," he commanded. "And sharp-like."

The crew hurried to oblige.

Laura gripped Alexander's arm but asked Treeve, "Can we outrun a revenue cutter?"

"Definitely. Dyer has done so in the past, times without number." He turned to the man. "Haven't you?"

John Dyer nodded, but his mouth remained a tight, thin line. "A long time ago."

"And you can do it again," Treeve assured him. "Evade that cruiser, skipper!"

Laura lowered her voice. "And if he can't?"

"If we can't outsail them, we shall have to outwit them, overpower them, or . . . bribe them to avoid arrest. Sadly, I haven't the funds required for the latter."

The skipper called more commands. As the cutter pursued, the lugger crew strove to outpace it.

"Better go below, Miss Callaway," Treeve said. "Don't want the boom knocking you into the water." He said it lightly, but she saw the tension in his face.

She acquiesced. "Very well."

Laura climbed below but kept the hatch

door open, watching the activity with anxious fascination.

Alexander stayed above, helping the crew. His years as a naval man served him well, giving him skills and experience with sails and rigging. The wind continued to build, the eight-foot waves breaking into gleaming streaks, like the manes of galloping white horses.

Treeve again studied the distant ship's progress through his glass. "She's still gaining on us."

The skipper cursed. He gave the helm to the first mate and grabbed the glass. "Lemme see." Another curse. "That's the *Dolphin* all right."

"Keep calm. We don't have any contraband on board. Yet."

"No? What about 'im?" The first mate lifted his chin toward Alexander.

"Would a revenue cutter have any interest in him?" Dyer asked.

"Mebbe. If the militia asked the preventive men to aid their search."

"Or they may think we look suspicious for some other reason," Treeve said.

Dyer scowled. "I don't want to be fined or arrested when the only illegal cargo we're hauling is a Frenchman and his sweetheart."

"If they stop us," Treeve said, "there's

probably enough equipment on board to fine us, what with the drift lines, sinking stones, bladders, and the like."

"I'll go stash 'em all in the hidden compartment," Jackson offered. "Unless you want me to throw 'em overboard?"

"Not yet. See if they get near enough to hoist the warning flag."

"You really think they may just be patrolling and have no interest in us?"

Treeve shrugged. "Possibly."

Dyer frowned. "Want to risk it?"

"Not really. What else do you suggest?"

"We're near Land's End. We'll soon approach the Longships."

"Right. We'll need to sail around them."

"Or we could stay between them and shore."

Treeve ran a hand over his face. "I thought there was no safe passage between Longships and Land's End, only shallow shoals and tidal eddies."

"There *is* a passage between," Dyer said. "It's narrow and complicated and therefore seldom used. We risk hitting Kettle's Bottom, but easier for us than a cutter with its deeper draught."

"If we make such a risky maneuver, we'll erase any doubt that we're trying to evade them."

"True. But we *will* evade them."

Treeve grimaced. "For how long? They will just sail around the hazards and catch up with us."

"It would buy us time."

"Time for what?"

Before Dyer could reply, Archie jerked a thumb in Alex's direction. "To get rid of 'im."

Alexander spoke up. "If you think I am why that ship is pursuing you, then by all means, get close to shore somewhere and let me off."

From the hatch, he heard Laura protest, "Alexander, no."

"I will not be like Jonah, bringing disaster on the entire ship."

"Jonah, ey?" With a glance at the rail, Archie said, "That do give me an idea."

"No, now . . . hold on." Treeve raised both hands. "No one is getting thrown overboard. But perhaps our skipper is right. We've no chance of outrunning that ship in open water all the way to Jersey. But we can land and hide anything . . . questionable . . . and then let them board us, if they like. When they find nothing and no one suspicious, they'll let us go. I hope." He turned to Dyer. "Can you do it?"

Dyer screwed up his face in thought. "Low tide is coming on with a racy current ebbing from the gap. To make it through those rocks, I'd need a chart and a compass."

Pucky retrieved both.

Captain Dyer spread out the chart and ran a finger over it, tracing a narrow gutway through the rocks. Alexander leaned close, studying the chart as well.

"Depth?"

"Sufficient, according to this. But the chart is old."

"It's the best we've got."

In the distance, southwest of Land's End, the granite tower of Longships appeared, a lighthouse set amid a formidable array of rocky outcroppings, including what Dyer called the nasty Shark's Fin. Alexander watched Dyer examine the gap between them and a pair of rocks marked as *Kettle's Bottom*, situated midway between Longships and the coast.

Dyer tapped the chart with his scarred finger. "We'd just make it over, but that revenue cutter will ground out if she follows us."

"Can you get her through?"

"I think so. With bearings and a lookout."

"Very well," Treeve said. "Through the passage it is."

Pucky crossed himself, and Jackson began praying under his breath.

Alexander prayed as well.

Decision made, Dyer's doubts seemed to

evaporate as duty called. Chest out, confident tilt to his chin, he called, "We're going through, lads. Attend to the set of the sails. Get the best you can out of 'er."

The other crewmen stood at the ready beside sheets and runners. Archie kept his eye on the captain, ready to throw his weight on the tiller.

"East, southeast, sir. Upon the instant."

"Down helm. Sheets there."

The *Merry Mary* came into the wind, spray bursting over the bow.

"Pucky, aloft there and watch for rocks, tide rips, and eddies."

"Aye, sir." He climbed the rigging and shouted down, "Run, sir. Fine to starboard!"

Danger was clearly visible on both sides. The Shark's Fin and Longships lay on the starboard quarter, the Kettle's Bottom to larboard. They sailed through the gap, the lugger's bowsprit surging forward like an aggressive porpoise.

The rise and fall of the crashing waves revealed rocks everywhere, the water foaming white around them, the passage even narrower than Alex had reckoned from the chart.

Behind them, the revenue cutter changed tack, moving westward around Longships.

The rocks drew abeam, the keel gave a creaking whine, and Alex heard the terrifying scrape of wood on rock. He noticed Laura grip the hatch and hold on tight.

But the creaking stopped. They had almost made it through the narrow tunnel of jagged grey rocks and white foam.

From the rigging, Pucky shouted, "Rock dead ahead, sir!"

"Up helm," Dyer shouted.

The bowsprit swung away, but the current pushed her stern around.

"Down helm!"

Alexander braced himself for the sound of cracking timber, for the ship's hull to be crushed.

Seeing the first mate struggle, Alex raced across the deck and added his weight, shoving the tiller to larboard.

A second passed. Two. Alexander held his breath but the sounds of calamity did not come.

"We're through, sir," Pucky called from above.

Alex met Laura's gaze across the deck and released a prayer of thanksgiving. The others threw fists in the air.

Captain Dyer closed his eyes in silent relief, while Treeve wore his as a foolish grin.

Having reached the other side, they saw no sign of the *Dolphin*, out of view somewhere behind the rocks and spray.

"Well done, men," Treeve called.

Newlyn's father made do with a nod, the tension in his jaw revealing the passage had been no mean feat.

The rigging strumming above their heads, the *Merry Mary* cruised on. At Dyer's command, the men brought down one of the sails to reduce their speed. The heeling eased.

A short while later, Dryer directed the lugger into a small cove partially hidden by large rocks on either side of its entrance. Alex hoped the secluded harbour meant less chance of being spotted by a passing ship.

Laura sagged against the bulkhead with a sigh of relief. How welcome it was to go from the wild open sea, pounding waves, and flying spray into the calm safety of harbour. The skipper uttered more commands. Soon the other sails were lowered, and they were moored snugly in the tranquil cove.

She gathered up her few possessions and climbed up on deck, uncertainty and fear rippling through her. This had not been part of the plan.

"What now?" she asked. "Where are we?"

Captain Dyer squinted over his charts. "Porthgwarra. Nothing here really. A few cottages and one inn, if memory serves. Porthcurno is a mile and a quarter eastward. And Penzance another ten."

Treeve hesitated. "Perhaps we can plan to meet you in Penzance tomorrow."

Dyer shook his head. "It's your ship, Mr. Kent, but I didn't like taking a Frenchman and a female aboard the first time. I'm sure not ready to do it again."

Archie nodded his agreement. "Let 'em find another way to Jersey."

Treeve looked sheepishly from the crew to Laura and back again. "But I gave them my word. Miss Callaway is a family friend."

"And my daughter works for her," Dyer said. "But I don't care if she is a crown princess—it's too dangerous with the *Dolphin* on our trail."

"It's all right," Alexander resolved. "I will find another way. Thank you for bringing me this far, Mr. Kent, men. I know you all took a risk to do so."

They lowered the small boat, and Alexander climbed in. Laura followed him.

Treeve protested, "Miss Callaway, what are you doing? I can deliver you safely back home. We may need to hide here for a time, but then—"

"Let her go if she wants," Archie said. "Like the skipper said, no good comes of having a woman on board. Nor a Frenchie either."

Alexander frowned. "Laura, no. This has

gone too far. We can't go wandering aimlessly across the country together."

"I agree. We are not going to wander aimlessly. We are going to Penzance. I know someone there who might help."

A few minutes later, Treeve and Pucky rowed them ashore in the tender, then Treeve took her aside. "What do I tell your family?"

Her family was all gone, but she knew he meant the Brays.

"Tell them I am well and grieved to worry them—that I have gone to visit my parents' grave and will return when I can."

Eagerness widened his eyes. "You need only write and I'll sail back for you. I regret I cannot take you there and back now." He pressed her hand. "I am sorry we failed you, little turnstone."

Hearing his sweet, silly pet name for her, nostalgia squeezed her heart. "Don't be. I will forever be grateful for your help."

He gave her a rueful grin. "Better wait and see how grateful you feel when all this is over. I hope you don't live to regret it."

Laura managed a wobbly smile in return. "Me too."

From June 1810 to June 1812, a total of 464 officers broke their parole, of which 307 made it across the Channel aided by smugglers.

—PAUL CHAMBERLAIN, *THE NAPOLEONIC PRISON OF NORMAN CROSS*

Chapter 19

Laura followed Alexander up the steep rocky path from the cove, his knapsack bobbing gently on his back. In the distance, she saw a few humble cottages and the public house Mr. Dyer had mentioned.

She eyed it hopefully. "Might it have a room to let?"

Alexander frowned. "Too risky. If the authorities find Kent's boat and begin searching for us, wouldn't that be the first place they'd look? We had better go farther."

"You are no doubt right." Laura forced a smile and trudged on. She didn't understand why she felt so very weary. She supposed it was all the tensions and trials of the last few days.

As they walked eastward through the twilight, rain began to fall. The damp wouldn't harm Alex's leather knapsack, but to protect her fabric traveling bag, she slipped it under her cape with a sigh.

After a mile or so, they reached Porthcurno. The village consisted of a two-story building signposted *Seaview Inn* and a cluster of low cottages huddled in a narrow valley.

"Shall we stay the night here and continue on in the morning?" she asked, her legs like lead.

He hesitated, wearing a grimace. "I think we should press on and get farther away from the ship." Then he looked at her, his eyes widening in concern.

"Laura, you look tired. Forgive me. Of course we shall rest here if they have rooms. What a day this has been for you."

He opened the door for her. Stepping inside, they greeted the innkeeper, who stood behind a counter.

"Good evening," Alexander said. "Have you rooms available?"

"I have one room, sir, with two sturdy beds. Just right for you and your missus. Well I remember when my good wife was expecting.

How she tossed and turned, striving to be comfortable."

Laura stared dumbly. *Why does he think . . . ?* She glanced down at her bulging midriff, and her face flamed. "Oh! I am not, that is . . ." She reached beneath her cape and pulled forth her traveling bag. "I was simply shielding this from the rain."

The publican reddened and chuckled awkwardly. "A thousand apologies, madam."

"That is all right. An understandable mistake." Laura swallowed and sent a nervous glance toward Alexander. "But he and I are not—"

"We are not particular," Alex interjected. "Are we, my dear?" He laid his hand over hers, covering the fact that it wore no ring. Brows high, Alex asked her, "Will one room suffice? I shall endeavor not to snore."

She looked at him, blinking with uncertainty. Then understanding dawned. "Oh, em, yes. I am so tired I could sleep through a gale."

The publican looked from one to the other. "Very good. And shall I send up a bit of supper on a tray?"

"Yes, thank you. You are very kind."

He handed Alexander the key. "Top of the stairs, first door on your right."

Alex took Laura's bag and gestured toward the landing. "After you."

Reaching the room, he unlocked it, and Laura entered first. Alexander closed the door but remained near it. In a low voice, he said, "Pray forgive my presumption. I was afraid the man would put us out if he knew we were not husband and wife traveling together."

"You were right. Good thinking."

Setting down their bags, he said, "I will wait awhile, then go downstairs to the taproom and find a quiet corner there."

She looked from the beds to him. "No need. There are two beds, as he said, and I trust you."

"Do you?"

She paused to consider. "Yes, I find that I do."

"Very well."

A knock on the door startled them both. When they didn't respond, a woman's voice called, "Your supper."

"Oh. Right." Alex turned and opened the door.

A chambermaid in her early thirties came in and set the tray down on the dressing table, whipping off a linen cloth with dramatic flair. "Wah-la!" she exclaimed, mispronouncing the French.

Alex cringed and corrected, "It is *voilà*."

"What?"

"Never mind. Thank you." He handed the woman a coin from his earnings. "Might you help my missus with whatever she needs while we're here?"

With an eager glance at the gleaming coin, the maid replied, "Happily, sir. I'll come back in half an hour to collect the tray and shall help her then, if that suits."

"Yes," Laura replied, thankful for Alexander's thoughtfulness. "That would be perfect, Miss . . . ?"

"You may call me Rennet, ma'am." The maid performed a deep, stage-worthy curtsy and slipped from the room.

At the woman's theatrical exit, Laura and Alex shared amused grins.

Then Laura looked at him with a mixture of wonder and gratitude. "You think of everything."

His eyes glimmered with sadness. "I only wish that were true."

Alexander hoped Laura would not come to regret traveling with him, but feared she would. He gestured for her to take the seat at the dressing table, while he sat on the only other chair in the room. She handed him one of the bowls of stew and a spoon, and they began eating.

The tender chunks of beef, carrots, and onions in rich gravy were delicious and warming, reminding him of his father's favorite, beef *bourguignon.*

They ate in silence, an awkward tension between them. They had spent many hours in the guest room in Fern Haven and had shared the same cabin on the ship, though they had rarely been alone, with the crew sleeping in shifts.

They were certainly alone now. Was that why this felt so different? So . . . dangerous?

When they finished eating, Laura stacked the used bowls and cutlery and set the tray aside. The uneasy silence stretched.

Laura reached up and began unpinning her hair. "I hope you don't mind. The pins are digging into my scalp."

"I don't mind at all."

Her long hair cascaded down around her shoulders in a veil of autumn colors—deep amber, cinnamon, maple leaves. His chest tightened.

She massaged her scalp, and his fingers itched to stroke the silky length.

"Your hair is beautiful," he said, unable to stop himself.

"Thank you." She dipped her head, clearly self-conscious.

Trying not to stare, he stood, searching

the room for some distraction. "I will, em, clean my teeth." He turned to the washbasin, scrubbed his teeth with the brush and tooth powder from his knapsack, and washed his face and hands, glad for the cold water.

The maid, Rennet, returned as promised, and Laura smiled at her. "If you could help me with the fastenings?"

"Yes, ma'am."

To keep up the pretense that he planned to spend the night with his "wife," Alexander remained in the room, instead of escaping like the interloper he knew himself to be.

He licked dry lips. "I will, em, just read while you change." He repositioned the chair, angling it away from them, and sat down, trying in vain to read the New Testament and Psalms he'd found on the side table.

The maid undid the back buttons and loosened the lacings of the shapeless black frock.

His rebellious eyes now and again shifted to the side, catching a glimpse of bare shoulder in the dressing table mirror.

Steady, Carnell. You are not really married, however you might wish you were at this moment. Think of something else. . . .

But he was losing the battle. A minute or two later, he cleared his throat and rose. Stepping to the door, he said, "I think I will go down for a glass of something while you ready for bed."

He quickly fled the room—and the tantalizing sight of Laura Callaway getting undressed, her gorgeous hair down around her shoulders.

Half an hour later, he knocked softly and let himself in. The room was darker now, the fire burned low and only one candle left alight—the one on the side table beside the empty bed.

Laura lay on her side in the other bed, facing the wall, blankets pulled up to her ear. Asleep or feigning it?

He removed his coat and hung it on a peg. He yanked off his boots, then removed his waistcoat and folded it with military precision. He pulled his shirt over his head, washed it out in the basin, and hung it near the fire to dry for the next day. He was too warm as it was, but remembering Laura's earlier shivering, he added a scoop of coal to the fire before climbing into bed, wondering if he would get any sleep lying this close to her.

Slumber had barely overtaken him when he was awoken by the sound of someone pounding on a distant door. Alex leapt from bed and crept to the window. Below, he saw two men holding lanterns and another official-looking man in uniform.

"Open up!"

A window squeaked open, and the inn-keeper called out, "We're full up, my good fellows, and the taproom closed for the night."

Laura joined Alex at the window, gripping his arm in fear.

"We don't want a room, we want a word," the officer called back. "We are searching for a Frenchman. An escaped prisoner of war. He may be traveling with a young woman."

Laura whispered, "I'm so sorry. You were right. We should have gone farther."

Clenching his jaw, Alex hissed, "We may have to make a run for it. Or at least I will. You have done nothing wrong."

"Except aiding and abetting you?"

"If need be, say I forced you to come." He pulled on his boots and stepped to the room's other window, this one facing the side of the inn. "I think I can lower myself to that porch roof and jump down from there."

"I am going with you," she whispered back.

"No."

He grabbed for the window latch, and again the publican's voice reached them from below. "We have no Frenchmen here. And our only female guest is a tetchy woman large with child, and woe to anyone who disturbs her slumber."

"You sure?" the officer asked.

"'Course I'm sure. You've searched my establishment before and found nothing and angered my guests and my good wife to no purpose. You've cost me custom."

The door to their room creaked open, and Laura barely stifled a gasp. Rennet slipped in, finger to her lips, candle lamp in her other hand. She beckoned them to follow her. They did so, tiptoeing to the far end of the room, to what looked like an ordinary wall. Her fingers worked some hidden latch, and a panel slid open. The flickering candlelight revealed a closet-sized compartment with several stacked half ankers and a crate of tea atop them. Smuggling contraband.

Laura and Alex stepped inside, the maid shoved his damp shirt, coat, and knapsack atop the crate, and then closed the panel, shutting them inside the compartment, just as the front door below opened.

In a loud, long-suffering manner, the innkeeper said, "Very well, if you insist on searching the house again, be quick about it."

In the darkness, Alexander slid a protective arm around Laura's waist, and she leaned against him, her soft hair against his bare chest. Could she feel his racing heart? He took a steadying breath and prayed they wouldn't be discovered.

Through a thin crack in the panels, they saw the maid tidy one bed, then stuff a pillow beneath her dressing gown and climb into the other.

The chamber door burst open, and the three men charged inside.

"Wha—!" the woman screeched in alarm, sitting up as best she could with her enlarged middle. "What'ee doin' in my room? Have'ee come to murder me in my bed? Get out this instant, or I shall scream. Out, out, I tell'ee. If'ee make my poor child come early, that innocent life will be on yer heads and the heads of yer own children!"

The officer held up a palm. "Calm down, madam, calm down. We are only searching for an escaped prisoner of war."

"Are'ee blind, sirs? I am no prisoner, not even a man. Out, out, I tell'ee!"

With a quick look under the bed, the men sheepishly left the chamber, and continued their search of the inn. Half an hour later, they left the premises with nothing to show for their efforts.

When all was quiet again, the maid whispered for them to wait and slipped from the room. She returned shortly to open the panel for them.

"I've brought some warm milk to help'ee

sleep," she said, as though nothing so very out of the ordinary had just occurred.

"Th-thank you," Laura managed.

"We are obliged to you," Alex added.

The maid nodded. "Good night, sir. Madam. I'll be back in the morning." And she let herself out without another word.

In the morning, Alex was up and out of the room before Laura awakened. Thoughtful of him to give her privacy to dress. The same maid came in with warm water, sent up by "yer mister."

When Laura asked the time, she was surprised to find the hour so advanced. She brushed her tangled hair and washed in the heavenly warm water. Again Rennet helped with her lacings and fastenings. In hindsight it had been very foolish of her not to bring only front-fastening gowns. Today she wore her own dress, rolled up Miss Chegwin's black one, and shoved it into the bag with the few other things she had packed. When she looked in the mirror, she saw that she looked more like her own self again.

"Thank you again for hiding us last night," Laura said. "That was quite a performance."

Rennet smiled. "Do'ee think so? I always wanted to be an actress on Drury Lane, but

Pa said it weren't proper. I said, 'Better'n cleaning chamber pots all my livelong day,' but, oh well, here I be."

"You are a talented actress."

The maid dimpled. "Thank'ee, ma'am. That makes me very happy to hear."

When Rennet left, Alex returned with bread, butter, and cups of hot strong tea for them both. Laura could have kissed him.

After they had eaten, she removed a few coins from her reticule and extended them. "For the room."

He shook his head. "No need. I have my earnings from the salvaging work."

"Save that for the journey."

"It would not be gentlemanly to allow you to pay my way."

"The money is from the sale of the jeweled salamander. Not mine, really. In fact, I would feel better about spending it on returning another treasure rather than on myself."

"A treasure now, am I? Better than flotsam, I suppose." He winked.

Her face warmed in embarrassment, but she saw that her words had pleased as well as amused him, so she could not regret saying them.

They packed their few remaining things and went downstairs.

Finding the publican alone, Laura said, "Thank you, sir, for your . . . discretion . . . last night."

The man nodded sagely. "I'm a publican in Porthcurno, madam. I make it a practice to deny anything the revenue men ask me." He cleared his throat. "Rennet told me where she hid you. I trust I can count on your discretion in return?"

"You may indeed."

They smiled at one another and settled their bill, and the two travelers began the long walk to Penzance. The day was cold, damp, and misty. A few carriages passed by, and Laura hoped one of them would stop and offer them a lift, but none did.

Ten miles was going to be a tiring trek, especially in the rain, which grew heavier as they trudged along the road.

Seeing her traveling bag getting wet, Laura again tucked it under her cape, wishing she had brought a stout leather valise instead, although it would have been heavier.

A wagon passed them, and the driver stopped his horses with a "Whoa now, boys." Then he called to them, "Where are you two bound?"

"Penzance."

"That's a long walk for a woman in her condition. Climb up."

Alex looked at her, brows high in surprise, then bit back a smile.

The farmer nodded toward the ewes in the wagon. "I wouldn't make my girls walk so far."

"You are right, sir," Alexander said humbly. "And we sincerely appreciate your offer."

He helped Laura up onto the bench and squeezed in beside her.

They continued on their way. The wagon would win no races, but it was better than walking the whole ten miles.

Reaching Penzance, Alex offered the man something for his kindness, which he waved away. After thanking him, they spent some time walking around the harbour, inquiring about a ship. Finding no one willing to help them, Laura asked a passerby for directions to Quayside Cottage. After their late start, slow pace, and futile inquiries, the sky was already darkening.

When they found their way to the house, Laura handed Alex her bag and whispered, "Let me talk to him first."

Alex nodded and stood off to the side behind her. Laura took a deep breath and knocked on the door.

A few minutes later, a short, rotund housemaid answered. "Iss?"

"Good evening. I am here to see Mr. Truscott. Is he at home?"

The woman hesitated, looking her up and down. Laura lifted her chin and managed a small smile, hoping to look more ladylike than she surely had over the last few days.

"I'll see. Wait there." She shut the door, leaving them out in the cold.

Lord, please let him remember me and look on us kindly.

The door opened again a few minutes later, and a thin, balding man stood staring at her, wariness etched into his features.

Laura swallowed. "Good evening, Mr. Truscott. I apologize for the unexpected call. But you did say if I were ever in Penzance, I should visit you."

"And you are?" he asked.

"Laura Callaway. I wrote to you about your first wife, some months back. And I received your kind and, may I say, unexpected response."

His expression transformed into one of wonder, then fell. "You've missed the wedding, I'm afraid."

"I know. I hope it went off well?"

"Yes, the new Mrs. Truscott and I are blissfully happy. I wish you could meet her, but her niece just had a child, and she has gone to stay the night with her so she can rest."

"How kind of her."

"Yes, that's Ruth." He shifted uneasily. "I know I offered you some reward, but now I fear you mistook me for a rich man. I hope you did not come all this way expecting a great deal of money."

"No, sir, I did not. We are . . . passing through, my friend and I, and our ship had to land unexpectedly and is unable to take us farther. If you happen to have a spare room—"

"Your friend?" he asked, leaning to the side and looking toward Alex.

Alexander stepped forward and bowed. "At your service, sir."

Mr. Truscott looked from one to the other, chewing his lip. "Traveling alone together, are you? I don't suppose you are married? I wouldn't scruple it myself, but as I wrote, the new Mrs. Truscott is very particular about proper behavior and avoiding even the appearance of sin. So while I could offer one of you lodging, I don't know that she would agree to the both of you, unless . . . may I tell her you are man and wife, recently wed? Then there can be no objection."

Laura hesitated. She did not want to lie, but she was cold and weary to the bone.

Alexander touched her arm. "You go in, Laura. You're exhausted. I will find shelter somewhere. A church or barn, perhaps."

Mr. Truscott grimaced. "No, no," he said. "I can't turn you away. Come in the both of you, I insist. You look dead on your feet. Leave the explanations to me, assuming you will behave like a gentleman while under my roof?" He sent Alex a piercing look.

"Upon my honor, sir."

"Good, good. That's settled, then. Come in, come in. You must be hungry and thirsty from your journey." He called down the hall, "Rozenn, some dinner for our guests, if you please."

A few minutes later, they sat down to a simple but hearty meal of cold chicken, beef, turnips, and bread and butter, with an apple tart for dessert.

After they had eaten and talked over tea and brandy for a time, Mr. Truscott led Laura upstairs and through a sitting room to a small guest room beyond.

Then he said to Alex, "And perhaps you might sleep here in the sitting room?" He gestured to a worn, upholstered sofa. "I have napped there plenty of times, I can tell you."

"Yes, perfect."

Mr. Truscott hesitated, then turned back to Laura. "I would, em, rather not involve the maid in our little ruse. She tells my wife everything. Can you manage on your own for one night?"

"Easily," Laura replied. "Thank you, Mr. Truscott."

Their host brought up a pitcher of water for the washstand, built up the fires in both rooms, and bid them good night.

When he departed, Alex whispered, "*Can you manage without a maid?*"

She shrugged. "I can sleep in my frock."

"Not very comfortably. I could help, if you don't mind."

Laura hesitated. She would have to wear the same dress the next day, so she hated to sleep in it. She'd far rather let it air than wake up in a wrinkled mess.

"If you could just undo the frock's back buttons and laces. I can sleep in my shift and stays."

Her ears heated to mention her underclothing, but she reminded herself that Alexander had been a married man at one point, so was probably well versed in female attire.

He approached, and she turned her back to him, grateful for an excuse to hide her flushing face.

His fingers seemed a bit unsteady as he fumbled over the buttons.

"Sorry. They are dashed tiny."

She clenched trembling hands. "That's all right."

He unstrung the laces more easily. His

hands paused, lingering on her waist a moment.

"Anything else?"

She was tempted to lean back in his arms but forced herself to turn her head and smile at him. "I can manage the rest. Thank you. Good night."

Laura gently shut the bedchamber door behind him, then leaned her back against it, wondering what might have happened had he stayed. She imagined leaning against his strong chest, his arms going around her. Alexander kissing her shoulder, the back of her neck . . . She pressed her eyes closed. No. They had done the right thing.

She sighed. Sometimes the right thing was a cold and lonely room.

Laura slipped off her frock, hung it from a peg, and pulled a nightdress over her shift and stays. She cleaned her teeth and climbed into the small, chilly bed. She tossed and turned, her mind alert even though her body was weary. She prayed for a time, then finally fell asleep.

Sometime in the middle of the night, she awoke and found herself shivering. She rose to add more fuel to her fire. By its light, she opened the trunk at the foot of the bed and from it drew two woolen blankets. She laid the first on her bed, then tucked the second under her arm. Hoping not to wake Alex, she opened the door gingerly and tiptoed to the sofa. He lay there, one arm bent over his head, one foot on the floor, knitted lap rug covering his torso. She carefully spread the wool blanket over him. For a moment she stood there, gazing at his handsome face by moonlight. Might she ever have another chance?

She leaned down and gently kissed his forehead. Alexander's eyes snapped open, and he caught her hand. He pulled her down to him and drew her close in a warm, lingering kiss. Laura's pulse raced. When the kiss ended, she lifted her head but made no move to leave.

In a low, gravelly whisper, he said, "You had better return to your room before I break my word to behave as a gentleman."

"I only came out to make sure you were warm enough."

He stroked her cheek. "I am now."

Heart beating hard, Laura returned to her bed on legs of jelly.

The next time she awoke, muted morning light shimmered through the shutters. She rose and opened them, revealing an overcast day, though at least it was no longer raining.

She combed her tangled hair and washed

in the now-cold water. When she looked into the mirror, she saw a strange brightness to her eyes and flush to her cheeks, though the room was quite chilly. She dressed as best she could, then knocked and slowly opened the door into the sitting room.

Alexander stood before the hearth mirror, tying his cravat.

"Good morning," she whispered.

He turned to look at her, his gaze softening and lingering as it moved over her hair and gown before returning to her face. "How are you feeling?"

"Anxious, but otherwise well. Would you mind, em, fastening my frock?"

"Not at all."

Again she turned her back, and he began the task, his hands steadier this morning.

As he finished, a door opened below, and both of them jumped.

Voices ascended the stairs. Mr. Truscott exclaimed, "My love, you are home early. I didn't expect you until this evening."

"I know, my dear, but I missed you, and Joan is getting on so well. . . ."

Laura and Alex exchanged uneasy looks. The particular Mrs. Truscott was back.

"I'll go first," Laura whispered.

"Wait," he hissed, pulling the ring from his hand and sliding it onto her ring finger.

She nodded, took a deep breath, then made her way downstairs.

Mr. Truscott turned as she descended. "Ah. You will never guess who has come to call, my love. It is Miss Laura Callaway, em, that was. She wrote the letter telling us of Prudie's passing. Remember?"

The middle-aged woman, still in cap and mantle, turned to her, eyes alight. "Oh! I do indeed. Miss Callaway, what a pleasure. How good of you to come."

"Um, I say the Miss Callaway that was, my dear, for she has recently married. She is, em, Mrs. . . ." He turned pleading eyes in Laura's direction.

"Carnell."

He smiled in relief. "Mrs. Carnell now."

"Congratulations, my dear." Mrs. Truscott said, her face plain but pleasant. "And your husband?"

"He should be down any minute. Ah, here he is."

Alexander came tentatively down the stairs and joined her at the bottom.

"Good morning, my good man," Mr. Truscott said a bit too loudly. "I was just telling my dear wife that you and this fine young lady are to be congratulated."

Alex frowned in confusion. "Are we?"

"For your recent nuptials, of course!" their host said, rather desperately.

Alexander's expression cleared. "Ah yes. Thank you. I am a blessed man indeed." He stepped closer to Laura, taking her hand in his.

Introductions were made, and then Mrs. Truscott suggested they all sit down to breakfast together. Dread filled Laura at the thought of having to make conversation over a meal and the lies that would be necessary to continue the ruse.

Mr. Truscott looked from person to person and wrung his fingers. "My dear, why do we not let the newly wedded couple dine on their own? I have already eaten, but you could bring a tray into my study. I relish a little time with you, my love. You can tell me all about your niece's new baby."

Mrs. Truscott smiled at her husband, the expression transforming her rather homely face into one of true loveliness.

"As do I, my love, but we should not neglect our guests."

"Not at all, Mrs. Truscott," Alex responded politely. "We were unexpected guests, and we don't mind a bit."

Mr. Truscott nodded. "You see, my dear. I am not the only recent bridegroom eager to spend time alone with his lovely wife."

"Thank you, but truly, I am eager to speak

with our guests," Mrs. Truscott gently but firmly insisted. "You and I can talk later."

Mr. Truscott reluctantly acquiesced. "As you like, my love."

They took their seats in the dining parlour, and the maid brought out a basin of porridge, a rack of toast, and platter of cold meat. On the table were already-arranged pots of jam, honey, and butter, as well as tea things.

Mrs. Truscott turned to Alexander. "Would you like to ask the blessing, Mr. Carnell?"

"With pleasure." He bowed his head, and Laura followed suit, though she didn't quite shut her eyes, eager to observe this demonstration of his faith.

"Almighty God, look with mercy on those here assembled and accept our humble petitions. We are grateful for this new day and for the gracious hospitality of our hosts. Please pardon our offenses of yesterday and guard us from evil today. You know our weaknesses and the temptations that surround us. We ask for your protection through any dangers ahead, and we pray for all who travel by land or by sea. Amen."

Everyone echoed his amen.

Mrs. Truscott thanked him and poured the tea. "You made no mention of your betrothal when you wrote, Miss Cal . . . er, Mrs.

Carnell. Your marriage must be even more recent than ours."

"Yes, I am as surprised as you are. It was most unexpected."

Between bites of porridge and toast, Mrs. Truscott asked, "Have you known one another long?"

"No, we only met last month."

John Truscott nodded sagely. "Love at first sight, was it?"

Alex looked at Laura and said with apparent sincerity, "Indeed it was. For me at least."

"And you, my dear?" Mrs. Truscott prompted, eyes twinkling.

Laura felt her face heat. "I was . . . certainly intrigued."

"How did you meet?"

"He . . . em, sailed into my life, as it were."

"My wife is all modesty," Alexander said. "I was injured during a shipwreck, and she rescued me and nursed me back to health."

Mrs. Truscott pressed a hand to her heart. "How romantic."

"I'm afraid it did not seem so at first," Laura said. "We were not sure he would live. And sadly, so many others died. Including one of his dear friends."

"I am very sorry to hear it."

A moment of respectful silence followed.

Mrs. Truscott sipped her tea, then asked, "And are you two on your wedding trip?"

"In a manner of speaking," Laura explained. "Mr. Carnell hopes to visit his family and I . . . to pay my respects to mine."

"They were unable to join you for the wedding?"

Laura looked down, unable to meet the woman's earnest gaze. "My parents are gone, I'm afraid. But they are buried on Jersey. Alexander's family lives near there, so we hope to pay our respects to both."

"Unfortunately, the vessel carrying us ran into difficulty near Longships," Alexander added.

"Oh no! Not another shipwreck, I hope?"

"No, thank the Lord. But the master thought it best to put into Porthgwarra for a time."

Mr. Truscott nodded. "Making repairs, are they? I do hope everyone is all right."

"They were all well when we left them. We decided to try to find another way to Jersey. I don't suppose you know of anyone who might be willing to take us?"

Mrs. Truscott's expression fell. "I am sorry. I wish we could help, but we have no ship, nor am I acquainted with anyone with any reason to travel so near to France, especially with a war on. Are you, my dear?"

Mr. Truscott winced and, with a telling glance at his wife, said to them, "I will give the matter some thought."

Later, after Mrs. Truscott left to attend a meeting of the church charity guild, Mr. Truscott took them aside.

"I do know someone who might take you to Jersey. I told you when I wrote that my first wife left me for a smuggler. He's long gone, but his brother is still here and has a small schooner. I'm ashamed to admit I've kept the connection from Ruth. She would not approve. But the French brandy we had last night and the fine tea at breakfast . . . ? Let's just say, I know several men who regularly participate in free trade with the Channel Islands. The brother owes me a favor. I will go and speak to him. You stay here, and if Ruth returns before I do, say I have gone to the warehouse to see about an order."

He turned back, giving them a sheepish look. "As you see, the missus is a saint, but her husband is not."

Alex smiled at the man and put an arm around Laura's shoulders. "Isn't that the way it usually is, Mrs. Carnell?" He winked at her, drawing her close in an affectionate sideways embrace.

She chuckled and wished she could remain there in his arms.

～

Later that afternoon, Alexander and Laura stood with Mr. Truscott on the quay. At the bottom of the stone steps, a man in a small boat awaited.

Laura turned to their host and held out her hand. "Thank you, Mr. Truscott."

He pressed her fingers. "My pleasure, my dear. After all, I offered you a reward. I am only sorry it could not be more."

She smiled up at him. "It is more than enough."

"I hope you don't think too poorly of me, keeping things from my wife. She is from Somersetshire, you see, and doesn't understand Cornish ways."

Laura nodded. "I can empathize."

He rocked on his heels, hands behind his back. "Perhaps knowing what you know now about my . . . activities . . . you think Ruth is too good for me." He grinned. "And you would be right." He shook Alex's hand and helped Laura into the tender that would deliver them to the schooner moored in the harbour.

A short while later, the *Curlew* raised anchor and hoisted sails, and they were on their way to Jersey. The captain and crew asked no questions of them, and Laura was relieved for their silence, weary of falsehood. Weary, in general. She found an out of the way corner and sat down on a crate, setting her bag beside her.

Alex came and sank to his haunches nearby. "All right?"

She nodded. But in truth she felt woozy, which was odd as she'd felt no touch of seasickness aboard Treeve's ship. Alex kissed her forehead, hesitated, then followed the caress with a lingering hand. "You're warm. Too warm."

"Just a little queasy."

"It's all been too much for you. All the tension and late-night traipsing about in the cold, not to mention the damp."

"I am all right," she insisted.

"I don't know that you are. But there's no turning back now. Lord willing, we'll arrive in Jersey sometime tomorrow."

He rose. "I'll be right back." After a brief conversation with the skipper, Alexander returned. "Come, the captain says you may rest in his cabin."

She put her hand in his, and he pulled her to her feet.

"Are you sure it's all right?" she asked.

He took her elbow and led her to the hatch.

"Yes, and I will be within calling distance if you need anything."

"Rest does sound heavenly, I own."

Helping her below deck, he led her to a small compartment with a bunk and side table.

There, he again kissed her brow and turned to go. "Rest, Laura. You've almost made it."

Alex gently woke her sometime later. "Laura? Time to wake up. I see the château in the distance. We'll soon reach Jersey."

"Oh?" She pushed up on her elbows. "That was fast."

"You slept through it all. It's the next day."

She stared at him in alarm. "No."

"Yes. I knew you were exhausted but not quite how much."

"The captain must be vexed."

"He got a few hours in the first mate's bunk. It's he who's vexed, but better him than the captain."

She handed him her purse. "Make recompense however you think best."

"If you'd like."

A few minutes later, they climbed on deck and stood at the rail, watching the island loom closer. Soon they passed a large fortified castle perched on an islet in the bay.

"What's that?" Laura asked.

"Château Elizabeth, a military fortress."

They continued into the busy harbour. Laura saw tall ships in the broad bay and many buildings along the curved waterfront and rising up the green hills of St. Helier beyond. Alexander pointed out several shipyards huddled on shore and Fort Regent standing guard over it all.

Laura stood transfixed, staring at the island of Jersey for the first time—the place her parents had died. Had it looked the same when they arrived? Ten long years had passed. She hoped she could find someone who still remembered them, who could tell her about their final days or at least show her where they were buried.

Mamma . . . Papa . . . I am here at last. And I miss you still.

The ship dropped anchor and lowered one of the boats.

"The tide is high," Alex said to the master. "Will you not approach the quay directly?"

The man shook his head. "Don't like getting too close to the authorities, you know. We'll let you out and be on our way, that lot none the wiser."

"Don't you sail here regularly?"

"Yes, but we usually land at a less heavily guarded port. We are only here for you."

"And we thank you." Alex pressed coins into the hands of the captain and first mate, then returned to the rail.

A crewman helped Laura and Alex into the boat, then rowed them ashore. When they reached the quay, Alex clambered up first, then reached down a hand to help Laura ascend. She felt strangely weak and in need of his strength.

Standing on solid stone at last, Laura should have felt steadier, but instead the earth continued to sway beneath her.

Alex placed a supporting hand under her elbow. "Are you all right? May take a few minutes to find your land legs again."

She nodded, drawing in long draughts of cool, salty air, wishing away the dizziness, the mounting nausea. What was happening to her? For her vision narrowed, tunneling into blackness. She felt her legs give way and knew no more.

She had been entangled in the fog, not knowing where she was, all her bearings lost.

—S. BARING-GOULD,
IN THE ROAR OF THE SEA

Chapter 20

Laura became aware of someone mopping her brow. Her vision returned in uneasy intervals, blurry at first, as though she peered through a thin layer of wax.

She glimpsed a wrinkled hand and heard a kind older voice. *Miss Chegwin?* Laura wondered.

Had she said the name aloud? For the voice gently hushed and soothed her. The woman spoke English but her accent was different. Not Cornish. French? Laura didn't think so.

"Shh, there now. Drink this." Warm, soothing liquid touched her lips, her throat, her stomach, and once more Laura slept.

She woke again with a spoon to her lips. "Come, Sara, you must eat something."

Sara? That was her mother's name. Why was this woman calling her Sara?

"Laura," she murmured, or tried to.

"Right. Laura. Sorry."

An unfamiliar male voice said something she could not make out.

The woman responded, "Is such a large dose necessary? Yes, yes, I know you're the doctor, but . . ."

Later, Laura heard a voice she did recognize. Alexander, suggesting something.

"You're right," the elderly woman replied. "Fresh air will do her good." Laura was conscious of being lifted and carried.

"Put me down," she mumbled, embarrassed at her weakness.

She was settled gently onto a chaise longue. Warm sun shone on her skin and fresh sea air filled her lungs, yet her stupor remained. Her eyelids felt unnaturally heavy, as if weighted. *What is wrong with me?*

"Go about your business, sir," the woman said. "I shall sit with her."

Laura felt a mixture of relief, confusion, and dismay that Alexander was still with her. Was there not somewhere he needed to be, something important he needed to do? What was it? Her brain refused to conjure the answer.

Laura felt a squeeze to her hand, smelled

a whiff of spicy shaving soap, and then he was gone.

She wasn't sure of the name of her nurse but was vaguely aware she was sitting in someone's small front garden, its stone walls protecting her from the wind. The sound of gulls told her the sea was nearby.

Time passed. Laura slept, stirred, slept some more, dreams and reality muddled together.

From beside her, the nurse said, "A cup of tea, I think. You rest here, and I shall return presently." She stood and laid yet another blanket over her.

Laura heard soft padding footsteps and a door quietly opening and closing. She was left in solitary peace.

Then a different sound penetrated her mind. Not the door, but a creaking hinge. The garden gate?

Another set of footsteps approached, this time on paving stones.

Laura turned her head and, with effort, opened her eyelids. The blurriness had lessened, but the sunlight hurt her eyes. She closed them again, save for the narrowest slit. Through the haze and her lashes, she saw a feminine figure. A woman in a long green cape closed the garden gate behind her. She had a halo of red hair—the color faded by sunlight or age. Her profile and the small spectacles she wore seemed familiar.

The woman turned toward her, and Laura's hand flew to her chest.

It was her mother, back from the dead.

Was she still dreaming? Yet she felt jolted awake. If her mother were alive, she would surely not have let all these years pass without sending word.

I must be hallucinating. She had heard that fevers could give people strange fancies. Just what had that doctor given her?

Or . . . another explanation seized her heart.

Had she died? Died and gone to heaven— and just as many predicted, her loved ones were there on that beautiful shore to meet her. At least . . . one loved one.

Laura felt twin waves of emotion wash over her. Yes, she was relieved to find herself in paradise, especially considering her recent untruths. She remembered Uncle Matthew describing God as merciful, assuring her that her sins would be forgiven if she confessed them, and for that she was grateful.

Yet, she was sad too. She wasn't ready to leave her world behind, to leave Alexander behind. He might blame himself for her illness, and he must not. It was not his fault. She had chosen this course and would choose it again.

The elderly nurse returned with the tea. She exclaimed, "Oh, you're back!" Turning to Laura, she asked, "Sara—I mean, Laura— can you hear me?"

Shock pinned her tongue to the roof of her mouth, leaving her unable to speak.

The older woman directed her next comment to the apparition. "The fever elixir Dr. Braun gave her contains a great deal of laudanum. A dose meant for a soldier or sailor, not a petite young woman. It's no wonder she's out of her senses. I'm not going to give her any more. Don't tell him when he comes back."

She gently touched Laura's arm and repeated, "Miss Callaway? Can you hear me?"

Laura slowly turned her head to get her first clear look at her nurse, a kindly looking woman of at least sixty, her fair hair streaked with silver.

The nurse smiled at Laura. "There is someone here most anxious to meet you."

Would the vision still be there? Laura turned her head the other way. Yes, still there—with a face blessedly familiar.

Laura's throat constricted and her eyes

418

heated. She felt stunned, elated, and betrayed all at once.

"Mamma?"

The brown eyes looking back at her filled with tears. She slowly shook her head, the movement sending glistening streaks down fair cheeks. "No, my dear. Your aunt Susan."

Laura blinked. "But you died too."

"No, I did not. I should have. But your father was the best physician I ever knew. I don't know why he succumbed to the illness I survived, but he did. Your mother as well. It was so unfair. I've felt terribly guilty all these years."

Laura stared at her, taking in her words and her appearance, trying to make sense of both. She had not seen her aunt Susan in many years, but she didn't remember her looking quite so identical to her mother, who had worn spectacles and been plumper than her thin sister. And had her aunt's hair not been darker? Or had Laura's memory of her mother faded so much over the years, that now her sister seemed her spit and image?

She murmured, "You look . . . different. Your hair . . . ?"

Her aunt nodded. "I hated having red hair when I was young, so my maid used to darken it with a boiled walnut solution. Foolish, I realize, especially now that I see how beautiful your hair is."

"You never wore glasses before."

"That's age, my dear. My eyes are not what they once were." She patted her plump abdomen with a self-conscious smile. "Nor the rest of me."

Laura slowly shook her head. "You look so much like her." Or so much as Laura remembered her, at any rate.

"I take that as a sincere compliment, though it's not surprising. We were twins after all, and so close. Not a day goes by I don't miss her."

Laura's heart ached. "Me too."

Her aunt squeezed her hand, and a few more tears escaped.

"Will you show me where they are buried?" Laura asked.

"Certainly—when you are more fully recovered. You are still quite weak."

Laura turned to the older woman, who watched the reunion with misty eyes of her own. "Did you know my mother? Is that why you called me Sara?"

The nurse nodded. "Yes. I was at the harbour buying fish when you collapsed. You resemble her a great deal. I thought I was seeing a ghost."

Laura smiled softly. "I know exactly what you mean."

"Mrs. Tobin insisted your friend bring you here so she could care for you," Aunt Susan explained. "She also devotedly nursed your mother throughout her illness."

The woman's chin trembled. "I only wish we could have saved her. Saved them both."

Laura reached for her hand. "Thank you for trying."

The wind picked up, and Mrs. Tobin insisted her patient move inside. So the women helped Laura to her feet and settled her in a snug parlour. Laura and her aunt sat near each other, Susan in a padded chair and Laura on the sofa. Mrs. Tobin discreetly left them to talk, only coming in to pour tea and offer sandwiches.

Laura sipped her tea, the questions she longed to ask lodged in her throat. Instead, she asked, "Do you live nearby?"

"I live here with Mrs. Tobin," Susan explained, "and have ever since my husband's death. I have been here all the while."

"Have you? I did not realize."

"I was getting over a cold when you arrived a few days ago, so I kept my distance. You were out of your senses from the fever, and the laudanum only made it worse. I was afraid you would not recover and I wouldn't have a chance to"—her voice hitched—"explain."

Laura swallowed hard and asked, "Why did you never contact me?"

Pain pinched the older woman's features. "I did try, my dear. Please remember that I was seriously ill at the time and barely survived. And when I did begin to recover physically, I was overwhelmed with grief—grief over the deaths of my husband, beloved sister, and your father as well. I was laid low in a deep melancholy for a long while, unable to rouse myself even from bed. I had no interest in living, almost wishing I had died with the others.

"Then I remembered you. My sister's daughter. I wrote to your parents' home address, but the house had been sold, and the new owners could provide no information about your whereabouts.

"I went through your mother's letters and found the name of the girls' seminary in one of them. I wrote to the school, and the matron wrote back with Mr. and Mrs. Bray's direction in Oxford. But that letter was returned as undeliverable. Apparently, they had moved away.

"I also wrote to your father's young partner and, through him, learned the name of your parents' solicitor. He helped me track down an address for your aunt and uncle in Truro, but I never received a reply to that letter either. I began to think that perhaps you did not wish to be in contact with me. Or that the Brays did not wish it for some reason."

Aunt Susan shook her head. "Had my husband lived, I might have been successful in discovering your whereabouts. But his connections to Britain, his access to official channels, died with him. And you must remember that France and England have been at war for years. It wasn't exactly easy to convince anyone to spend time on what seemed to them a trivial domestic matter. I am ashamed to say I gave it up, figuring you were better off with your aunt Anne than with me, a guilty shell of a woman living in far-off Jersey."

"Aunt Anne died in childbirth, not long after I went to live with them," Laura said. "Uncle Matthew was a broken man as well. But eventually he rallied and married again. Through his second wife, he came into a living in the north of Cornwall."

"Where?"

"St. Minver is the name of the parish. Near Padstow."

"No wonder my letters went unanswered."

Laura nodded. "Matthew Bray wrote to Uncle Hilgrove via the garrison, but the letter was returned, marked *Deceased*."

Aunt Susan winced at the word. "Yes. I was convalescing here with Mrs. Tobin by then. Eventually, the new garrison commander moved into our former house. I was ill for so long, and my fate so uncertain, that I became a forgotten woman."

"I am sorry."

Susan rose and restlessly paced the room. "You have nothing to be sorry for. I should have tried harder, not given up. Will you forgive me?"

Laura looked up at her and saw not only her mother's sister but also her mother herself, looking at her with pleading brown eyes so like her own, asking for forgiveness for leaving her. For losing her.

"Yes, of course I forgive you," Laura said, thinking, *I forgive you both.*

Alexander walked through the *Havre des Pas* neighborhood, thinking about Laura. He knew he would soon have to leave her to go to France, and he was resolved to go alone. With his and his family's futures so uncertain, he was in no position to do otherwise. But in the meantime, he prayed for her full recovery.

Here and there small streams ran across the street—water from the surrounding hills finding its way to the sea after recent rains.

He made use of the planks left by helpful residents to cross over them without getting wet. The town had clearly grown in the years since he'd spent his summers there. Many new houses and streets had been built, while some of the old streets had been widened and the names changed from French to English. He reached a narrow street only eight feet wide he thought he remembered as *Rue des Trois Pigeons*, but the sign read *Hill Street*. He'd found the original street name amusing as a boy and did not think the change an improvement.

In the distance, above the rooftops, he glimpsed a castellated church tower he recognized, probably the very church his grandparents had attended. He decided to make his way to it and find his grandparents' former home from there.

Before he could, an aroma caught his nose. A delicious, familiar aroma. And on its scent, he was transported to the happy days of his childhood, when his grandmother would take him to the local *pâtisserie* for his choice of *vraic* buns or deep-fried twists of dough called *mèrvelles*.

He walked on. In his boyhood, the north side of King Street had looked out over green fields; now more houses and businesses filled the once-open space. He turned the corner, passed an ironmonger's, a greengrocer's, a hat shop, and a newsagent's, and then—there it was. *Egre Bakers & Confectioners.* The bow windows gleamed, the displays of honey-brown bread loaves, cakes, and every good thing drew him to the familiar doors. He smelled warm yeasty bread, cardamom, and *chocolat*, and could almost feel his grandmother's hand holding his.

He entered the establishment with a sense of stepping back in time. The man behind the counter greeted him and asked how he could help.

"I came here regularly as a boy. It's one place that seems blessedly much the same."

Alexander ended up buying several *vraic* buns dotted with raisins, and half a dozen golden-brown *mèrvelles*, still warm. He would share them with Laura and her aunt, he decided. If he resisted eating them all himself.

He then asked the man if he might direct him to *Rue des Vignes.*

"You mean Vine Street? Certainly . . ."

Following the man's directions, Alex turned onto a lane of vine-covered houses. There he saw it, surrounded by other houses, when it had at one time enjoyed sprawling lawns on two sides.

It seemed smaller than he remembered.

The wrought-iron gates less high. But he recognized it, even so.

He stood at that gate and selected a pastry from the bag, lifting it to his grandmother in a toast of sorts and then savoring every bite.

Eventually, he walked back to the harbour and relished the sight of all those ships moored there, recalling his first long-ago glimpse of the *Victorine*.

He noticed an older man in a tweed coat and slouch hat, watching him with friendly interest. When Alex looked over, the man asked, "Are you admiring the ships or daydreaming?"

"Both, actually. I especially admire that brig, there."

The man's broad shoulders straightened, and his chest seemed to expand. "You have a good eye, sir, for that is my own ship."

"Is it? You must be proud indeed."

"I am. Just back from several weeks at sea." The man nodded toward Alex's parcel. "And I see you also have a good eye for bakeries."

"Yes. In truth, I have been enjoying a little stroll into the past. My grandmother used to take me to Egre's bakery. Here, help yourself." He extended the grease-stained brown paper bag.

The bushy eyebrows rose. "That is prodigious generous of you. Ah, Jersey wonders. You must be a local lad, then?"

Alex shrugged. "I spent summers here as a boy. Take two. My eyes were bigger than my stomach."

The older man patted his rounded abdomen. "That is not a problem for me, as you see." He took a big bite. "Delicious."

"I agree."

The man chewed, then said, "Your accent . . . Do my ears mistake me, or do I recognize something of the French . . . perhaps Normandy?"

Alex reared back his head in surprise. "Close. Brittany. You have very skilled ears, sir, for although I have not been home in a few years, my honored father lives near Quimper."

The man nodded. "I have been there. Beautiful country. Though Camaret-sur-Mer is my favorite."

"Camaret-sur-Mer! We used to take holidays to the seashore there in my childhood. You have refined taste as well as hearing, I see."

The man wiped crumbs from his mouth with the back of his hand. "I have spent a great deal of time in France and learned to hear the differences. I've grown quite fond of the country. In fact, I had thought that when this blasted war is over, I might live there.

But, well, Jersey has a . . . certain beauty . . . that keeps me here."

Alexander watched the older man's face and guessed, "And does this 'certain beauty' have a name?"

"Ah, you are too clever for me, my friend."

"I came to Jersey with a beauty of my own."

"Oh? Perhaps I know this lady. St. Helier is not such a big town. Bigger than it once was, yes, but still not such a metropolis that one does not know his neighbors."

"Miss Callaway is niece to Mrs. Hilgrove," Alex explained. "She lives with a local nurse, Mrs. Tobin."

"Susan Hilgrove . . . That is . . . Mrs. Hilgrove, yes. A . . . gracious lady."

"You are well acquainted?"

"Not as well as I should like, but I shall say no more. Not gentlemanlike, I reckon, to talk about a lady. Her niece, you say? I did not know she had a niece coming to visit."

"I think it's fair to say our arrival was most unexpected."

"Well, I shall have to pay a call and learn all about it." A flash of eagerness shone in the man's eyes.

"Then, perhaps I shall see you again."

"I hope so." The older man extended a strong, rough hand. "Bert Gillan."

Alex took it. "Alexander Carnell . . . That is, Captain Carnell."

Again the bushy eyebrows rose. "Captain, is it? Well, well. I won't ask which side. I am neutral, after all, since I do business with both France and England."

"Glad to hear it."

"Staying with Mrs. Hilgrove, are you?" the man asked wistfully.

"No, I've taken a room at La Folie." Alex pointed to the small inn tucked away in a sheltered corner of the harbour.

The man glanced at it and nodded. "Lot of character in that old place. And a lot of characters frequent it too. It's a favorite with sailors, pilots, dockers, and the like. Local fishermen sell their catch right outside its doors."

Yes, Alexander had seen and smelled the mounds of fish and hoped he didn't carry the smell with him when he visited Miss Callaway.

Alex turned to take his leave, saying in parting, "May I mention to Mrs. Hilgrove that I met you?"

"Yes, and put in a good word for me while you're at it, ey?"

Alexander grinned. "Indeed I shall."

Her aunt insisted Laura rest, but later that evening, after a nap and a good dinner, the two sat together once more. Mrs. Tobin joined them.

Laura asked about Captain Carnell.

"We have not seen him since this morning," Mrs. Tobin said. "He walked off in the direction of the harbour."

He was looking for a ship to take him to France, Laura guessed, her heart aching at the thought. It was only a matter of time until he sailed away from her. As her parents had . . .

Turning to her aunt, Laura began, "When Mamma and Papa left me to the fickle mercies of an English boarding school, I felt abandoned, like an inconvenience sent off so that they could travel without impediment. Then again, I was an irritable adolescent."

The two shared knowing looks at that.

"I received no letters from them, and assumed they had forgotten all about me as they enjoyed the delights of their new island home."

Mrs. Tobin shook her head. "They did not forget about you, my dear. I can vouch for that." The nurse handed her something. "Your mother wore this almost continually."

Laura accepted the locket and stared

down at the golden oval. She'd all but forgotten about it. Opening it, she saw the miniature portraits within—her father, and herself as a girl.

"She loved you both very much," the nurse said. "She clutched that to her heart as she drew her final breaths."

Tears burned Laura's eyes. She had misjudged her mother. *I am sorry, Mamma,* she whispered in her heart. *Please forgive me.*

"Your mother wrote you a final letter," Aunt Susan added. "I planned to forward it, once I had located your direction, but as I never did . . . well . . . I still have it."

She retrieved the letter and handed it to Laura. Then the women left her to read in private. She recognized her mother's handwriting, but the words were shaky, and hard to read at times.

My dearest Laura,

I am afraid our trip to Jersey did not turn out as we had hoped. I know you resented being left behind. But in hindsight I cannot regret leaving you in England, for you have escaped this illness that has claimed so many.

I am sorry to tell you that your dear papa died four days ago. He was too weak during his final days to leave his bed, but before that he was tireless in visiting the sick here and doing all he could to relieve their suffering. This fever, whatever it is, has swept through the barracks and much of St. Helier.

I had hoped to be spared. I thought God would surely not take us both. Not leave you orphaned.

I was wrong.

I am so sorry, my darling daughter. I had hoped to watch you grow up. To guide you a little and love you a lot along the way. Apparently that is not to be. My own sister is gravely ill as well, but I trust your father's sister—your aunt Anne— will fill my shoes and become a second mother to you. I hope you will allow her to love you and care for you as I am sure she will be eager to do.

You have always had a strong will and strong mind, Laura Callaway. And though it saddens me to send you into adulthood alone, I know that you will live a good and God-honoring life that would make me, your father, and your heavenly Father proud.

Life may disappoint you. Friends may desert you. But God is faithful. Stay close to Him, and you won't stray far from the right path.

I am praying for you even now, my dearest, and I will always love you.

Mamma

Tears overflowed, streaking her cheeks and cleansing the final traces of resentment from her heart.

One of our most familiar little waders, especially on rocky, seaweed-covered shores at all times of the year, is the Turnstone. But it has never nested here, despite claims to the contrary.

—R. D. Penhallurick, *Birds of Cornwall*

Chapter 21

The following days passed in quiet, comfortable routine. The women took meals together, and talked while they sewed or read in the evenings. Mrs. Tobin regularly went out to visit ailing elderly people in the town and did what she could for them. Both women were active in charity work, but now that Laura had come, Aunt Susan stayed home with her so she would not be left alone.

They had not seen Alexander in a few days, and Laura began to fear he had left the island without saying good-bye.

That afternoon, Mrs. Tobin came into

the parlour, eyes alight. "A gentleman to see you, my dear. Do you feel equal to a visitor?"

Anticipation tingled through Laura's chest at the thought of seeing Captain Carnell again. "Indeed I do."

She rose, smoothing back her hair and then her bodice, pausing to press a palm to her pounding heart. *Be calm.*

But the handsome gentleman who strode into the room, hat in hand, was not the man she'd expected.

"Treeve! What a surprise."

His lips pursed in an uncertain grin, and he twisted the hat brim. "Not an . . . unhappy surprise, I hope?"

She had rarely seen him look less confident. "No, of course not. I have been wondering how you fared after we parted, what, nearly a week ago?"

"Ten days."

"Really? I'm afraid I have been ill, so my awareness of time passing has been unclear."

"Ill?" His golden eyebrows rose, and he looked sincerely concerned.

"Never fear. I am well on my way to a full recovery."

"I am glad to hear it. Do sit down. Don't stand on my account."

"Very well." She reclaimed her seat and gestured to the one near it.

He sat in the low chair, his knees high, his long legs looking decidedly coltish.

"And I am glad to see you have not been arrested," Laura said. "What happened with the revenue cutter?"

"They never searched that cove, thankfully. To be safe, however, we hid our tools of the trade in a nearby field, most of which the locals carried off. It will be costly to replace them."

"Then, perhaps you should not. Perhaps this is a sign to you. A chance to choose a new path."

He looked down, again twisting his hat brim in restless fingers.

She changed tack. "How did you find me?"

"Was not difficult. I knew you were coming to St. Helier, so I asked around the harbour until I found someone who had seen you or Captain Carnell. A ship owner who'd met the captain directed me here."

"It was kind of you to seek me out."

He shrugged. "I wanted to assure myself you had made it to Jersey as you'd intended. I still feel terrible I was unable to deliver you myself."

Was that the only reason he had come? Laura wondered. Or in hopes of something else?

"There is no need to feel bad."

"It is a relief to find you safe and whole and . . . in at least reasonably good health. I would have come sooner, but the men and I decided it would be wise to wait for a time before we made another attempt to cross the Channel." Treeve glanced around the small parlour. "Is . . . the good captain not with you?"

Laura hesitated, for in truth she did not know where he was. "He was here in St. Helier, but we have not seen him in a few days."

Treeve, she noticed, watched her carefully. Laura hoped her expression did not reveal her disappointment. She added more brightly, "I imagine he is busy trying to find a ship to take him to France."

Treeve winced apologetically. "I'm afraid I can't volunteer for that duty. Our narrow escape had a sobering effect on us all. I believe Dyer would mutiny if I suggested he sail into enemy waters, and I would not blame him."

"Nor I," Laura agreed. "After all, he has a family at home. As do you, Treeve—don't forget."

"But Dyer has a wife, and I do not." He shifted uneasily in his chair. "Had I a wife encouraging me to get out of smuggling as Dyer has, it might be easier to do so."

Laura slowly shook her head. "Don't

change for a woman, Treeve. Change because it's the right thing to do. To live inside the law and your God-given conscience. I know you said your family is facing financial hardships, but imagine the far worse hardship and heartache if their eldest son and heir were to be imprisoned."

Again he looked at the floor, and regret stabbed Laura. "Forgive me. I did not intend to speak harshly or to judge your actions. It is not my place."

He looked up at her through blond lashes. "It could be."

"Oh, Treeve." Laura's heart thumped and her stomach knotted. "Thank you. I am flattered truly, but you and I are not suited. Besides, I could not bear the thought of my home and livelihood being supported by ill-gotten gain. To worry every time my husband sailed away that he would be arrested." She shook her head and attempted a teasing tone. "Once an up-country lass, always an up-country lass, I suppose."

She leaned forward. "But there is a woman worthy of your admiration and respect who knows what you are involved in and cares for you deeply even so. She too might demand you stop, but she would happily marry you. You have been fortunate indeed to win Miss Roskilly's regard. I hope you will be mature enough not to disdain her for the flaw of admiring you. I daresay if I had flirted with you as devotedly as she or Eseld had, you would disdain me too."

He managed a dry chuckle. "Sadly true. Aware of my faults as I am, I can't respect any woman who admires me."

She studied his vulnerable expression. "You have always seemed so confident, but I have wondered if that was truly the case. It's nothing to be ashamed of. We all lack assurance in some areas, and we all have flaws."

"And what possible flaws have you, Miss Callaway?"

"Many. I have been proud. I have stood in judgment of my neighbors because their ways seemed foreign and wrong to me. I have felt superior to them, and at the same time, unworthy of their acceptance. I have been unforgiving and resentful. Oh, and let's not forget my red hair."

A shadow of a grin flickered over his lips. "And is Carnell aware of these so-called flaws of yours? He clearly admires you anyway."

"I believe he is aware of my faults, yes. As to the extent of his admiration, that remains to be seen."

"Shall I wait until the future is decided between you? Or is there no hope for me?"

Laura considered. It was tempting to

leave this door open. A sure way to return to Cornwall and visit Uncle Matthew. But no, it wouldn't be right. Nor fair. Not to Treeve, and not to Kayna Roskilly.

She slowly shook her head. "We shall always be friends, Treeve. And I shall always care about you. But don't wait. Go home to your family, and to Miss Roskilly."

He rose. "I thought you'd say that. Still, I had to try. Once more for old times' sake."

She rose as well. "I sincerely appreciate your visit. Please do greet my uncle and Eseld for me, won't you?" Her voice cracked. "And Perry, and Miss Chegwin, and . . . Well, I don't suppose you often socialize with Mary Chegwin, but—"

He raised a staying palm, accompanied by a brave smile. "I will happily pass along your greetings to all who love and miss you. I include myself in that number."

He took her hand and raised it to his lips. "Good-bye, little turnstone."

Laura blinked back tears, her throat burning. "Good-bye, Treeve Kent."

The sound of footsteps penetrated the poignant moment. At the creaking of the door, Laura turned. There stood Captain Carnell. He stopped abruptly in the threshold, expression inscrutable as he looked from Laura to her visitor.

Laura extracted her hand from Treeve's. "Look who has come to visit!"

Treeve Kent's bravado reasserted itself, and he straightened to his full lanky height. Hand to heart, he said in gallant tones, "I could not rest until I assured myself all was well with Miss Callaway. And with you too, of course."

A wary light shone in Alexander's eyes. "I did not realize you planned to visit, Mr. Kent."

"Nor I," Laura added. "I was stunned but relieved to see him well and free. I worried he might have landed in a spot of trouble after trying to help us."

"I worried about that too," Alexander said. "Though I imagine Mr. Kent is too charming and too well connected to face any serious consequences."

"Your confidence in me is heartening, Captain. But I would not have been the first gentleman to face legal consequences for smuggling."

"Is that why you are here? To free trade?" Alex asked. "Or simply to see Miss Callaway?"

"Both. We hope for one more profitable haul to cover our expenses and help see us all through the long winter ahead. After that, Dyer is out. I can't speak for the others."

"And you?"

"I have not yet decided."

"In the meantime, do be careful," Laura said earnestly. She touched Treeve's arm, immediately drawing both men's gazes. Noticing, she quickly removed her hand.

"I shall be. Thank you. Well, I had better take my leave." He bowed. "A pleasure to see you both again."

"And you," Laura said. "Godspeed."

Laura and Alexander stood there awkwardly as Treeve's footfalls faded down the corridor and the sound of a closing door echoed through the house.

"Well, that was a surprise," she said.

"Agreed, but perhaps it should not have been. The man obviously cares for you."

Laura shifted uneasily. "Well, we are friends, after all."

He studied her face. "How are you feeling?"

About seeing Treeve again or physically? she wondered, and chose to respond to the latter. "So much better. Still a little weak and I tire easily, but overall, I am remarkably well."

"I am glad to hear it. You gave me a scare."

"And what have you been doing? I have not seen you in days."

"I did not wish to intrude on your reunion with your aunt. And along with seeking a ship, I searched for my grandparents' former house. Turns out, it's not far from here."

"I would like to see it."

"I . . . could give you the direction, but I may not be here long enough to show you. I have found a merchant who might be willing to take me to France on one of his ships."

"Oh. Well . . . Well done." She forced a smile.

He did not ask her to join him, she noticed. Alexander had a family, after all—a father, brother, sister-in-law, and nephew—who, she guessed, would rejoice at his return despite past arguments. She did not belong at a Carnell family reunion. Besides, she had made it to Jersey, which had been her goal.

She began, "I would like to see you returned home, but—"

He held up his hand. "I know. You have just found your aunt again and are reluctant to leave her."

"True," she allowed. Nor would she beg to go along.

Aunt Susan entered, and Laura turned to include her in the conversation. "Have you met my aunt, Susan Hilgrove?"

"I have, yes. A pleasure to see you again, madam."

"And I you, Captain. Thank you, again, for bringing my niece to me."

"In truth, she brought me."

"Well, however you got here, thank you. I know you have done your best to take care of her and see to her safety."

He winced. "I regret the journey stole so much of her strength."

"Do not blame yourself," Laura said. "It was my choice, and I am growing stronger every day."

"And what will you do now, Captain Carnell?" Aunt Susan asked.

"I hope to sail to Brittany as soon as may be. A Mr. Gillan has offered to take me on one of his ships. Regularly trades there, apparently. He also mentioned being acquainted with you."

A surprising blush rose to her aunt's cheeks. "Yes, a charming man, if a bit . . . eccentric."

Alexander nodded. "My impression as well."

"And when you reach Brittany?"

"I shall visit my father, and my brother in prison, and see what I might do to help secure his release."

"In prison . . . why?"

Shame colored his features. "He has been charged with treason for spying. I hope to prove another man was the informant officials tracked to our village."

Laura knew he referred to François La-Roche. Might he manage to escape the militia and return to Jersey?

"Spying for the British?" Aunt Susan asked.

"Perhaps."

"Then you ought to speak to Admiral d'Auvergne."

Wariness washed over Laura. That was the man LaRoche had worked for.

The captain's brows rose in surprise. "Are you acquainted with him?"

Susan nodded. "My husband was. He might call here at my invitation, if and when his duties allow."

Alexander made a wry face. "He might also arrest me."

"True," her aunt allowed, studying him. "Shall I inquire?"

Alexander nodded decisively. "Yes, please do."

The women invited Mr. Gillan and Alexander for dinner the next night. They all helped prepare the meal, as Aunt Susan and Mrs. Tobin had no official cook—only the assistance of a young maid-of-all-work, who was not clever in the kitchen.

Their menu consisted of a rich conger

soup, fish with a savory sauce, potatoes, and *bourdelots aux pommes*—apples baked in pastry.

At the appointed hour, Mr. Gillan arrived bearing a pot of boiled ormers, while Alexander brought flowers for their hostesses.

When they had all taken their places, Aunt Susan rose somewhat shyly and said, "I believe some sort of toast is in order. I feel rather like the woman in Scripture who lost one precious coin, and when she found it again, called her friends and neighbors together, saying, 'Rejoice with me, for I have found the treasure I had lost.'" She raised her glass to her niece, tears sparkling in her eyes. "To Laura."

"To Laura," the others echoed, glasses high.

Laura's heart squeezed with poignant pleasure.

"Now, let us eat, and be merry," Susan added.

"Hear, hear," Mr. Gillan agreed, beaming at her.

Her aunt sat back down, clearly feeling self-conscious but pleased too.

The meal began, and after several minutes of general conversation, Laura decided Mr. Gillan was a pleasant man. He had thick, bristly dark hair streaked with silver, and bushy side-whiskers, weathered skin, and jolly blue eyes. He was not tall, only an inch or so above Aunt Susan's height, but he seemed larger, with his broad shoulders, stout stature, and vibrant personality.

He was a bit loud and coarse, but only from lack of breeding, Laura thought, not from any smallness or meanness of character. On the contrary, he seemed kind and noble hearted. His table manners were not all they might be, but considering he usually ate alone or in the company of rough sailors, she did not hold it against him.

And most telling of all, he was clearly besotted with Susan Hilgrove, which spoke well of his character and discernment.

His gaze lingered on her many times during the meal, and he was quick to offer her seconds and to refill her glass.

"You are too thin, my dear lady. A strong wind would blow you right off the deck." And "Here, have some more ormers. Gathered these from the rocks myself. Delicious."

Mrs. Tobin spoke up. "Enjoy ormering, do you?"

"Indeed I do. Enjoy eating them even more." He patted his straining waistcoat buttons. "And I cooked these long and slow for you."

"In fish stock?"

"What else?"

Susan politely ate another of the boiled snail-like creatures. Laura could only be glad the man was not besotted with *her*.

As if guessing her thoughts, Alexander turned to her, a teasing light in his eyes. "Another for you as well, Miss Callaway?"

"No, thank you. I could not eat another bite."

Laura had come to enjoy many Jersey specialties—bean crock, sweet cakes, lobster, crab, and more—but was still not fond of mollusks.

As they ate, the men talked companionably of their seafaring experiences, and it pleased Laura to see them getting along so well.

After dessert, Aunt Susan rose again. "Shall we leave you two to cigars and port?"

Standing abruptly, Mr. Gillan said, "Not on my account, I beg you. Please stay, ladies. That is, if that meets with your approval, Captain."

"Indeed it does," Alexander agreed.

So together they lingered over tea, coffee, and genial conversation for another hour. Mr. Gillan insisted Alexander give up his room at the inn and stay with him instead, saying, "Any friend of Mrs. Hilgrove is a friend of mine, and we men need to stick together. I've bought myself a fine little house not far from here. Not that I'm on dry land often enough to truly get my money's worth, but I hope, someday, to settle down and have a real home."

His gaze strayed to Susan at the words, then returned to Alex once more. "I would be honored to have you as my guest."

"Thank you, sir. I accept," Alexander said. "Though I shan't be here much longer."

Laura watched him as he said it, but he didn't look her way.

The next day, Laura again rested in the protected garden, her shawl tucked around herself, a blanket on her lap. It was warmer in Jersey than in England, and she enjoyed the mild late-autumn sunshine and sea breezes. She was feeling almost like her old self, with a clear mind, though she still tired more easily than before.

Aunt Susan and Mrs. Tobin were busy in the kitchen, and Alexander was with Mr. Gillan, finalizing arrangements for their departure.

Portly Dr. Braun came out to see her again, carrying a bottle of his prized fever elixir. "How are you this morning, Miss Callaway?"

"I am well, Dr. Braun, thank you."

"Have you had your dose of medicine yet today?"

"Um . . . not yet. I don't think I need it any longer. I—"

"It's important to continue the regimen for a full fortnight. Here, allow me." He poured a generous dose into her cup of tea. "I shall leave the bottle with Mrs. Tobin and remind her to be more punctual in administering it."

She managed a wan smile and dutifully picked up the teacup as the man returned to the house. As soon as the door closed behind him, however, she set the cup back down, planning to dump it out at an opportune moment.

Laura had just drifted off to sleep when the now-familiar creak of the garden gate woke her from her doze.

She opened her eyes, expecting to see Mr. Gillan or Alexander, but her anticipatory smile fell away.

François LaRoche.

"Well, well. Miss Callaway. We meet again." He gave her a sly smile, and alarm bells sounded in her brain.

"Monsieur LaRoche." Laura swallowed and sat up straighter. "What are you doing here?"

He sauntered nearer, Laura's heart rate accelerating with each step.

"I have been to Jersey on several occasions in the past, though not in some time. I am here to renew old acquaintances."

"Captain Carnell is not here," she said, both relieved and grieved that Alexander was absent.

"Not now, perhaps, but as you are here, I know he cannot be far away, any more than a bee can resist the fair flower."

His words might have been flattering from anyone else, but coming from him, it sounded suggestive and insulting. Should she call for help, and end up endangering her aunt and Mrs. Tobin in the process? She told herself to remain calm. To think.

Last she'd seen LaRoche, he was being held by the militia. She licked dry lips and said, "May I ask how you came to be here?"

"The usual way. By ship. Your friend Tom Parsons was happy to oblige. Always eager for an excuse to trade on the Channel Islands. I would have arrived sooner, but it took time to extricate myself from the *stupide* authorities."

"They let you go?"

He smirked. "Parsons is a persuasive man."

Without invitation, he sat down beside her. She noticed him eye the tea tray on the table.

"May I offer you some refreshment, *monsieur*? You must be hungry and thirsty after your journey."

"Pretending to be polite, are we?" He shrugged. *"Eh bien.* Don't mind if I do."

He wolfed down a biscuit, and she slid the untouched cup closer to him. "Help yourself."

He ate another biscuit and drained the tea, then said, "I also hoped to see my old friend Philippe d'Auvergne. With his connections, he could arrange a new passport for me and enough money to start a new life. I am owed some reward for the hardships I've suffered while his informant—inconvenience, imprisonment, shipwreck . . ."

Mrs. Tobin, likely spotting a strange man with her young guest, flew outside like a protective mother hen, apron stained and meat mallet in hand. Aunt Susan stepped out behind her.

"Who is this, Laura?" the nurse asked.

"Monsieur LaRoche. He was shipwrecked with Alexander."

Would they remember what Laura had told them about the man?

The women stilled. "And what brings you to Jersey, *monsieur*?" Aunt Susan asked.

"Came to see my old friends, including Philippe d'Auvergne. You know him?"

"Everyone on Jersey knows him. He has recently been promoted again. Vice admiral of the white. He divides his time between here, London, and the sea."

"How nice for him," LaRoche said dryly. "Perhaps that explains why I was told he was busy when I went to see him. Too important now for those who risked their lives for him. At least his aide told me where I might find Miss Callaway."

Her aunt must have mentioned her when she wrote to invite d'Auvergne to call. If only she had not . . .

At that moment, Alexander strolled through the gate. He drew up short, and his face stiffened. "François."

Laura's stomach dropped. *Dear God, help us.*

François remained slouched in the chair near Laura. *"Bonjour,* old friend."

Alexander's nostrils flared. "We are friends no longer."

"Is that any way to greet me? The man with a pistol pointed at the woman you love?"

Laura sucked in a breath and glanced over. LaRoche held a gun at his waist.

Alex stopped where he was. "Leave her alone. She has done nothing."

"You call rescuing you, nothing? Hiding you, helping you escape, nothing?"

"Nothing to you."

"There you are wrong. For I want to see you destroyed."

"Why?"

"You know why, and her name was Enora."

Alexander spoke in a surprisingly calm voice. "I truly believed you were not coming back."

"You believed what you wished to believe. First you break Léonie's heart, then mine."

"Léonie? What has she to do with this?"

"She expected you to marry her. We all did. But instead you stole my Enora." He gave a dismissive wave with his free hand. "No matter. I stole her back."

A muscle in Alexander's jaw pulsed, yet he held himself in check. "Then you have had your revenge."

"And that is not all I did to you," François went on. "Shall I tell you more before I shoot you?"

Heart beating hard, Laura noticed Alexander's eyes dart from side to side. Searching for a way to evade LaRoche's gun, she guessed.

"Yes, tell me," Alex urged, drawing him out. Stalling. "I know you felt betrayed when we married, but it was *you* Enora loved. You who fathered her child. Why do you still wish to destroy me?"

François pointed an accusing finger. "Because you grew up with everything I wanted and deserved, simply because of the family you were born into. Wealth, education, influence . . ."

He leaned forward. "Do you know, I even reported your father as a *Royaliste* sympathizer, but because you were serving Napoleon, he was spared. So I set out to destroy you another way." He sat back rather heavily against the chair.

Alexander's nostrils flared. "Are you talking about Alan?"

"Al*an*." François stressed the second syllable in the French pronunciation. "So earnest. So idealistic. So easy to persuade."

"You recruited him to spite me."

François raised an unconcerned shoulder. "I simply convinced him that helping the British foil Napoleon would help the *Royalistes*."

Alex gritted his teeth. "Alan was arrested. But you escaped—what is the English saying—scot-free."

François smirked again. "I am too cunning to be caught."

"Cunning?" another voice interrupted. "Is that what you call it?"

François lurched to his feet, and Alexander whirled about in surprise.

An impressive-looking older man in British naval uniform strode into the garden, hat under one arm, grey hair tied back and neatly trimmed at the brow.

Laura noticed two soldiers just beyond the garden gate, but LaRoche seemed to have eyes only for the man she assumed to be d'Auvergne.

He stood as though at attention. "Vice Admiral, sir!"

The older man bowed toward the ladies. "Pray forgive the intrusion. Shall I tell you how Monsieur LaRoche escaped, when my other agents were arrested?"

The women nodded. Alex, Laura noticed, kept his eye on François's gun as he tucked it away.

"LaRoche was one of my couriers. He and several others traveled from here to France for me many times, gathering information, which I then sent to London. On that fateful last journey, however, the men found all the usual safe havens closed to them. They spent a number of weeks traveling around Brittany and living rough, but after several failed attempts to sneak back to Jersey, LaRoche turned himself in to the French. He then led the secret police to his companions. He gave up every detail he knew about our correspondence, including landing places, hiding places, and codes. In return, they let him go while the others were imprisoned."

"That is not true, sir," François said, his smirk fading. "I told you when I made my way back to Jersey, it was Prigent who informed. I managed to hide in a ditch and later escape."

"I believed you at the time. But since then I've had reason to revise my opinion. I talked to one of the others, who told me the truth."

"Then he lied."

"No, LaRoche. You lied. Worse, you were not only spying for us, but you were also sharing British intelligence with the French. Playing both sides. I call that treasonous."

LaRoche raised his hands and began an impassioned appeal in rapid-fire French, which Laura could not follow. D'Auvergne answered in kind, his neck and jowls reddening with barely controlled anger.

"I hold you responsible for the lives of my men," the admiral bellowed.

Alexander spoke up. "Are the others . . . dead?"

The admiral looked at him. "I don't know. Since my sources of information have been cut off, I can't say for sure. If they haven't yet been executed, I fear it is only a matter of time."

Alex said something in French under his

breath, and the admiral nodded his grim agreement.

"I am going to find out," Alexander declared.

The older man's eyes narrowed. "Who are you?"

"Alexander Carnell. Alan Carnell's brother."

"Arrest him, sir," François exclaimed. "He is an officer in Napoleon's navy and an escaped prisoner of war."

"I am not here as an officer," Alexander calmly replied. "I am here as a brother. If Alan is alive, I want to free him."

"I want that too," d'Auvergne said. "If you are determined, I will deliver you to the Brittany coast in my own ship."

"Thank you for the offer, sir, but I have already arranged a less conspicuous means of travel."

The admiral's brows rose, impressed. Then he turned to the waiting soldiers. "Officers, arrest this man."

François grinned slyly at Alex, but the expression soon faded, for the uniformed men marched right past Alexander and advanced on him instead.

"Careful," Alex warned. "He is armed."

François pulled out the pistol he had briefly tucked away. "*Arrêtez!* Stop where you are."

He stumbled slightly, as though dizzy, and aimed the gun at Laura. Standing to one side of him, Mrs. Tobin struck him with her meat mallet. The blow glanced off his head, not enough to kill him but certainly enough to infuriate him. He whirled on the older woman and raised his gun.

From the corner of her eye, Laura saw Alex lunge. He threw himself at François, tackling him to the veranda. The gun went off with a loud pop, and Laura screamed.

The soldiers sprang into action, pulling Alexander from François and yanking away the gun. Blood stained both men's chests bright red.

Alex groaned and rolled to his feet, winded but otherwise unhurt. François leapt up and, evading the soldiers, bolted through the house and out the front door. Alex ran after him. Emerging out the front of the house, he saw François trip over a plank, hand clutched to his chest. He splashed through one of the small streams crossing the road and turned up Hill Street and out of view. Alexander followed, lungs burning.

He rounded a corner, and there saw François, half-sitting, half-lying, head propped against a wooden fence, legs sprawled, bloody hand pressed over his heart. Alexander's own heart beat painfully at the sight.

He advanced cautiously, as though approaching an injured but beloved animal who might bite out of fear or pain.

When he didn't lash out, Alexander knelt beside him. And suddenly François was no longer man or enemy, but boy, friend, and neighbor.

François looked up at him, and for the first time in years, his scowl fell away and the customary hatred in his blue eyes faded. It was just the two of them, as it had been all those years ago in Bretagne, sharing hopes, dreams, and the losses of loved ones.

"Alexandre . . ." François murmured. "I have missed you."

"And I you, Fañch."

Rapid footfalls drew nearer.

François winced. "Go. Leave me to my fate."

"*Non.*" Struggling to speak over the burning lump in his throat, Alexander said hoarsely, "Friends share everything, remember?"

François reached out a trembling hand and laid it on Alex's arm. In the language of their childhood, he said, "*Ma digarez, breur kozh.*"

"No. *I* am sorry, my brother."

"I forgive you," François whispered. "May God forgive me."

"He will, *mon ami, par la grâce de Jésus.*"

François nodded, then glanced heavenward. "Enora is waiting?"

"*Oui.* There is nothing to be afraid of."

"I am not . . ." And he was gone, blue eyes wide to the sky.

But let him ask in faith, with no doubting,
for the one who doubts is like a wave of the
sea that is driven and tossed by the wind.

—JAMES 1:6 ESV

Chapter 22

After François LaRoche's body had been carried away and the admiral and his men departed, Alexander and Laura sat together in the parlour, sipping soothing cups of chocolate.

"It was strange to see François unsteady like that," Alex said. "He's usually deadly accurate with a gun and fast on his feet. I wonder if he had been drinking."

"He drank the tea I gave him," Laura explained, "which contained a large dose of potent fever medicine. Dr. Braun poured it for me when he was here. François came before I could dispose of it, so I offered it to him. I hoped it would put him out as it did me, but at least it hindered his ability to react quickly."

"Clever girl." Alexander watched her closely. "And you are sure you are all right? François didn't hurt you?"

"Shaken but otherwise perfectly well. He did not touch me."

"Good."

"And how are you faring with all this?" she asked in turn. "Being an officer, you have probably seen men shot before, although with an old friend, it must still have been difficult."

He looked up, eyes distant in thought. "More difficult than I would have imagined. I am relieved he isn't here any longer to endanger us, yet I am grieved as well." His voice thickened. "Despite everything, we were once as close as brothers."

Laura nodded her understanding.

"It reminds me of Alan," he went on. "I know now he was working for d'Auvergne, yet he is still my brother, and I love him."

"Of course you do." Laura reached over and squeezed his hand. "I will pray for him and his family. Which reminds me, I am planning to venture out to church tomorrow with my aunt and Mrs. Tobin. Will you join us?"

Alexander hesitated. He seemed about to refuse, then relented. "Yes. Much needed in my case. It has been too long."

The next day as they readied for church, Aunt Susan came into the guest bedchamber and handed Laura her father's prayer book. Laura held it to her chest, then kissed her aunt's cheek. "Thank you. I shall treasure it."

Alexander arrived as prearranged to go to church with them. He offered Laura his arm, and she laced hers through it, glad for his support during her first lengthy walk since falling ill.

Together they strolled through the streets of St. Helier amid warm sunshine and cool breezes until they reached the parish church. From the church's tall tower, the bell rang as they entered the nave. Around them, the congregation filled the pews. Laura decided it felt good to be in the church where her parents—and Alexander's grandparents— had worshiped.

As they waited for the service to begin, Laura prayed for Alexander's family, as promised, and thanked God François hadn't injured or killed anyone the day before.

The parish clerk rose to call the service to order and announced a hymn.

Aunt Susan stood on one side of her and Alexander on the other. How pleasant to stand beside him, to share a hymnal and her father's prayer book. Alexander sang quietly and tentatively, perhaps not as familiar with the English lyrics. Even so, his rich, deep baritone voice was like warm chocolate, and she leaned nearer to better hear him.

Later, when the vicar climbed into the three-tiered pulpit, Laura felt a stab of nostalgia, thinking of dear Uncle Matthew, her favorite, much-loved clergyman.

The vicar read from the letter of James. "'But let him ask in faith, nothing wavering. For he that wavereth is like a wave of the sea driven with the wind and tossed. . . .'"

As Laura listened to the sermon, she slowly realized that while she had believed in God since a young girl, after losing her brother, parents, and Aunt Anne, her faith and trust in Him had wavered and diminished. She prayed, attended church, and went through the motions but didn't really believe God acted in her life. Had she come to the wrong conclusion?

God had not spared her family or given her everything she wanted as her doting papa had. But did that mean He did not care? Did not hear her or answer?

As if sensing Laura's inner thoughts, Aunt Susan squeezed her hand, and beside her, Alexander subtly pressed his shoulder into hers. The presence of these two people seemed proof of something. Of God's love, if nothing else. Did He hold her future in His hands? And did Alexander figure into that future?

After the service, Alexander walked home with them. Aunt Susan and Mrs. Tobin went to the kitchen to prepare Sunday dinner, but they insisted Laura rest in the parlour and keep the captain company.

Laura was happy to oblige them, but Alexander, she quickly noticed, was restless. He briefly sat, then rose and paced across the room.

"You are not overtired?" he asked her.

"No. I enjoyed the walk and the service."

"Good." He took a few more steps, then turned to her. "Laura, now that you are out of danger, it is time I left for Brittany."

She had guessed this was coming, but dread weighed down her stomach even so.

"Though Alan and I chose different allegiances, we are both Carnells and Bretons and Frenchmen. I must try to help him."

"I understand."

"In other circumstances I might have asked you to accompany me to Brittany, but look how far you have brought me. To a French-speaking island only twelve nautical miles from the French coast." He reached down and touched her shoulder. "You have done well, Laura. It is enough. Please remember, France is a dangerous place, especially for a British subject. We are still at war, and conflict continues between the *Royalistes* and those who support Napoleon."

"Including you?"

Alexander pressed his eyes closed. "It seemed so clear to me as an idealistic younger man. Change was needed. But neighbors turning against neighbors, and executions of anyone who dared question the new regime?" He shook his head. "I did not agree with that. When Napoleon crowned himself emperor, I was already gone to sea and was soon responsible for a ship full of men who deserved a strong leader. I did my best in a bad situation. But it has become an ugly war, both within and without. And I am no longer certain I am on the right side. I spoke privately with the admiral before he left the house, and he intimated the end of the war is in sight. I hope he is right. It is one of the reasons he has decided not to detain me—besides wanting his men freed, if there is any chance. Being a French officer, I will have more access to the prison than most."

Confusing emotions swamped Laura's soul. Alexander was leaving. Yes, she had wanted to see the lost man return home, but she was disappointed he said nothing about returning to Jersey. She had begun to hope for a future between them and had thought he did as well.

She'd presumed too much.

Her chest ached, and his dear face blurred through her tears. A face she might never see again.

"Laura, there is another war going on here." He pressed a fist to his chest. "Our countries are at odds. Our desires . . ."

"I think our desires are very much aligned," she said softly.

"This is something I must do. Alone."

Pain lanced her heart, but she took a deep breath and stood. "Then I have something to give you." She walked to her room on leaden legs, and returned a few moments later with the blue uniform coat with red cuffs. The coat she had purchased from Martyn. She held it out to him. "You will need this."

He looked up at her in wonder. "Where did you get this?"

"Remember the ferryman's son, who took us to Padstow? He found it after the shipwreck."

He nodded. "I had it in my satchel during our escape. It must have been washed overboard."

"Well, here it is. I sewed the epaulet back on. I thought you might like to return home in it." She held it up like a valet might, and he turned and allowed her to help him slip into it.

"I should indeed. Thank you."

"My pleasure."

He turned again to face her. Her dear castaway transformed into a French officer. She reached out to smooth a few wrinkles, then let her hand drop to her side.

"It looks good on you. It looks . . . right." She smiled, but felt her lips tremble and turned away to hide her grief.

The following day, Laura stood on the esplanade, watching the ship that would carry Alexander away on the final leg of his journey home. She was dressed in her warmest clothing, along with shawl, muffler, and gloves, but still felt cold to the bone. Hot tears escaped her eyes and streaked down her chilled cheeks, as salty as the sea air, their warmth fleeting.

"Godspeed," she whispered.

Beside her, Aunt Susan gripped her hand. The sails were hoisted, and the ship moved out of the harbour and into open water. Captain Carnell was sailing away from Jersey, away from her, perhaps forever. She stood there, eyes fastened on the vessel as it grew smaller and smaller on the horizon. With each passing mile, a part of her heart, and her home, departed with him.

It's no coincidence that Cornouaille sounds rather like Cornwall—it looks like it too. When 6th century Celts crossed the Channel from England to escape religious persecution, they found a rugged landscape strikingly similar to the Cornish countryside of their homeland.

—GILLIAN THORNTON

Chapter 23

Alexander returned to the Cornouaille region in the southwest corner of Brittany. He was struck by how much the rugged coastline reminded him of Cornwall. After leaving Mr. Gillan's ship and the sea behind, Alex rode with a farmer inland for a time, then walked the rest of the way on foot.

As he neared his family's estate on the outskirts of a country village, memories and nostalgia swept over him. A cool breeze caressed his face and brought the faint smell of apples. Old Jacques was likely busy in the *cidrerie*, making the last of the year's cider.

Alex continued to the house. He had been gone for years. Did he let himself in or knock? He tried the door and found it locked. Little wonder in such uncertain times. Taking a deep breath, he rapped on the solid oak.

Then rapped again.

After another moment, slow footsteps approached. He heard the jingle of keys, then the door to his childhood home opened.

An older woman stood there, narrow-eyed in suspicion. *"Bonjour. Qu'est-ce que vous voulez?"*

It was Betty—his mother's English maid, who had stayed on with them after her death. Even after all these years living there, she still spoke French with a British accent.

Her gaze swept over his coat and face, then recognition bolted across her features. "Master Alexander. Saints be praised!"

"Good to see you too, Betty. Is my father at home?"

She shook her head, eyes filling with tears. "Oh, Master Alexander . . ."

His chest tightened, fearing he was too late. "Is he . . . is he gone?"

Again she shook her head. "Not yet. But he is bad, *très mal*, indeed."

She led the way to the snug morning room.

"Your father uses this as his bedchamber now to avoid the stairs."

The shutters were closed, although it was afternoon. Faint light shone through the transoms above, and a low fire burned in the grate.

In the shadows, Alexander made out a slumbering form propped up by pillows on a bed set up near the hearth.

Alexander approached slowly. "Papa? *C'est moi.*"

His father's eyelids fluttered. "Alan?"

Shafts of hurt and hope stabbed him. Hurt that his father had not recognized his voice, and perhaps wished to see Alan more than him. But also hope that it meant his brother was still alive.

"No, Papa. Alexander."

"Alexandre?" The man's weary eyes opened and fixed on him.

Mamma had named him Alexander, with the English spelling, but his father still pronounced it as the French *Alexandre.*

He held his breath. What would his reaction be? Would his father welcome him back or remain aloof because of the harsh words spoken in parting?

"My boy. My dear boy." Pierre Carnell addressed him in French and held out shaky hands. "Forgive me. My mind wanders. I was dreaming of Alan, and when I heard your voice I thought it was him, foolish old man that I am."

"Is Alan still alive?"

His father pressed his eyes closed and shook his head. "*Non.*"

Alexander's stomach twisted. "When?"

If Alex had missed his opportunity to save his brother, or at least to reconcile with him, by a few days or weeks while he was lingering in Cornwall and Jersey he would never forgive himself.

"About ten months ago, though I did not hear the news until several weeks afterward."

Alexander sat heavily in the nearest chair, winded. His brother had been dead for nearly a year. His heart beat dully within him at the news. He felt empty. Hopeless. Stupid. All his efforts to return—the escape, Daniel's death, lies and deception—all in vain. *God forgive me.*

"I am sorry, Papa. I tried to get home to help him, but I failed."

"It is not your fault. Nothing you could do, *mon fils*, except pray. Last I heard news of you, you were being held in a prisoner-of-war camp."

He nodded. "I escaped. I should have done so sooner."

"Then you risked your own life, which is more than I have done. Thank you for trying. I know you loved Alan, despite your differences, and he knew it too. Don't blame yourself."

"I shall try not to, but that will be difficult." Alexander swallowed. "I am sorry too, Papa, for the tensions between us during my last leave. The arguments about Alan and politics. I know I spoke harshly, and I regret it. Please forgive me."

"I do. I forgave you long ago. And I hope you forgive me. I know I did not respond well. My own loyalties torn. The struggle within my own soul played out in real life by my beloved sons. . . . I fear God is not pleased with me."

"God is merciful, Papa. You taught me that. He will forgive us if we ask Him for His Son's sake."

His father nodded. "I will meet my Maker soon, I believe. If He will accept me."

"He will, Papa. But please don't be in a hurry to go." Alex's voice grew thick with emotion. How old his father looked, how frail, how dear. "We have just been reunited, and I have missed you."

"And I you, my dear boy."

The door creaked open, and Alexander turned. A small head appeared, with a pair of large dark eyes. Alan's eyes.

"Grandpapa?"

A five-year-old boy hurried into the room,

then stopped short at seeing another man there—a stranger for all intents and purposes, as Alex had not seen his nephew in years.

His father held out his hand to the little boy. "Don't be afraid. This is your uncle."

"*Mon oncle?*"

His father nodded. "*Oui. Oncle* Alexandre."

Alexander managed a tremulous smile. "*Bonjour*, Jean-Philippe. You have grown big since I saw you last."

The door opened wider, and an elegant dark-haired woman appeared, framed in the threshold. His brother's wife was even more beautiful than he remembered.

"I hope Jean-Philippe does not disturb y . . ." Her eyes widened. "Oh."

"*Bonjour*, Léonie." Alexander rose and bowed.

"Alexander!" She curtsied. "I am stunned to see you here. What a"—her voice cracked—"happy surprise."

Her pretty face crumpled, and her dark eyes filled with tears, belying her words.

He saw then that she was dressed in black, and his heart squeezed with empathy. "I am sorry, *ma sœur*."

She pulled a handkerchief from her sleeve and wiped her eyes. "*Je t'en prie, pardonne-moi*. It is only that you are so much like him."

Her beautifully accented French was music in his ears, even though the words and her obvious grief pained him.

"That is a compliment, indeed."

"Is it?" she asked, studying him as she walked closer.

"Yes. He was my brother, and I will always love him."

She kissed his cheek. "Me too."

The following day, on a chilly grey afternoon, Alexander and Léonie visited the churchyard together.

"Your father's connections were not powerful enough to save Alan," she said, "but at least they were able to return his body to our home parish."

Alexander nodded, unable to speak over the lump in his throat.

"The headstone just arrived last week," she added.

Alexander read the inscription, the carved words searing pain into his chest.

Ici Repose le Corps De
Alan Philippe Carnell
1784–1813
REGRETS ÉTERNELS

Tears filled his eyes as he whispered, "*Je suis désolé, mon frère.*"

Eternal regrets, indeed.

After a few quiet moments, his sister-in-law asked, "Would you like to see the grave of Enora and the infant?"

Alexander hesitated only a moment. "*Oui.*"

She led him to a simple headstone carved with small figures of Madonna and child, and her name: *Enora Angelle Carnell.*

She had borne his name at the end, though not his child.

I forgive you, he whispered in his heart. He sincerely hoped both Enora and François rested in peace.

Beside him, Léonie slipped her hand into his in silent comfort and empathy.

⁊〜

A few days later, Alexander undertook the visit he knew he could not put off any longer. Knapsack over his shoulder, he went to see Daniel's widow, Vivienne.

He found her in lodgings in Quimper, a newborn child in arms.

His heart expanded at the sight. How was it that such a small, innocent face could look so much like his dearest friend? There was no doubt who this boy's father was.

The realization brought both pain and pleasure. "I can see Daniel in him."

She nodded. "So can I."

"I am so sorry, Vivienne."

She looked up from the swaddled babe, eyes wide. "He isn't coming home?"

Alex shook his head. Throat tight, he managed only one syllable. "*Non*."

Tears filled her eyes, and answering tears filled his.

"He died in a shipwreck," Alexander explained. "We were trying to get home. He was so eager to return in time for the birth of your child. I wish I had been able to save him. I tried. . . ."

"Could you not have tried harder?" Vivienne's voice broke, and Alexander's heart broke with it.

Dear God, why? Oh, to exchange his life for Daniel's . . .

"Forgive me," she said, swiping a hand across wet cheeks. "I know you loved Daniel too. I am only shocked and hurt."

"I understand completely."

She laid the child in a nearby cradle, gazing down at the little face. "What are we going to do, my love? How shall we go on without your papa?"

Alex squeezed his eyes shut, but the hot tears escaped anyway.

When she straightened, Alexander took a deep breath and pulled the gift from his bag. He had repaired the intricate Noah's ark as best he could and completed the missing pairs of animals himself.

Seeing it, her tears increased, and she whispered hoarsely, "He made this?"

"Yes, for his child."

She held it to her chest. "We will both treasure it always."

Why do we rouse Brittany and La Vendée?
Why bring civil war into France?
—Honoré de Balzac, *The Chouans*

Chapter 24

After Alexander's departure, Laura wrote letters to Eseld and Uncle Matthew, letting them know she planned to stay on Jersey with Aunt Susan for the foreseeable future. She also sought out the former house of Alexander's grandparents and spent time helping her aunt and Mrs. Tobin with their charity work.

When Mr. Gillan returned from his voyage, he came by the house to tell Laura that he had delivered Captain Carnell safely home to Brittany.

He added, "I asked him to command one of my ships when his business there is finished. He thanked me but turned me down. Said he was not certain what the future held.

I replied, 'Who of us is?' But he would not be moved."

Disappointment sank in Laura's stomach. It was as she feared. He had no plans to return. Even so, she thanked Mr. Gillan for bringing her the news and led him into the parlour to visit Aunt Susan.

A fortnight after Alexander left, Mrs. Tobin brought in the post. "Letter for you, Laura. From France."

Laura's pulse quickened. Would it contain good news or bad?

Dear Miss Callaway,

I pray this letter finds you in good health. I hope neither you nor your aunt mind my taking the liberty of writing. I realize that after all we have been through together, it might seem a little late to worry about propriety, but I want you to know that I respect you as a gentlewoman of the highest character. I regret that my coming to Cornwall caused you to throw caution to the wind. I appreciate your sacrifices on my behalf and hope your reputation and relationships have not suffered irreparable harm because of me. I trust you and your uncle have been in contact. I have written to him myself, to apologize for exposing you to danger and gossip. I have not heard back, but with the war slogging on, perhaps the post is not yet getting through to England. I hope my letter to you does not meet a similar fate.

I'm afraid I have some bad news to relay. My brother, Alan, died almost a year ago, executed by firing squad. I was unable to help him or even see him before he died, to my deep regret.

My brother leaves behind a wife, Léonie, and a five-year-old son who live with my father. My nephew's name is Jean-Philippe. He is the handsomest boy I ever saw, with his mother's beauty and his father's keen mind. He has won my heart already, and I am very much enjoying my role as "Oncle Alexander."

Sadly, my father is in poor health, and his heart is failing. The doctors say it is only a matter of time. I am forever grateful that I am here with him for however many days, weeks, or months God grants us. We have forgiven one another and have been reconciled. Our daily conversations are sweet and precious to me, knowing each may be the last. I will never forget that it is you I have to thank for returning me home to his side.

> *Most sincerely,*
> *ALC*

Her aunt came in as Laura was reading the letter a second time. "Mrs. Tobin mentioned a letter from France. Good news, I hope?"

"I am afraid not," Laura replied. "Alexander's brother was executed, and his father is near the end of his life. He was unable to see his brother, but at least he has been reunited with his father."

"That is thanks to you, my dear."

Laura shrugged. "He would have managed, one way or another, but yes, he expresses his gratitude." She wondered if gratitude was all he felt for her now that he was home.

She added, "He mentions he is enjoying spending time with his young nephew. He and his widowed mamma live with the Carnells. Both very handsome apparently."

The words Alexander had written echoed through her mind, *The handsomest boy I ever saw, with his mother's beauty.* What was it François LaRoche had said about Léonie? *"She expected you to marry her. We all did."* And now that she was a widow . . .

Her aunt watched her closely, her eyes downturned with concern and far too knowing.

"Anything about his plans for the future?" she asked. "Has the French navy given him another commission?"

"He does not say."

"Well, perhaps in his next letter. You will reply, I trust?"

"Yes, if you don't mind. I wish to express my condolences." *And so much more.*

A few weeks after his homecoming, Alexander sat reading the newspaper after dinner, his father propped on pillows on his daybed and Léonie seated near the fire screen for light and warmth as she sewed. Jean-Philippe came in with a book and climbed onto the sofa beside him. Alexander smiled at the boy, pulled him onto his lap, and the two read together.

Léonie looked up from her needlework to watch them, her lovely dark eyes glimmering with affection . . . and something more? Alexander quickly returned his attention to the book.

Later, after Léonie had taken Jean-Philippe up to bed, his father said, "Léonie is very pretty, is she not?"

"Yes, though black does not suit her."

The older man's eyes twinkled. "She will not wear black much longer."

Awareness prickled over Alexander. "Papa . . ."

His father raised a hand to forestall his protests. "Don't say anything. I realize it is too soon to be thinking of such things. I won't be here much longer, or I would have waited to mention it. But it would ease my mind. Léonie and Jean-Philippe would be provided for. You could share this house together, and I could die in peace."

"She is my sister."

"Bah. Not every country shares England's laws. In some traditions, a man is encouraged to marry his brother's widow."

That was true—although Alex thought it wiser not to concede the point. Instead, he said, "Rest assured, I will make certain Léonie and Jean-Philippe are provided for after you are gone. And she has a sister yet living as well. She will never know want, whether she remarries or not."

"Just consider it. I can tell she still admires you, and you've allowed she is attractive."

"Yes, but I don't—"

Again his father raised a palm to cut him off. "Don't answer me now. Just tell me you won't dismiss the idea out of hand."

Alex felt torn. He wanted to please his

ailing father but felt guilty at the same time. Was it a betrayal to agree?

"Very well. I will think about it, to make you happy."

"Thank you." His father settled back against his pillows and closed his eyes, a small smile on his lips.

Wary, Alexander asked, "Tell me you have not said anything to Léonie?"

"I . . . may have mentioned something."

Alexander groaned. "Papa . . ."

In his mind's eye, he saw Laura Callaway's beautiful face, looking at him with affection and even desire in her golden brown eyes.

Where did his duty lie?

The following morning, his mother's former maid brought in the post. "Letter for you, Master Alexander."

"Thank you, Betty."

His father slept on, undisturbed, but Léonie watched him with interest.

Alexander saw the St. Helier postmark, and his heart instantly lightened. *Laura.* He pried open the seal and read.

> *Dear Captain Carnell,*
> *Thank you for your letter. I very much appreciated hearing from you al-*

though I was dreadfully sorry to hear the news of your brother. It must have been difficult for you to learn he died.

I know how hard you tried to get home to help him. You did your best, and that's all any of us can do. I hope you are not being too severe with yourself for not being able to rescue him. Alan chose his own path in life. Though I imagine leaving behind a beautiful wife and young son must have been his greatest regret.

I pray this war ends soon and am sure you do as well. My aunt asks if you have been called back into active duty or given another ship like your old favorite, the Victorine*? I suppose you would be gratified, but I for one would be sorry to see you rejoin the fighting, especially now that the end is in sight, at least, if the newspapers can be believed.*

Aunt Susan, Mrs. Tobin, and I are doing well here, three women living as a little clutch of hens. Mrs. Tobin is all graciousness, and I am enjoying every minute with my aunt. However, I believe, if Mr. Gillan has his way, one of us will find herself living elsewhere before much longer. I think my aunt hesitates to accept him because of me, but I have assured her that her happiness is mine.

I have finally received a reply from my uncle. You will be glad to know that he has forgiven us both, and that he and Mrs. Bray are well and in good health. They are delighted with Eseld's recent engagement to Perry Kent and eagerly anticipate their upcoming wedding.

I hope your father still lives and that God grants you many days together to store up in your heart and treasure for years to come. In spending time with my mother's sister and nurse, and hearing their reminiscences of my parents' final days, I feel I have been given back some of our lost hours to treasure in my heart as well.

Your sister-in-law and your nephew have my condolences. May God grant them comfort as they grieve their loss. How good of Him to bring you home just when they needed you most.

Most sincerely,
Miss Laura Callaway

When he refolded the letter, Léonie said, "I hope it is not from the navy, offering you another commission."

Funny that his sister-in-law should express the same concern Laura had. Duty had compelled Alexander to write to his superiors to inform them he was back in France. But his letter had been met with silence.

"No. A letter from a . . . friend."

"So the post is now getting through?"

"At least from Jersey."

"Ah. The woman who rescued you and nursed you to health?"

He had already given them an abbreviated account of his escape, shipwreck, and journey from Cornwall. But he had left out certain details.

"Yes, though she had help from the nurse next door and a young doctor." He chuckled awkwardly. "It was a group effort."

"But she is the one who helped you get home."

"Yes."

Léonie watched him closely. "She remains on Jersey?"

He nodded. "Her aunt lives there. Her last living blood relative. They have been reunited after many years apart. She hasn't anyone else."

"Has she not?"

He looked at his sister-in-law, saw the arched brow, and said, "She is not remaining on my account, if that is what you are implying."

"What is her name, this rescuer of yours?"

"Laura. Er, Miss Callaway."

With a mischievous grin, Léonie asked, "And is Laura Er Miss Callaway pretty?"

He took a deep breath. "She is."

"And young?"

"Perhaps too young. Only three and twenty."

"I was even younger when I married Alan." Léonie ran her fingers over the pillow fringe. "Had she no suitors before you came along?"

He considered. "There is one young man who admires her. He took us as far as he could in his ship until a revenue cutter forced him to set us ashore. He would do anything for her, I think." He recalled coming upon the two of them in Mrs. Tobin's parlour, hand in hand. Laura had said they were only friends, but Treeve, he guessed, wanted more.

"She did not return his admiration?" Léonie asked.

"Not then, no, though perhaps in time."

"Why did you not bring her here?"

"Why would I? There is a war on. I am a French officer, and she is British. Besides, I was focused on Father and Alan. There were too many uncertainties."

"And now?"

He looked at her, then away again. "There are still too many uncertainties."

The dark drear days of November came along, and with them hurried mists and sweeping rains, wrapping the headlands in their mantle of grey, shutting out from the Padstow folk all sight of what lay beyond.

—GRATIANA LONGWORTH
KNOCKER, *TREBETHERICK*

Chapter 25

Winter passed in quiet domesticity. Together Alexander, his father, sister-in-law, and nephew celebrated Christmas and the New Year. His father seemed to rally since his return and even joined them at the table for a delicious Christmas dinner and indulged in a few sips of *Manoir de Carnell* cider, made from apples grown in their own orchard.

Alex had still not received another commission. Perhaps this was due to the blockades and the fact that the fighting focused on land versus sea. Or perhaps because they considered him compromised after his time in England and his relationships with Alan and François—two known spies. Whatever the reason, Alexander was not sorry. He felt he was where he was supposed to be. At his father's side.

By February, his father's rally lagged and his beleaguered heart began its slow final march, like the last labored ticks of an ancient clock. He died peacefully in his sleep the following month, Alexander holding his hand.

At the end of March, France's allied enemies invaded and captured Paris, forcing Napoleon to abdicate.

Due to this news and Pierre Carnell's death, the family's Easter celebration was rather reserved, yet Alexander relished every word of the divine service, taking solace in the solemn yet joyous reminder that Christ had triumphed over death. Because of His resurrection, Alexander knew he would see his father again one day in heaven.

On a beautiful spring day near the end of April, Alexander walked around the kitchen gardens Betty tended so carefully, and then out to the orchard and small family vineyard beyond. The air was warm and carried the scent of apple blossoms, but Alexander was too distracted to appreciate it, striving to get his thoughts in order. Torn between keeping his word to his father and his feelings for Laura.

Was he obligated to marry his sister-in-law after their mourning periods ended? It would not be a hardship. Léonie was beautiful, and they had always liked and respected one another. Many marriages were forged on far flimsier foundations. And then there was Jean-Philippe. The little boy pulled on his heartstrings whenever he saw him. So young to be without a father. So innocent. So much like Alan.

He saw Léonie on a bench beneath a grape arbor, reminding him of the similar trellis-covered bench at Fern Haven. Was she too considering the future?

Alexander looked around the *verger de pommiers* but saw no sign of its tender. "Where is old Jacques?" he asked.

"Laid low with the rheumatism, poor dear," Léonie replied.

A younger man appeared among the blossoming trees. He walked with a decided limp yet looked to be no more than thirty. His hat, pulled low against the sun, shadowed his face. Alexander lifted his chin toward him. "And who is that?"

"His son, Jacques Marec. Do you not remember him?"

"Ah, of course. I thought he had enlisted in the infantry?"

"He had, but he came home to recover from his injuries and stayed to help his ailing papa. Your father offered him the place, and he accepted. He is very capable."

"So the estate is in good hands, then?"

"I believe so." She looked up at him. "That is not to say you are not welcome or needed. You are the new master now that your father has passed on."

Alexander sat beside her, chewing his lip, considering. He wondered if he ought to visit the family lawyer in Quimper, or ask the man to come here.

"Alexander . . ." Léonie laid a hand on his sleeve. "I want to ask you something."

He looked into her lovely face, her beseeching eyes. This was his old friend, his brother's widow, and his beloved nephew's mother. He knew whatever she asked of him, he could not, would not, refuse. He steeled himself. "Yes? What is it you want?"

She held his gaze intensely, warmly, intimately. "I want you to be happy. I know your marriage to Enora was not a happy one. I hope you will choose more wisely the next time."

When he hesitated, she added, "I trust your Laura is a superior woman?"

"In every way, but—"

"Come. I know you love her. I saw your face when you read her letter. And whenever you speak of her, your features soften, and your eyes glow like sunlit honey."

He looked away, self-conscious under her words, her scrutiny, her *vérité*.

"What holds you back?"

"How can it work?" He grimaced. "I am French—she is English. Our countries are enemies."

"So? Your mother was English."

"Those were different times."

"Human nature changes little, I find. And besides, the war is over."

"For now."

"Come, *mon frère*. What is the real reason you hesitate?"

Should he tell her? He looked away. If he was going to ask her to marry him, divulging that his father had urged him to do so was not a romantic way to begin.

She faced him on the bench, taking her hands in his. "I can guess why. Your father, he was not very subtle. He hinted to me as well. But he only wanted reassurance that Jean-Philippe and I would always be provided for."

"You will be. I promise."

She squeezed his hands. "I believe you.

And I beg you not to let feelings of obligation impede you."

From the orchard came the sound of laughter. They both looked over, and there was Jean-Philippe on Jacques Marec's broad shoulders.

Léonie's gaze rested on the distant pair. Her features softened, and her eyes glowed just like the sunlit honey she had described.

"We will be all right," she said softly. Decisively. Léonie looked from the orchard to the house and gave a little sigh. "I often miss your mother." She glanced over at him and grinned. "Another *Anglaise* would be good for the Carnell family, I think."

Alexander relaxed and smiled back. "I think you are right."

Laura and her aunt stood in the church-yard on a lovely late-April day. The winter had passed, and spring had arrived on the island. Laura saw signs of new life every-where she looked—the new leaves on trees, the spring blossoms, the new bloom in her aunt's cheeks every time Mr. Gillan called, and in her own heart as well.

She, Aunt Susan, and Mrs. Tobin had spent a quiet Christmas together, followed by reserved celebrations of the New Year and the news that the war was ending. They observed Eastertide by attending church, making hot cross buns, *fliottes*, and simnel cake, and inviting several neighbors, including Mr. Gillan, to dine with them. They also had "Jersey wonders" from Alexander's favorite bakery.

Laura had quickly grown to love her aunt, to know her as true family. *Her* family. Laura was an orphan no longer.

She and Aunt Susan had visited the churchyard several times before but returned today, on her mother's birthday, with a bouquet of lilies—Mamma's favorite—and laid them on her parents' grave.

Stanley and Sara Callaway
Beloved Brother and Father, Sister and
Mother
Gone to Their Redeemer
~1803~
Gone but Never Forgotten

Never forgotten. How true.

Arm in arm, the women returned to the house overlooking the harbour. The rocky shoreline and rhythmic waves reminded Laura, as always, of Cornwall, and she was surprised to find she missed it—the beaches and hidden coves, Uncle Matthew, Eseld, Miss Chegwin, and Newlyn. Even Perry and

Treeve. She and her uncle had exchanged several more letters over recent months, and he assured her all was well and she was welcome to return anytime she wished. Would she ever return to Fern Haven? She didn't know.

Laura had also received a chatty letter from Eseld, describing her wedding to Perry and joyous in her expressions of happiness over her new wedded state. Eseld had written, *Mamm was angry with you at first for running off like that, fearing it would harm my reputation and chances of an advantageous match, but Perry's proposal set her mind at ease. In fact, now that you and I are both gone from Fern Haven, she seems to be filling the role of parson's wife more actively than before.*

She also wrote, *Treeve has sold his ship. He continues to flirt with Kayna Roskilly, but she is giving him the cold shoulder, so I doubt if there is any hope of another Kent wedding anytime soon.*

Laura smiled, thinking, *Wise, Miss Roskilly.*

Eseld also mentioned that Dr. Dawe decided to remain with his sister, so Perry faced no opposition or even competition in establishing a practice in the parish of St. Minver. Even though some were wary of being treated by one so young, most were quick to accept Dr. Kent. After all, he had been born there and was one of them.

Eseld ended the letter with a postscript: *Perry insists I add these lines. He thinks you will be pleased to know that he has officially engaged our neighbor Miss Chegwin as his chamber nurse. Between them, he says, their ages average to a very respectable fifty years.*

Laura chuckled. "Always knew you were an excellent man, Perran Kent."

She was pleased indeed.

I know so well this turfy mile,
These clumps of sea-pink
withered brown,
The breezy cliff, the awkward stile,
The sandy path that takes me down.
—JOHN BETJEMAN, "GREENAWAY"

Chapter 26

Glorious spring weather continued on Jersey. Flowers bloomed even earlier there than they did in the southwest of England. Laura took to walking the beaches of St. Helier as she had at Trebetherick, her eyes keen for treasure. She rarely found anything worth salvaging, besides a seashell or tide-smoothed rock, but the fresh air revived her, and the sand and surf reminded her of Cornwall. Reminded her of home.

How was it that only by leaving a place, could one sometimes learn to appreciate it? To miss it, and those who lived there? But she did.

One beautiful morning, Laura strolled along her favorite beach, amazed anew that she had at last made it to Jersey, the place where her parents had died and her aunt, thankfully, still lived.

She heard a voice and turned to look behind her. In the distance, she saw a man striding toward her. There was no one else around, and she felt a pang of unease at being on this lonely stretch of sand with a stranger. She noticed a greatcoat, tall boots, and beaver hat—the attire of a gentleman. As the man neared, her unease melted away. The face was familiar, in fact, often recalled and dearly missed. Alexander. Her heart tripped, and anticipation needled her stomach.

He quickened his pace to catch up with her. "I hope you don't mind. Your aunt told me you walk here . . . most . . . every morning." His English sounded a little rusty after half a year in Brittany. Or perhaps there was another reason he spoke somewhat haltingly.

"I don't mind at all," she replied.

He watched her reaction closely, expression tinged with uncertainty. "I . . . hope I find you well."

"Yes. And you?" Her eyes slid to the black armband he wore. Stomach sinking, she asked, "Your father?"

He nodded. "He died in March. I am glad I was able to be with him at the end."

"Me too."

"I suppose you have heard the monarchy has been reinstated?"

"Yes."

"So Alan got what he wanted in the end, though he didn't live long enough to see it. The new government is supposedly a democratic monarchy, but we shall see. At all events, the result is my brother did not die in vain, and I take solace in that."

She longed to reach out and take his hand but made do with lacing her own fingers together. "Again, I am sorry for your losses."

"Thank you." He shifted, then cleared his throat. "Sorry. I did not come here to bring sad news."

"Seeing you again is good news. It was kind of you to come and tell me about your father in person."

She supposed he was duty bound to go back. After all, he was his father's heir and had a sister-in-law and nephew to provide for. And what about his obligation to the French navy? But Laura wasn't ready to ask him those questions. She needed a little time to steel her heart. "Come, let's walk awhile."

Hands behind their backs, the two continued along her usual route.

Several yards ahead on the sand, something caught Laura's eye—light green glass sparkling in the morning sunshine. Excitement prickled over her, reminding her of former times when she went searching for treasure on the beaches near Fern Haven.

"Excuse me a moment." She hurried toward the glinting glass and picked it up. A corked bottle. And inside, a whisper of white paper.

Her pulse rate accelerated. Had she finally found something of value on Jersey? She pulled up the cork and worked out the piece of paper with her little finger. Successful, she unfurled the slip and read the words written there: *My dearest Laura, will you marry me?*

She sucked in a breath and whirled to face Alexander. "How did you . . . ?"

A crooked grin lifted one corner of his mouth. "I could not resist."

She hesitated. Was he asking her to live in France with him, or . . . ?

Perhaps guessing her thoughts, he added, "I have resigned my commission. I remained long enough to bury my father and deed the family home to Alan's wife and son."

"But that is your home."

He shook his head. "My heart is not there any longer."

"But . . . are you sure?"

He nodded and walked nearer. "One thing I've learned while being apart from you. Wherever you are, Laura Callaway, is my home." He reached out and caressed her cheek. "If you will have me."

Her heart beat hard. Her stomach seemed to be filled with a hundred fledgling skylarks, longing to fly. "Yes," she breathed.

With a relieved smile, he wrapped his arms around her waist.

She looked up into his dear face and teased, "Unless . . . did you only come back to Jersey because so many people here speak French?"

He pursed his lips. "I admit a French oasis amid the British empire sounds *parfait* to me. But only with you at my side."

He drew her closer, his gaze tracing her cheeks, her eyes, her mouth. Then he leaned down and kissed her with love, adoration, and a pent-up passion that mirrored her own.

Raising his head at last, he said, "Come, let's walk to the harbour. Mr. Gillan said he has something very important to show me."

"Mr. Gillan? He mentioned he'd asked you to command one of his ships, but you did not accept."

"At the time, I had unfinished business in Bretagne. Now he assures me he has, how do you say, sweetened the deal? He has something up his sleeve. Do you know what it is?"

"No, but let's go and find out."

They continued to the harbour and walked along the old stone quay.

Several ships were moored in the calm waters of the protected bay, and there they saw Mr. Gillan in a smaller boat with a crewman rowing to shore.

He waved to them. "Ah! You came. Excellent, Captain. And Miss Callaway too. Good."

"Morning, sir," Alex replied as the men drew closer.

The boat reached the stone steps, and the older man climbed nimbly up them.

"I have exciting news," he said, rubbing his hands together. "I bought a French privateer for a very good price. The Royal Navy captured her on the way back from the Indies with a cargo of spices, sugar, and coffee. The British crew shared the prize money, but for some reason they did not take her back into service. Their loss is our gain."

"How so?" Alexander asked.

"She sails remarkably well and has a history I think you'll find interesting. The ship was originally a Spanish brig until the British captured her. After that she was captured by the French, and then recaptured by the

British. She's seen more changes of home port, names, and loyalties than most can boast."

Alexander smiled sheepishly. "I can relate."

Mr. Gillan swept his arm toward a stately ship moored in the harbour. "Would you like to guess her original name?"

"How would I . . ." Alexander stared at the vessel. "Wait. Are you saying this ship was the *Victorine*?"

"That's right."

"It can't be. I never thought I'd see her again."

"You can do better than see her, you can command her, if you're willing, Captain Carnell."

Alex turned to Laura. "I am willing, but it is up to my wife."

Mr. Gillan's brows lifted. "Wife, ey?"

Laura laughed. "Give us time. First there is the wedding to take care of, and the honeymoon to enjoy. . . ."

"Hear, hear." Alexander slipped his arm around her waist and pulled her close to his side. Then he said, "You know, my love, with such a ship at my command, we might visit your family and friends in Cornwall, as well as my sister-in-law and nephew in Brittany."

"Good point."

"So you agree?" he asked.

"*Absolument.*"

His eyes gleamed. "Your French has improved, I see."

"*Merci, mon amour.*" She rose on tiptoes and kissed him again, right there on the quay, in front of God, and for the whole world to see.

Standing on the quarterdeck, surrounded by the sounds of the splashing sea, flapping sails, and snapping rigging, Laura counted the hours until she would reach Fern Haven. Nearby, Alexander consulted with Mr. Gillan over a chart and instructed the helmsman at the wheel. They were sailing to Cornwall together—Alexander and Laura, Aunt Susan and Mr. Gillan, and a modest crew.

It was Aunt Susan's first trip back to the mainland in more than fifteen years, and Laura and Alexander's first voyage as man and wife.

They'd had a small, simple wedding, with Aunt Susan, Mrs. Tobin, and Mr. Gillan in attendance. They had enjoyed a few days at a seaside inn before embarking. And now, their honeymoon continued aboard the *Victorine II*. The newly wedded couple shared the great cabin together at Mr. Gillan's insistence, while he and Aunt Susan each had small cabins of their own. Aunt Susan and Mr. Gillan had not yet married but planned to do so soon.

Laura's heart rate accelerated as they passed Trevose Head, then neared Stepper Point. As the ship approached Padstow Bay and the estuary, Laura searched each familiar headland and cove with growing excitement. Recognizing Trebetherick Point in the distance, she strained her eyes for a glimpse of Fern Haven at its summit. Understanding her longing, Alexander handed her a glass, and through it she saw the dear whitewashed house at last and smaller Brea Cottage as well.

Within the hour, she was once again in Uncle Matthew's embrace.

He held her close, as if he would never let her go. "How I have missed you, my girl."

"And I you," she whispered over a tight lump in her throat.

Eseld greeted her next, throwing her slim arms around her in an enthusiastic embrace. "My dear cousin! I could not wait to see you, so I came here to await your arrival."

"I am glad. How goes life at Roserrow?"

"Very well. I could not be happier. Did I not tell you the apple peels would reveal our future husbands?"

"You did, and you were right."

Eseld stepped back and gave her a satisfied grin.

While Uncle Matthew shook Alexander's hand, Laura turned hesitantly to Eseld's mother. "I hope you are well, Mrs. Bray?"

"I am indeed." She leaned forward and kissed Laura's cheek. "Welcome back. I am glad to see you."

Amazement flooded Laura. "Are you?"

"Absolutely."

Laura took a steadying breath and turned to introduce Aunt Susan.

In his last letter, Uncle Matthew had invited Susan to stay with them at Fern Haven as well. Mr. Gillan, however, preferred to stay at an inn near the harbour with most of the crew.

Greetings over, Eseld announced in a singsong voice, "We have a surprise for you! We are hosting a party in your honor."

"Really?"

"Yes, to celebrate your homecoming and your marriage."

"My goodness . . . how kind," Laura breathed. "Thank you."

"It is planned for tomorrow."

"We thought you would need to rest from your journey first," Mrs. Bray added. "Your old room is ready for you and your husband."

"Unless you'd prefer the guest room again?" Uncle Matthew sent Alexander a teasing grin.

With a mischievous glimmer in his eyes, Alex replied, "No, thank you. I will happily share with my wife."

After showing Aunt Susan to the guest room Alexander had once occupied, Laura and her groom retreated to her old room.

There, he helped with her fastenings and bent to kiss her neck. "Are you glad to be home?"

"I don't know that Fern Haven is home, but I am certainly glad to be back."

"Did you ever imagine the two of us sharing a room here? At least, with your aunt and uncle's consent?" He winked.

"No. Feels strange, does it not?"

"Feels good," he replied, turning her in his arms and murmuring against her lips. "Feels right."

❦

In the morning, Laura rose before anyone else in the family and dressed herself simply. Quietly letting herself out of the house, she hurried over to Brea Cottage, eager to see Miss Chegwin.

Mary was in the kitchen, pouring tea.

She looked up at her entrance. "Laura!

Dynnargh dhis." She threw wide her arms, and Laura entered the older woman's embrace.

"*Myttin da, Mamm-wynn.*"

Hearing the commotion, Jago came in, hair in more disarray than usual. "Ah. Our Laura. *Myttin da.*"

"Good morning to you too, old friend. You are keeping well, I trust?"

"Indeed I am."

"Good. And you are both coming to the party?"

Mary nodded. "We wouldn't miss it. Newlyn asked Jago to help with preparations and to play during the festivities."

"Did she? I am glad to hear it."

Laura visited with them awhile longer, then returned to Fern Haven.

The party preparations began a short while later. The men set up a white open tent on the sands of Greenaway, Laura's favorite beach, just down the path from Fern Haven. Then they set up a long table. Everyone helped carry down chairs for the older folks as well as plenty of blankets for a picnic-style meal.

Later that afternoon, Laura watched as Jago helped Newlyn carry big heaping platters and urns of tea, the usually timid maid smiling her thanks at the big man. Soon, the long buffet table was overflowing with food of all descriptions, including a large cake and a bowl of punch.

Laura walked over to the old cook-housekeeper. "What a feast you've prepared, Wenna," she praised. "You must have been working for days."

"Indeed I was," she replied. "But many were eager to help—Newlyn, Miss Chegwin, and several other neighbors."

"The captain and I sincerely appreciate it."

"Oh, miss." Wenna squeezed her hand. "You know we would do anything fer ye. Fern Haven just ain't the same without ye."

Laura hugged her and went to thank the others who'd contributed to the feast.

The Trenean family came bearing their instruments and began playing joyful music. When Jago finished his work, he went to join them, playing his hurdy-gurdy with skill. Newlyn watched him, admiration shining in her eyes, and Laura was delighted to see it. Delighted for them both.

Alexander brought her a plate of food, and Laura ate every morsel, savoring the delicious, familiar tastes of home, and the beauty of the day.

Eseld stepped near her and asked, "Are you enjoying yourself?"

"Oh yes. Everything is perfect. Thank you for suggesting the party."

"It was Mamm's idea."

Surprise flashed through Laura. "Was it?"

"Yes. Though I eagerly seconded the notion!"

Taking Eseld's arm, Laura led her through the crowd to Mrs. Bray. Reaching her, she began, "Thank you, Mrs. Bray. Eseld tells me the party was your idea, and I sincerely appreciate it."

Looking self-conscious, Lamorna Bray glanced at her daughter. "Was it? Well, we were speaking of your return, and it just sprang to mind."

"It was definitely your idea, Mamm," Eseld said. "An excellent one I heartily agreed with."

Mrs. Bray tried in vain to suppress a smile. "It was my pleasure. I wish you and your husband every happiness, Laura."

"Thank you. Will you come and visit us on Jersey? You would be most welcome."

"That is very kind. And I hope it goes without saying that you will always have a place to stay with us when you visit here. You will visit again, I trust?"

"Yes. We hope to."

"Good."

Eseld returned to Perry's side, but Mrs. Bray lingered near Laura. She shifted and bit her lip. "Laura, I know I was not . . . that I did not treat you as . . . warmly . . . as I should have when you lived here. I apologize. My dearest wish and indeed, duty, was to pave the way for a good marriage for Eseld. And having you here . . . with your eye-catching hair and ladylike graces . . . seemed like a threat to my plans. Now that Eseld is happily married, and you as well, I hope we can put all that behind us and start anew."

"With all my heart," Laura agreed.

"Good." The older woman sighed in relief. "And I know I did not encourage it before, but I would be honored if you would call me Aunt instead of Mrs. Bray."

Laura blinked. Yet another surprise. "Th-thank you . . . Aunt Lamorna."

"You are more than welcome." She nodded in apparent satisfaction and went to rejoin her husband.

Heart overflowing, Laura stood alone for a few moments to reflect, enjoying the warmth of the sun and the sweet sounds of waves, Cornish accents, and congenial laughter. Across the tent, her groom stood talking with her uncle and aunt. His uncle and aunt now too.

Seeing her alone, Treeve Kent walked over to join her. "Well, Mrs. Carnell, I wish you happy."

"Thank you, Mr. Kent. And thank you again for visiting us on Jersey."

"You're welcome. I am glad things have worked out for you."

She cocked an eyebrow at him.

"I mean it! You were right in what you said to me. But I am growing up, by and by. And I find the effort has had its rewards."

"In the shape of one Miss Kayna Roskilly?"

They turned to pick her out among the crowd. There she was, laughing with her father. She looked beautiful in her green dress with a sprig of flowers in her dark hair, and an affectionate smile on her face.

"She is lovely, is she not?" Treeve said.

"She is indeed."

He squeezed Laura's hand, held her gaze a moment, and turned to go.

She watched as he walked over and bent to whisper in Miss Roskilly's ear, causing the young woman's smile to brighten. Another wedding in the near future, Laura guessed.

Near them, Perry sat on a blanket with his arm around his wife, a besotted smile on his boyish face. How good to see the two so happy together. Even Mrs. Bray—er, Aunt Lamorna—looked contented and relaxed surrounded by her family.

Family . . . Tears heated Laura's eyes at

the thought. She was deeply grateful she had been able to come back to Cornwall to see them. And with Aunt Susan too. *Oh, Lord, thank you!* Yet her gratitude was threaded with sadness, knowing they would soon have to leave.

She felt Miss Chegwin's gaze on her. The older woman crossed the tent to her, hand extended.

Laura silently took it, and for several moments the two stood there, hand in hand.

Mary tilted her head to one side. "I know yer happy with Alexander. But do I sense sadness as well?"

"Yes, both. How can that be?"

"That is life, my dear. Joy and loss in the same moment."

Laura nodded and squeezed Mary's fingers. "I miss you, you know."

"And I you, up-country lass," Mary teased even as tears glistened in her eyes.

Then she brightened, saying, "Have you heard the news? Dr. Kent has asked me to serve as his chamber nurse. I am busier and happier than ever."

"Yes. And I was delighted to hear it."

They talked for a few minutes longer, then Laura embraced the woman and excused herself. She helped herself to two pieces of cake and went to find her uncle among the guests.

She handed him one of the pieces. "Thank you, Uncle Matthew. For everything."

He accepted it with a smile. "I did little, in all honesty. Though I was happy to foot the bill." He winked and fondly pinched her chin. "And happier still to be reunited with you, my dear girl."

"I am so very thankful to be here." Laura looked over to where her former neighbors and, yes, friends gathered. Her uncle followed the direction of her gaze. Then she felt his pensive look return to her profile.

"Have you decided where you will live?"

Laura took a deep breath. "Alexander has agreed to captain a ship for Mr. Gillan. So for the foreseeable future, when I am not sailing with him, I will live on Jersey."

His expression turned wistful. "Sounds perfect. Though I shall miss you."

"I hope you are not too disappointed. We will visit as often as we can."

His eyes misted over. "I am glad to hear it."

The party continued for several hours, guests enjoying the good company, good music, and good food, and reluctant to see the occasion end. Alexander and Laura walked from person to person, thanking everyone for coming and accepting well-wishes and fond embraces in return. How touching to be welcomed back so warmly.

The musicians continued to play, their notes harmonizing beautifully with the sound of the sea. For an instant, Laura closed her eyes to relish the moment and commit it to memory.

Beside her, Alexander whispered, "Everything all right?"

She took a deep breath and smiled up at him. "More than all right, my love."

Laura gazed around at the delightful scene, and her heart expanded with aching joy. Her whole family was together: Alexander, Aunt Susan, Uncle Matthew, Aunt Lamorna, and Eseld, along with dear Miss Chegwin, Jago, Perry, Kayna, and Treeve. Laura could not recall ever being happier.

She leaned near Alexander. "Remember when you asked me to describe my favorite memory?"

He nodded.

"This moment is my new favorite."

He smiled deeply into her eyes. "Mine too."

Epilogue

A year has passed. And with it, the unexpected return of Napoleon Bonaparte, the bloody battle of Waterloo, and Bonaparte's second and, hopefully, final abdication and exile. Now that peace has returned, Alexander and I have sailed back to Trebetherick to visit our friends and family as promised.

I rise early in the mornings, as is my habit. Leaving Alexander still asleep in my old bed, I quietly dress and slip out of Fern Haven alone.

As in former days, I walk along Greenaway Beach, the golden crescent lapped by foaming blue-green water. Up, down, and over I go, stepping from beach to beach grass and from rock to rock pool. The call of a seagull draws my gaze skyward, and I look up to admire the beautiful heavens. I have so much to thank heaven for.

Balmy summer weather reigns in Cornwall, and vibrant life is everywhere—gorse in yellow bloom lines the paths, and sea pinks dot the grassy cliff tops. Other dainty plants and flowers grow even on the hard rocks and sandy shore. Beauty amid harsh conditions. Life where nothing should thrive.

Like these hardy plants, I am no longer simply surviving but am instead thriving.

At the thought, I touch my slightly rounded middle. A new life is on the way, thank God. My family is soon to gain a precious little member. If it is a girl, we shall name her after our mothers. If a boy, after our fathers, or maybe our brothers.

Standing on a rock, wind tugging at my bonnet, I realize I no longer feel like a castaway. Whether here in Cornwall or on Jersey or at sea, I am where I was always meant to be—close to my extended and growing family, and at Alexander Carnell's side.

I used to wonder if there was a plan in all the loss I experienced. Now I know the answer.

Yes.

Once, I feared I would never belong anywhere again. But I no longer ask myself if I am flotsam or jetsam, cast off and unwanted. I finally understand that in God's hands, and now in Alexander's arms, I am truly home.

Author's Note

Thank you for traveling with me to North Cornwall within the pages of this book, and the real places of Padstow, Trebetherick, and Rock (formerly known as Black Rock). For this novel's setting, I chose an area known for shipwrecks, some say second only to the Lizard Peninsula in the south of Cornwall. In fact, this stretch of coastline is sometimes referred to as "The Lizard of the North." I enjoyed learning about the history and traditions of this region, which is now far more developed than it was during the novel's time frame over two hundred years ago and is today a popular holiday destination.

My husband and I had planned to travel there, but when the COVID-19 pandemic canceled those plans, Peter Long of the Elite Duchy Touring Company stepped in to help with setting research. I am grateful for his assistance and his knowledge of the area. I am also grateful for the helpful volunteers at the Padstow Museum for answering my questions by email.

If you were surprised to read that more people on shore did not try to help those trapped on foundering ships, or that so many died in shipwrecks, remember that few people knew how to swim in previous centuries, and this period is before the creation of the Coastguard, or the proliferation of the rocket lifesaving device and breeches buoy, etc. The first Padstow lifeboat was not established until 1827. Before that, shipyard gig crews, fishermen, and others did what they could to save those in distress, though many perished.

Most of the characters in this novel are fictional. However, when I read that a legendary wrecker named Tom Parsons lived near Padstow, I decided to incorporate him into the novel. Tom Parsons's Hut sits right on the coast path at Booby's Bay and is owned by the National Trust. Little is known of Parsons, so beyond his name, the character is a figment of my imagination.

Philippe d'Auvergne was an actual British official who led a spy ring from Jersey. I took the liberty of incorporating the arrest of his couriers into the novel, although in real life it happened earlier (1807). The names of most of his informants have also been changed—François LaRoche and Alan Carnell are fictional.

St. Enodoc is a real place. From the sixteenth to the middle of the nineteenth century, the chapel was virtually buried by sand. To maintain tithing rights and consecration required by the church, the vicar had to host services there at least once a year, so he and his parishioners descended into the sanctuary through a hole in the roof. By 1864, the sand was removed and the church restored, primarily through the efforts of the vicar of St. Minver, Rev. W. Hart Smith. His son later wrote,

> The sands had blown higher than the eastern gable, the wet came in freely, the high pews were mouldy-green. The sand was removed, the little churchyard cleared, and the roof renewed. I remember the pains and energy my father spent to raise the money to restore the building.

So although the character of Matthew Bray is fictional, he represents the campaigning clergyman who was finally able to bring about the chapel's restoration—along with, of course, the help of skilled masons and other workmen. Also, while many shipwreck victims are buried in the area's churchyards, old headstones are difficult to read. Therefore, the inscriptions used are fictional, though based on actual epitaphs.

A note about the Cornish words used in this novel. You may have read that a woman named Dolly Pentreath was "the last Cornish speaker" before her death in 1777. However, other Cornish speakers were identified decades after Dolly died, and well into the nineteenth century. Nowadays, the Kernewek language is experiencing a revival, and I hope experienced speakers will view my no doubt imperfect attempt to include a few words as a tribute to this revival.

When I read about the ancient Celtic ties between Cornwall and Brittany, France (especially the Cornouaille region), and their similar languages, I was intrigued and decided to incorporate that fact into the novel. The region has a long, colorful—and may I say, complicated—history that I don't pretend to thoroughly understand, even after research. Warmest thanks to Alexandra Caucutt and Yves Marhic, Brittany residents, who kindly helped me with the French and Breton sections. Thanks also to author Louisa Treyborac. Any unintentional errors are mine.

The list of "treasures" my heroine collected was inspired by the artifacts I saw at the Shipwreck Treasure Museum in the historic port of Charlestown, Cornwall, a must-visit for *Poldark* fans.

To learn about England's first purpose-built prisoner-of-war camp and those who worked and resided there, my husband and I visited the Peterborough Museum north of Cambridge with its excellent exhibits about the Norman Cross Depot and its impressive collection of crafts created by former (and primarily French) inmates. Also very helpful was the book *The Napoleonic Prison of Norman Cross* by Paul Chamberlain.

Keen readers may notice a nod to Elizabeth Gaskell's *Wives and Daughters* in the description of how a young Laura helped her physician-father with a patient. And Alexander's prayer in chapter 19 was inspired by the beautiful prayers of Jane Austen.

For sailing descriptions and terms, I owe a debt of gratitude to experienced sailors Heidi and Mark Green, and to Richard Woodman and his book *A King's Cutter*.

If you'd like to read more about the history and traditions of Cornwall, I recommend *Cornish Wrecking* by Cathryn Pearce and any of the books quoted in the epigraphs at the beginning of each chapter.

Thank you to my editors, Karen Schurrer, Kate Deppe, Jolene Steffer, and Raela Schoenherr, and my entire team at Bethany House Publishers, including Jennifer Parker, who designed yet another gorgeous cover. Thanks also to my first reader, Cari Weber, as well as Anna Paulson, Michelle Griep, and my agent, Wendy Lawton.

Finally, thank *you* for reading *A Castaway in Cornwall*. I appreciate you! For more information about me and my other books, please follow me on Facebook or visit my website, www.julieklassen.com.

Discussion Questions

1. Did you enjoy the novel's seaside setting? Are you personally drawn more to the beach, mountains, woods, or some other setting?

2. How did these opening Bible verses play out in the book?

"What woman, having ten silver coins, if she loses one coin, does not light a lamp, sweep the house, and search carefully until she finds it? And when she has found it, she calls her friends and neighbors together, saying, 'Rejoice with me, for I have found the piece which I lost!'"

Luke 15:8–9 NKJV

3. Who would you say is the castaway in the novel? Alexander, Laura, or both? Explain your answer.

4. Who was your favorite character? Least favorite? Did your opinion of

any of the characters change throughout the course of the novel?

5. Have you visited Cornwall? If
not, are you more or less interested in
doing so after reading this novel?

6. Which historical tidbit (e.g.,
about smuggling, prisoners of war,
Cornwall, Jersey, Brittany, etc.) intrigued you or made you want to learn
more? Did anything surprise you?

7. In chapter 16 Miss Roskilly tells
Laura, "You have made no secret of
wishing to be anywhere but here since
you arrived. Why do you think you
were never fully accepted?" Do you
agree or disagree with her assertion?
Was Laura's original disdain of Cornwall and its customs the reason she'd
never belonged? Or was the explanation more complicated?

8. Alexander says he loves his
brother and wants to help him even
though they strongly disagree politically. Is this a relevant situation in
today's world? Have you experienced
anything similar, striving to relate
with family members or friends whose
beliefs and views differ from your
own?

9. Laura was made to feel like an outsider by her uncle's wife, Mrs. Bray. Through a second marriage or other circumstance, are you a part of a blended family? If so, has your experience been similar, or is it one of general acceptance and fondness?

10. After experiencing loss (the deaths of her brother and parents) Laura's trust in God wavered, and she doesn't really believe God hears her prayers and acts in her life. Have you struggled to persevere in faith when it seems your prayers go unanswered? What would you say to someone struggling in this way?

Look for Julie Klassen's
next historical romantic mystery
coming in December 2021!

In a grand hotel shadowed by secrets, a lady's companion must face an old love and a murder where everyone is a suspect . . . including her. Will she lose her heart, and everything else as well?

Read on for an excerpt
from *The Bridge to Belle Island*,
Julie Klassen's latest historical
romantic mystery,
available wherever books are sold.

That afternoon, Benjamin found himself bounced, jostled, and thoroughly shaken on the *Emerald*, a day-coach traveling westward from London. The journey into Berkshire was only some thirty miles, but it felt interminable. Ben worried he would become ill or, heaven forbid, have one of his . . . episodes.

Ben closed his eyes, drawing deep breaths of fresh air, trying to stave off his own nausea. Again and again, he inhaled deeply and exhaled with a long "Hooo." The spell began to pass.

He hoped the worst was over, for he wanted to perform this assignment well and make Mr. Hardy proud. To do so, he needed to arrive on Belle Island looking the picture of a competent, composed lawyer.

If he concentrated, he could still feel Mr. Hardy's comforting hand resting upon his shoulder after his failure. It was the closest thing to fatherly affection Benjamin had experienced in years. He supposed he should have been the one offering comfort, since

Robert Hardy had lost not only a partner in the law firm but also an old friend.

You can do this, Benjamin admonished himself. *For his sake, you must.*

Finally reaching Maidenhead's Bear Inn, Benjamin hired a driver—a young man with a small gig pulled by a single horse—to take him the rest of the way. The rickety vehicle listed to one side and possessed not a single spring or ounce of comfort.

After fifteen bone-jarring minutes, they reached the outskirts of Riverton. The little hamlet curved around the riverbank, its church, homes, and shops situated on a low rise and, at present, enveloped in fog.

The driver pointed to a wooden bridge spanning the river, just wide enough to allow a carriage to pass.

"That takes you to the island, sir," the young man said. "The Wilders have lived there for ages. You'll see the house better once the fog burns off. All right if I set you down here?"

"Hm? Yes, all right." Benjamin paid the driver, climbed down on rubbery legs, and turned to study the scene. He faintly heard the driver's "Walk on," and the gig continue on its way, but his gaze remained fixed on the opposite shore.

Through the filmy grey fog, he made out

a tall stone manor house shrouded in climbing vines and mist. Nearer shore, trees overhung the river—prickly junipers and chestnuts, weeping willows and elms, their hoary heads bowed in grief, their arms reaching out, pushing him back. Warning him away.

Benjamin frowned. What a foolish notion. The journey had clearly addled his brains.

As he stood staring across the bridge, it seemed to undulate, the rails to compress to a narrow tunnel, and then widen again. He grasped a post for support. *Good heavens*. No wonder he rarely traveled.

Movement caught his eye. Across the bridge, a figure appeared through the mist—a woman in a long red coat, her deep bonnet concealing her face. She stood out against the grey background like a rosefinch in winter.

Benjamin blinked and looked again, and the woman was gone. Disappeared into the fog . . . or had it been an apparition?

He shivered.

Stepping onto the bridge, he felt it tremble beneath his feet. For a moment, he stopped where he was, everything in him longing to be back in his shabby, comfortable rooms in London. Something told him if he crossed the bridge his life would never be the same again.

He closed his eyes, breathed deeply, and

prayed for wisdom and direction. He again reminded himself of his purpose in coming. He was there on behalf of the firm—to offer legal advice to Miss Wilder after Percival Norris's death, and to discreetly discover if she or a member of her family was to blame for it. His success would go a long way toward redeeming his recent mistakes.

Soon he felt a bit steadier. When he opened his eyes again, the fog was beginning to lift.

He wondered about the female figure he'd glimpsed—or imagined. Had it been Isabelle Wilder? He had not seen the woman's face. He wondered how old Miss Lawrence's maiden aunt would be. Forty? Five and forty? For some reason, he imagined an angry spinster with a hooknose and an evil glint in her eye.

Through the lingering mist, a few more details of the island began to emerge. Beyond the bridge, a lawn led up to a broad veranda that wrapped around the front and side of the stone manor house. Columns flanked its entryway, and a three-story bay projected on the right. His gaze traveled up to a high rooftop parapet, and an unpleasant jolt of nerves shot through him. Not fond of heights, he quickly looked away and walked on.

As he stepped from the bridge onto the island, a woman near his own age appeared from behind the house, a shaggy dog trailing slowly behind. The woman was tall and slender. Light brown hair with streaks of gold shone from beneath her dark red bonnet. Now that he could see her face, he realized she was far too young and attractive to be the spinster he'd imagined. A companion, perhaps?

She noticed him and stopped. "Oh. Good day."

He took a deep breath and began, "I am here to see to Miss Wilder."

The woman replied, "I am she."

Incredulity flared. Her face was oval and smooth, her eyes large and blue, though dark circles shadowed them at present, like faint crescent bruises. She seemed a pretty, pleasant young woman, not evil looking at all. Though he knew too well that looks were often deceiving.

"*You* are Isabelle Wilder?"

"Guilty."

Interesting word choice, Benjamin thought. A wave of dizziness washed over him, but he tried to ignore it.

She looked down. "I'm sorry. You've caught me."

"Caught you?" he echoed stupidly. Was she going to confess on the spot?

"Just coming down for the day. I usually rise early, but I was not quite the thing this morning." The dog lay at her feet, tongue lolling, as if as weary as she.

"Oh? I . . ." he stammered lamely. "I have just arrived myself."

He set down his valise and gave her his card, hoping she did not notice the slight tremor of his hand. "Benjamin Booker. With Norris, Hardy, and Hunt."

She glanced at it. "Uncle Percy's firm, of course." She started up the veranda steps and gestured for him to follow.

"Oddly enough, I was just thinking about Percival. In fact, I dreamt about him last night."

"You did?"

"Um-hm," she replied casually. "Not surprising, I suppose. He was just here a few weeks ago."

"So I heard."

As they crossed the veranda, she asked, "What brings you here? I suppose you brought something I need to sign?"

Benjamin hesitated. He recalled Mr. Hardy's advice to more than one young barrister. *"State what you* suspect *as fact with confidence, and nine times out of ten people will believe you in possession of the evidence and respond accordingly."*

With this in mind, he said, "The two of you had quite a row, I understand. And afterward, you sent him a rather unpleasant letter."

She grimaced. "Yes. I suppose he told you all about it."

Benjamin sketched a noncommittal shrug.

She sighed. "I was angry. He is insisting we lease part of the island to a . . . stranger. It would spoil everything I have tried to do here."

"Well, with him dead, there's that problem sorted."

Her head whipped toward him, mouth parted, face elongated in shock or a convincing imitation. "What? Percival is dead?"

He nodded, the dizziness mounting. *No, no, not now. Hold yourself together, Booker.*

Taking a deep breath he asked, "Where were you last night?"

"Here on the island."

"Can anyone vouch for that?"

"Um . . . yes."

Suddenly unsteady, Ben teetered and grasped a nearby column for support.

Her eyes widened in alarm. "Are you all right?"

He shook his head, the act making him woozier yet. Heaven help him, he was going to faint. Not in front of this woman of all people!

"Are you unwell, Mr. Booker? Truly, you look very ill."

He pressed his other hand over his eyes. "Just . . . dizzy. It will pass."

"Do sit down, before you fall down." She took his arm and guided him to a nearby chair, her grip surprisingly strong.

Strong enough to kill a man?

A Castaway in Cornwall